THE CHARLETON HOUSE MYSTERIES

BOOKS 1 - 3

KATE P ADAMS

Copyright © Kate P Adams 2020

The right of Kate P Adams to be identified as the author of this work has been asserted by her in accordance with the Copyright, Designs and Patents Act 1988.

All rights reserved. No part of this publication may be reproduced, transmitted, or stored in a retrieval system, in any form or by any means, without permission in writing from the author, nor be otherwise circulated in any form of binding or cover other than that in which it is published and without similar condition being imposed on the subsequent purchaser.

All characters in this publication, other than those clearly in the public domain, are fictitious and any resemblance to real people, alive or dead, is purely coincidental.

Paperback ISBN

Cover design by Dar Albert

CONTENTS

Death by Dark Roast   1
A Killer Wedding   175
Sleep Like the Dead   357

DEATH BY DARK ROAST

For Mum and Dad,
who brought me into a world full of books.

CHAPTER 1

There were delicate macarons in a rainbow of colours, chocolates with ingredients from chilli to lavender, and even bacon. Enormous wheels of cheese, fresh handmade doughnuts, pies and pastries. I found old-fashioned puddings that brought childhood memories rushing back, like sticky toffee and spotted dick. I saw at least three kinds of gin and multiple stalls selling honey, olive oils and chutneys. The list of locally produced mouth-watering foods went on and on.

One stall really stood out for me, though: 'Hayfield Haggis'. While many people looked down their noses at the dish made famous by the Scots, the traditional ingredients of oatmeal, liver, heart and lungs turning their stomach, I had already declared it as worthy of being my last meal, should such an occasion arise. In reality, most haggis no longer contains the more unappetising ingredients. Besides which, there are plenty more questionable items in things like hot dogs.

It doesn't need to be Burns Night for me to savour the heavenly haggis, and I'm not a whisky drinker so I bypass that tradition too. Haggis for me is a delicious treat at any time of the year, and now I had found a local farmer who had turned her hand to making it. Although it was yet to open to the public, as far as I was concerned the Charleton House Food Festival was already a resounding success.

Tomorrow was to be the first day of the festival and today the gardens were a hive of activity as stallholders set up their banners and displays. Over one hundred little white tents formed two circles around the Great Pond at the rear of the house, all of the action being watched over by two enormous lions that were part of the central fountain design. If visitors looked up from their artisan burgers or churros long enough, they'd witness it shooting fifty metres into the air.

The house gardeners were on hand, both to help stallholders and to make sure no one damaged the beautiful flowerbeds which had taken months to carefully prepare and nurture, so I had taken the opportunity to escape my endless to-do list and get a sneaky advance look at the delights that awaited my stomach and wallet. Food was one of my passions, that and history, and I had been able to combine the two perfectly when I was offered a job at Charleton House, a five-hundred-year-old stately home in glorious Derbyshire.

After a career in London, running cafés and restaurants that were frequented mainly by suited and booted City types, I was now the manager of three lovely visitor cafés at the house, and regularly catering dinners and events for the owners, the Duke and Duchess of Ravensbury – the heads of the Fitzwilliam-Scott family. Right now, today's visitors were being looked after by my teams, and I was enjoying the sunshine and teasing my taste buds with Mark, one of the house tour guides. I had been meant to meet someone else, but they had cancelled so I'd called Mark, and he hadn't thought twice before agreeing to join me to wander around the stalls, making ourselves hungry. Mark had taken me under his wing when I'd arrived almost a year ago and had quickly become a friend as well as my fount of all knowledge.

'It's looking good, Sophie.' Mark's eyes were practically out on stalks. He loved food as much as I did and was more than happy to be my official taster – and recipient of free pastries and coffees when I was feeling generous. 'There's a couple of ale stalls which I'll be checking out, and look! Raclette cheese grilled sandwiches. That's tomorrow's lunch sorted.'

The quickest path to Mark's heart was definitely through his stomach.

I had spotted my first choice for lunch within minutes of arriving when I'd seen the sign for a hog roast. I'd be sure my serving came with a mountain of crackling, the delicious, crisply roasted rind being my favourite bit.

'So who dared to cancel on you? Do they not realise how important and busy you are?'

I scowled and feigned annoyance at the healthy dollop of sarcasm in Mark's suggestion that I was anything other than rushed off my feet. 'Oh please, you were probably sitting in your office watching videos of cats online and hoping someone would call.'

'How dare you! It's dogs all the way for me.'

I laughed. 'Apologies, videos of puppies. It was one of my suppliers, Bruce from the Northern Bean Company. They supply our coffee. He said something about managing to get a last-minute appointment with someone in the area that he couldn't afford to miss out on. He sounded like he was in a foul temper, so I didn't mind not seeing him. Anyway, our meeting was just a check in, nothing important.'

'I thought you weren't keen on them?' Mark stretched his arm out to stop me walking into the path of a woman who was loaded up with enormous tubs of mustard and tomato ketchup, and not watching where she was going. Once she was out of the way, we set off again.

'I'm not. I'm seriously thinking about jettisoning them and finding another supplier, but that's going to be a difficult conversation so I don't mind delaying it by a day. I said I'd meet him tomorrow.'

'Tomorrow is often the busiest day of the week.' Mark had put on his best orator voice so I knew he was quoting someone.

'Who said that?'

'No idea. It's a Spanish proverb I think. Soph, over here. I know where we'll find you for the next three days.' I followed Mark until we were standing in front of a cherry-red VW campervan which had been beautifully transformed into a mobile coffee shop. Its roof had been raised so that staff could comfortably stand while working, the coffee equipment gleamed in the August sunshine, and shelves held bags of coffee beans and mugs that matched the colour of the van. The vision before me, combining my favourite colour with my favourite drink, was possibly the most stunning thing I had ever seen.

A young woman held up a remote control and the awning sprang to life, revealing red and white stripes. She was wearing a red t-shirt that matched the van, the sleeves rolled up revealing tanned, muscular arms. I guessed she didn't have any issues lugging around big sacks of beans.

'Nice, isn't it?' she said, smiling.

'Amazing, you've done an incredible job.'

'Can I get you a coffee?' With the awning in place, she jumped back into the body of the van. 'We roast our own beans.'

'Are you up and running? I don't want to get in your way.'

She made a start on the coffee, her movements quick and well-choreographed. There was no excessive banging like you'd hear in chain cafés; this was an art.

'It's all good to go, it doesn't take too much to set up. I'm Lucy Wright, and this is Kathy, my sister.'

A young woman with long, dark hair – a stark contrast to her sister's short blonde cut – appeared at the counter having popped up from the floor of the van and gave a little wave before disappearing again.

'Sophie Lockwood, I work here.' I pointed over my shoulder in the direction of the house. 'We've come for a sneaky peek.' As I said this, I realised that Mark was no longer beside me, having likely concluded that he was about to lose me to the bean that had an obsessive hold over my life.

I was handed a brown cardboard take-out cup that was emblazoned with a cherry-red logo saying 'Signal Box Coffee'. A little drawing of an old-fashioned railway signal box took pride of place in the centre. It was rather adorable, but I wondered about its significance.

It seemed that Lucy had spotted the question in my face. 'Our grandfather worked on the railways and had a replica signal box built in his garden. We used to play in it when we were kids. When he died, Kathy and I moved into the house and the signal box is where we roast the coffee.'

What a lovely story. As I took my first mouthful, I imagined how proud their grandfather would have been that his own interest was still playing a part in his grandchildren's lives in some way.

The coffee was rich and smooth. It was exactly the kind of pick-me-up that I enjoyed.

'Kenyan?' I looked at Lucy.

'Very good, yes.'

'I'm a bit obsessed with coffee and Kenyan AA is my go-to.' I took another mouthful, holding it there for a moment before swallowing. Only the best Kenyan beans were given an AA grade, the top tier of the country's grading system. 'This is particularly good. Nice and silky.'

'I have Kathy to thank for that, she's our buyer.'

Kathy had stepped out of the van by this point and reached out to shake my hand. She had a firm grip and her wrist was covered in dozens of small leather bands, a few brightly coloured string bracelets mixed in. They were all well-worn and looked like mementos of trips overseas.

She took over from her sister, filling me in on the company's operation. 'We might be a small business, but I wanted to make sure we had the best beans. I went to Kenya to learn as much as I could and this is what I came back with. Their growing conditions are fantastic. I'm glad you like it.'

Mark reappeared at my side and Kathy spoke to him as she started to move back towards the van. 'Would you like some?'

'No thanks. But I reckon you'll be seeing a lot of this one over the weekend' – he nodded in my direction – 'not that she needs help feeding her addiction.'

Kathy laughed. 'Well make sure you stop by whenever you need topping up.'

I thanked both Kathy and her sister, then steered Mark in the direction of more stalls.

We stepped carefully over trailing cables as the gardeners helped stallholders to connect to power supplies or hook up to enormous portable water tanks. There were still a number of vans arriving, their drivers trying to follow the map of the garden and figure out where they would be based for the duration of the festival. One vehicle in particular caught my eye: a large Airstream was being pulled into place by a Land Rover. The long silver bullet-like trailer had become all the rage a few years ago and was one of the coolest ways to explore the world, or your own back yard, but most people would need a second mortgage to be able to afford one of those things.

Demonstrating impressive skill, the driver reverse parked the trailer into position and three men jumped out of the Land Rover to start work on setting up. I checked out the writing on the side: 'Silver Bullet Coffee'. It looked like a slick operation. With well-practised ease, the workers propped the side of the van open, unfurled the canopy and started to transform the inside into a professionally presented coffee shop, albeit a little too modern and clinical looking for my taste.

A dark-haired man with the sleeves of his shirt rolled up caught my eye. 'Coffee?'

'Thanks, but I've just had one.' I held my coffee cup out to show him. 'Tomorrow, maybe?'

'Ah, the competition. Come on, just a taste. I have to make a few anyway, make sure everything's set up properly.' He spoke with confidence, like there was no question about my accepting a cup, not breaking eye contact with me until Mark spoke.

'Of course she will.' Mark stepped forward. 'The stuff is practically running through her veins at the best of times. I've yet to see her reach a limit. Plus she'll be so curious about it, she won't rest until she tries it.'

The man laughed, leaned over the counter and offered me his hand. He had a firm grip.

'Guy Glover, Silver Bullet Coffee. Nice to meet you both. Bear with me and I'll rustle a couple up.'

I stepped back and looked again at the van. 'This is quite the set up, you must be doing very well.'

'Thanks, we are. We've no shortage of bookings. We're particularly popular with music festivals – the young crowds love the trailer and we end up all over Instagram. It's great publicity.'

He looked a little too old to be spending time at festivals; not quite middle-aged, but no longer part of the 'young crowd' either.

'We're not always so keen on the music, though,' another member of the team grumbled through a smile as he carried a box past us. 'I swear my ears are still ringing after that last one.'

Guy chuckled. 'Yeah, he got stuck next to a rock stage last weekend. Sadly I couldn't be there to help out.'

'Sadly? You couldn't find an excuse fast enough.' The man carrying the box raised an eyebrow. He had a warm smile and appeared to be enjoying the banter with Guy. His Silver Bullet t-shirt was clinging to his body with sweat and he shook his head to get his hair out of his eyes. I avoided looking at Mark; I imagined his mouth hanging open as he pictured the slim, healthy-looking man minus the t-shirt.

Guy introduced us. 'This is Ben. You might need to shout to get his attention until his hearing returns to normal.'

We introduced ourselves and took the coffee Guy was offering to us. Mark was right: I couldn't recall ever having turned down a cup. Guy watched as we took our first sips; it was a bit too hot, but I nodded my approval as I had a second taste.

'It's good. Nutty, nice after-taste.'

'Here,' Guy handed over a small bag of beans, 'take some with you, but be sure to come back and see us over the weekend.' A third man had joined Guy and acknowledged me with a nod. 'That's Kyle, my business partner.'

Kyle looked as if he'd just got out of bed and needed a coffee more than any of us. I returned his nod, then turned back to Guy, thanking him. As we walked away, Mark bent down and whispered conspiratorially in my ear.

'Go on, spill the beans, so to speak. What did you really think of their coffee? You weren't exactly bubbling over with enthusiasm.'

'Ha, you know me too well. Pedestrian at best. It was OK, but not very complex. It tasted no different to the dark roast we serve in the cafés and you know I'd love to replace that with something more interesting.' I'd been so unimpressed with the coffee when I first arrived at Charleton House that I'd taken to keeping a stash of my favourite beans tucked away in a filing cabinet in my office, and I rarely touched the coffee we sold to the visitors.

As I mulled over the similarities between what I had just tasted and what I sold in the cafés, a weight slammed into my shoulder. I staggered into Mark, who managed to keep me upright as pain shot through my arm. It was as if I'd been hit by a truck.

As I steadied myself, I turned to see who had almost knocked me off my feet. A man in a gardens team t-shirt and baseball cap was striding with purpose towards the Airstream and clearly nothing was going to get in his way. I watched as he grabbed Ben's arm and swung him round to face him. Either I was too far away or the gardener was keeping his voice down, but I couldn't hear what he was saying. However, I could see that his face had an expression of fury chiselled into it, and whatever he was saying to Ben wasn't pretty and was probably delivered with a ton of angry spittle. Ben was saying nothing, just looking shocked.

As quickly as it had happened, it was over. The gardener spun round and marched back the way he had come, his face red, his hard eyes staring ahead. His fists were clenched into tight balls as though he was trying to control an urge to use them. Despite coming close enough for me to hear his ragged breathing, he didn't appear to see me and didn't apologise for having barged into me.

I turned to look at Ben, who was watching the man walk away. Then with a look of resigned sadness, he shook his head and slowly carried on with his work.

'Are you OK?' I looked up at Mark and nodded. He was staring at the angry gardener's retreating back. 'Remind me never to annoy him; I'd hate to see those fists get some action. Come on, Soph, let's go.'

Mark put an arm around my shoulders and we crunched our way up the gravel path towards the house.

CHAPTER 2

Charleton House is, from the outside at least, a glorious show of Baroque opulence and power, and could easily be mistaken for a royal palace. When the sun glints off its gilded window frames, it's easy to imagine generations of family members looking out onto manicured lawns, colourful planting and delicately sculptured topiary, the gardens providing a restful break between plotting political takeovers and attempts to cosy up to the reigning monarch. The honey-coloured sandstone building has been the home of the Fitzwilliam-Scott family for over five hundred years, its 300 rooms bearing witnesses to history of both the romantic and scandalous kind. This weekend, the current Duke and Duchess would be using the magnificent house as a backdrop against which to showcase some of the finest food in the area, and I was like a kid at Christmas. I was going to need regular reminding that I was here to work and not just eat and drink my way through the three-day weekend.

Mark and I took a short cut through a door marked 'Private', making our way into the house and down a flagstone corridor. We cut across a courtyard that looked distinctly different from the rest of the building, as it and the ground floor rooms around it dated back to the original Tudor house, and gradually wound our way to the Library Café and my office.

The Library Café is my favourite of the three cafés I am responsible for, although I'm sure that, like parents with more than one child, I should never admit to having a favourite. As the name suggests, it's decorated and furnished to look like the luxurious library of one of the earlier Dukes. Hundreds of books line the shelves that cover every wall; armchairs you could sink into rest in front of a large, ornate fireplace; tables of different sizes and shapes fill the rest of the room. It is popular with staff who want to hold meetings outside their office, or bring paperwork and escape their phones and emails, as well as visitors in search of lunch and a chance to rest their feet.

Today, the dark space was refreshingly cool after we'd been spending so much time in the heat of the garden. Mark plonked himself down in the nearest armchair and I sat on the arm of one opposite, not wanting to get too comfortable. My day was far from over.

Mark let out an exaggerated sigh. 'The diet's off, then, or at least delayed. I couldn't see a food stall that wasn't tempting.'

'Diet?' Wide-eyed, I looked him up and down. 'You're stick thin as it is. I'm trying to fatten you up with as much cake as possible, but I think you've got worms.'

'That was what my mother used to say. As a kid, I'd stand in front of cupboards and "graze", as she called it, but it never made any difference.' He shrugged his shoulders in mock defeat. 'Don't stop trying, though, I'm sure the cake is helping in some way.'

'Sophie, sorry to disturb.' Tina, the supervisor who looked after the Library Café for me, appeared by my side. 'Terry is here.'

'Thanks, Tina, tell him I'll be right out.'

'Who is this Terry?' enquired Mark, turning his head to give me a sly look. 'Is he a thing of beauty that you've been hiding from me?'

'Terry Mercer is a short, bald twenty-two-stone culinary

genius who owns an award-winning restaurant in Sheffield and is catering tonight's event. He's not my type and I have no idea if I'm his. So you can curb that imagination of yours. I need to help him set up. Be off with you.' I waved my arms in the direction of the door as though I was shooing out a cat. It had the desired effect and Mark got up to leave. Sadly, he didn't get far before the leather-clad figure of Detective Constable Joe Greene walked in.

When I first started working at Charleton House almost twelve months ago, Joe was coming to the end of his time as a motorcycle police officer whose bike was regularly parked up outside the security office while he conducted 'important police business', also known as eating his way through my profits, in one of the cafés. Now, he was a plainclothes detective constable, but he didn't seem to spend any less time dropping by the house. He was also Mark's brother-in-law, so we were party to more local gossip than was probably legal. Between Joe and me, we playfully kept Mark on his toes.

Today Joe was in his own bike leathers and appeared to be on his way home.

'Ello, 'ello, 'ello,' was Mark's version of a welcome. 'Here to arrest me, officer?'

'Society should be so lucky,' Joe replied quickly. If anyone could give Mark as good as they got, it was Joe. 'It's pretty much the weekend, give or take, so I was wondering if you two were free to get it started with a visit to the pub?'

'Sorry, chaps' – I shook my head – 'you're on your own. I'm working the Food Festival drinks reception. Have a drink for me, though.'

'I'm up for it.' Mark made his way over to his brother-in-law. 'I'm not going on the back of the bike, though. I consider myself highly adventurous of mind and spirit, less so of body.'

'I couldn't risk you raising the centre of gravity anyway.'

Joe and I both laughed. It was funny to imagine Mark's tall, skinny frame sticking upright like the mast of a ship, while Joe crouched over the handlebars of his powerful sports bike. It was even funnier to imagine Mark carefully squeezing his perfectly groomed handlebar moustache under a motorcycle helmet without damaging it.

'I'll head home, drop off the bike and change, then I'll get a taxi so I can have a drink. See you there in an hour?'

Mark turned towards me just as I was rearranging my hair in the glass of a framed picture on the wall. I wanted to look my best for tonight's event, but I was short on time so I checked that my artistically ruffled short hair hadn't gone flat in the heat.

'I hate to be the one to tell you, Sophie, but you've got a few grey hairs coming through.'

I gave Mark a hard stare, trying not to laugh. Not only was I entirely grey but, despite me only being in my forties, the majority of it was already turning silver.

'Idiot!' Joe smacked Mark on the back of the head with one of his gloves. 'That's no way to talk to a lady.'

'Lady?' Mark exclaimed. 'Since when has she...' Joe hit him again. I laughed out loud.

'To be fair, I've never claimed to be at all ladylike...'

The banter was interrupted by the sound of Joe's phone. 'DC Greene... Hey, Julie, what's up?... That's right, off for a pint... Oh, OK, I guess not. I'll head straight there, thanks.' Joe finished the call and looked forlornly at Mark. 'Sorry, you're drinking alone. Looks like I'm not off duty after all. There's been a theft up at Berwick Hall.' Nine-hundred-year-old Berwick Hall was another magnificent historic building that was open to the public, about thirty minutes' drive from Charleton.

'What's happened? Nothing serious, I hope.'

'A painting's been stolen from a public area. No one noticed it was missing until they were closing up for the day, so I can only assume it wasn't some enormous portrait. Either that or a visitor was carrying the world's biggest handbag. I better head off. Are you going to the pub anyway, Mark? I might be able to catch up with you later.'

'I'd like to. I'll see if Bill wants to join me, turn it into a date night.' Built like the ex-professional rugby player he was, Bill was the opposite of his skinny husband, and always enjoyed challenging stereotypes with his tough, no-nonsense broken-nosed looks.

Joe walked out the door, calling, 'Hope to see you and my big brother later, then, Mark,' over his shoulder. Time was ticking and I knew I had to get on. I packed Mark off to the pub, grabbed my notebook and went to find Terry; I'd already left him waiting too long.

CHAPTER 3

The Library Café kitchen looked out onto a lane that was out of bounds to visitors. Here staff took short cuts, deliveries were made, and it was where the security office was based. There were always people coming and going, but when an event was being set up, it became a hive of activity. You had to be careful to make sure you didn't get hit by distracted people carrying furniture, trip over cables for lighting, or get run over by trolleys piled high with food or bottles of wine.

This evening's event was pretty small and relaxed in comparison to some of those held within the more decadent rooms of the house. There would be no ballgowns or tuxedos, but there was still plenty to do. I'd collected Terry from his van on the lane and was walking him through to the Gilded Hall, a magnificent room with a grand staircase ideal for making speeches and representing the grandiosity of the house. The ceiling was home to a brilliant Baroque mural by Antonio Verrio, a favourite of kings and queens. The staircase, a grand carving of alabaster, marble and the local mineral Blue John, led up to a balcony that ran the full length of the south side of the room. Every inch of the elaborately decorated railing was covered in gold leaf, hence the name of the room. There was no doubting the wealth and status of the Fitzwilliam-Scott family throughout the centuries. It was an awe-inspiring space which could hearten or intimidate you, depending on your frame of mind and the tone of the event you were attending.

'So the canapés will be served in here?' Terry asked.

'Yes, canapés and champagne in here. The Duke will make a speech, thank the main sponsors, then mingling will take place while the string quartet plays. At the same time, small groups will be taken off on short tours of the state rooms. The whole thing will be done and dusted by 8pm. Nice and simple.'

'That's easy for you to say' – Terry rubbed his hand over the top of his head – 'you're used to this place. I followed all the food guidelines, but I'm still terrified that something I made will stain the floor if it gets dropped.' All caterers were told what could and couldn't be served in order to help protect the historic environment and objects, so no greasy or highly coloured foods. If guests were going to be standing, then they were limited to clear drinks such as champagne, white wine and water.

'You'll be fine; you've had everything checked over. If our event manager is happy then you're good to go.' As if on cue, the Charleton House event manager, Yeshim, arrived, a little flustered and tucking her shirt in as she ran across the room.

'Sorry, sorry, I was stuck on the phone with a supplier. Everything OK, Terry? You look terrified! Don't worry, your food is great, and the Duchess loves your restaurant. Thanks for looking after him, Sophie, I'll take over from here.' Yeshim had incredible energy levels and rarely seemed to take a breath. She was great fun to work with, but exhausting company. I usually made sure I had an enormous mug of coffee with me when I joined her for meetings.

Even though I wasn't catering this event, I'd offered to help out. As a relatively new member of staff, I took every opportunity to learn how the place ran. I was also still in the starry-eyed stage of my career at Charleton where I'd happily sacrifice a Friday night to work, even if it wasn't necessary.

The event was starting to take shape. The string quartet had arrived and was setting up in an alcove at the bottom of the stairs. An electrician was adding a few additional lights and making the room feel a little more dramatic, not that it took much. Ellie Bryant, a member of the conservation team, hovered in the background, making sure no one did anything that could cause any damage. She might resemble a waif-like creature who would prefer to disappear into the background, but I have witnessed Ellie launch herself at a teenager who, for a bet, had clambered over a rope and made himself comfortable in an eye-wateringly beautiful gilt wood armchair designed by William Kent for the Third Duke in the eighteenth century. Ellie was passing in time to see his bottom reach the padded seat covered in a navy blue damask and gave him a verbal dressing down which probably left him in therapy for years.

A group of tour guides made their way upstairs, ensuring that the rooms they planned on taking guests through didn't hold any surprises, the paintings they would be talking about were still in place, and nothing had been removed for cleaning or loaned to exhibitions. I pictured my favourite tour guide, Mark, in the Black Swan, enjoying a pint of local ale and a mountain of fish and chips while I would be spending the next hour helping to line up 150 wine glasses, passing the electrician his tools, finding some safety pins to help a waitress secure her skirt after the zip had broken, and fetching a plumber to unblock a toilet. It was a good job I didn't aspire to a life of glamour.

Eventually, calm descended alongside a gentle air of anticipation. Being as this was such a small event, none of us were on edge. Occasions like this gave us the chance to savour our surroundings almost as much as the guests did.

As the guests started to arrive, serving staff offered champagne round, the bottles having been opened in a back corridor to avoid flying corks damaging precious artwork. The Duke and Duchess worked the room, welcoming everyone in their usual down-to-earth fashion and thanking them for their support. Terry's canapés were clearly a hit, and I watched as a couple of the guests cut across the room and homed in on a server who was carrying their favourite little taste bomb to grab a few more. Honey coloured lighting glinted off gilt mirror frames and the string quartet sent waves of Beethoven out across the gradually filling room.

'So far, so good.' I jumped as Yeshim appeared by my side. 'Terry finally calmed down, with the help of a glass of champagne, but I'm going to have to keep an eye on him. It went down far too quickly. The last thing we need is him sliding down the banisters as the Duke makes his speech. There he is.' She pointed across the room to a slightly wobbly looking Terry. 'And yes, there's another glass of champagne in his hand.'

I looked over in time to see Terry exchange an empty champagne glass for a full one as a server with a tray of drinks walked by.

'Oh no, there's the Duchess, and she's joining him.' Standing beside Yeshim was like having my own private sports commentary, and I wasn't sure I could get a word in if I tried. 'No, he's not... he won't... he has.' Yeshim let out a loud, exasperated sigh as Terry put his arm round the Duchess's waist and laughed far too loudly at something she said. Like a bird of prey, Yeshim swept in, had a quiet word in the Duchess's ear and steered her away from Terry's grasp, no doubt having thought of someone she could claim it was important the Duchess meet.

Well done, Yeshim.

As I scanned the party, my eyes rested on a man in a dark suit talking to the Duke and gesturing around the room. It was Detective Inspector Mike Flynn, who had got wind of my involvement in police business during the summer and wasn't my biggest fan. I wasn't surprised to see him here. Joe had told me just how ambitious Flynn was, and cultivating a friendship with someone as important as the Duke was no doubt part of the plan to help him shoot up the ranks.

DI Flynn scanned the room until his eyes came to rest on me. He raised his glass of champagne in my direction, but the expression on his face remained indifferent. It looked as if we wouldn't become friends anytime soon.

A hush came over the crowd and I noticed that the string quartet had stopped playing. Yeshim was talking to the Duke at the bottom of the stairs. A broad-shouldered, tall and handsome man, he had the stature and presence of one of the stags that roamed the Charleton estate. Wearing a navy blue pinstriped suit that was perfectly tailored to his figure, his pale-blue shirt open at the collar, he'd chosen to go without a tie. He cut a classical figure that matched his exquisite surroundings: a man of power, influence and style.

The Duke climbed halfway up the stairs, where he turned and waited patiently for silence to descend. With a charming, welcoming smile, he scanned the room.

'Ladies and gentlemen, it is such a pleasure to welcome you all to Charleton this evening. My wife and I gain so much joy from sharing this wonderful house with others and I thank you all for joining us. The Charleton Food Festival is one of my personal highlights of the year, and here in Derbyshire we are fortunate to have some of the country's finest artisan producers. This is a fabulous opportunity for them to showcase their talents, and we are so grateful to you, our many sponsors, for helping to make this possible...'

As the Duke spoke, my mind started to wander. It wasn't that he was a poor public speaker; just the opposite, in fact. He was an accomplished speech writer, and although his cut-glass accent was a throwback to more socially divided times, with the Duke it was just another part of his charming and gentlemanly image rather than an attempt to make his audience feel that they were in the presence of someone superior to them. But I'd heard him speak on many previous occasions and this was a fairly run-of-the-mill event, so I was able to tune out what he was saying.

I found myself wondering about the gardener who had barged into me earlier in the day, and I instinctively rubbed the spot on my arm where we'd collided. I was bound to have a bruise by now. It was a long time since I'd seen someone look quite so angry; he had been a rather frightening figure as he'd barrelled past Mark and me. Whatever Ben had done, it must have been pretty awful.

My thoughts were interrupted by laughter as the crowd reacted warmly to something the Duke had said.

'...So please, help me prove my wife wrong, just once.' He smiled in the direction of the Duchess who was laughing at his comments. 'Now, please enjoy the champagne and delicious food, take one of the tours with our extremely knowledgeable guides and have a lovely evening. Thank you again for all of your support.' He raised the champagne glass he had been cradling in his hand, smiled and slowly nodded his appreciation. His words were met with rapturous applause, and as he descended back into the crowd, the string quartet began to play again.

'I've never seen him fail to capture an audience.' A deep voice came from over my right shoulder and I turned to see a smiling ruddy-faced man. Wearing a checked shirt and tweed jacket, he looked as if he'd just come in from a hunt. 'Malcolm,' – he offered me his hand – 'Malcolm De Witt. I was up at Oxford with the Duke. He was forever jumping on tables to make speeches after a drink or two. It's good to see he's calmed down a little from his student days.'

'Sophie, I work here. You're a friend of the family?'

'I was. We're just getting reacquainted after a few years in the friendship wilderness. No one's fault, adult life just gets in the way. We used to ski together every year when the children were young, ran into each other at a university alumni event a couple of months ago and he invited me to stay for the week as I was due to be in the area on business.' Malcolm had a far off look in his eyes, like he wasn't fully engaging with me but just wanted to kill the time with someone – anyone. He was nice enough, though.

'Have you been here before?'

'Many times. A gang of us used to come up for a month every summer while we were students, got up to all sorts of mischief. Then there was the occasional Christmas party. Once his father died and Alex became Duke, he got too busy and my work took me overseas so we lost touch.' He was watching as the Duke entertained a group of fawning ladies who were gathered around him like twelve-year-olds around a pop star. 'Look at him. We're exactly the same age, give or take a week or two, and yet he looks twenty years younger than me. I, on the other hand, am carrying every single one of my sixty years.' He patted his stomach. 'Well, we only get one go around, may as well enjoy it. Lovely chatting, Sophie, I'm sure I'll see you again.' He drained his champagne glass, and with that, he was off, homing in on some bite-sized cheesecakes that were being offered to the guests.

'Sophie?' I had just said goodbye to Yeshim, who I had agreed could have an early night. I was more than capable of overseeing the end of the drinks reception. 'Sophie, I need to talk to you.'

Domenico Negri was trying to get my attention. Despite Negri being over 200 years old and long since dead and buried, this wasn't as crazy as it sounds. A couple of members of the live interpretation team had been employed to attend the reception dressed as significant food-related characters who had links with the house and engage with the guests. During the day, they would dress as historical characters and talk to the visitors, often recreating events from throughout the history of Charleton House. They weren't simply actors who memorised lines and hoped no one asked them an awkward question; they carried out in-depth research and took pride in remaining in character, no matter what they were asked or how visitors behaved around them.

Negri had been an Italian confectioner who, in the 1760s, had supplied the 5th Duke of Ravensbury with a spectacular dessert for his wife's birthday. Negri had presented an enormous, delicately handcrafted spread of sweetmeats, macarons, biscuits, marshmallow, fruits and creams, which would have been displayed like a work of art with sugar ornaments creating country scenes, fountains and buildings.

I took Negri over to a quiet corner.

'What's wrong?'

'It might be nothing. I might just have missed it, but I don't think so.' The Italian accent he had been using with the guests had gone. I rested my hand on his arm.

'What might you have missed? I don't understand.'

Negri took a deep breath, glanced around, then carried on, almost whispering.

'I was walking through the Stone Gallery. I know it's not officially open tonight, but we've been allowed to use it to get from our changing room to here. Well, I've been back and forth a couple of times, but when I came back through it a few minutes ago, I noticed that something was missing. Do you know the big green bowl with a brown rim? Looks like chocolate has been smeared round the edge and is melting into the bowl? It always sits on the table below the painting of the girl and dog?' His description rang bells, but I honestly couldn't be sure I knew what he was referring to. 'I could have sworn it was there earlier in the night, but now it's gone. The table is empty.'

My heart sank. I had dealt with drunken guests and fire alarms, running out of wine, and guests and staff alike being taken ill, but never this. Now I wished I hadn't let Yeshim go home. I called the security office on the radio and let them know we had a possible missing object, then searched around for the conservation team member who had been keeping an eye on things. When I found her, I pulled her aside.

'Ellie, quick, I need you to come with me.'

'What's wrong?'

'Not here.' I led her out of the room, trying to look calm and composed, and took her through to the Stone Gallery, a simple stone-floored corridor where some of the Duke's art was on display. Beneath the picture of a girl and a dog stood an empty table.

'Is there normally a bowl here?' I asked.

'Yes,' – she looked confused – 'the St Ives Bowl. Where is it?'

'I was hoping you could tell me. It's not gone for conservation work or been loaned out?'

'No, we never loan it out. It's a personal piece of the Duke's, a gift to his mother by the ceramicist who made it. It has no financial value, but he loves it.' The Dowager Duchess had been a real firebrand: a remarkable character who loomed large over the more recent history of Charleton House. It was she and her husband, the 11th Duke of Ravensbury, who had first opened the house to the public. Glamorous, outspoken and possessed of a wicked sense of humour, she was rarely seen without a martini in her hand in her later years, and martini would always be found on the Garden Café menu in her honour. I wished that she had lived long enough for me to meet her; I know I would have been terrified of her, but in awe of her nonetheless.

Ellie glanced around, as though expecting to find the bowl on another shelf or above one of the fireplaces along the wall.

'What's going on, girls?' I recoiled at the use of 'girls', but chose to ignore it and turned to face Pat, a security officer.

'We're missing a bowl.' I pointed at the table. 'It was there at the start of the evening, now it's gone.'

Pat thought for a moment. 'You positive?' He looked at me like I was a small child. 'Sure you're not mistaken, mislaid it, your memory going?'

'Very sure.' My teeth were clenched. I took a deep breath and spoke slowly and clearly. 'I'm reporting a missing item to you. I trust I can now leave this in your hands and…'

'Is everything alright?' Before I had the chance to start using four-letter words, DI Flynn walked in. 'I saw security come through.' He nodded at Pat. 'Can I be of assistance?'

'A significant item from the collection has gone missing, sir.' Pat stood ramrod straight, his voice having changed to one of control and respect. He seemed determined to make me punch him this evening. 'I was just about to take appropriate action when you walked in, sir.'

I stepped forward, glaring at Pat as I did so, daring him to stop me carrying out my role. As onsite manager for the event, I quickly filled DI Flynn in on the situation and that we were about to call the police.

'Well, as the police are already onsite' – the corner of his mouth showed the beginnings of a smile – 'I'll take over.' He nodded at Pat. 'You head back to the security office and get your team to start shutting this place down. I don't want anyone leaving. I'll have a quick word with the Duke, break the news to him. All clear?'

'Absolutely, sir.' Pat dashed off down the corridor, looking as if it was the first time he'd done any 'dashing' in years and he was probably regretting the family-sized pizza I'd seen him ploughing his way through earlier in the evening.

DI Flynn turned back to us. 'I'll need everyone to remain onsite, so please let your teams know. Now if you'll excuse me, I need to break the news to the Duke.'

With that, he strode purposefully down the corridor, and I prepared to spend the rest of the evening placating guests who were trapped here. Mind you, there were worse places to be trapped.

. . .

Fortunately, the majority of the guests didn't notice that there was a problem. We just kept pouring wine, and when we were out of canapés, I ran back to the Library Café kitchens and pulled a few cakes out of the fridge. Alcohol and cake – it was a sure-fire way to keep people occupied and onside.

In the meantime, the Stone Gallery had been closed off and declared a potential crime scene. DI Flynn, with the help of the security team, had conducted a sweep of nearby rooms to check the bowl hadn't found its way elsewhere, and all the live interpreters who had used the gallery as a short cut had been put in a separate room. When I'd taken them some refreshments, I'd been met by a bizarre sight: two eighteenth-century characters, one male, one female, sitting on a very modern sofa, killing time on their mobile phones. It wasn't an unfamiliar sight, but it never failed to amuse me.

After a thorough search of staff bags, eventually DI Flynn declared that the reception guests could leave, but anyone with a bag large enough to conceal the bowl would need to be searched. Once the guests had gone, he pulled me aside.

'I just wanted to give you a quick update. The Stone Gallery is off limits and I have a team in there now, taking fingerprints. We've completed bag searches and found nothing, so we'll let the staff leave shortly. There's currently no sign of anything on CCTV, and the likelihood is that the bowl is long gone.' He sighed. 'The Duke is of course devastated, but equally he's realistic about it all, especially with the lack of any sort of art alarm system attached to the item. I was rather hoping that he would have invested in some upgrades to the security system by now, especially after recent events.'

He was referring to a murder that had occurred onsite a couple of months ago. Much to DI Flynn's annoyance, I had identified the killer before anyone else. This event was the first time our paths had crossed since the murder and I was a little surprised by how civil he was being, but I took it as a sign of his professionalism and gave him a brownie point.

'Do you think this is related to the theft up at Berwick?'

'I don't know, but it seems a bit of a coincidence that something goes missing from two historic buildings not far apart on the same day.' He paused, then looked at me intently. 'But what I do know is that the police don't need any help.' His eyes drilled into mine. 'OK?'

I nodded. 'The thought had never crossed my mind, Inspector.'

CHAPTER 4

I'd been warned that the cafés would be quiet over the weekend of the Food Festival, but my staff weren't allowed to take it easy. When I arrived at work the next morning, I helped to set up the Garden Café, a beautiful Baroque orangery with enormous ceiling-high windows that looked out onto the gardens. When it was built in the 1700s, it had been heated with stoves, and in the winter it was used as a conservatory for delicate plants. Now it was an elegant café where visitors came for afternoon tea and a glass of champagne. When the British weather was behaving itself, the doors were fastened back and tables placed among the lime and lemon trees that decorated the patio.

Most of my team had yet to arrive so I had the opportunity to enjoy my surroundings in peace. The sunlight streamed in and cast a gauze-like veil over the tables. The glassware had been polished to within an inch of its life and sparkled, ready to hold fine wines, glasses waiting to be clinked together in moments of celebration. The freesias that had been delivered by the gardens team were ready to go in delicate vases and bring some subtle colour to each table.

'Morniiiing,' Mark trilled as he flew through the door. 'The sun is shining, you need more coffee and I need gossip, so we're heading out to the garden where you can fill up on caffeine and loosen that tongue of yours.' He put his arm through mine and marched me towards the patio doors that were already open. We let ourselves out through a gate and made our way down the path towards the Food Festival stalls.

There was already a buzz of activity, even though it was only 9am. It was still an hour until the visitors would be let in, but there was bound to be plenty to do before then. Robin Scrimshaw, the head gardener, was heading in the same direction as us with an enormous roll of black bin bags under his arm.

'Bit early, aren't ya?' he asked.

'We reckoned we could have a bit of a wander before the hordes arrive,' Mark replied. 'Besides which, if I don't get some good quality coffee in this one, then… well, it's just not worth thinking about.'

I smiled and shrugged in agreement. 'Will you get a chance to explore the stalls?' I asked Robin.

'Sort of. The whole garden team is being kept busy, whether it's emptyin' bins' – he pointed at the bin bags under his arm – 'or keeping people off the flowers, but we always get given treats by the stallholders for free, especially if we help 'em out with somethin.'

We'd reached the circle of stalls and Robin set off to distribute rubbish bags. Lucy and Kathy were still setting up Signal Box Coffee. The cherry-red van immediately put a smile on my face, and Lucy spotted me straight away.

'Morning, Sophie, can we get you a coffee?'

'That would be great, thank you.'

'And…' She looked at Mark.

'Mark. I'd love some, thank you.'

As Lucy got to work, I spotted Kathy carrying some boxes

into the van. She nodded in our direction when she saw us, but she looked tired and not quite as happy to be there as her sister.

'So, how did the Duke take it?' Mark brought me back to last night's events. 'He must have been furious to have it taken right from under his nose.'

'It wasn't exactly under his nose. It was hard to tell, he seemed quite business-like. Maybe "subdued" would be the right word. When I saw him, he was just listening to DI Flynn as he updated him.'

Mark shook his head. 'Poor man, he loves that piece. The previous Duchess cherished it, and so did he once his mother passed away.'

'If it was so precious, why was it on display in a public route? Why didn't he keep it in his study or somewhere off limits?'

'The artist became quite well known, and when she died, the Duke felt it was important to share her work with the public. That's just the way he is. He doesn't believe art should be locked away and enjoyed only by those with vast amounts of money. Also, it doesn't have a great deal of financial value. The artist became recognised as a superb ceramicist, but she wasn't hugely collectable. So in theory, it wasn't at risk.'

'Then why would someone steal it if it's not valuable?' I asked. Mark shrugged his shoulders.

'No idea. The thrill? The mistaken belief that it was valuable?'

'Here you are, two mugs of coffee. You can keep the mugs.' Lucy had appeared with two wonderful Signal Box Coffee mugs; they were the classic chunky diner shape and mine felt great in my hand. A little illustration of a signal box and the name of the company were painted on the side in white; the mug itself was a red that matched the van.

She had made my morning. 'Thanks, Lucy, they're great,' – I took a sip – 'and so is the coffee. I held off having my usual cup when I got to work; I wanted to wait for this.' I breathed in the rich aroma and took a bigger mouthful. Lucy looked over at Mark and smiled.

'Sorry, did you have to suffer while she deprived herself of caffeine?'

'She wasn't too bad, but I keep a taser to hand just to be on the safe side.' He smirked, clearly delighted that he'd found someone to engage with in some banter at my expense.

'Don't encourage him. It was worth the wait. Look, I've been thinking, I'd love to sit down with you sometime and learn a bit more about the company.'

I was about to suggest we catch up once the festival was over when I was interrupted by a voice in my ear. 'Ours is much better.'

I turned quickly and spilt hot coffee on the back of my hand, which hurt like hell and brought tears to my eyes. 'Ow, dammit!'

'Oh God, I'm sorry, that was my fault. Here.' Guy handed me a handkerchief that he'd pulled out of his pocket. 'Sorry, I didn't mean to make you jump. Are you OK?' He looked genuinely worried. Kyle was with him, and he simply looked embarrassed.

'I'm fine, honestly.' I dried my hand and wiped the mug before handing back the coffee-stained handkerchief.

'Guy, you idiot!' Lucy didn't look best pleased as she reached for the mug. 'Let me top you up, Sophie.'

'No, it's fine, honestly, I didn't lose much.' Looking up to see Kathy glaring at Guy, I sensed a little tension. 'You must have lots to do, we should get back to work.'

'Not really.' Guy put his hands in his pockets. 'We did most of it yesterday and Ben was planning on getting here early to finish off. He'll be in there now.' He nodded towards the Airstream. 'He's more of an early bird than us.' Turning towards Kathy's retreating back, he bellowed, 'Morning, Kathy.' There was no response, but she'd have had to have been deaf not to hear him. She'd made no effort to come and talk to us once he'd arrived, and now she was ignoring his greeting, which seemed out of character for the friendly woman I'd been introduced to yesterday.

The Airstream was still closed up. Ben hadn't opened the serving hatch or put out any signage, so it looked like an enormous silver bullet: very cool, but a bit soulless. I watched as Robin headed towards the back door, brandishing a handful of bin bags.

Lucy turned back towards the campervan. 'Well, I must get on. Thanks for stopping by, Sophie, and yes, it would be great to meet up. Just let me know when you're free.'

'I guess we should give Ben a hand.' I was surprised to hear Kyle's voice; he had been so quiet. 'Guy, are you coming?'

'Of course. Sorry again, Sophie. I definitely owe you a coffee now, so drop by when you're ready for your next top-up.' He smiled and turned, but had barely taken a step before the back door to the Airstream was flung open and Robin burst out.

'HELP, SOMEONE, HELP,' he cried. 'HE'S DEAD!'

CHAPTER 5

'I thought you were working on the theft at Berwick Hall.'

Joe sat next to me on a bench that had a great view of the Airstream. 'I am, I'm multi-tasking, and we're not exactly flush with officers right now.'

I still had hold of my Signal Box Coffee mug and turned it slowly in my hands. 'So how bad is it?'

'Pretty bad,' he replied. 'Poor guy had his head bashed in. It looks like whoever did it used one of those coffee things. You know – you bang it really hard, and then put coffee grounds in it before slotting it into the machine.' He mimed the actions of a barista.

'You mean the portafilter?'

He shrugged and gave me a blank look. 'If you say so. Anyway, one of those. It was lying on the floor covered in... well, you don't need to know, but there's a bloody great hole in his head.'

'Poor Ben. That's a horrible way to go. Is there any sign of a struggle?'

Joe nodded. 'Some, and it looks like a few things might have been taken. I'll need Guy or Kyle to confirm.'

Guy was talking to a uniformed police officer; Kyle was pacing up and down, seemingly in a different world. I nudged Joe and pointed in Kyle's direction.

'He looks like he's in shock, is there someone who can take care of him?'

'I'll make sure he's looked after. Now, you sure you didn't see anything unusual, anyone around the van?'

'You mean the Airstream? No, only Robin Scrimshaw. He was going round to every stall and handing out bin bags. We were all just chatting; Guy and Kyle thought Ben was in there working.'

Joe stood up and adjusted his belt. 'I'll send someone over to take a statement from you later.'

Before he had a chance to walk away, I had a question for him. 'Look, you're going to get this a lot, but when are the stalls around here going to be allowed to reopen?' Joe had told me not long after he'd arrived that the Food Festival was going to have to be closed, and now the area was buzzing with forensic officers in white suits, a number of them going in and out of the Airstream while police officers were carrying out interviews.

He was about to answer, but paused and looked intently at me. 'Are you concerned about the festival, the stallholders and the enjoyment of the visitors, or are you just wondering when you can get your hands on another coffee?' His eyes glanced down towards the mug in my hands, but when he looked back up at me, he was smiling. 'I know you have a severe addiction, but that's taking it a bit far.'

'It wasn't what I was thinking. I was just pre-empting the question you are going to start getting bombarded with, but now you mention it...' I looked over towards the red campervan. Lucy and Kathy were sitting silently outside, waiting their turn to be interviewed, and any desire to lighten the mood vanished. 'This is a pretty small community. Most of the stallholders know each other – they often end up at the same events, so this will hit a lot of people quite hard.'

I felt Joe's hand on my shoulder. 'I know. We'll get them back up and running as quickly as possible. I would imagine being able to get back to work will make it easier for them. There'll be a point when we can move the Airstream, which will make it all more bearable. Now, don't you have some cafés to run?'

'They're all really quiet during the festival; everyone comes out here to eat, so my team are probably twiddling their fingers.'

'Not all of them.' Joe nodded towards a couple of my Library team who were standing off to one side, watching the drama. They were probably on their break, but still, it wasn't very professional, especially as their uniforms were on display.

'Bloody hell!' I stood up, annoyed. 'I'll have a word. A bit of common sense wouldn't go amiss.'

'Go for it, dragon lady, speak later.' Joe walked off, pulling a notebook out of his back pocket. I marched off in the opposite direction to have a word with my team members. After metaphorically giving them a clip around the ear, I sent them back to work. With the festival closed, there was a good chance that visitors would make their way to the cafés.

Mark had already returned to the house to deliver a tour, but I didn't feel like following him yet. It seemed important to me to hang around; I was certain it wasn't some sort of gratuitous rubbernecking, which would have been a bad case of hypocrisy after sending my team members away for doing just that, but I'd been here when the body had been found, with the people who'd had the closest connection to Ben, and I felt the need to stay nearby. I was also, if I was honest, interested in finding out more.

I watched Kyle. He still looked slightly dazed, but at least he was holding a mug of something warm and hopefully sugary. He walked away from the police officer who had been questioning him, ducked under a strip of crime scene tape and sat down on the bench I'd just left. I returned and sat next to him.

'I'm so sorry.' I didn't know what else to say.

'Thanks. I can't believe it.'

'Had he worked for you for long?'

Kyle nodded. 'Couple of years. I'd gone to school with him not far from here – we're both local. We hadn't seen each other for years, then I went into business with Guy and we set up the office here in Derbyshire. Guy lives in London, but is on the road a lot so it didn't matter to him where the office was. I wanted to be near my family.' Kyle paused for a moment, his head hanging down. He hadn't looked at me since we'd started talking. 'I ran into Ben in a pub. He was looking for work and we needed an extra set of hands at events like this, so he came on board. He was great, a real hard worker. Pretty quiet, but he knew how to make a great cup of coffee.' He sat back on the bench and sighed. For the first time, I noticed that there were tears in his eyes. 'He was so excited about coming here – he loved Charleton, told us how his parents used to bring him here as a kid every summer.'

'He sounds like a nice guy.'

'He was.'

'So who would want to hurt him? Do you know if he'd crossed someone?'

Kyle shook his head. 'No, I really don't. I know he'd got himself into debt a couple of years ago, but that was all cleared up, or at least I thought it was. He...' Kyle shrugged and fell silent. I felt like I'd pushed him as far as I could.

'Kyle?' It was Joe, walking towards us. 'I'm sorry, but I'm going to need you down at the station. Routine, nothing to worry about.'

Kyle rose from his seat and turned towards me. He attempted to smile, but there were still tears in his eyes. Joe touched his arm gently and directed him towards a car that was waiting on the nearest gravel path.

As I stood up, I saw the next item on my agenda heading my way. Bruce from the Northern Bean Company was striding across the grass. Of course, when we'd agreed to reschedule our meeting to this morning, we'd had no idea that coffee would be the last thing on our minds.

The Northern Bean Company was a medium-sized business based in Manchester, our nearest large city, supplying numerous cafés and restaurants in the area. It was big enough to keep its prices lower than companies like Signal Box or Silver Bullet, but small enough that customers could feel pleased with themselves for not using the big international coffee roasters. The Northern Bean coffee was OK, but not particularly special. In my experience, it was quite dark and had a sort of smoky carbon flavour, so it was hard to taste the origins of the bean. It wasn't awful, just a bit on the predictable, commercial side for me.

'Hi, Bruce, I was just about to come looking for you. The police are closing off the gardens, so I'll walk you back towards the car park.'

'OK, fine,' he replied, looking rattled and sweaty.

'Are you OK?'

He nodded and pulled a bottle of water out of a pocket in his baggy cargo shorts. 'What a horrendous start to the day. I was meant to meet Ben yesterday. Poor guy. I just don't know what to say.' Bruce was glancing around as he spoke, looking as if his eyes weren't taking in anything that he saw. After a few moments' silence, he finally looked at me. 'Sorry I couldn't see you yesterday, something came up. I just wanted to check in with you. We have a new line of beans that you might be interested in, but now doesn't seem like the time to discuss it.'

It wasn't, and it certainly wasn't the time to tell him I was planning on finding someone else to supply our coffee beans.

Bruce was tugging at his shaggy beard as he spoke. With that and his shorts, he looked like the climbers on boulders and rock faces in the Peak District, practising their skills before heading off to climb mountains in Scotland or further afield in the Alps, maybe even fulfilling a dream of making it up Mount Everest.

All of a sudden, he seemed to pull himself together. 'Look,

Sophie, Charleton is a really important contract for us. I'll send you a couple of bags of the new stuff gratis and I'll do you a decent discount on your first order.' He sounded pretty confident that I'd like it, but I didn't have high hopes. I just nodded and politely thanked him. I hadn't been at Charleton House long before I'd learnt that Bruce was all about the sale; I don't think I'd ever had a conversation with him about the origins of his beans or what the company was doing to support the farmers, let alone what flavours he was passionate about or why he had got into the coffee business. It didn't look as if I was about to today, either.

'Any idea what happened?' It took me a minute to realise he had switched the conversation to Ben.

'No, none.'

We'd reached the path that would lead him to the car park. There were a couple of police officers standing guard, making sure no one came back into the gardens.

'Right, well, I'd better be off.' He stared back across the gardens to the stalls and the police activity around them before finally looking at me and shaking my hand. 'I'll have someone deliver those bags to you.'

With that, he was gone, his long strides powering him across the grass. He looked as if he was in a rush, but I wasn't at all sorry that our meeting had been shorter than usual.

I dismissed Bruce from my mind and set off towards the house. There were plenty of far more important and productive things I needed to do with my time. My feet crunched up the wide gravel path and I caught a glimpse of Mark in one of the windows, pointing out towards the gardens and probably explaining the history of the estate to a group of Russian businessmen. They'd asked for somewhere to land their helicopter, to borrow one of the Duke's private rooms to smoke cigars and drink champagne, and that none of the public go anywhere near them. What they'd got was the address of a football club ten miles away that might be prepared for them to land on the pitch, a tour with Mark in the same parts of the house as the general public, and extra members of our security team keeping an eye on them just in case they got difficult. The Duke and Duchess were happy to accommodate all sorts of requests, so long as they were reasonable and not the by-product of arrogance and wads of laundered cash.

I stopped to run my hand through a row of lavender plants that filled a long bed along the side of the path, and then brought it up to my nose, taking a deep breath. I'd picked up this habit from my father when I was a child and now I couldn't walk past a lavender plant without trailing my hand through it.

'*Lavandula angustifolia*, or common lavender.' Malcolm walked over to join me. 'Not a huge fan myself, reminds me of old aunts and grandmothers, but I once dated a girl whose family ran an enormous lavender farm in Provence so I know a bit about it. Beautiful – both the fields of lavender and the girl.' He was wearing, appropriately enough, a lavender coloured t-shirt tucked into cream cargo shorts and straining over his stomach. He was as ruddy faced as he had been at the drinks reception; even more so, if that was possible.

'Thought it was time I got out and about, got a bit of fresh air. Alex and I finished off a bottle of port last night. Well, I finished it off and he kept me company. Quite a night, eh?' He seemed to have no clue that the morning had been infinitely more eventful. I didn't have the energy to break it to him, and he'd find out soon enough if he tried to get into the gardens, so I played along.

'How was the Duke? Was he very upset?'

'Stoic, I guess you'd say. He talked a lot about the ceramicist. It was all rather dull; it's never been my kind of thing, but I guess it was part of my role as supportive friend to listen to him.' Malcolm didn't seem too concerned about any of it, but if he hadn't been in the Duke's life for a while, then maybe some of the emotional connection between the two men had waned.

'Were you very close when you were at university?'

Malcolm thought about the question for a moment. 'I suppose we were, not that we discussed that kind of thing. We left that for the girls. I was a little surprised, to be honest with you; I didn't think I had enough money to be accepted by his crowd as I had a very different upbringing. Normal, you'd probably call it. Father was the manager of a small local bank, mother stayed at home and looked after the children. It was the talk of the town when I got into Oxford. Of course, that was expected for Alex. Grandfather went, father went, Alex was next in line.

'There was a group of us who always dined together. Lots of champagne flowed and late nights drinking extortionately priced whisky. Of course, none of them had to worry about money. They spent summers in French châteaux, enjoyed endless skiing trips, that sort of thing. They were good enough to invite me on a couple of their jaunts and pay my way – very generous, but it certainly stung a bit, I can tell you. Sense of pride and all that.' He laughed, although it sounded more like a snort. 'They probably viewed it as a charitable act. Made me work damned hard, though. I was determined I'd be able to pay my own way once we graduated, show them I could match them pound for pound.'

He stopped and stared off into the distance. After what felt like a few awkward minutes, but was probably only seconds, he turned to look at me and smiled, and with a much more upbeat tone brought the subject to a close.

'Well, it seems to have worked. I've done pretty well for myself and the Duke remains a very generous man. I'm off for a stroll; it's too nice a day to be inside. Hope to run into you again later, Sally.'

I was about to correct him, but he had already set off.

I had expected the Library Café to be quiet, but not this quiet. However, I couldn't imagine it staying this way for long, unless the visitors assumed that the entire house was closed too. Tina was sitting at a table in the far corner, catching up on paperwork, a cappuccino and chocolate cookie beside her. A young member of staff stood behind the till, looking bored until she saw it was me who had walked in, at which point she jumped like someone had poked her from behind with something sharp.

'Sophie, is it true?' She started talking nineteen to the dozen. 'We saw all the police cars and someone said something about a dead body in the Great Pond, but I'm not due on a break yet so I've not been able to go and find out. Were you there?'

Tina joined us and tried to calm the girl down. 'Breathe, Chelsea, breathe. Let the poor woman sit down, I'm sure she'll tell us what she can in a moment.'

Tina had always been a steady, calming influence on the staff, and I often reminded myself how lucky I was to have her. When I'd arrived at Charleton House, she'd made my transition into a new job so much easier by keeping things running smoothly while I'd spent my time in endless meetings and learning the ropes.

I sank into one of the armchairs, the cold leather against my skin a relief after the intense heat out in the gardens.

'So, what's the gossip?' Tina was as keen as anyone to hear what had been going on.

'The body wasn't in the lake, it was in the back of that coffee Airstream. One of their staff. He'd been hit over the back of the head.'

'Was it a break in?'

'Joe said there were signs of a disturbance and things were missing, so that would make sense.'

I looked around the room. Only one table was taken and I recognised the customer as the Charleton House Health and Safety Manager. In a stiff grey suit, Anthony Leggett looked every inch a rule-making bureaucratic robot, but having sat in countless meetings with him, I knew that his exterior concealed a wicked sense of humour and someone with a firm grasp on the realities of working with the public.

'You can't account for the stupidity of people,' was one of his most often-used comments.

'Has it been this quiet all morning?' I asked Tina.

'Don't worry, it's not as bad as it looks. We had a mid-morning rush, three muffins and a packet of nuts. You'll be able to give us all pay rises.' She grinned. 'Really, don't worry, this happens every year. No one expects the cafés to make any money when the festival is on. Well, maybe a little in the Garden Café. Some of our older regulars still like to go in there for their afternoon tea, and dog walkers stop by the Stables Café.' Visitors didn't need a ticket to the house to reach the Stables Café, which took up a small space in an attractive cobbled courtyard within the eighteenth-century stable block, so it was hugely popular with cyclists, hikers and others exploring the 40,000 acre estate.

'Here in the Library,' Tina continued, 'we'll only see the staff who are too busy to go into the garden, which as it's a weekend is down to three people in IT with deadlines to meet and Anthony who's here to check everything's OK at the Food Festival. Mind you, that might change now. I'll make some extra sandwiches.'

I looked over at Anthony; he had his phone wedged between his shoulder and ear and was frantically making notes. I wondered if he'd expected to spend the day getting free food, when instead he'd got a dead body and a mountain of paperwork.

Tina looked up. 'Hang on, we're saved, the rush has arrived. We're about to sell at least one blueberry muffin, I'll go and book a cruise.'

I turned round to be greeted by a stony-faced Mark.

'Are you alright?'

'This is the face of a man who has spent the last ninety minutes talking into the wind.' He dropped into the armchair next to me. 'I love my job, I love telling the stories of this amazing house, and often I have to do that to people who aren't as interested in it as I am. You know, schoolkids who would rather be chasing the ducks on the Great Pond, journalists who are here because nothing has happened and their editor has forced them to go and do a piece on local tourist hot spots, or corporate guests who are only interested in the free alcohol. But this lot took the biscuit. They spent their time pointing at things and laughing, presumably claiming they have "three of these at home", ogling female visitors in shorts and checking their phones.'

'You mean the Russian group?'

'I do. But on the upside, a couple of little old ladies from Newcastle who attached themselves to the back of the group got a top quality tour for free, and the Russians' interpreter, who, to be fair, was hugely apologetic, gave me two hundred quid as a tip.'

'Bloody hell!' Chelsea shouted out. 'Maybe I should become a tour guide.'

Mark rolled his eyes at me and shouted back, 'Don't get too excited, I can't keep it. I'll take it down to the ticket office and get it recorded and put in the till.'

Chelsea looked disappointed and started straightening packets of nuts. Mark waited until she looked preoccupied by her own thoughts, and then focused on me again.

'So, any more developments? Does Joe have any leads?' As he talked, he removed his tie and rolled up his sleeves.

'No. I think he reckons a robbery, but he didn't say much. Far too early, I guess.'

'Well, he's supposed to be coming round for dinner tonight, so I'll see what I can get out of him. Bill has promised to make his favourite Eton Mess for dessert, but I might threaten to withhold it if he doesn't tell us what he's got so far. Do you want to come? There'll be plenty of food, and I could swear our friendly local bobby gets a twinkle in his eye every time he sees you.'

'Don't be ridiculous, Mark, there's no twinkling of any kind, nor will there be. We're friends, end of story.'

Mark pouted like a four-year-old. 'Spoilsport. Well, are you coming tonight?'

'Thanks, but no. I need a quiet night in after all this drama.' I dragged myself out of the chair. 'Promise me, no twinkle references over dinner. Don't go putting any ideas in Joe's head.'

'Like I said, spoilsport.' Mark stood up, spun dramatically and marched off towards the door. I knew I'd see him later; he could only go for a couple of hours before coming begging for free baked goods.

I liked to work in the Library Café kitchens, overlooking the back lane. Sometimes colleagues would stop for a chat through the window if they saw me there, and I felt like I had a reasonably good handle on life at the house as a result. Despite the festival being closed, not many visitors had made it to the Library Café yet, and Tina and her team were more than able to cope with those who had come in, so I'd decided to spend the afternoon trying out a couple of recipes.

I wasn't a trained pastry chef. I'd been employed at Charleton House to manage the cafés, and most of the cooking and baking was done by a husband-and-wife team Gregg and Ruth Danforth and the staff who worked for them, but I loved baking, and if I managed my time well, I was able to help out. Ruth was a great tutor and my skills were improving all the time, so I'd also been able to cut a few costs this way.

Right now, I was working on a very special project. Ruth had handed me the intimidating job of making the Duchess's birthday cake: an over-the-top super-indulgent chocolate creation. Ruth had been giving me hints and tips as I practised over the last couple of weeks, and I wanted to be able to present my final recipe to her on her return from holiday in a week's time.

I was measuring out ingredients when I spotted a familiar figure walking down the lane. It was the gardener who had almost knocked me to the ground and shouted at Ben yesterday afternoon, and he looked surprisingly tired for a guy with a healthy physique and muscles that popped out from under his t-shirt sleeves. I hadn't put two and two together before now, but an angry gardener and a dead body seemed, under the circumstances, to add up to a pretty reasonable four.

CHAPTER 6

I could feel four little feet pressing into the small of my back. I was cosy and had no desire to move, but the sun was streaming into my bedroom, and even with my eyes closed it was too much.

I rolled over, much to the frustration of Pumpkin, the enormous tabby cat who was under the sheets and pressing her feet against me like a toddler who had taken up half the bed and was after even more space. She let out an angry meow and repositioned herself, the end of her tail flicking back and forth. I was in trouble.

After climbing out of bed, I picked the book I'd been reading up from the floor, where it had fallen when I'd dozed off, rubbed the top of Pumpkin's head, pulled the sheets up over her and left her to it. She was most definitely in charge of the household, and I didn't want to disturb Her Majesty any more than was necessary. Especially on a Sunday, one of her seven days of rest.

I managed to make my way to the kitchen without falling down the stairs: a daily accomplishment which never fails to amaze me. Without my first coffee of the day, I doubt I could even tell anyone my name. On autopilot, I ground some beans in an antique cast-iron coffee grinder and set off the espresso maker. Pumpkin, who had deigned to venture down into the servants' quarters for breakfast, head-butted my leg as she passed by. I seemed to have been forgiven for the too-early wake-up call.

I sat at the kitchen table and stared at the logo on the side of the paper bag the coffee beans had come in: 'Signal Box Coffee'. My finished espresso was as good as the coffees Lucy had served me from the campervan, the quality was consistently high, and I knew I'd found my new favourite. Through bleary eyes, I registered the way the red of the Signal Box logo matched my red espresso maker and the enormous red fridge in the corner of the room. Everything about Lucy and Kathy's business suited me; it would be great to serve their coffee in the cafés.

I didn't know whether it was the espresso or the force of my idea, but I was wide awake. I wanted to start making changes in the cafés and this would be one of them: I was going to ask Signal Box Coffee to come on board and supply the coffee for Charleton House.

With that decision made, I found a spring in my step. I decided to forgo breakfast and made my way straight to the bathroom to get ready. Oh God, that was a mistake. The idea of looking in the mirror before I'd had my first coffee of the day had been a step too far, but not doing so before I put my glasses on was an unforgivable error. Most days, I thought that my spiky silver-grey hair looked cool; this morning, I just looked as if I had shoved my fingers in a plug socket. Well at least I didn't need to stress about roots showing or the cost of getting my hair dyed. This morning I might be capable of frightening small children, but it was all me and I loved it.

'Where's that scarf I gave you? I've told you before, you need brightening up. It's a beautiful summer's day and you look like you're off to a funeral.'

Joyce Brocklehurst was our brash retail manager and she wasn't one to beat around the bush. To be fair, she did have a point. After she had given me a bright colour-splotched scarf a couple of months ago, I had made a half-hearted attempt to look more like the creative café manager for an art-loving stately home, but it had soon petered out. My argument was that I rarely had time to go shopping and my wardrobe still reflected my previous life, managing restaurants and cafés in the business districts of London. Joyce's wardrobe, on the other hand, would probably require sunglasses and an active imagination. Today, her neck-breaking lime-green stilettos were paired with a peacock-blue pencil skirt that was so tight, I was amazed she could walk, and showed off her trademark 'visible panty line'. A purple silk shirt displaying an impressive cleavage finished the look.

Joyce had joined me in the Garden Café to see what gossip I could impart. After making us both a coffee, a smooth, creamy latte for Joyce and an espresso for myself, I walked behind her to a table, unable to take my eyes off her blonde bouffant hair which, combined with her heels, must have added almost a foot to her height. Every time I saw her, I wondered how she was able to walk around a house with cobbled courtyards, gravel pathways and uneven flagstones and not break an ankle every time she left one of the shops.

As we made our way through the café, more than a few eyes turned to take her in. Peacocks are not an uncommon sight in the stately homes of England, and it seemed Joyce was trying to ensure that Charleton House wasn't left out. We tucked ourselves away in a corner and she focused on me with her piercing blue eyes.

'So tell me, is it true that the body you found belonged to the young man who worked in that silver coffee van?' She peered at me over the china cup, her little finger raised in the air.

'It wasn't me who found him. Poor Robin from gardens was the one who stumbled across him, but yes, it was Ben.'

Joyce nodded. 'Ben Hines. I remember him running around in his football kit, muddy knees n'all. Always very polite.' That information surprised me, but then I knew he was local, so it shouldn't have been an enormous stretch that someone at Charleton would have known him. 'He went to school with my youngest daughter. I vaguely recall she had a crush on him, he was a nice lad. Such a shame.'

'If he was such a nice lad, how come he's ended up dead? Surely not everyone could have liked him.'

Joyce took her time placing the cup on the saucer, deep in thought.

'I've been wondering that since I heard. He must have been twenty-nine by now, so we're talking thirteen years since he was at school. I did hear that he'd got himself into a bit of trouble a while back…'

'Debt?' I interrupted, thinking back to what Kyle had said.

'Yes, that's it. We're not talking huge amounts of money, but enough for people to be unhappy with him. That was a while ago, though.'

'Do you think someone came back to collect and killed him when he didn't pay up?'

She looked at me intently for a moment or two. 'Sophie, dear, this is Derbyshire. The days of sheep rustling are long gone, and the Mafia have never, as far as I'm aware, taken control of any criminal underworld in the valleys. At worst, he'd have received a thumping round the back of the pub; at best, a cold shoulder or two. No, he was small time, and as far as I know, he'd sorted himself out.'

'But it's such an odd location for a random theft, we're in the middle of a country estate. It's not like someone could just happen to be passing and see an opportunity.'

'Think of all the dog walkers, hikers, tourists, locals out for a drive. There are no gates on the roads that run through here; locals use them to take short cuts on their commutes. That wouldn't explain how they got into the grounds of the house, I admit, but almost anyone could be in the general area.'

That didn't ease my mind. If this was an opportunist murder by someone who just wanted to empty the till and run, then maybe Charleton wasn't as idyllic as I had always thought.

Joyce appeared to read my mind. 'Still, it's a darned sight safer than that London and you must have been used to all the crime after, what? Fifteen years living there? Muggings on every street corner; having to walk everywhere clinging to your handbag in case someone snatches it; drinks being spiked in pubs; no one giving up their seats to old ladies on the bus. It's no wonder you moved back north.'

I couldn't help but chuckle at the mention of old ladies, but resisted the urge to make a joke at Joyce's expense. I'd rather be mugged on a street corner than offend Joyce with an ill-judged quip about her age.

'It's really not that bad. Anyway, Charleton looks far more dubious this morning. Police still crawling all over the garden; photographers trying to get past security to find a vantage point in the house where they can take pictures of where it happened.'

'Ah, but these are special circumstances. It happens all the time in London.'

'You're spending too much time reading scare stories on the internet. I loved London; I was just ready to come home.'

'Well, I'm a born-and-bred Derbyshire lass,' Joyce replied with pride, slipping back into the northern accent that she was, ironically and unsuccessfully, forever trying to tame, especially around the Duke and Duchess. 'I've never left and I never will. There isn't anythin' you can get in London that you can't get up 'ere, whether it's style, food or culture, and all in a much better setting.'

In many ways I couldn't argue with her, and when it came to

style, she certainly didn't have any competition. Mainly because she'd scared it all off.

'You can lead a quiet life round here if you want, Sophie, although you're still a bit too young for the pipe and slippers routine. Whatever you returned north looking for, it was a good move. Joe will figure out who killed poor Ben and we can all go back to smelling the roses, or your baking, without having to worry about a killer being on the loose, which is a permanent possibility in London.'

'Was that meant to be comforting, Joyce? The words "killer on the loose" aren't going to help me sleep tonight.'

'Don't be soft, girl. Knock back a glass of something strong before you go to sleep, then when you wake, put on your brightest, sunniest outfit. Works for me when I've got something on my mind.' I looked at her lime-green fingernails and her matching earrings – solid discs at least an inch wide that swung with every movement. Now I was keen to see her choice of outfit on a day she was feeling depressed. That thought alone perked me up and I smiled at her, grateful that this slightly bonkers, slightly scary, but wonderful rainbow of a woman had entered my life.

'That's more like it.' She beamed back at me. 'Now, another slice of cake each and all will be well in the world.'

CHAPTER 7

Within Charleton House are two outdoor courtyards. From above, the building looks like a square-cornered figure of eight. One of these courtyards is cobbled and dates back to the original Tudor building – it is said that Henry VIII dropped by during one of his processions north. On one wall is a stone archway, housing a heavy wooden door, low enough to cause taller visitors to duck their heads as they make their way into the room beyond. Previously a wine cellar, on normal days it is full of replica wine barrels.

Today, however, the space had been transformed into a seventeenth-century coffeehouse to complement the Food Festival, the wine theme having already been brought to life the previous year. The windows had been covered up and faux candles flickered along the windowsills. A small amount of 'smoke' hovered in the air and a long table dominated the room. Visitors of all ages sat around the table, and others stood around the walls awaiting the eleven o'clock performance. With my own coffee obsession, there had been no way I was going to miss this. I was keen to learn more about the bean that kept me functioning and pleasant to be around.

The chatter of the crowd hushed as a tall man ducked under the doorway and made his way into the room. He was a startling figure in a low-crowned beaver-fur hat trimmed with ribbons and feathers. Below that he wore a wig, which must have been unbearably hot in the August heat. As he came down the stairs, I got a good look at the rest of him. He was wearing a suit of biscuit brown wool: a long straight-cut knee-length coat with elbow-length sleeves over a waistcoat almost as long. His full-sleeved shirt was worn with a cravat tied in a knot at his throat. Breeches that finished just below the knee over stockings and square-toed shoes tied at the instep with ribbons finished the look, and his entire outfit was dotted with knots of brown and beige silk. In one hand, he carried a pair of gloves; his other rested on the hilt of a sword that hung from his waist.

He scanned the room, a smile forming on his lips. 'How wonderful to see so many enquiring minds, seeking knowledge and good conversation over that most virtuous of drinks, coffee. I see some familiar faces, but for those of you who don't know me, I am Samuel Pepys, diarist and politician. I have of course filled my life with other noble professions, but I won't bore you with that for now, for we are here in the year of Our Lord 1676, in this simple yet welcoming coffeehouse, to debate matters of the day, learn of mathematics and science. If we feel the need for something a little more light hearted, we can take bets on a bear fight. You can even get a haircut – not something I'll be doing, of course.'

He smiled and winked as he tossed some of the long hair of his wig over his shoulder.

'You see, ladies and gentleman,' – he paused – 'although I am surprised to see ladies in here. Normally the fairer sex never frequent a coffeehouse; it's really not the place for you respectable ladies. Do you know' – he spoke quietly, sharing his surprise with the crowd – 'there are some women who would like to see coffeehouses closed down, saying that their menfolk are wasting their time here, that coffee weakens us, turns us into babbling fools and makes us unable to... well, erm, fulfil our, shall we say, manly duties.'

He slowly circled the table, stopping from time to time to make a point or single out a visitor, looking them in the eyes and bringing them into his confidence.

'I find coffee a marvellous stimulant, and it contains, so I am told, many medicinal qualities. It will cure you of gout and scurvy. Children in particular can be found in much better health after consuming it. However, I don't recommend drinking it after dinner, unless you wish to avoid sleep for some hours. But it's not just the coffee that brings me here to this "penny university", for that is what the coffeehouses are sometimes called. I assume you all paid your penny at the door in order to enter? And once you're here, the learning available to you makes them worthy of that name. Literature, politics, science – just sit down next to a stranger and discuss any subject that takes your fancy. Revolutions have been planned, scientific experiments carried out. It is said that one Isaac Newton dissected a dolphin on a table in a coffeehouse that goes by the name of Grecian.'

He was pointing at the table, indicating the length of the dolphin and getting the visitors to picture the scene.

'My personal favourite is Will's near Covent Garden. It is a particularly literary crowd that you'll find in attendance and it is there that you will find me enjoying a dish of coffee. I'm not short of choice, however, as we are well on our way to having over a thousand coffeehouses in London alone.'

As Samuel Pepys talked to the crowd, a few visitors quietly came and went through the door in the corner. One of them caught my eye: Kathy from Signal Box Coffee, the quieter of the two sisters. She looked tired and distracted. Tucked away in the shadows, she watched the performance with glassy eyes, but didn't really seem to be taking it in. She just stared in the general direction of Pepys.

As I returned my attention to the action, I spotted another familiar face enter the room: Guy Glover. This was turning into some sort of coffee roasters' reunion. He scanned the room, paying no attention to Pepys and his performance. Spotting Kathy, he made his way over to her, stood by her side and whispered into her ear. She jumped and turned, realising who it was. Her face taking on an expression of fury, she immediately turned and left. With a look of amusement, Guy shook his head and casually leant against the wall, clearly in no rush to follow her.

I turned back to hear Samuel Pepys asking a visitor if he could have his seat as his feet were weary. Then, loud enough for everyone to hear, he directed his comments at those around the table. He was telling them all of King Charles II's 1675 proclamation, which attempted to suppress coffeehouses.

'You see, my friends, his fear was that political debate, which had previously only been the activity of the elite, was now being encouraged among the middle classes, and that coffeehouses were hotbeds of revolutionary talk and possible violence against authority, including the Crown. He lost that battle. I have a feeling that coffeehouses will be here for a very long time to come. Now if you'll excuse me, I need to fetch my wife. I would never allow her to join me in a coffeehouse and she has the good sense not to ask. It has been a pleasure speaking with you all.'

With that, he swept out of the door and disappeared. The visitors applauded and gradually left the room until only a few remained to read through the replica seventeenth-century newspapers and pamphlets that were scattered on the table.

Guy had already gone.

Inspired by my encounter with Samuel Pepys, I felt the need for another coffee. Making myself a latte, very different from the gritty, overly sweetened jet-black sludge that Pepys himself would have found pleasure in, I took the mug into my office, hidden behind a door at the back of the Library Café kitchen.

I immediately regretted it. One of the quirks of working in a building like Charleton House is the varying degrees of temperature you experience throughout the year. In the winter, my office is cold enough to freeze ice cubes; in the summer, when I could do with those ice cubes, I feel like I'm sitting in one of my ovens. At least my matchbox-sized office is homely and close to some of my team. I have colleagues who are in attic spaces and can't stand up straight. One shares a corridor with a photocopier and another is convinced his room is haunted by the ghost of an old housekeeper. He never works beyond six o'clock at night, when he swears she comes in and tries to share the desk with him.

Right now, however, I felt no sympathy for any of them as a bead of sweat ran down my forehead, and I'd only been in my office long enough to turn on my computer.

'Sophie, have you got a minute?' Chelsea called from the end of the kitchen. With no regret, I abandoned my office, went out to the café and found myself face to face with Kathy.

'I'm really sorry to bother you, but I was wondering if you had heard anything about when, or if, the festival will be reopening. It's just, I saw you with that detective, and no one else is telling us anything. Lucy thought it was worth seeing if you knew anything – maybe there has been a staff memo?'

'No, I'd be the last to know. I'm sure the police will hand the gardens back over to us as soon as they can.'

'I guess so. We saw the Airstream being taken away on a trailer, so maybe it won't be too long. Sorry to disturb you, we're just frustrated. This weekend was a big opportunity for us.'

She looked more than just frustrated; she was pale and distracted.

'Is everything OK? You look a bit under the weather; can I get you a drink or something to eat?'

She shook her head. 'I'm just tired, and this has all been a bit of a shock.'

'Did you know Ben well?'

'In a way. We often ended up at the same events. I can't believe what's happened. He was one of those gentle giants, built like a rugby player, but really sweet and kind. We always helped each other out if we ran out of anything. He gave us a hand when we ran out of petrol once and couldn't get off site at a concert.'

I decided to chance my arm. 'What about Guy? Did he work with Ben a lot or was he mainly in the background of the operation?'

At the mention of Guy's name, she met my eyes and froze, then glanced away.

'I better go. I've left Lucy on her own.' With that, she was off and out of the door, and I was left staring after her, a little surprised at how quickly she'd managed to scurry away. Something was going on between her and Guy, and as much as it was none of my business, I was curious to know more.

'No gin? Really? Are you sure you're feeling alright?'

Mark and I had decided to end the day at the Black Swan, a beautiful English country pub that would look at home on the front of a postcard. It was our nearest pub in the pretty village of Hadshaw, just within the boundary of the Charleton House estate, and was another property owned by the Fitzwilliam-Scott family. It was everything that an English pub should be and we were lucky to be able to call it our local. I was doubly lucky to live only a couple of doors away, so getting home safely was never a problem. Not that I often over indulge; I value my early mornings far too much.

Mark and I had found a table to sit at out in the garden. It was a warm evening, and to my mind it was worthy of a glass of Pimm's. As has become the tradition, I only ever indulge in this quintessentially English gin-based liqueur when the sun draws me outside without the need for a sweater. Combined with lemonade, the glass filled with chopped cucumber, oranges, lemons and strawberries, and a few mint leaves, the drink screams 'English summer'.

'There's gin in it, so near enough,' I responded.

'But I enjoy picking one out for you, finding the most ridiculous name.' Mark knew I was attempting to try every one of the seventy gins that the Black Swan served. 'You're ruining my evening.' He moved off towards the door, ducking to avoid the roses that were hanging low off the trellis that surrounded it.

I closed my eyes…

'You're snoring.'

I woke with a start as Mark put the glasses on the table. 'What?'

'You were snoring. The poor family at the next table had to move, it was so bad.' He gestured to the family two tables over, making sure he spoke loudly enough for them to hear.

'I was not.'

I turned to see the family all trying to stifle laughs, looking back and forth between them and Mark a couple of times.

Mark eventually smirked. 'You are so easy, of course you weren't.'

I smiled sheepishly at the family, and then turned back to Mark, stealing the bag of crisps he had brought out with him as punishment. We enjoyed an easy silence as we savoured the first few mouthfuls of our drinks.

Mark was the first to break the peace. 'Do you think the two thefts are related? Berwick Hall and here at the house? It's too much of a coincidence.'

'True, but they're very different. Berwick Hall was during the day when visitors were around. Or at least, Joe got the call during visitor hours, so I assume that's what happened. The St Ives bowl was taken during a private evening event, so only specific people were allowed onsite. It would have been a mighty coincidence for someone working the event to have also been a visitor at Berwick.'

'True.' Mark thought for a little while. 'And the body?'

'Joe's first thoughts were a robbery. Ben did owe some people money, but only small amounts and he seemed to be well liked.'

Mark took a big gulp of beer. 'Maybe we're dealing with an over-caffeinated rivalry.' His voice was dripping in comic conspiracy. 'The Signal Box women are tired of being in the shadow of the big shiny Airstream, their coffee sales are falling as their cute campervan just can't compete with the hypnotising gleam of the silver bullet. One of them snaps and suffocates Ben in a bag of beans. The autopsy is going to reveal hundreds of coffee beans in his ears, up his nose and down the back of his throat. The only clue will be that a single bean among all those found on him will come from the Signal Box.' He looked at me through half open eyes, as though assessing a potential suspect.

'Did you enjoy that?' I asked. He had certainly seemed to get a lot of pleasure out of his little fantasy. He shrugged and returned to his normal voice.

'It's a thought, I'll run it past our resident detective in the morning. He'll be forever in my debt for solving the crime.'

I loved Mark, but he could be an idiot sometimes. 'Well the first problem you have is he was killed with a portafilter, not beans.'

'But that still means he was killed by coffee, sort of. I keep telling you that too much of that stuff isn't good for you.'

I spluttered as my laughter coincided with a mouthful of Pimm's, then moved him on to something more serious.

'Kathy wasn't happy today. Each time I saw her, she looked miserable and on edge. Something is certainly bothering her.'

'The one with the long hair? I didn't notice. I remember seeing her in here on Friday night, though. She must be staying here as she went up to the guestrooms.'

Not only was the Black Swan the sweetest English pub with a killer gin list, but it also had the most exquisitely designed guest rooms. The Duchess herself had led the interior design, and I'd experienced one of the rooms first hand when I'd come for my interview at Charleton House and needed somewhere to stay the night before. I hadn't wanted to leave the next morning, the room was so nice, but I figured trying to claim squatter's rights wouldn't have gone down too well with my new employers.

'But they're local, aren't they? I don't see why they'd book to stay here during the festival.' I instinctively looked around the garden, just in case either of the sisters was there and could hear us.

'It's not uncommon. Some just decide it's easier and like the idea of not having to cook for themselves, or they want to make a weekend of it and enjoy being on the estate the whole time. If there are celebrity guests who aren't important enough to stay with the Duke and Duchess, they'll be put up here.'

I thought about what Mark had just said. There was one easy way to find out, plus it was my turn to get the drinks in. I gathered up our empty glasses and made my way into the cool, dark pub. The low ceilings were covered in wooden beams and an enormous stone fireplace stood at the far end of the room, but it was too hot a day to appreciate the cosy atmosphere.

After choosing a glass of Crooked Spire Summer Gin and tonic, I watched the landlord hand pull Mark's pint of English porter.

'Such a shame, what happened up at the house.' The landlord had seen me often enough to recognise me. 'I hope the police catch who did it quickly, then we can all rest in our beds again.'

I nodded. 'Am I right in thinking that some of the stallholders are staying here?'

'You are. All five rooms are booked and all to people working the festival. Two of them to that poor lad's friends.'

'Ben's friends? Do you mean Guy and Kyle who worked with him?'

'That's them. He wasn't staying here, but they've both got rooms.'

'What about the other coffee company, run by two women?'

He shook his head. 'We've got a cheesemaker and his wife, and two chocolatiers, but no more coffee roasters. It's marvellous having them stay, mind. We've had some great conversations and I might end up doing business with the cheesemakers. There you are, love, enjoy.'

He handed me the two glasses and I walked back out to Mark with a spring in my step.

'What do you look so cheerful about?'

'The mystery continues.' I peered over the top of my glasses at him, attempting to look conspiratorial, but I probably just looked drunk. 'Kathy isn't staying here so she must have been visiting someone. The question is, who?'

'Well I remember that Ben followed almost immediately after her, but I just assumed he was staying here too.'

I took a long, cool drink. A honey blossom infused gin had sounded perfect for summer, but to be honest, it was a bit odd.

'Ben being here kind of makes sense. If his colleagues were staying here, then they might have been meeting to discuss business, or just having a relaxing drink in the quiet of one of their rooms after setting up for the festival. That seems reasonable enough, but why would Kathy be here? I didn't get the impression that the two coffee companies were particularly friendly.'

'What if...' Mark let the words hang in the air and attempted to wink. 'What if there was a bit of "how's ya father" going on?'

'Don't be daft, she was not sleeping with any of them.'

'Why not? They end up at events together, they get to know each other. The next thing is they're falling in love over a bag of coffee beans, very romantic.'

It didn't make sense to me. There hadn't been many signs of a professional relationship between the two companies, let alone simmering sexual desire.

'Kathy was always keeping to herself, not fluttering her eyelashes at the Silver Bullet crew.'

'What if that was intentional? What if she's sleeping with the enemy, so to speak, and is hiding it from her sister?' He paused for a moment, thinking it all through. 'She's hiding the relationship and comes over here for a sneaky fumble. Ben arrives at the pub at the same time to go and meet whichever one she isn't sleeping with and follows her upstairs. She sees Ben, or he later says something to her, and out of fear of all being revealed to her sister, she bashes him on the back of the head and her dirty little secret dies with him.'

Mark looked very pleased with himself. I wasn't sure how to respond so I sat back and drank some gin. Personally I felt the angry gardener was a stronger suspect, but sex had played a part in plenty of murders before, and as much as I didn't really know Kathy, she was definitely a woman with something on her mind.

'Are you planning on putting your deerstalker hat on?' Mark disturbed me from my thoughts.

'Am I what?'

'Sherlock Holmes's deerstalker hat. I can hear the cogs turning, I think you're trying to figure out who killed Ben.'

I couldn't deny I was more than a bit curious, and there were already two suspects. This was going to need another gin and tonic to oil the cogs.

CHAPTER 8

After upsetting Pumpkin because I wouldn't lounge around in bed all day with her sprawled on my chest, her nose in my face, I made myself a quick espresso and then jumped in the car. I always enjoyed coming in to work, but today I was especially keen. The cogs had continued to turn as I lay in bed last night, but I had so little information to go on, I didn't get very far. I needed to know more.

I'd received a text from Joe in the early hours: the festival had received the all clear and could open again. The stallholders were never going to make up for their lost takings, but hopefully a combination of good weather, passionate foodies and, let's face it, macabre curiosity would lead to a decent number of visitors and the weekend wouldn't be a complete failure for them.

This morning I had decided to shower some love and attention on my Stables Café staff, also known as checking up on them and making sure everything had been kept to a high standard while I'd been distracted with events at the festival. This was the one café that would still have done a reasonable amount of trade while the festival was on, and that hadn't changed just because the garden had been closed, so the team hadn't been able to take it easy. The Stables Café was popular with people who wanted to spend time outdoors, and another hot day had been forecast so it was likely they would be busy.

The café shared a large cobbled courtyard with a gift shop and a number of horse-related exhibitions that reflected the Fitzwilliam-Scott family's love of the animal. The café team was doing a good job, so after a quick meeting with the supervisor, fending off dozens of questions about the murder from the team while helping them open up and serve the first few customers of the day, I was ready to leave them to it. I knew they would be distracted and eager for gossip, but under the circumstances there was little I could do to prevent that, so long as it didn't get out of hand.

'Excuse me, are you the manager?' Queries that started like this were rarely good news. 'I have a complaint to make.' As I turned and looked at the owner of the voice, I laughed. It was Joe.

'Oh, give me strength. I hope you're not expecting a coffee.' His mouth fell, forming a cartoon-like sad face. 'Walk with me to the Library Café and by the time we get there I might have changed my mind.'

We set off out of the courtyard, took a short cut through a sweet little walled garden and down the lane to the staff entrance into the house. I was enjoying the warmth of the sun on my face; as far as the weather went, the Food Festival had been lucky. I'd heard tales of thunderstorms in previous years, of flooded gardens and sausage rolls floating away, never to be seen again. Staff drove past us on golf buggies, and I felt a brief childlike stab of jealousy. I loved the idea of whizzing around the grounds on one of those, but I never had a reason to do so.

Joe woke me from my mental meanderings. 'Penny for your thoughts.'

'Hmm? Oh, nothing special. I've been thinking about the murder.'

'You and me both, and if you've any ideas, I'd love to hear them. Everyone is alibied up to the hilt.'

'Did you know Ben? You both grew up around here.'

'No, he's much younger than me, but thanks for the compliment. Plus he went to a different school to me where the kids tended to be from another area.'

We turned the corner into the Library Café, our eyes quickly adjusting to its shadows, the natural light being limited to a couple of tiny windows and the few rays that escaped from the kitchen every time someone opened the door. I pointed in the direction of a table tucked away in the corner.

'Go and grab a seat, and I'll fetch some coffees.'

'Already sorted,' Tina called out across the room, making her way towards me and smiling. 'I saw you coming down the lane when I was in the kitchen.'

I was impressed, although it suggested she also knew how to soften me up.

'Can I grab a moment with you and Joe?'

'Sure, come on.'

Tina pulled up a chair. 'It's nothing major, it's just that I was in The Old Oak pub last night and there was a young lad in there selling off some of the coffee from that van.'

'From Silver Bullet Coffee?' Joe sat up straight.

'Yeah, the silver van thing, where the guy was killed.'

The Old Oak was a pub in a small village about five miles from Charleton House. I'd been told it was nothing special – there was the occasional fight or drugs-related issue, but it was mainly the work of small-time local troublemakers and not particularly newsworthy.

'Did you recognise him?' Joe had pulled out a notepad and pen.

'No, but he seemed to know quite a few of the locals. No one wanted to bother with him.'

'That's great, Tina. I'll have a catch up with Sophie, then I'll arrange for you to make a formal statement. Thanks for letting me know.'

Tina stood as the drinks were brought to our table. 'Not a problem, you know where to find me.'

Once we were alone, Joe grinned at me. 'Well that helps my theft theory.'

'So you still think that's what happened? Ben was the victim of a robbery?'

'Maybe. I really don't have much to go on. Everyone else who was in the area has a pretty solid alibi.'

'Even the angry gardener?'

'What angry gardener?'

'Oh sorry, I thought Mark would have told you. He barged into me on Friday afternoon, shortly before confronting Ben, and he was seriously mad. I'm afraid he was too far away for us to hear what he was saying to Ben.'

'Ah, that angry gardener. Yes, Lucy told me he nearly sent you flying. He's called Elliot Forrester and he was working with Robin, his supervisor, when Ben was killed. Robin's a fan of spreadsheets, so he knows exactly what's being worked on when, where and who's doing it.'

'What about Kyle and Guy?'

He shook his head. 'All spoken for. Kyle was having breakfast at the Black Swan and was seen by the landlord, and Guy was meeting Malcolm De Witt up in his room.'

'The Duke's friend? What was Guy doing in his room? A secret assignation?' I couldn't imagine anything less likely, but people could surprise you.

'Ha! Hardly – what a thought. No, Guy was giving him advice on investing in restaurants. Apparently that's Guy's background and he sometimes works as a consultant. Malcolm is thinking of investing in a new restaurant in London.' I must have still looked a bit nonplussed, because Joe added, 'Malcolm has a separate sitting room to himself, they weren't having a meeting on the bed.'

I laughed. 'I was starting to picture that. What about Kathy from the Signal Box?'

Joe took another mouthful of coffee and put the mug down. 'What about her?'

I explained what Mark had seen and the theory that was knocking around my head.

'A crime of passion?' Joe looked thoughtful. 'That's a damn sight more interesting than a robbery, it would certainly liven things up. I'll double check her alibi and keep it in mind, but I don't think we're going to get a "made for TV" sex and murder special out of this. It'll be something much more mundane.'

'Mundane? A murder at Charleton House? You're kidding, right? You could be fishing bodies out of the Manchester Ship Canal, but instead you're in the glorious surroundings of one of the country's finest historic houses. Don't start taking it for granted.'

I peered at him over the top of my glasses, looking for signs of a twinkle I really didn't want to find. Bloody Mark, putting thoughts into my head. I needed a distraction so gathered up our empty mugs.

'Any word on the thefts, are they related?'

Joe was straightening his tie and tucking in his shirt. He always had a slight air of a dishevelled schoolboy.

'You need to stop asking me questions I can't answer.' He sighed dramatically. 'Well, one happened long enough after the other that they could have been done by the same person, but the Berwick theft was during public opening hours and was a miniature painting that could have been slipped into someone's bag. Charleton was a private event, and you would have had a hard time sneaking the bowl out unless you had a decent sized holdall to put it in. And everyone with a big bag was checked as they left, guests and staff.'

'So it was an inside job?'

'No, I'm not saying that, but I reckon it was planned. I'm sure that Berwick was the work of an opportunist who saw a chance and took it. Sadly they're both on the backburner now; the murder comes first and we haven't got the resources to focus on the robberies too. I'm still technically on the Berwick case and I'll do my best, but it's not a priority right now.' It looked as if his two days of dead ends were getting to him. 'But I've been really lucky. Most new detectives would be shuffling papers back at the station, checking statements, doing background checks, that sort of thing. DS Harnby only has me out and about because we're short of feet on the ground, and she knows that people are used to seeing me around here so are likely to open up. I need to come up with something useful, though, or she'll have me chained to a chair again.'

Concern was scored into the crease across his forehead. I went back to the counter and wrapped up a huge slice of lemon drizzle cake; I couldn't tell him who had murdered Ben, but I could give him a sugar rush and a reason to loosen his belt a notch!

I angled the bratwurst so the tomato sauce wouldn't drip onto my skirt, tilted my head back and took another enormous bite. This was no scrawny hotdog, but really good-quality meat from Derbyshire born-and-bred farm stock and I was already thinking about having a second.

Mark and I were sitting facing the Great Pond, soaking up the sun and watching a family of ducks swim in single file across the water. The gardens team had installed little ramps on either side of the pond's concrete base to make it easier for the ducks, who were clearly considered part of the family, to climb in and out. I watched the crowds of visitors as they shuffled from stall to stall, countless different languages and accents filling the air along with the sweet scents of freshly baked cookies and breads. A gentle breeze could change everything and the smells of sizzling bratwurst or melting cheese would take over. I shuffled along the bench a little; I seemed to be in prime position for getting my knees bashed by shopping bags as people passed by.

On the opposite side of the pond was a gap where the Airstream had been, and the immediate area remained closed off. A few visitors were milling around looking at the gap, no doubt speculating as to what had happened, but the majority weren't paying it any attention. For those not immediately involved, Ben's murder was quickly becoming yesterday's news, and that didn't feel right. I couldn't stop picturing the gentle-looking man who had seemed so dejected when Elliot Forrester had confronted him.

'There you are.'

I looked up for the source of the voice and found myself face to face with a wall of navy and white checked fabric that turned out to be a summer dress clinging to Joyce's various curves. She had adorned it with every fuchsia pink accessory you could think of: a wide belt with an enormous buckle; a cluster of bangles on each wrist; a chunky necklace that could be mistaken for a string of child's toy bricks. Fuchsia-pink sunglasses were balanced on the top of her head and a pair of fuchsia pink stilettos made me wonder how she didn't get vertigo. I also couldn't understand how she wasn't sinking into the grass, so I took a closer look and saw she had an ingenious plastic plug on each heel that stopped them acting like sharp blades.

'Brilliant!' I hadn't meant to say it out loud.

'What's that, dear?' Joyce followed my eye line. 'Oh yes, stops me looking like a drunk guest at a garden party. Also means I can come and find you two and not miss out on all the fun. Budge up.' She had a plastic flute of prosecco in her hand; she shouldn't have been drinking while at work, but I couldn't think of anyone brave enough to confront her. Settling herself next to me, she looked across the water at the gap in the stalls.

'So sad. I'm really struggling to picture someone wanting to kill the boy I remember at the school gates all those years ago.' She stared off into the distance, I assumed picturing Ben as a kid in his school uniform.

'Did you ever hear of him getting involved in anything? I know about the debt, but anything else? He seemed like such a nice, mild-mannered man, but he must have been involved in something.'

Joyce shook her head. 'Like I said, love, it's been years since I last saw him. I've certainly not heard of anything. Tom might know more.' She was looking across the crowds in the direction of the stall we'd got our bratwursts from. 'Tom Bidwell, the butcher. He was one of those Ben owed money to for a while. He might know more about what was going on with him. Tell him how much you liked your sausage and I'm sure he'll talk to you.'

'Will he give us a couple more of these?' asked Mark. I'd almost forgotten he was there. He took the last bite of his bratwurst, a large drip of mustard making a bid for freedom and landing on his tie.

I had a better idea. 'How about I get a serving of haggis, neeps and tatties for us all to share instead?'

I felt two sets of eyes swivel in my direction. 'I beg your pardon?' Joyce sounded horrified.

'Haggis, neeps and tatties. Haggis is traditionally served with mashed swede – neeps – and potatoes – tatties.'

'I know very well what it's served with. You could serve it with caviar and a jeroboam of Dom Pérignon and you'd still not get me anywhere near it. I'm stunned that you'd suggest I'd consume peasant food. You do know what it's made from?'

'I do, it's fantastic stuff. I'd choose it as my last meal if I found myself on death row.'

'Bring it anywhere near me and you might have that opportunity.'

'Ladies.' Mark had found the nerve to come between my love for haggis and Joyce's strong feelings. 'Don't worry, Joyce. Sophie is going to wait until we have both gone before she goes anywhere near that stall.'

'Of course she is,' agreed Joyce, 'she knows what's good for her.' She peered into the distance again, distracted by something. 'Bugger. Well I guess my break has come to a sudden end. Those two are meant to be looking after the courtyard gift shop while I'm in meetings.'

We followed her eye line to a couple of young women on the other side of the pond.

'What meetings?' Mark was clearly feeling brave.

'This meeting, Mark, this meeting. You can call it cross-departmental integration and development if you like, but whatever it is, it's over. I need to go and round up my errant staff.' She swallowed what was left of the prosecco in one gulp and handed the empty flute to Mark. 'Make sure you recycle it, we can save the planet one drink at a time.' Then she tottered off, slowly but with fierce determination.

Tom Bidwell was taking a break at the back of the stall, sitting on top of a wooden box, writing a message on his phone as I came round the corner.

'Tom?'

He didn't look up. 'Who wants to know?'

'Sophie, I'm a friend of Joyce's.'

'Who?'

'Joyce Brocklehurst, I work at the house with her.'

He stood up and looked at me for the first time. 'Any friend of Joyce is a friend of mine. Fine woman. How can I help you, Sophie?'

'It's about Ben, the man who…'

'Died, I know. Bloody awful. What about him?'

I was unsure about talking to a stranger about their financial affairs, but I got the impression that mentioning Joyce hadn't just unlocked a door for me, it had firmly wedged it open.

'Sorry for being quite so personal, but I believe that he used to owe you money.'

He stared at me. 'Joyce told you, I assume. Yes, he did. Why are you interested?'

I wasn't entirely sure how to answer that, so I decided to be honest. 'I don't know. I was there when his body was found and I can't stop thinking about it. I guess I need to make sense of it.'

'Isn't this in the hands of the police?'

'Yes, but… well, I'm here onsite. Maybe I'll find something that can help them.'

Tom laughed. 'I don't know what your job is, but it must leave you with a lot of spare time on your hands. Either that or you're management and have a talent for delegation.'

I couldn't help but laugh at that. He read my response perfectly.

'Management, eh? Well, I better not waste your time. Have a seat.' He removed a bag of bread rolls from the top of another box and gestured towards it. I sat down. 'I had a lot of time for Ben. He worked for me and was a real grafter. I had no problem lending him money when he asked a few years back; I trusted him, but not long after that, he just stopped coming into work. I'd see him cross the road to avoid me. If I did catch him, he always promised I'd get the money back and then made an excuse, so after a while I gave up. It was only a couple of hundred quid; it wasn't worth making a fuss.'

'When was this?'

Tom closed his eyes. 'Hmm, about three years ago. Yeah, three years ago. I remember because it was the year we had that awful summer and it didn't stop raining. A couple of times I ran into him and he was wearing sunglasses, which was ridiculous because we barely saw the sun that year. I eventually realised he was hiding one hell of a black eye.' He laughed at the memory. 'The daft sod, should have just claimed that the other guy looked a lot worse. Turned out he owed some bloke down the pub fifty quid and he was more worried about getting the cash back than I was.'

Tom didn't sound like a man who was bitter. In fact, he didn't seem to bear Ben any ill will at all.

'What happened to him after that? Did you hear any more about him?'

'Only that he was in and out of work, owed a few others money, and then I got wind of this coffee job and I started to see him at some of the food events in the area. Far as I know, he didn't pay off any of his debts, but he seemed to sort himself out. You know, he was always working, and he had that money he'd borrowed off folks and not repaid, yet he was always in the same jeans and rugby shirts, and drove an old car his mother had given him years ago. Still lived with her too. Most blokes his age would get themselves a flash car or fancy watch, but there was nothing like that. I don't know what he was doing with his money, but he wasn't spending it on himself, that's for sure. I can't tell you much else, I'm afraid. He was a good lad; I don't know what he got himself mixed up in, but I'm sure he didn't deserve this.'

I thanked Tom. It had been a brief but incredibly helpful conversation, and I was starting to build up a picture of Ben. Not a detailed one, but enough to give me a slight sense of him. I'd also ended up with even more questions to answer, and a couple of free bratwursts.

It had definitely been a fruitful ten minutes.

After lunch and a wander round the gardens to work off the sweetcorn and honey ice cream we'd had for dessert, Mark and I went our separate ways. I needed to get on top of my budgets, and while the festival was still on and the cafés were quiet, it was the ideal chance to lock myself away in my office and get them out of the way. If the heat inside my office caused me to sweat off a couple of pounds, then that was an added bonus.

I was pulling up the spreadsheets on my computer when Chelsea stuck her head around the door.

'Sophie, there's a bloke to see you. Bruce someone.'

'Thanks. Er, Chelsea...' I picked up the waste basket from under my desk and held it out to her. 'Chewing gum.'

She rolled her eyes and removed the gum from her mouth. I didn't say anything else; she'd get the idea. I stretched my back out as I stood and took a deep breath; I still wasn't in the right frame of mind to talk to Bruce about ending our business relationship, and anyway, I needed to know exactly what I was going to use instead before I did anything. The last thing I needed was our final few deliveries being late, or being sent the wrong stuff because Bruce was annoyed or just focusing on the customers who were sticking with him. Added to that, I was a coward and was choosing to avoid what was likely to be a difficult conversation.

Bruce Keen from the Northern Bean Company was sitting at the end of a table, tapping his foot madly and picking at a label on the side of the box he had brought with him. He stood up when he saw me coming.

'Sophie, hi, hope I'm not disturbing something.'

'No, it's fine. I'm just surprised to see you, you don't normally make deliveries. Plus it's a Bank Holiday, aren't you meant to be taking the day off?'

He glanced around the room. 'No, no, too much to do, you know how it is. I've brought you the samples I was telling you about.' He patted the box. 'We've added another Ethiopian farm to our list, so I've brought you some of the beans I'm getting from them, both a single and a blend, and then there's a couple of flavoured ones that are kind of fun. A cinnamon and rum one and a toasted coconut.' He pushed the box towards me. 'So how are things here? Are the police still around or have they moved on?'

'A couple of them are still here, but the festival is doing OK.' I wanted to get back to my budgets, so I hoped that short answers would help encourage him out of the door.

'Have the police any idea who did it?'

I shook my head. 'They've not made any arrests as far as I know.'

Bruce nodded. 'Have you heard if they've got any leads? Are they hopeful?'

This was quickly becoming an odd conversation. No chitchat, no talk about the coffee, just straight into the murder. It wasn't like we knew each other well and regularly exchanged gossip.

'I've really no idea, Bruce. I know they've interviewed some of the staff here and a lot of the stallholders, but I'm unlikely to find out what they've discovered, if anything.' That wasn't strictly true. Give him a piece of cake and a coffee, and I could probably wheedle the information out of Joe, but I wasn't planning on telling Bruce that.

'OK, well, I just wondered. I should be going.' He stood and moved the box even closer to me. 'Let me know what you think. We're roasting all this week, so if you like them, I can get a few more boxes out to you by the end of the week.' He paused and I thought for a brief moment that he was going to shake my hand, but instead he turned and walked out. I'd avoided a difficult conversation, but got rather a strange one instead.

'So he was frugal. I'm not sure how that helps us.' Mark was driving me home and I was bringing him up to date on my conversation with Tom. 'Unless this meant he had one enormous debt and he was taking on smaller ones in order to pay off the angriest of his creditors.'

'He could have had a gambling problem, or maybe drugs,' I suggested. I didn't believe either of these ideas; I was just throwing things out there in the hope one of them might stick or trigger an idea.

Mark was clearly thinking along the same lines as me. 'No, nobody has said anything that would indicate that.' He drove slowly through the beautiful Charleton estate, keeping an eye out for any deer coming close to the side of the road. Charleton House was set in 40,000 acres of rolling countryside, the wooded hillsides home to red and fallow deer. There were trout ponds and miles of stunning walks, and in the distance, a church steeple peeped out from between the trees. It was an idyllic English setting that sent the tourists wild, inspired artists and brought a tear to my eye. Moving back here was proving to be the best decision I had ever made.

'Are you looking forward to getting back to normal?'

I looked over at Mark, unsure what he meant. 'Hmm?'

'Now the fair is over, you'll be busy again.'

'Funnily enough, I am. I thought I'd welcome the break, but I enjoy it when we're busy. I have a good team, like a well-oiled machine.'

'So long as you keep greasing the cogs with coffee it will stay that way. Talking of greasing the cogs, do you fancy a drink?' We were pulling into the village and could see the Black Swan up ahead, but I wasn't really in the mood.

'Not tonight, thanks all the same. I think I'm just going to relax, spend a bit of time with Pumpkin, maybe plan some menus.'

'OK, well promise me you'll do it with a gin and tonic in one hand and something unhealthy in the other.'

'A gin and tonic isn't unhealthy?'

'Darling, put a slice of lime in it and it's one of your five a day.'

We were both distracted by the sound of shouting as we neared the pub car park and our heads swivelled in the direction of two men who looked as if they were about to come to blows. Mark slowed down to a crawl, but the men were too focused on trying to hit one another to notice that they had an audience.

As we got nearer, I recognised them. 'That's Guy and Kyle. Can you hear what they're saying?'

Mark wound down his window, but we still couldn't make out what they were shouting at each other over the noise of the engine. Guy was clearly furious; his face was red and he was jumping about as if the tarmac under his feet was red hot. Kyle on the other hand was standing his ground. He looked just as angry, but more in control.

'What was his alibi?' Mark had read my thoughts. Right now, Guy looked angry enough to kill.

'He was with Malcolm, having a breakfast meeting. Although to be fair, they both look angry enough to take a swipe at someone.'

As though he had heard me, Kyle threw his arms up in the air and shook his head. He started to walk towards the rear door of the pub, but Guy grabbed his shoulder and spun him around, his fist raised. I tensed my body, waiting for Guy's fist to make impact, but something stopped him. Guy froze, and Kyle, who had seemed ready to take it, walked calmly inside. Guy stood with his head resting against the stone wall, looking as if he was trying to calm down. After a couple of minutes, he followed Kyle inside.

I'd been so engrossed that I hadn't even noticed that the car had come to a stop. Mark and I looked at each other, wide-eyed.

'Well, that's enough drama for tonight. Are you sure you don't want to go in for a drink, try and find out what was going on?'

I was tempted, but decided against it.

'My guess is they'll go to their rooms and stew for the rest of the night. We're not going to find out anything tonight.' I opened the car door and got out. 'Drive safely, morning coffee in Library?'

'Throw in some chocolate croissants and you have a date.' And with his order placed, Mark drove off. I walked round the corner to my little house and, I was guessing, a grumpy and demanding cat.

Pumpkin was on the mat, waiting for me as I walked in. I was getting home later than she would have liked, or at least that was how I read the expression on her face as I followed her swaying tail into the kitchen and reached for a glass out of the cupboard. This was my first chance to really savour the Twenty Trees Gin that I had bought from the fair, so I was going to take Mark's advice and pour myself a glass of gin and tonic.

Sitting down at the kitchen table, I let Pumpkin jump up onto my lap. I couldn't remember the last time she had been weighed, but I would have sworn she was the same weight as a small child, with the attitude of a haughty teenager under the illusion that the world revolves around them. In Pumpkin's case, it's not an illusion; the world really does revolve around her.

She rubbed her face against my chin, purring, then against the side of my glass. I only narrowly avoided losing its contents. After sticking her claws into my shirt and probably making a number of holes, she considered her duty complete and jumped off my knee to collapse in a heap by my feet. Her large tabby mass spread across the floor until she was the size of the small dog that she seemed to believe she was.

I sat back and put my feet on the chair next to me. Swirling the ice around my glass, I breathed in and liked what I discovered. The drink's grassy notes made me think of fresh country air, hibiscus and lemongrass, maybe a touch of pine. My love of gin wasn't something that I allowed to cross over into work too much; this was for pleasure only, when the working day was over and I could fully relax. Only tonight my mind wouldn't stop whirring. The conversations I'd been having about Ben were buzzing around my brain and showed no signs of quietening down, even under the influence of alcohol.

Taking centre stage right now was the image of Kyle and Guy fighting outside the pub. I couldn't be sure that it was related to Ben's murder; maybe they were under a lot of stress and emotions were simply running high after the death of their colleague. That wasn't hard to imagine. Maybe they had found Ben stealing their profits, killed him in a moment of anger, and then made it look like a robbery to hide their tracks, only now they were worried they were going to get caught and were taking it out on each other. The problem with that idea was that they both had rock-solid alibis. Perhaps the murder *was* the result of a robbery and the guy who had been selling the coffee down the pub was going to find himself serving a life sentence once Joe got hold of him. That I did find hard to believe. You'd have to be pretty stupid to kill someone and then start selling the evidence at a pub under five miles away.

My next thought was of Elliot Forrester, the gardener Mark and I had seen having a go at Ben, having almost barrelled me to the ground. He wasn't afraid of being seen shouting at Ben and had no problem expressing whatever was annoying him, so it didn't seem like there would be unreleased rage simmering inside him, ready to bubble over into violence. At least, not the murderous kind.

But I could look at that another way. A man not afraid of showing his temper in public, not caring what others thought, might just be able to get angry enough to kill someone. After all, he didn't seem to have a self-control button.

Tom Bidwell didn't appear to be carrying any residual anger; instead, he remembered Ben fondly. As far as he was concerned, no one else was baying for Ben's blood over a couple of hundred quid here or there, either. Ben was coming across as an unremarkable man who, with the exception of Elliot, few people felt any ill will towards. None of it seemed to fit easily. It was like a jigsaw puzzle that looked, from a distance, as if all the pieces would slot together, but once you tried to match them, they were misshapen and wouldn't flatten into place.

I looked at my glass. It was empty. That wasn't going to help things. I needed another drink.

With a second drink in my hand, I moved next door to the sitting room and sat on the sofa, opening my laptop on my knee. Pumpkin made a half-hearted attempt to sit on the keypad, but realised for herself it was unworkable before I had to shoo her off. She settled instead for curling up in a ball by my side. Something had been bugging me, and I didn't know if it was connected to anything. It was just there in my mind and I wanted to do something about it.

I'd been wondering about the art theft at Berwick, and then at Charleton House. Joe had said they were very different crimes carried out in different circumstances, but I wanted to check them out anyway. It wasn't because I thought they were connected to Ben, but I felt so bad for the Duke. It was hard to spend any time with him and not realise just how important art was in his life, especially a piece that had meant a lot to his mother. I wondered if I could help, plus my brain would not settle. I was beginning to wish I was into meditation or distracting myself with muscle-aching exercise, but neither of those things were up my alley, so I just had to run with it and see what I could find.

I spent the next hour searching for art thefts from historic houses, focusing on Derbyshire, but taking into account anything in the neighbouring counties. There had been five in Derbyshire over the last six months, and three in neighbouring areas, the bulk of them carried out since April. Then I looked further back in time and found that over the preceding twelve months, there had been eight reported thefts in the area, starting in March and ending in September. That timeline made sense as many historic houses closed over the winter and couldn't be accessed by the public.

I looked at the houses. Some were run by charities, some were privately owned, but all were open to the public at some point during the year. Two of the thefts had been of paintings small enough to be hidden in a bag, the rest were either silverware or ceramics of one kind or another. I couldn't see any pattern of locations or kinds of houses. I even started reading about the history of the houses – maybe there was a connection from centuries ago, but I wasn't finding anything. Adding to this the fact that I was getting my information mainly from press reports, so it could have been that not all the relevant information had been made public, I started to feel like I was wasting my time.

If there were any links, then Joe stood a better chance of finding them than I did. Joe had already given Mark and me far more information than he ever should, and part of me felt guilty that he could get in a lot of trouble if he was found out. Not guilty enough, however, to stop me sending him a text message and promising him fresh chocolate croissants and as much free coffee as he could drink if he came round tomorrow morning before we opened to the public. I was really hoping that under the influence of my baking, he'd forget all pretence of professionalism and bring me up to speed on what he'd found out so far.

CHAPTER 9

'You're kidding, right?' Joe looked over at Mark hopefully. 'She is kidding?'

I placed a tray of muffins in front of them, the result of my early arrival at work and a quick baking session before any of my staff arrived. I'd promised Joe and Mark some freshly baked chocolate croissants, which were coming, but first I wanted them to try my latest experiment.

'Chocolate and beetroot muffins?' Mark looked as nonplussed as Joe. 'What would Ruth say? I will tell her.' His threat of revealing my experimentation to our pastry chef wouldn't come to anything. After all, it had been Ruth who'd encouraged me to have fun and try new things when baking.

I decided to ignore Mark's comments. 'The chocolate is produced by a local artisanal chocolatier and the beetroots are from the Duchess's own vegetable garden.' I'd been inspired by the Food Festival and the idea had come to me last night as my online research became a journey down an internet black hole of food ideas. I was pretty impressed with myself; Joe and Mark less so, it seemed, but I put that down to surprise and not having heard of the combination before.

They both reached for a muffin and examined them more closely, then looked at each other like soldiers about to go over the top. I swear they were a heartbeat from a manly pat on the shoulder and a good luck wish. Each took a bite and chewed slowly while looking at me, back at each other, at the muffins, and then back at me again.

Mark swallowed.

'So?' I asked him. I loved the idea of the muffins, and thought that with the backstory of the ingredients, they'd make a great addition to the menus in the Stables and Library Cafés. Mark took a mouthful of coffee, looking as if he was thinking – hard.

'Well, you know how much I love chocolate, and I'm up for trying pretty much anything. The chocolate, yep, great. Those chunks are fabulous, you can tell it's good quality.' He paused and looked over at Joe. 'And I think this is a great example of a project that combines the work of the kitchens and the gardens, largely because it tastes like I've just eaten a mouthful of Charleton's finest artisanal soil.'

Joe sniggered as Mark took another mouthful of coffee and swilled his mouth out with it.

'Sophie, I've become very fond of you, and I love being one of your chief tasters, but please don't pursue this or I might have to resign from my position.'

'They're not that bad, surely?' I reached for a muffin and took an enormous bite. After a couple of chews, I saw his point. I felt like I'd just licked one of the gardeners' spades. 'Oh God, alright, point taken. I can't argue. Can't blame me for trying, though.'

It was Joe's turn to speak up. 'No, you're right, we can't. But we can blame you for trying them out on us. I thought you liked us.'

I laughed at them. 'Oh shut up, the pair of you. I'll go and get the croissants.'

I let them eat a croissant each in silence, the looks on their faces oddly serene.

'Better?' I raised an eyebrow at them, daring them to make a cheeky comeback, but all I got were synchronised 'mmmms' and a 'God, yes' from Mark. Deciding that I had Joe in a moment of chocolate-induced weakness, I enquired after the murder investigation and how it was going.

'Slowly,' he answered. 'We just can't get hold of anything concrete. Friends, family, they all say the same thing about him: a nice guy who couldn't get any real purchase on life. I've spoken to a bunch of people he owed money to, but none of them seem particularly angry. They're just really sorry he's been killed. I guess that's the thing about small town life: he's one of theirs and they care about that more than a couple of hundred quid. It's a reminder of why I like it round here. There's so much awful stuff going on in the world, but they seem to have their priorities straight.'

His comment about money reminded me of my conversation with Tom. 'From what I've heard, there wasn't much evidence of him spending the money he borrowed, or earned for that matter. Any idea what was going on? Was he gambling?'

'Who have you been talking to?' Joe looked both curious and slightly annoyed. As he'd finished his croissant, it seemed the window on his moment of weakness had closed. 'You shouldn't be getting involved, Sophie. I've already told you far too much. You need to leave this to the police.'

'It was just a couple of locals who were working at the festival. We got chatting about Ben. It's a hard subject to avoid when he was killed right here and many of them knew him.'

That seemed to placate him, but he did pause for a moment before replying.

'We haven't found evidence of gambling. He seemed to travel quite a bit with the job, but mainly around Derbyshire. Sometimes further north in England – presumably the company covered his expenses for that.'

'What about the lad Tina saw selling coffee in The Old Oak?'

Mark asked. I hadn't realised that he'd been paying attention; I'd assumed he was still in a croissant-shaped world of his own.

Joe smiled, his lecture forgotten. 'Local lad was romancing his girlfriend in the back of his car in a layby north of here. They got out to have a smoke and he found the coffee abandoned in the grass.'

Mark snorted. 'And they say romance is dead. Presumably the sweet Juliet can confirm her Romeo's story?'

'She certainly can. We also found a couple of bags they'd missed when we visited the site. Problem is, we can't know if the lad selling them knew they were stolen goods, so it will be difficult to prove any kind of offence. Either way, it doesn't help our investigation at all.'

Talk of Romeo and Juliet got me thinking. 'Did Ben have a girlfriend, or boyfriend? Maybe this is the work of an aggrieved partner.'

'You still fancy the crime of passion route? No, not that we can find. He lived a pretty quiet life with his mum when he wasn't on the road. He has a brother down in London he phoned occasionally, a few friends he'd go to the pub with. We did find a picture of a kid in his wallet, but his mum didn't recognise her and thinks she might belong to a friend of his. She said he was always good with youngsters and got quite attached to his friends' children – a sort of honorary uncle.'

'He sounds a bit too good to be true,' Mark commented. 'He has to have had a murky side hidden away for someone to have killed him.'

I wasn't sure I agreed. I'd heard enough stories from Mark over the last year to know that history was littered with innocent victims.

'Think about all the research you've done. There must be countless people who have been wrongly accused of things, or became the target of treacherous kings and noblemen just because they were in the way of their dastardly ambitions.'

'Fair enough.' In the silence that followed, Mark stared into his mug, and then looked up, his puppy dog eyes sending a clear message. I reached out for his mug.

'You really need to work on your subtlety. Joe, more coffee?'

'No thanks, I should be going. I need to head back to Berwick Hall – a member of staff I need to interview about the theft has just returned from holiday. I'm hoping I can get something from him that is tantamount to a lead; that's another case that's grinding along far too slowly.'

I held the plate of muffins out towards him. 'One for the road?' A look of mock horror appeared on his face and, with wide eyes, he pretended to sprint for the door, stopping briefly to wave before he disappeared.

'You'll never see him again,' was Mark's response. 'Wave those things at me and I'll run for the hills too.'

I couldn't resist.

After sending Mark on his way, clearing up our coffee mugs and finding precisely no one who wanted me to add chocolate and beetroot muffins to the menu, I wandered off to the events team office so Yeshim could give me the run down on a corporate booking. Nothing hugely exciting: the board members of a local art gallery were holding their annual away day here at Charleton House. It was their chance to discuss profit and loss and future exhibition sponsorship underneath a chandelier that would kill if it fell on them, in a room with a view that would take their breath away. I was providing the refreshments, among them a buffet lunch that included a beetroot salad – I was determined to get beetroot in somewhere.

After a brief conversation, I left Yeshim to it when she got a phone call from a bridezilla from hell who was holding her wedding here in the autumn. As I left the office, I made a mental note to return with cake for the worn-down looking events manager. I sensed that she was going to need it.

Ambling down the private lane, enjoying the warmth of the

sunshine and exchanging pleasantries with staff I passed on my way, I spotted a familiar figure walking towards me: Guy Glover. He had the swagger of a man with a lot of confidence who always liked what he saw in the mirror.

'Morning, Sophie,' he called out once he'd spotted me. 'Getting some fresh air?' He clearly had no idea that I'd witnessed his fight with Kyle. Either that, or he didn't care.

'Something like that. What about you? The festival is over, so why are you still here?'

'I have some paperwork to drop off with Yeshim. I wanted to get everything squared off before we move on to the next event.'

'Does that mean the police have given you the van back?'

'No, not yet, and to be honest, I don't think we'll use it again. We'll sell it and invest in a new one. I'll admit to not being overly sentimental, but I have my limits. I don't think anyone wants to stand serving coffee where... well, you know what I mean. I'm sure I can find someone who will take it off my hands for a reasonable price. They're worth a lot of money, and if a buyer isn't aware of its more recent history, then I'm sure I can get a decent amount for it.'

I'd gone from impressed by an apparent display of feelings to appalled by how quickly he'd turned the conversation to making money out of someone's ignorance about Ben's murder. I hadn't been sure before, but now I knew I didn't like him, and I decided I wasn't going to be shy about last night.

'I saw you at the pub yesterday. You and Kyle didn't seem to be getting on very well.'

He looked momentarily confused, then realised what I was referring to.

'You saw that? I didn't spot you.'

'You wouldn't have done. We were driving past and you were a bit preoccupied.' He wedged his hands firmly in his pockets and looked uncomfortable. 'Do you and Kyle often argue like that?'

He gave an awkward laugh. 'It was nothing. We argue all the

time. I've known Kyle since he was sixteen, so I guess he's like a brother to me. We have a bit of rough and tumble every now and then; next thing we're happily having a pint together.' He was clearly growing in confidence, and when he laughed again, it sounded a lot less awkward. 'We'll probably have another argument in a week or two. Hopefully you won't have to witness it next time, though.'

He smiled as though we were in on a great joke together. I wasn't falling for it.

'It must have been pretty serious to cause an actual fight, though. You seemed really mad at him.'

He looked away briefly, and then turned back to face me.

'It really was nothing, Sophie. You don't need to give it another moment's thought. Now, I need to make sure I catch Yeshim, then I have a diary full of appointments.'

Before I had a chance to say anything else, he walked off. 'Take care, Sophie, see you next year,' he shouted over his shoulder as he strode away at great speed, making sure our conversation couldn't continue. While it might be over for him, I knew he was lying, so as far as I was concerned, this was far from over for me.

CHAPTER 10

*Y*ou might think that a dark room with walls covered in shelves groaning under the weight of thousands of books, dark leather armchairs and dark wood tables all around would be the last place you'd want to spend time on a warm summer's day, but no matter what was going on outside, I always found the Library Café comfortable and welcoming. In the winter, it was a cosy escape from the worst of the weather; in the summer, it transformed into a cool respite from the sun's rays. I had yet to find a season in which this wasn't my favourite of the three cafés.

Today it seemed like the visitors agreed. With the Food Festival packing up and the stallholders moving on, the visitors had returned to the cafés for lunch and their restorative coffee and cake. Staff members also reappeared in their droves for a caffeine-fuelled pick-me-up before meetings; others held their meetings in here with coffee and cake to make it all the more bearable. Visitors would browse the shelves, taking in the selection of books that the Duke had demanded would not merely be decoration, but would reflect the interests and history of the house and generations of the family that had lived here. Art, architecture, gardening, social history, Shakespeare – books of all kinds were there on the walls of the café, sourced from second-hand bookshops throughout Derbyshire, giving visitors a glimpse into the minds of the Fitzwilliam-Scotts. It amazed me that so few books were stolen, but the first time I'd mentioned to the Duke that there *were* some gaps on the shelves, he'd simply smiled and said he hoped that the books gave their new owners great pleasure.

I had spent the morning helping to keep the shelves of sandwiches stocked, serving iced coffee and clearing tables. It was a day for mucking in and I didn't mind; it was a nice change from spreadsheets and emails, and anyway, my office was unbearably hot and I'd grab any excuse to stay out of there. I'd just finished advising a couple of American visitors on what I felt were the 'must see' parts of the house and was wiping down tables when Kathy Wright came in. She looked tired and distracted, but smiled when she spotted me.

'Hi, Kathy, lovely to see you. Can I get you a coffee, or is that not the generous offer it sounds?'

She laughed. 'I wouldn't say no. My morning cup just doesn't seem to be enough today.' Despite the smile that had crossed her face, she still looked tired. Her eyes flitted around the café, unable to settle on me, or anything else for that matter. 'I'm actually here to drop this off for you while Lucy is up at the events office with Yeshim. We thought you might like some more samples, have a chance to try some of the coffee that we didn't have on sale at the festival.'

Kathy handed me a cardboard box. I opened it to find six beautifully packaged sample bags with the adorable Signal Box logo printed on every one.

'What a wonderful surprise, you've made my day. Grab a seat and I'll be back with the coffee.'

After stashing the box of coffee in my office – there was no way I wanted anyone accidentally serving the samples along with our usual stuff – I made two cups of coffee using some of the sample Kathy and Lucy had given me over the weekend and went to sit down with her.

'Are you all packed up now?'

'We are. We drove the van straight off last night. It's so easy to pack up and go; it's one of the things we love about it.'

We sat in uncomfortable silence for a moment or two while Kathy played with sachets of sugar. I was struggling to find anything to say that wasn't pure business and this didn't seem like the time. Kathy must have had enough of that over the weekend.

'Was it a success for you?'

'Hmm, sorry?' She looked at me blankly

'The festival, was it a success for you?'

'Yes. It was the first one at Charleton House we'd been part of and we'll definitely come again.'

'Well, I'm glad to hear that Ben's murder hasn't put you off.'

She picked up another packet of sugar and started folding it in her fingers. I couldn't stand it anymore and didn't care that I hardly knew the woman.

'Look, Kathy, I don't mean to intrude, but is everything alright? When I first met you on Friday, you seemed really happy to be here, but I haven't seen you smile once over the weekend. Well, not while I've been around, and I'm wondering if I should take it personally or if there's something wrong I can help with. I hardly know you, but I like you and your sister, and I'd like to do some business with you, so it would be good for us to get off on the right foot and have clear air between us.'

Kathy looked up, surprised. 'Oh God, no, it's not you, or the fair, or the house. This whole weekend has been great. I just, well...' – she glanced around the room – 'I did something really stupid, and if my sister finds out, I don't think she'll react well. We've put our hearts and souls into this business, and I don't want to screw it up, but I think I might have done.'

She looked genuinely worried as, for the first time, she looked directly at me.

'I have no idea why I'm telling you this; I hardly know you.' She stopped and took a deep breath. 'Friday night, a few of us had gone to the pub after we'd finished setting up. The Black Swan, just down the road. Well, Lucy went home early. She wanted to get a good night's sleep, but I stayed for another drink. I ended up sat with Guy from Silver Bullet. One thing led to another and, well, I spent the night with him. That wouldn't be a big deal, but he's the competition and someone that neither Lucy nor I have a lot of respect for professionally. I was an idiot after a couple of drinks too many and Lucy is going to kill me.

'Of course, it also made it awkward for the rest of the weekend. He attempted to get me alone a couple of times. He seemed to give up fairly quickly and didn't try anything on, or really say anything, but he had a knowing look in his eye, like he had something he could use against me. He's a bit of a sleaze.'

She sat back in her chair. I didn't know why she'd just told me all that, either, but if it helped her, then I was OK with it. I remembered the live interpretation with Samuel Pepys on Sunday morning when Guy had followed Kathy into the room. She'd been trying to avoid him. He, on the other hand, had looked rather amused by it all.

'You need to talk to your sister. There's no way she doesn't know something is bothering you. If I could tell, then she will. You're never going to be able to move on from this if you don't talk to her. You're bound to end up at the same events as Guy for years to come.'

She nodded. 'I know, I'm being ridiculous. I was just so mad at myself; I'm not a one-night stand kind of girl, and the one time I actually do it, it's with him. It creeps me out just thinking about it.' The more she talked, the more emboldened she became. Her voice had stopped sounding so weary and downtrodden, and she was looking me in the eyes again. It seemed that unburdening herself had made a difference.

I decided to dig a bit deeper. 'Did you see Ben before you went up to Guy's room?'

She thought about it for a moment. 'No, he wasn't at the pub. He said he was going to join us, but I didn't see him. Guy went up first and I followed a couple of minutes later, we didn't want to make it obvious. He might have arrived after that and spent time with Kyle or the others.'

My gut told me she was telling the truth. 'What time did you leave in the morning?'

'About five. I wanted to get home and make it look like I'd just gone to bed late, be there when Lucy got up, so I crept out like a guilty teenager.' She shook her head at her own behaviour, then looked directly at me. 'Why the questions? My messed up love life can't be of that much interest to you.'

I was about to answer with some vague version of the truth when I saw Lucy walk into the café and scan the room. She smiled and waved as she walked over.

I looked back at Kathy. 'This is your chance to come clean. I'll get you both a drink.'

I stood up and said hello to Lucy as she joined us, then made two cups of coffee and plated up a couple of chocolate brownies and took them over to the table.

'Are you not joining us?' Lucy enquired as she reached for a brownie.

'I've got a couple of things I need to do, I'll be back in a bit.'

With that, I left them to their heart to heart and kept myself busy. The visitors were still arriving in a steady flow, and the café hummed to the sound of their chatter as I fetched more cakes to put on display. A small child was running between the tables, so I scanned the room, trying to identify his parents, and noticed two women in the far corner. One had a child on her lap, the other an empty pushchair next to her. They were engrossed in something on a phone, scrolling through photos and laughing, taking no interest at all in where the young boy was.

As I asked the boy what his teddy bear was called, one of the women looked over. I pointed at her and with a big smile encouraged the lad to go back to her, but once he reached her, my smile disappeared and I made sure his mother realised I wasn't overly pleased. I love kids; I'd just rather not go flying over one when I'm carrying a pile of dishes or a bowl of hot soup.

After telling a couple of old ladies from Yorkshire which part of the gardens were my favourite as they didn't have much time and wanted to know where they should head first, I helped a father attempt to convince his teenage daughter that this was one of the coolest buildings in the country and she'd get some amazing photos for social media. (I'm not sure we succeeded.) Next I had to ask a grumpy looking bloke to stop manhandling the sandwiches if he wasn't going to buy them. When he reluctantly apologised, I accepted his apology with mildly sarcastic grace.

'It's OK, I'm used to telling children to stop doing it all the time.'

After a while, I was able to slow down and look over to where Kathy and Lucy were sitting. Lucy had hold of her sister's hands and was smiling; Kathy looked incredibly relieved. Suddenly they both laughed. It looked as if all had been forgiven, not that I was sure there had been much to forgive. I was relieved that Kathy seemed genuinely not to have seen Ben on Friday night, so if he had seen her going into Guy's room, she wasn't aware. For a moment, I wondered if Ben had caught up with Kathy later and threatened to blackmail her. It seemed he was always in need of money, but I couldn't think when she would have seen him if she had left the pub at 5am, and by 8am he was dead. No, she could be ruled out, I was sure of that.

Once it became clear that Kathy and Lucy's discussion had become more light-hearted, I made my way over.

'Mind if I join you?' A daft question as I'd just turned up with three coffees.

'Of course not.' Lucy pulled out a chair for me. I looked across at Kathy, who smiled at me in a way I hadn't seen since Friday. She looked so much more relaxed.

'We were just trying to predict what you might want to talk to us about,' Kathy said with a glint in her eye. I imagined that they already had a pretty good idea.

'Probably not hard to guess, but why don't we go back a bit and you tell me more about the company.'

Kathy indicated towards her sister, allowing Lucy to start talking.

'Well, like we said, our grandfather had a replica signal box at the bottom of his garden. He'd worked on the railways all his life and he loved it. He built the signal box when we were only small, so I don't remember a time when it wasn't there. It had two floors. The ground floor was used as a garden shed, but above that was where we loved to go as kids. He had a model railway set up there – it was incredible. He'd made all the little buildings and landscaped it to look like part of Derbyshire. He'd recreated the Edale Valley and some of its stations. It was beautiful. He used to make up stories about the people on the trains and the little figures at the stations.'

Lucy looked across the table at her sister and I noticed that they had exactly the same smiles. As they looked at each other, I guessed they were picturing the same scene and recalling the same memories.

Kathy continued. 'Our grandmother had died when we were tiny and he was devastated. They were so in love. The model railway was his distraction; he spent most of his time down there. I don't think he was trying to forget; the opposite, in fact. He was always telling us stories about her. There were pictures of them together on the walls. I'm sure he talked to her when we weren't there.'

She paused for a moment, then took a deep breath.

'When he died and left the house to us, Lucy and I decided to move in together. We were both renting small flats in Sheffield and couldn't afford to buy property. This way we had our own place, could save money and eventually do something we'd always talked about doing.'

Lucy raised her coffee mug to me. 'It was our dad who got us into coffee. He isn't hugely knowledgeable about it, but he always started his day with a big mug of coffee. As soon as we were old enough, he taught us how to make it just the way he liked it: a large pot in a French press and a jug of cream. We thought it was a huge honour to be shown how to make it, like we were finally adults.' She laughed. 'Of course, it actually meant we could make him coffee whenever he wanted it.'

'Even take it to him and mum in bed on a weekend.' Kathy rolled her eyes. 'Only instead of resenting it, we started to try and make the perfect coffee. After a while, we would take them new things. We bought different kinds of coffee, made it using different methods, and before long we were obsessed.

'Fast forward fifteen years and we'd moved into our grandfather's house and saved to buy a coffee roaster of our own. We knew exactly where it would go and what we'd call our company. Lucy kept working for a few months and then went part time, but I quit my job and read everything I could get my hands on. I did a few courses and travelled to Ethiopia, Kenya, India. We don't make much money at the moment, but Lucy has been able to join me full time now and we're getting a lot of attention with the van at festivals, so business is picking up.'

Kathy spoke with such passion. Once she had finished talking, I knew I wanted to work with her and her sister.

'So, how would you like to gain another customer and supply the coffee to one of the country's finest historic houses?'

The two sisters looked at each other, their eyes wide. Lucy was the first to speak.

'We thought this might be what you were going to say, but... well, now you've said it out loud, wow! Yeah, of course. That's amazing.'

Kathy threw her head back and laughed. 'Oh my God, suppliers to Charleton House. It's incredible.' She leaned over and flung her arms around me. I wasn't expecting it and nearly fell off my chair, but I hugged her back. She was a different woman to the one I'd seen over the weekend.

'But don't you need to check with the Duke and Duchess?' Lucy asked, looking concerned.

'No, the Duchess never drinks coffee so wouldn't be able to offer an opinion, and the Duke would never get involved with this level of detail. I sometimes run menus past them for their own events, but in the main they leave food- and drink-related decisions up to me.'

'I feel like we should be drinking something other than coffee.' Lucy stared into her empty mug.

'Don't worry, we will,' I replied. 'We'll get the details sorted, then we'll crack open the champagne. But for now, cheers.'

I offered them my mug, they raised theirs, and in a chorus of 'cheers' we saluted our new venture.

After I'd said goodbye to Lucy and Kathy, I made my way through to the kitchen. The café had quietened down and I felt I could leave my extremely competent team to it, so I tidied up the kitchen to look less like a bombsite and started to lay out some ingredients. Following the magnificent fail of the chocolate and beetroot muffins, I wanted another go at experimenting, only this time with a much safer recipe.

After coffee, my favourite liquid to drink is gin – only much less liberally, of course – and I'd had an idea. I was about to get started when there was a loud rapping at the window, so I looked up and found myself face to face with Malcolm. I'd forgotten all about him and it was quite nice to see him. He wasn't someone

I'd choose to socialise with, but he was always friendly and upbeat.

I opened the window.

'Hello, Sophie, hope I'm not disturbing you?'

'Not at all, I was just about to experiment. What are you up to?'

'Not much, stretching my legs. I'm on my way to say goodbye to the Duke and Duchess; I'm heading off shortly.'

'I thought you were staying all week.'

'I was, but something came up in Paris. I'm getting the Eurostar later today, so sadly my little break has been curtailed. It was lovely while it lasted, if a little lively. Is murder a common event around here?'

He laughed, a deep throaty laugh that I imagined being formed by long nights with whisky and cigars.

'Fortunately not.' I decided not to tell him about a murder that had taken place a couple of months earlier. 'It certainly livens things up a bit, though.'

He leaned through the window. 'What delights are you whipping up, or is it top secret?'

'Not at all: gin and tonic cupcakes. I thought they'd be rather nice for some of the events we hold. The Duchess has a few coming up with "ladies who lunch" types, and with it being summer...'

'Sounds delicious. Shame I won't be here long enough to try them, although I'm more of a whisky man myself. Mind you, cake of any kind hits the spot.' He had stepped back from the window and patted his stomach. 'As you can see.'

As he gave another of his throaty laughs, I remembered his meeting with Guy and his interest in restaurants.

'I believe food is a professional interest as well?'

'In what way?'

'I might have got it wrong, but I thought I heard someone say you were interested in opening up a restaurant. Guy is advising you?'

'A restaurant?' He thought briefly. 'Oh yes, of course. Well, not so much opening one myself, but investing in one back in Paris. I don't know much about it so I do a bit of research whenever I can. Guy's done this kind of thing in the past.'

A restaurant in Paris. It all sounded rather romantic, but then anything associated with Paris ended up sounding romantic.

'What sort of food? I ran a couple of restaurants in London over the years, I might be able to help. I'm happy to give you my email address.'

He looked a little flustered; embarrassed, perhaps. Maybe it was a project he was trying to keep secret until more had been confirmed. I was exactly the same way; I hadn't told any of my friends or family about the job at Charleton House until I'd been offered it and accepted.

'Well, it's sort of a mix. Fusion, I guess you'd call it. We're still playing with ideas. Well, the chef is. As the owner, I'd just be the backing.'

He didn't seem very sure. I was used to working with chefs who had a very distinctive style, but I knew that wasn't always the way.

'Whereabouts in Paris will be it? It must have been hard to decide, there are so many beautiful neighbourhoods.'

'Absolutely.' It was as though he hadn't heard my question. 'Well, sorry to say I ought to be getting off. I want to say goodbye to the Duke and Duchess.' He was stepping back from the window as he spoke. 'It's been an absolute delight, Sophie, hope to see you when I next stop by.'

With that, he was off up the lane and out of sight.

I made a start on measuring out the ingredients for the cupcakes, pouring in the two tablespoons of gin the recipe called for, then I reconsidered. I was much more comfortable with the sound of four tablespoons. When it came to boozy cakes, too much was a risk I was always prepared to take. As I worked, I pondered over Malcolm's obvious anxiety to get away from me. What was it with men avoiding conversations? Both Malcolm and Guy had been keen to escape my company as quickly as possible. Maybe I'd made them uncomfortable. Maybe my questions were just a little too close to the bone.

CHAPTER 11

Unusually for England, the hot weather wasn't showing any signs of letting up, so the next morning I welcomed the opportunity to escape my kitchens and head off into the Derbyshire countryside. My car windows were wound down and fresh air buffeted me as I blasted my way round the country lanes. I had spent the morning visiting one of my suppliers, a farm about twenty miles away that supplied all the bacon and sausages I used at Charleton House. It had turned out that the farmer was a bit of a history buff and enjoyed playing with interesting sausage recipes, and I'd been selling one that combined pork, beef, sage and nutmeg. Simple, but delicious and authentic, it had ensured I'd sold record numbers of sausage barms – or sandwiches – to staff in particular. Once I'd arrived, it had been fun to put on my wellies and get a short tour of his farm. The packet of sausages that were now sitting in a cooler in the boot of my car, destined for my own fridge, were a nice bonus.

I swung the car round the tight bends, past farms and cottages selling honey and jams at their gate with an honesty box for money. The cottage gardens held wonderful displays of foxgloves, sweet peas and delphiniums that sang 'English country garden'. Their scents wafted in through my window and I slowed down to admire them, their delicate pinks and cream colours easy on the eye.

I crossed over some train tracks, drove down a steep hill and passed the sign for an industrial estate that was hidden in some trees down a lane. One of the company names on the notice board caught my eye: 'Silver Bullet Coffee Roasters'. Of course, this was where Guy and Kyle had based their company and roasting operation. I wondered idly if they would all be at work, roasting more beans for their next event. In a split second I decided to turn the car round and drop in unannounced. It would be easy for me to claim I was interested in their operation. It wasn't too far away from the truth, and maybe I would find out something more about Ben.

I drove slowly down the pot-holed lane and eventually came to a large clearing. There were five industrial buildings and a number of cars, vans and trucks scattered about, the red-brick walls and metal roofs of the buildings a million miles away from the artistic splendour and show of wealth that the architects of Charleton House had created. I drove slowly past them, looking for one that had a sign referencing coffee.

There it was, on the third building along, next to some external stairs. I parked up the car and got out just as a man appeared from a large open door a few feet away.

'Can I help you, love?'

'I'm looking for Silver Bullet Coffee, I'm guessing they're up there?' I pointed up the metal staircase.

'Sure are. I saw one of them around earlier, but he left about half an hour ago. Why don't you wait upstairs? If he's coming back, it'll be open. I'm guessing you'll be able to make yourself a coffee.'

He laughed at his own joke as I climbed up the metal staircase to the door at the top. The man had been right: the door was unlocked and I let myself in, calling out as I entered, not wanting to take anyone by surprise if it turned out someone was still in there.

No response.

The Silver Bullet offices consisted of two large rooms, connected by a single door. The white walls shone as the sunlight bounced around the room. A couple of desks along one wall held a few untidy piles of paperwork and cables where laptops would be plugged in when someone was working there. On the opposite side of the room was a long, tall shelving unit, filled with cardboard boxes. A couple of the boxes were open and I could see they contained the bags that would go on to hold the Silver Bullet Coffee beans. A few of the empty coffee bags had fallen on the floor; a couple littered one of the desks. There were brown flecks here and there on the pale grey carpet, and the occasional pile of brown powder. I bent down to investigate more closely and realised it was coffee granules.

It made sense. Some customers wanted beans they could grind at home, others wanted them ready ground, avoiding the fuss of that extra step. I for one always ground the coffee myself; I enjoyed playing an additional part in the process of getting the coffee into my cup, and it meant the room filled with the wonderful aroma of fresh beans.

It looked as if the Silver Bullet guys packaged the coffee in here. I stepped through the door, expecting to see the roasting machine in pride of place and waiting to get to work on another batch, but there was nothing. No roaster; no sacks of coffee beans waiting to go in; no sign of a coffee operation at all. But I could tell from indentations on the carpet that large boxes had recently been stored in here, and there were some coffee beans scattered about.

It didn't make any sense. I knew that this was Silver Bullet's registered office and warehouse; I'd looked the company up online as I often did with independent coffee roasters I came across. A small company like this wouldn't be able to afford multiple locations, and if Guy and Kyle had a backer who did enable them to expand, they would have also had the money to make these rooms look a lot more welcoming. There wasn't even a cheap inspirational poster on the wall, let alone empty coffee sacks with interesting designs framed and turned into art. I'd have expected maps of the world that showed where the beans had come from, perhaps a large version of their logo proudly displayed on the front door, but there wasn't any of that here. Yes, there were all the bags that would later be filled with the coffee, but that was it.

The offices were beginning to look like somewhere that had been abandoned in a hurry, like the company had collapsed, the bailiffs had been in, and Guy and Kyle could no longer pay the rent on the space and had just walked out. But I knew that wasn't the case. They had a beautiful Airstream that they took around the country, an employee in the form of Ben – well, an ex-employee – and they were selling their reasonable if uninspired coffee very successfully. I was sure these rooms had not been abandoned. Besides which, the man I had spoken to outside had said that one of them had been here this morning. None of it made any sense.

Returning to the first room, I started to flick through the paperwork on the desk. I was a bit unnerved by how little guilt I felt about that; I wasn't sure if that made me a great snoop or a great detective! There were the usual letters from events companies about upcoming festivals, late payment letters for the rental of this industrial unit, and delivery notes for the boxes on the shelves. There was the receipt for the Airstream, which had been paid off in one lump sum twelve months ago. There was also paperwork relating to the Sheffield Roasting Hub. I'd heard of it before, but I quickly pulled the information up on my phone to refresh my memory.

The Sheffield Roasting Hub was a coffee roasting facility

where people could rent the space by the half day and roast their own coffee using the equipment provided. It was a great solution for small companies that couldn't afford the huge financial investment of buying their own roasting equipment. I pulled some of the paperwork together – it looked as if Silver Bullet had stopped using the Roasting Hub roughly twelve months ago. That would usually mean that a company had finally been able to afford its own equipment, but not Silver Bullet. Or at least, there was no sign of it here.

What were Guy and Kyle playing at? They weren't using the Roasting Hub, they hadn't bought their own equipment, and yet they had the money to buy an enormous, gleaming Airstream. The more unusual it seemed, the more uncomfortable I started to feel, and I decided it was time to leave.

As I turned towards the door, I spotted a small piece of card on the floor. It was a business card for Bruce Keen from the Northern Bean Company. I was now doubly confused as I couldn't imagine what Bruce had been doing here, unless he was planning on going into business with Guy and Kyle, which I found unlikely. One of the attractions for customers to companies like Silver Bullet was their independence and small-scale operation. Mind you, without any equipment, Silver Bullet's operation was so small it was virtually non-existent.

I stepped back out into the summer heat and down the stairs, my footsteps making the metal steps clang as I went. Next to the stairs was a large metal skip and I glanced inside as I went down, using my temporary bird's-eye view. There were dozens of empty folded cardboard boxes inside. I was hoping that the Silver Bullet lads were planning on recycling them when I spotted something familiar on the side of one of the boxes. It was an image of a pile of coffee beans with three letters underneath: 'NBC' – the logo for The Northern Bean Company.

I stopped a couple of steps from the bottom of the stairs and stared at the boxes. Silver Bullet's coffee had tasted exactly like that of NBC – I'd used the same words to describe them both. That was because they *were* the same.

Silver Bullet Coffee and NBC coffee were one and the same.

As I stood there, staring into the skip, it all became clear. Guy and Kyle were decanting NBC coffee into Silver Bullet branded bags and selling it as their own, with a healthy mark up on the price because people were happy to pay more when they thought they were supporting a small local company. I was horrified by what they were doing, and I couldn't help but wonder if this had some bearing on Ben's murder. Was Ben in on it to the same extent as Guy and Kyle, assuming, of course, that as the owners of the company, Guy and Kyle were both happily behind this idea? Had Ben been supportive of the scheme, or was he a reluctant participant, in it solely to keep his job? Had he developed a conscience about what they were doing and been threatening to blow the whistle on the whole operation? That of course would put Guy and Kyle directly in the spotlight as having motives.

On the other hand, Bruce must have been furious when he realised what was happening. I was sure he would have put it together in the same way I had. When had he visited and dropped the business card? I knew he'd been in the area on Friday and Saturday – surely this now gave him a motive.

I started to feel distinctly vulnerable. The last thing I needed were any potential killers turning up and discovering that I was in on their secret, so I went back to my car. I was about forty minutes' drive from Charleton House and that would give me some thinking time; I'd call Joe when I was back at the office.

The route from the industrial estate to Charleton House took me past my home and the Black Swan Pub. I'd already decided on my next plan of action and I pulled into the car park.

There were a few customers sitting in the beer garden, enjoying the sunshine and an early afternoon pint as I went in. It was nice to get inside, my eyes welcoming the rest after the glare of the sunshine, especially as I'd left my sunglasses in my office. I looked about for the landlord and found him wiping down a table in the far corner.

'Steve, do you have a minute?'

'Of course, can I get you a drink?'

'No thanks, I can't stop. This is going to be a bit of an odd question, but you know the two guys from the coffee company that have been staying here? Well, one of them was here for breakfast the day of the murder up at the house. Do you remember him?'

'Of course, Kyle. The police were asking about him.'

'Do you remember what time he left?'

'Sure. Like I told the police, I saw him leave at about nine. I remember because I had a delivery arrive as he was leaving and the brewery is always dead on time. Sorry, that's not a good way of putting it under the circumstances.'

I smiled so he knew he hadn't offended me.

'That was quite late for breakfast.'

'He wasn't eating breakfast that late; he had it delivered to his room at seven. We started doing room service about six months ago. Just for breakfast, mind, and it's been really popular. He did that each morning he was here. I took the tray up to his room at seven, then collected the dirty dishes after I saw him leave at nine.'

We'd moved over to the bar and Steve started emptying a dishwasher as we spoke. The hot steam from the machine hit me in the face and I stepped back.

'Sorry, luv, I should have warned you.'

I removed my glasses and wiped the steam from them. 'Did you tell the police that?'

'What, that he ate in his room?' He thought for a moment, and then shook his head. 'No, they wanted to know if he'd had breakfast here and what time he'd left, so that's what I told them. Is everything OK?'

I didn't want to give too much away; I had no idea if Steve was one of those gossipy landlords who enjoy knowing everyone's business and coming across as the fount of all knowledge, so I kept my feelings to myself.

'Everything's fine, thanks, I just wanted to check. See you soon.' After promising to return for a drink as soon as possible, I jumped back in the car, noting exactly what time I set off. I wanted to be 100% sure how long it took me to get back up to the house.

'So you think he might have snuck out after he'd had his breakfast delivered, killed Ben, and then returned so he could be seen leaving the pub later on?'

I was sitting in my stuffy office with the door closed, beads of sweat running down my forehead. I felt sticky and disgusting, but I had to make sure no one could overhear my phone conversation with Joe. To be extra sure, I'd turned the dishwasher on in the kitchen. The noise drowned out any conversation that escaped under the door, but it just added to the heat. At this rate I was going to sweat off a few pounds – no bad thing.

'It's possible. It took me nine minutes to drive from the pub to the car park. Kyle had two hours from the point of breakfast being delivered to being seen leaving the pub. You said that Ben had been murdered around about 8am. That gives Kyle loads of time to get here, argue with Ben, kill him and get back.'

'True.' Joe didn't sound entirely convinced. 'But how did he manage it without appearing on camera? The car park is almost fully covered, and if he took the route stallholders take to get to their stalls, he'd definitely have been seen. And the security staff would have had to sign him in anyway. Nobody said anything about seeing him.'

He had a point, but I wasn't giving up that easily. 'Kyle grew up around here, which means he probably knew the estate reasonably well and knew how to get in and out unseen. Most locals have walked the estate countless times over the years, and they drive through here regularly. It's not uncommon for the security team to find some drunken teenagers daring each other to climb over walls and go for a dip in the Great Pond.'

'And his motive?' Joe didn't sound like he was completely dismissing my theory. If anything, I imagined he was annoyed with the police officers who had interviewed Steve and not got the details about Kyle having breakfast in his room, out of sight of anyone else: a distinctly less watertight alibi than they had previously believed.

'Kyle and Guy are passing off someone else's coffee as their own. It means they have considerably less overheads as they haven't had to buy a roaster. They're not paying the costs associated with running it and they're not dealing with the hassle of importing beans. They're repackaging someone else's coffee, marking up the price and selling it for a decent profit. Buying expensive locally produced products is all the rage now. You should have seen the prices at some of the stalls over the weekend, and yet people were still happily handing over their cash. It wouldn't take much to run, and Kyle and Guy could have been leaving Ben to do all the work, while they're off making more money through other business ventures.'

There was silence on the other end as Joe took in what I was saying.

'None of this is without logic, Sophie, but I just don't know how Kyle could have got in and out of the gardens without being spotted by someone. The gardens team, for example – there were about half a dozen of them preparing for the start of the festival, and many of them had been onsite since 6am and were working within the vicinity of the festival stalls. But none of them saw anything out of the ordinary. It would have made more sense for

Elliot to have done it. He was actually meant to be in the gardens at that time, but he has an alibi too.

'I'll talk to DS Harnby and we'll get someone over to the industrial estate. At the very least, Kyle and Guy are going to have to answer some awkward questions from the Trading Standards Office about how they run their business, and they're bound to wind up in court over that. And you're right, if Ben got tired of how they were doing business, then both Kyle and Guy have suddenly got a substantial motive for wanting him out of the way. But alibis and access to the gardens are problematic. Leave it with me.'

'There's something else you ought to be aware of as well.' As I told Joe about Bruce's business card and that he probably knew about the scam, I heard him breathe out, hard. I could imagine him leaning back in his chair and messing with his hair as he thought about what I'd told him; I'd seen him do it before when he was taken by surprise. He didn't seem to realise doing it would leave his hair in a straggly mess, but it was rather endearing nonetheless.

'Well that's a new one. I'll add it to my list of things for DS Harnby... Thanks, I owe you.' I'd yet to meet her, but I knew that Detective Sergeant Harnby was proving to be a tough, though fair, boss, so I was pleased to be able to give Joe something he could take to her and maybe gain a few extra brownie points at the same time.

CHAPTER 12

I still have plenty of days when I need to pinch myself. It can be hard to take in the fact that I work in one of the most stunningly beautiful houses in England, especially as it's a common occurrence for me to sit chatting with the Duke or Duchess of Ravensbury. Today was one of those days. I had a meeting with the Duchess to discuss the catering for a private event she was hosting, and so here I was, on a seemingly ordinary Thursday morning, looking out of the window of the private study she shared with her husband.

The Duchess is a handsome woman; slim, but not waiflike. There is a physical strength in her posture and figure that is matched by a determination and focus in her eyes. The expression 'eyes in the back of their head' seems to have been invented for her, yet she doesn't instil a sense of fear. Instead, she inspires great loyalty, and I have never heard a single negative word directed towards the Duchess. People find her impressive and warm. She loves Charleton House and talks about that love openly. Fascinated by the history of the family she has married into, she doesn't shy away from discussing the more colourful Fitzwilliam-Scott characters and their exploits. The Duke has the same attitude; there are no skeletons in their closets, the Duke having long since invited them all to dinner.

The only thing about the Duchess that's difficult to fathom is her dislike of coffee. She hates the stuff, an attitude I find impossible to relate to.

'It's not the most spectacular of views,' the Duchess said as she handed me a delicate china cup of coffee and glanced out of the window, 'but as the courtyard below is off limits to the public, it does make for a quiet working life.' Outside were brightly coloured window boxes along the sills of all the lower windows, and Robin was currently replanting a number of them. Beyond that, it was a simple, small stone courtyard that I wasn't aware served any particular purpose; at least, not anymore.

The Duchess took a seat behind an enormous wooden desk that would have needed an army of men to move. I guessed everything stayed where it was in this room; no spur of the moment furniture rearranging, and if it wasn't feng shui, then so be it. A second desk, the Duke's, sat at a right angle to the Duchess's. Against the other two walls were waist-high bookcases and a couple of ancient wooden filing cabinets, which I imagined getting stuck on a regular basis and requiring a lot of cursing and shoving to open. Although bearing in mind this was the office of a duke and duchess, the likelihood was the furniture behaved as well as the staff did when they were nearby.

Dozens of photos in exquisite silver frames lined the tops of bookcases and the walls were home to portraits, both painted and photographed, of family members and friends. Photos of presidents and prime ministers being welcomed to the house were interspersed with group photos of university students: a much younger Duke stood among his mainly male classmates, all in bow ties and tails at Oxford University. Privilege and confidence oozed from every pore.

I spotted Malcolm; even in a black-and-white photo, it was possible to make out his ruddy cheeks. In his youth, he'd had a sturdier build than all the others. He looked as if he would have been the life and soul of the party, always inviting people – friends and strangers alike – back to his rooms. It was likely, of course, that he would have done that to fit in with a class of people very different to his own.

Recalling my reason for being there, I sat opposite the Duchess and opened my notebook. We were planning a simple afternoon tea for a group of women who were paying a lot of money to have a tour of some of the private areas of the house with the Duchess. I would make sure there was an almost endless supply of champagne, sandwiches with the crusts removed and cakes so delicately decorated, they would be worthy of going in a display case alongside works of art. Or at least, I knew that was what was expected of me and I would spend the next three weeks working with Ruth, practising until our knuckles cramped and we never wanted to ice another cake in our lives.

'I love the idea of gin and tonic cupcakes. Would you mind making me some for this weekend? I have a friend staying and I just know she'll adore them.'

I was pleased the Duchess was so taken with the idea. 'Absolutely, and if you have any particular requests for the other cakes, please let me know.'

The Duchess considered the question for a moment. 'I'll leave that in your hands, Sophie. I have quite a lot on and don't want to give this event any more thought than absolutely necessary.'

We both turned as the door opened to admit her husband. I stood.

'Good morning, Duke.'

'Sit, please, none of that. I just need to collect some papers off my desk. How are you, Sophie?'

'Well, thank you.' When I had first met the Duke and Duchess, I had referred to them by the appropriate address of 'Your Grace' and 'Ma'am', but Mark had quickly put me right. He told me that they were a little more laid back than that, and insisted that staff simply call them Duke or Duchess. It had made me feel part of the 'inner sanctum'.

'Where did I put the damned thing?' As he rooted through a mound of paper on his untidy desk, the Duchess and I finalised a few more aspects of afternoon tea: which kinds of tea would be served; how many choices of coffee; different milk options. We really were catering to all potential requirements.

'Got it.' The Duke interrupted our conversation. 'I swear I'd lose my head if it wasn't screwed on. Sophie, you often have your ear to the ground. Any updates on the murder of that poor man?' He perched on the edge of his desk and turned to face me.

'Nothing substantial that I'm aware of. A lot of dead ends and anyone of interest has an alibi, but I know that DC Greene and his colleagues are working extremely hard.'

'Oh absolutely, I wouldn't suggest otherwise, but I do hate loose ends and we'd all like to move on.'

I was confused. 'I saw you with DI Flynn at the reception on the night of the theft. Hasn't he been keeping you up to date with events?'

The Duke smiled. 'Ah yes, your friend the detective inspector. Seems to think that any assistance you gave his team in the past was unnecessary, and feels the same way about current or future cases.'

I glanced down at my hands – was this a warning?

'Of course, my view is that if anything you did helped speed things along, then you were clearly essential, and I for one don't have an issue with that. Not that I'd say that to the inspector.' He had an impish smile on his face. Every time I met the Duke, he gave me another reason to like him. As he seemed talkative and supportive of my curious nature, I took the chance to question him.

'Is there any more news about your mother's bowl?'

He sighed deeply. 'None. My greatest frustration is that it is of absolutely no value to anyone else, so there is no gain from the theft, just the great sense of loss that is left behind. It's utterly pointless.'

'So it had to be an opportunist. If anyone knew of its lack of value, they wouldn't have bothered taking it, I presume?'

I'd meant that to be more rhetorical than it had sounded and I wasn't sure I'd meant to say it out loud, but the Duke took hold of my thoughts.

'Are you saying that if there was a chance it was chosen intentionally, then it must have been taken by someone who knew its loss would cause emotional distress?'

I hadn't actually been saying that; I hadn't even thought it, but he was onto something and I wanted to build on it.

'Who knows how much it means to you? I mean, visitors see it all the time and know the history, but don't necessarily know the sentimental value attached to it.'

'Only the family, I think. Of course, I often talk fondly of my mother, and there are a lot of items in the house that you could assume I attached a sentimental value to, but I can't see why anyone other than family would be aware of the additional significance of this piece. I've been in touch with various friends in the antiques business and they're all on the lookout for it. If anyone tries to sell it to a respected dealer, we'll know about it, so I guess I just have to play a waiting game. Well, on that slightly sombre note, I must be off.'

As he reached the door, he paused and looked over at his wife.

'Don't forget, we're meeting Jeremy and Belinda for cocktails at four. Are you planning on wearing the blue number I saw hanging on the back of the door?'

'I am.' The Duchess sounded a little uncertain, as though she expected him to say he didn't like the dress.

'Good.' He smiled and winked at her before heading out of the door. The Duchess laughed and looked at me.

'He can be such a lad sometimes.' She paused before adding, 'I'm very lucky.'

I left the Duchess to her work and thoughts of her young-at-heart husband, keen to talk to Robin, who was still working in the courtyard below. My route took me down a short, narrow staircase with whitewashed walls and plain wooden steps. In the past, it would have been used by servants making their way to their quarters at the end of a long working day.

I appeared from behind a hidden door at the top of an enormous, imposing oak staircase. Every inch of the walls was covered with muskets, bayonets, pistols, swords, daggers and body armour. Early generations of the Fitzwilliam-Scott family had fought for King and Country, this magnificent display a reminder of their role in bloody battles and the fight to win the approval of reigning monarchs. The weapons had been hung like works of art: concentric circles of swords and daggers formed a starburst around a silver chest plate; the crossed muzzles of muskets made blocks of patterns. I briefly considered how the tools of war could be used to create something so beautiful as I passed visitors reading guidebooks or listening intently to their audio guides, and those who were experiencing the house entirely from behind the lens of their camera-phone.

I quickly stepped out of the way as a visitor walked into the centre of the staircase without looking in order to take a selfie. Touching her arm gently, I drew her attention to how close she was to the edge of the step and she smiled gratefully. I didn't want any Darwin Awards handed out to visitors of Charleton House; not today, anyway.

I found the window that Robin had used to access the courtyard and, in a very unladylike fashion, clambered out to join him.

'Sophie, let me give you a hand.' I already had two feet on the ground by the time he reached me. 'What on earth are you doin'?'

'I wanted a quick word with you, do you have a minute?'

'Of course, let's sit over here in the sunlight. What's so important that you're prepared to climb through windows to see me? I'd be flattered, but I'm a little old to be your type.'

I'd warmed to Robin as soon as I'd met him last summer. He had a slightly old-fashioned way about him, but he was never offensive; more of a gentleman with a cheeky wit.

'I wanted to ask you about Saturday morning, if you don't mind. I know the police have spoken to you, but I just want to get something straight in my mind.'

'Get somethin' straight in your mind? Are you moonlighting for the police now? Cupcakes and crime, that's quite a mix.'

'I know. Technically it's none of my business. I can't quite explain why I'm so interested, but I have so many snippets of information coming my way that they end up swimming about my head and I need to make sense of them. It's a bit like someone has put a load of ingredients down in front of me; I can't help but wonder what I could make with them, what they'll look like once I've worked out quantities and what order they should be added into the mix.'

I'd never thought of my interest in Ben's murder in this way before. Sitting in the quiet courtyard with nothing to disturb me but the seemingly genuine interest of a sweet man like Robin made it easier for me to throw some light on why I was digging into motives and alibis; why I was so determined to find out what had happened. My mind instinctively wanted to piece things together, only this time it was a murder, not a meringue or a muffin.

'You said that on the morning of the murder, you were working with Elliot?'

'That's right, we were up near the Rock Garden. I knew the night before that we were on top of everything for the festival, so I'd scheduled in some other jobs for the team until about 9am when we knew the stallholders would start arriving so we needed to be back by the Great Pond and available to help them.

Elliot's rather fond of the Rock Garden so I had him up there with me.'

'You were up there all morning?'

'Let me think. I have it all on a spreadsheet back at the office, but off the top of my head, we started work at six. A number of us were in the greenhouses until seven, and then Elliot and I went up to the Rock Garden. We were there until eight-thirty, we grabbed a quick coffee together back in the break room, and then we both made our way over to the stalls to start helping there.' He laughed. 'You don't think I did it, do you?'

I smiled and nudged him with my elbow. 'Even weeds get handled gently by you, so I doubt it. Look, this is a bit awkward, but how well do you know Elliot?'

He looked at me with one raised eyebrow. 'Really? You think he did it?'

'I'm not saying that. It's just... well, did you see him flip out at Ben on Friday when they were setting up? Elliot was really mad, I thought he was going to hit Ben.'

Robin shook his head. 'I didn't see it, but I heard about it. Elliot can get a bit hot-headed; people often describe him as someone who shouldn't be crossed, but he's the kind of person that explodes and then comes back down to earth almost as quickly. I've never known him actually hit someone.'

I found that hard to believe; I'd never seen someone have to rein themselves in quite so much. Elliot had been as mad as hell.

'Can you think back to Saturday morning? Are you sure that Elliot was with you the whole time you were up at the Rock Garden? Was he ever out of your sight, no matter for how short a period of time?'

Robin rubbed his soil-covered hands across his face, leaving a brown streak on one of his cheeks. 'You're barking up the wrong tree, Sophie, honestly, love. Like I told the police, I was with him the whole time. We were tidying up the borders, making notes of what areas might need refreshing, picking up some rubbish, then I had to...'

He stopped and thought for a moment.

'Hang on, there was a point where... oh God, I forgot all about it. I didn't mention it to the police.'

'What?'

'Look, I still don't think for one minute that Elliot had anything to do with Ben's murder, but there was a point when I left him to it. You know the old shepherd's hut on the path that leads to the Rock Garden? We used to use it to sell ice cream in the summer, and then your predecessor decided it wasn't profitable enough. Well I'd noticed on the way past that a couple of the panes of glass in the small windows had been broken, so I went in to tidy them up and put a couple of pieces of cardboard in the holes, make them safe. I must have been in there twenty, maybe thirty minutes at the most. When I got back, Elliot was right where I had left him.

'He's a good man, Sophie. Hot-headed, yes, but he's a kind, reliable man who dotes on his family and loves his job. He wouldn't jeopardise that, no matter what it was that Ben had done to make him so angry.'

There was a pleading look in Robin's eyes. I liked him a lot, and I trusted him. But I didn't know Elliot, and I certainly had no idea if he could be trusted.

CHAPTER 13

*L*eaving Robin looking pensive, I felt bad for spoiling his day like that, but at least I had jogged his memory. I knew how easy it was for things to be so routine or instinctive that they didn't stand out in your mind, so I didn't blame him for not remembering that bit of information when he had been questioned by the police. No wonder detectives on police shows always handed out their card and said, 'Call me if you think of anything else.'

I didn't have any more meetings until after lunch, so decided to check out the Rock Garden. The glaring summer sun was still hanging around, but it was a little chillier than it had been at the weekend, and every time I walked into shadows, I shivered. The Rock Garden was about fifteen minutes' walk from the house if you knew where you were going, but I wanted to be sure.

Most visitors stumbled upon the Rock Garden accidentally as it was tucked away behind a small thicket of trees, and the pathways that brought you to it were winding and branched off in different directions at numerous junctions, but you were in for a treat when you made it. A waterfall tumbled over a mountain of dark grey rocks, then down a steep bank, round a few twists and turns, and finally into a large rocky pond. A maze of paths meandered their way up and down the surrounding ground, past rocks and displays of beautiful flowers.

I recognised a swathe of purple as a bank of irises. Pretty little violet-blue flowers covered the ground immediately next to the water, and the colour theme continued with deep purple flowers that had round pin cushion-like heads on tall green stalks. I was determined to learn more about horticulture now I was here and I made a mental note to ask Robin to walk me round this area and teach me a few things.

There were some visitors around, stopping to bend over and smell the flowers, or read the miniature wooden signs that said what they were. An elderly couple sat on a bench opposite the pond, holding hands as they took in their surroundings, occasionally following the flight path of a bird or pointing something out to one another. It seemed like everyone who walked these paths found themselves afraid to disturb the sounds of nature, opting to whisper to their companions if they deemed any conversation necessary.

I checked my watch; it was two thirty-two. Setting off down the path at a decent pace, round the pond, back up the other side of the waterfall, around the trees, over a miniature meadow and along a gravel path, I had a few more twists and turns and two gates to walk through. Once I made it to roughly where Silver Bullet Coffee had been based on Saturday morning, I checked my watch. It had taken me nine minutes. Bearing in mind that I didn't know any short cuts, I wasn't wearing the right footwear for cutting across flowerbeds, and I had walked at a steady but not particularly fast pace, I figured that Elliot could have made it in six or seven minutes. That gave him time to have a ten-minute argument with Ben, kill him and make it back to the Rock Garden in time for Robin to find him at work. OK, so it was cutting it fine, I knew that, but it was possible. If Elliot was already in a bad mood and had been quietly fuming all morning over whatever Ben had said and done, then it wouldn't have taken long for him to get mad enough to kill him. I couldn't explain how Elliot would have known Ben was alone in the van, but maybe he didn't. Maybe he just took a chance and got lucky. Either way, Elliot had the opportunity to kill Ben. Now I just needed to find out if he had a motive strong enough to kill someone.

Behind Charleton House, just beyond the back lane, is an enormous yard that's home to the gardens team. Five huge greenhouses stand side by side; surrounding these are old single-storey stone buildings, and every corner of the yard is dedicated to something: oversized plant pots; trees waiting to go into the gardens; a miniature allotment; small electric-powered vehicles; free-standing signage waiting to be called into use. It looks like well-organised chaos; it is busy and definitely lacks space.

I walked past the greenhouses, peering in as I went by. A number of them were empty, but in some there were signs that the team was starting to prepare the winter bedding plants. Small plant pots stood in hundreds of rows, some containing fresh soil, others waiting to be filled.

A black and white cat trotted past me, then backtracked and rubbed itself around my ankles before disappearing into another greenhouse. I spotted a cat bed and bag of dried cat food in the corner and guessed it was a stray who had been made welcome and, if it was anything like Pumpkin, now ran the show.

I spotted Elliot ahead of me, sitting on a low red-brick wall, cleaning tools. He was using a wire brush to scrub off the worst of the muck and had a focused look on his face.

'Elliot?'

He looked up. 'Yes?'

'I'm Sophie, we've not met before. I run the cafés.'

He nodded and turned back to the tools. 'What can I do for you?'

'This will sound a bit odd, but I wanted to ask you about Ben, the man who was killed.'

Elliot immediately stiffened and stopped what he was doing, but he didn't look at me.

'I know you knew him and I thought maybe you could tell me about him.'

'I've nuthin' to say.'

'So you did know him?'

'I told you, I've nuthin' to say.' Elliot started cleaning the tool again, only this time with even more vigour. It was only at that point that I noticed the size of the blade on the large pair of shears he had in his hands.

'Elliot, I saw the way you spoke to him on Friday. A lot of people did…'

'I've already spoken to the police, it's none of your business.'

'You nearly broke my arm when you slammed into me as you walked towards him. The resultant bruise rather makes it my business.'

Elliot stood. As much as I'm used to being the smallest person in the room, having him stand over me with a large, sharp blade in his hands made him seem about ten feet tall. I slightly regretted being so brusque with him, but I didn't warm to the silent, moody type at the best of times, and he was being foolish if he didn't think people were going to be interested in him after his display of anger towards Ben.

'It's none of your damned business.' He scooped up a couple more tools and marched off across the yard. I followed close on his heels.

'Elliot, I'm not saying you're involved, I just want to know if there's anything you can tell me that will help. I'm trying to figure out what happened.'

'What the hell has it got to do with you anyway?' He didn't wait for an answer and strode through a large open door into one of the stone buildings. Hanging in perfect order along the back wall were dozens of tools: hoes, shears, scissors, knives, shovels – you name it. They were spotless and clearly cared for; many of them also looked extremely sharp and I started to regret following him in.

Elliot hung up the tools he had been cleaning, and then turned to face me. 'Back off, I'm warning you.' His eyes were wide and there was a fury in them as he stormed past me, bashing into me as he went. 'Oh, I'm sorry,' he shouted sarcastically over his shoulder.

I was relieved that he'd gone. I knew there were cameras in the yard, but I still didn't feel safe around him, no matter what Robin had said about his temper flaring up but crashing down just as quickly.

I watched Elliot walk into the gardeners' break room. It was three o'clock and the first shift would be clocking off now. A number of gardeners were already leaving for the day, bags over their shoulders, striding towards freedom and a chance to rest their weary bodies. I left them to it and walked back towards the lane, wondering how on earth I was going to find out what Ben and Elliot had been arguing about.

It turned out that Elliot had taken a different route to the lane, and by the time I arrived, he was already standing by the security gate, chatting to one of the guards and looking a lot calmer. I hovered in the background and watched as a small car pulled up next to him. Elliot drew his conversation to a close as a woman with long blonde hair tied back in a ponytail got out and walked over to him. They briefly kissed, and after she'd exchanged a few words with the guard, they both got in the car. She performed a nifty three-point turn, and as they drove off, Elliot stuck his arm out of the window and waved at the guard. A small child I hadn't noticed before did the same thing, its arm barely visible from within the child seat.

'Sophie?' The car had just driven past Joyce and she was heading my way. 'Are you alright? You look miles away, have you been neglecting to top up your caffeine levels? Nice top – I keep telling you that brighter colours suit you, and I'm glad to see you're listening.'

'Hmm?' I looked down to see what she was talking about. I'd gone for a loose-fitting wide-necked t-shirt that was bright red on one side and navy blue on the other. Bold, but still smart enough to wear when meeting the Duchess.

'Now, if I were you, I'd finish it off with an extremely chunky necklace, either bright red or navy. A pair of bright red shoes would be perfect and… ooh, you ought to get yourself some glasses with a red frame. Daring, but with your silver hair you could pull it off. You'd look marvellous.'

Once I assumed that my fashion consultation was over, I changed the subject. 'What do you know about Elliot?'

'Forrester? Been here for years, wouldn't surprise me if he came here straight from school. Never quite become one of the old guard, though. Not old enough for a start, but he's also a bit aloof, hard to warm to. You've heard about the girlfriend, right?'

I shook my head.

'Well, a few years ago…' Joyce linked her arm through mine and steered me towards the side door that would take us to the Library Café. I mentally checked that I had some decent cake to offer her, and then tuned back into what she was saying.

'…Carla had only been here about a month…'

'Hang on, who's Carla?'

'Pay attention, girl! The woman in the car, Elliot's girlfriend. I'll start again. Carla started working as a gardener here a few years back and had only been here a month or so when she and Elliot got together. Love's young dream, they were. We were quite relieved; Elliot had always been a bit sour faced, but he seemed to perk up when she arrived. We actually started to see him smile – personally I thought his face was going to crack. Well, they were together about six months when things seemed to get a bit rocky. Elliot's period of smiling was over and she got a bit withdrawn.'

We'd reached the café and I got Joyce to take a break and grab us a table. There was plenty of choice as the visitors were starting to thin out. I cut a couple of slices of lemon drizzle cake, made two mugs of coffee and returned to join her. The enormous chunk of cake that Joyce indelicately shovelled into her mouth kept her quiet for a minute, and I took the time to admire today's choice of nail polish. She had opted for a delicate pale pink, but each nail had the added detail of a small – I presume fake – diamond. I just hoped one didn't come off and get swallowed up with the cake. Joyce wasn't the most delicate woman I'd come across, but she was inhaling the cake like she hadn't eaten for a week.

She paused and looked at me, at the plate, then at the full slice of cake I was holding, and smiled coyly. 'It's been a busy day, I barely had time for lunch.'

'But you did have time for it?'

'Well, yes, but… oh, be quiet. Are you going to eat that?'

I quickly took an enormous bite of my own slice and grinned at her triumphantly as crumbs fell from the corners of my mouth onto the table. Joyce laughed and I covered my mouth with my hand to avoid hitting her with crumbs as I joined in. Some people found Joyce intimidating, but I found myself able to relax easily around her, and I loved her upfront nature.

Once I'd swallowed my mouthful, I got her back on track. 'You were saying something about a rocky patch between Carla and Elliot.'

'Ah yes. Well, we all thought that things were going to be short-lived – this was just six months after they'd started dating. Neither of them looked happy, and then all of a sudden, she left. No one knew why – here one minute, gone the next.

'Things got back to normal and no one talked about it anymore. Elliot was back to sulking around the place, and then three months later, he perked up again. We started to wonder if he was dating someone else, but no, it turned out that he and Carla had never actually split up and he was grinning like the Cheshire Cat because she was pregnant.'

I tried to do the maths. 'What are we talking here? Two, three years ago?'

Joyce paused, the mug just in front of her lips, the jewels glinting on her impossibly long nails.

'Little Isabella was born three years ago, so Carla must have started a year or two before that.'

'You made it sound like there was something scandalous. That just sounds like normal relationship ups and downs, with a baby thrown in, albeit quite quickly.'

Joyce waved a glittery nail in my direction. 'Hold your horses. When Isabella was about three months old, a rumour started going round my team. Heaven knows how they got hold of it, but once I got wind of it, I gave them all a lecture on spreading gossip and the damage it can do. I wasn't specific, of course, but they must have known what I was talking about. That put an immediate stop to it.'

I wasn't surprised – Joyce had instilled the fear of God in her team. They loved her and were terrified of her in equal parts.

'They were saying that the baby wasn't Elliot's and Carla had stopped working here because she'd had an affair with someone. He'd forgiven her on the understanding that she quit her job and stay away from "him", whoever "he" was.'

'So she'd slept with someone they worked with?'

'That was the assumption.' Joyce didn't sound in the slightest bit judgmental, but that didn't surprise me. I knew that she had, until recently, been 'the other woman' in a relationship. 'We never found out who it was; there's always some turnover in the gardens team, so he might still be working here, he might not. After a while it became yesterday's news. We often see Carla picking Elliot up from work and they seem happy enough. He dotes on Isabella, that's for sure; he's still a miserable devil, but not when his little girl is around.'

Joyce changed the subject, her story at an end. 'Now, tell me, when are you going to let me take you shopping?'

I smiled as the image of flying pigs appeared in my mind.

CHAPTER 14

There was a knock at the door. I knew it was Mark so I called out that it was open.

'It's just me, I come bearing gifts. Bloody hell, what's that?'

I dropped my knife and walked out into the hallway. Mark and Pumpkin were standing stock still opposite each other. They'd never got on.

'That's Pumpkin. You met her the last time you were here, and the time before that.'

'I know, but she wasn't this big last time, was she? I think Pumpkin's eaten a pumpkin. A large one. More than one.'

'Oi, you're talking about a family member, and you're on her home turf, so be nice.'

'I will, I will, for fear she'll eat me if I don't.' He tentatively stepped past her. She gave him a look that made it very clear she still wasn't warming to him.

Once we were back in the kitchen, I put my hand out. 'Come on, then, where's this gift?'

He handed me a narrow paper bag with string handles. 'You might have already bought it for yourself, but if so, I doubt you'll mind having two.'

I reached in and pulled out a bottle of Twenty Trees Gin. The small distiller – and by small, I mean one man and a garden shed – had been at the food festival and I'd had a taste. It was delicious. Mark was right, I had bought myself a bottle, but I was so impressed that I was very happy to have a second ready and waiting.

I handed him a couple of glass tumblers and the bottle I'd already opened. Setting him to making us both drinks, I returned to preparing a salad and the swordfish steaks I was going to serve. After we'd raised a toast to gin distillers everywhere, Mark sat at the table and watched me chop a multi-coloured array of tomatoes.

'Nice job above the fireplace. Have you ever thought about moonlighting as an interior designer?' From where he was, Mark could see into the sitting room and he'd spotted the four splotches of paint on the chimney breast. I'd moved in twelve months ago and had been slow at making my mark on the place.

'I know, I know, I just can't decide.'

'Between white, white, white or white? Tough choice.' He had a thoughtful look on his face, but I knew he was teasing.

'Get up close and they're very different. I want the room to feel bathed in light, but not too sterile.' I handed him a pencil. 'Go and rank them, I'm sure you have an opinion.' He went through and stared intently at the wall while we continued our conversation through the doorway.

'I saw you sniffing around the gardeners' yard today, do you have any updates for me?' he asked as he wrote on the wall.

'Not really, but I have a question. Were you aware of the rumour about Elliot's girlfriend having an affair?'

He nodded. 'Most people were, but it's old news.'

'Any idea who she slept with?'

'Not a clue, and it was probably better that no one found out. I'm sure we'd have had a murder on our hands a couple of years ago if that had got out. Why?' Mark returned and sat back at the table, the pencil tucked behind his ear.

'I'm trying to find things that link back to Ben. Guy, Kyle and Elliot are the most closely associated with him, plus they all had a good idea of where he would be on Saturday morning. Kyle is the first one I'm inclined to rule out. When I spoke to him after Ben was found dead, he seemed genuinely shocked and upset. I really don't think it was him, although his alibi is a bit shaky.

'Guy has Malcolm as an alibi and the time he signed in at reception matches his story. They were discussing a restaurant project in Paris, although Malcolm seemed a bit cagey about it, and I'm not sure I'd want advice from Guy. If Guy's involved with, or even just supportive of a company rebranding someone else's product as their own, then he's not a very ethical businessman. Who knows what he gets up to in London? I know for sure I wouldn't want to eat at any restaurant he was involved with.

'There's the dodgy business with the coffee which could be behind this, but as far as we know, Ben might have supported the whole thing. It might even have been his idea, so I don't think he was killed because he was against them doing that. Elliot, on the other hand, had the opportunity, and he clearly had an issue with Ben, but we don't know any details. Then, of course, there's Bruce Keen. If he has found out what the Silver Bullet lads were up to, then he's certainly got a motive; I just don't know if it's enough to make him want to kill someone over it.'

'Did Bruce have the opportunity?' Mark asked.

'Possibly. He was at the festival that morning to meet me, but I have no idea what time he arrived. He has enough contacts among the stallholders for someone to have signed him in as one of their team. There's often a change in staffing at the last minute, so sometimes our security staff are told how many people are coming from one organisation, but not given their names. It's not great and the security team shouldn't be doing it, but it's the reality. He's also been taking a lot of interest to how the investigation is going. When he came to drop off some samples, it was all he would talk about. It's all just swimming around in my head.'

'You do realise...' Mark let his thought hang temptingly in the air for a moment. 'If Elliot was out of Robin's sight for thirty minutes or so, then no one saw Robin either. His alibi has just gone to pot.'

I'd already thought of that. 'True, but I checked the shepherd's hut and you can see where he's repaired the windows. He's in the clear.'

'Oh.' Mark looked deflated. 'I've no idea then. I need food. Maybe then I'll be able to think straight' – he smirked – 'although that would be a first.'

We spent the rest of the evening discussing Bill and Mark's ongoing debate about where they were next going on holiday and who we should attempt to set Joyce up with. Neither topic reached any conclusion. At one point Pumpkin wandered into the room, hoping for a chunk of swordfish. I'd already saved her a big piece and put it on a saucer for her. Once she had finished trying to lick the enamel off the plate and was satisfied there wasn't even so much as a sniff of fish left, she leapt from floor to window ledge to the top of the fridge and took a bath while keeping half an eye on us.

Mark was impressed. 'I would have thought she'd need a hydraulic lift to make it up there.'

I offered Mark coffee.

'Aren't you missing something?' I looked at him blankly. 'There's no dessert?' He looked genuinely horrified. It had completely slipped my mind, but then I had spent all day feeding him cakes, pastries and any other sweet goods that didn't make it from the oven to the display cases fast enough to avoid his gaze. I could have argued, but his desire for 'something naughty' was stronger than any argument I could present.

'Get your coat,' I ordered him.

'What? I only asked where dessert was, you don't have to kick me out.'

'Get your coat, we're going over the road. I'll buy you one of those crème brûlées you love so much.'

Despite it being a warm evening, we opted to stay inside at the Black Swan. We grabbed the seat in the large window that overlooked the beer garden and I went to order a crème brûlée and a glass of white port for Mark – I figured that the port would make up for me neglecting to make dessert. For myself, I opted for summer berry pudding and a decaf coffee.

As I returned to our seats, Mark pointed in the direction of the beer garden. I followed the line of his finger and saw Guy sitting on his own under a large umbrella. His attention was focused on his phone.

'Inevitable, I suppose, he is staying here.'

'Why is that?' asked Mark. 'If Silver Bullet is a local company, why didn't he go home once the festival finished?'

'The company is local, but he's not. He lives in London and leaves Kyle and Ben – well, Kyle now – to manage things here. He seems to come along for the fun stuff. The police told him he had to stay around.'

Our desserts and drinks arrived and Mark tucked in. Between each bite, he cleaned the spoon as thoroughly as Pumpkin had cleaned her saucer. He didn't speak until his dish was empty.

'That filled the spot, thank you. Chin-chin.' He clinked his glass against my coffee cup. I was about to ask him if he had a busy day tomorrow when his eyes swivelled from one side of the room to the other. I turned to see what had caught his attention.

'Don't look,' he hissed. 'Wait, I don't want them to know I've spotted them.' He'd dropped a little lower in his seat, using my head as something to hide behind.

'Oh for heaven's sake, it's a pub. Everyone is always checking out everyone else, especially the locals, and I like to consider myself a local now.'

I turned to see the back of Guy's head at the bar. He was handed two pints, one of which he passed to a man standing next to him. Then he led the way through the door that accessed the bedrooms.

I turned back to Mark. 'Do you recognise him?'

'No, never seen him before, but they're pretty pally. I watched him arrive. They had one of those man hugs – you know, lots of back slapping but keeping about an inch apart, just in case someone should think they're anything other than men's men who do manly things and love the ladies.'

I laughed at his description; I knew exactly what he meant.

'Wait here, I might be able to find out.' Mark drained what was left of his port and got up. I watched him out of the window as he walked down the centre of the garden and through a wooden gate. From where I sat, I could just see the corner of the car park and the first four spaces. One of them was filled by a racing green Jaguar, and Mark slowly circled it. He nodded a few times and scratched his chin, to all intents and purposes looking like a car buff who was impressed with what he saw. In reality, I didn't know anyone less interested in cars, but he was doing a fine job of looking otherwise. He got closer and peered in through a window, then moved to the rear window and did the same. Finally, he stepped back, gave another nod of approval, then sauntered down the path and back into the pub.

'You're a natural.'

'What?' It came out as a grunt as he landed on the seat.

'You looked like a true petrol-head.'

'Ha, it's all these years of pretending that my tour groups have just asked the most interesting questions I've ever heard. It hones my acting skills. Now, do you want to know who Guy's pal is or not?'

'You know?'

He looked very pleased with himself. 'There's a stack of paperwork on the back seat and a couple of his business cards are scattered on the passenger seat. Guy is currently meeting with Chester Manning, an antiques dealer from Buxton, specialising in rare antiquities.' He folded his arms and sat back. 'You, my darling girl, owe me a drink.'

CHAPTER 15

Despite the events of last night, and the gin and tonic I'd eventually succumbed to at the pub, I'd managed to get a decent night's sleep, which was a good thing; the cafés were packed. The continuing good weather was bringing people to Charleton House in their droves, and no matter how warm it got, they still wanted a cup of hot tea or coffee.

I started by helping the Stables Café team set up, leaving them to it as they were swamped by a group of dog walkers who had started their day early. Then I hot-footed it back to a meeting in the Garden Café, where I reprimanded a couple of staff members for the scruffy state of their shoes. In the Library Café, I threw half a dozen trays of pastries in the oven, prepared what felt like hundreds of single-serve quiches, and then gave the team a hand clearing tables. I was hot and sweaty, but happy. This was one of the many reasons I loved my job. I couldn't spend all day in an office or in meetings, or I'd go crazy. Nor could I spend all day on my feet in a café, but combine all these things and I was in my element.

I was carrying a tray piled high with dirty dishes when Mark appeared. He was followed by a group of about ten elderly women, covered head to toe in floral prints, and every one was wearing straw hats with purple ribbons around them.

'Well, girls,' he called out across the group, 'I must say goodbye to you, but as promised, I am leaving you with easy access to tea and cake.'

The women oohed and aahed with relief.

'I can highly recommend the chocolate croissants, and they do a mean lemon drizzle cake here. There's a large table in the corner that's free, so why don't you make yourselves comfortable and I'll arrange for someone to come and take your order.'

As a rule we didn't do table service in the Library Café, but we sometimes made an exception if Mark appeared with a group that he had clearly become fond of and wanted to go the extra mile for. I fetched a staff member and sent them over to the table.

Once Mark had freed himself from the overly eager octogenarians, he walked over to me and dramatically leant on my shoulder.

'They are adorable, every one of the old dears, but I am exhausted. I haven't been drilled so thoroughly or laughed so hard in years.'

'I'll refuel you, don't worry. Go and say goodbye to your fan club and I'll prepare your favourites.'

I watched as Mark returned to his group. All eyes were on him as the women thanked him and told him how wonderful he'd been. His hands were clasped, his arm held firmly, and he was kissed until his cheeks were covered in bright pink lipstick. They all insisted on photos being taken, and after he'd fought off their attempts to give him tips – and no doubt a few offers to take him home – he was released and joined me at a small table on the far side of the room. I handed him a napkin and he discreetly wiped the lipstick kisses from his face.

I laughed. 'That's a very eager fan club.'

'Bright as a button, every one of them. I almost feel sorry for their husbands.'

'Or wives,' I added.

'Of course, one shouldn't assume, although based on their fawning over me, I doubt it. I don't know what it is about little old ladies, they're like moths to a flamer.' He waited to see if I got the joke.

I groaned. 'That's dreadful.'

'But true. Now back to the most important business of the day – do you have a plan?' He sank his teeth into a chocolate croissant.

'Not really. I looked up Chester Manning on the internet when I got home. His website isn't very extensive, it just looks like your average antiques store. There are a few auctions coming up and there's a link to a very old newspaper interview he did, talking about French side tables from the eighteenth century, but nothing of any interest.'

'Nothing that links him and Guy?'

'Nothing at all.'

I waited while he gulped down half his mug of coffee in one go; I must have been staring.

'What? I've been talking non-stop all morning, I'm parched.'

I caught the eye of the team member who had just carried a tray of cakes over to Mark's group. 'Can you bring him another coffee? I'm concerned he's going to pass out if we don't get more fluid in him.'

The young woman looked at him; all my staff were used to Mark. 'You do realise coffee dehydrates?' she advised him, the smallest hint of humour detectable in her voice.

'You do realise I know your boss quite well and I'm sure she expects nothing but "yes sir, no sir" from all her staff?' he replied.

'Feel free to add pepper into his coffee, maybe some chilli powder.' I smirked at Mark as the grinning server walked off to the kitchen. 'I love my staff like you love your old ladies. Look, I don't have any meetings in my diary this afternoon, and I was thinking' – I scanned the room – 'this place could do with some antique French side tables. Maybe some lamps, perhaps even a couple more armchairs. It's a nice day out there, so we should go and browse some antiques. I've heard about a place in Buxton that might be worth checking out.'

'I couldn't think of anything I'd rather do. Why don't you collect me from my office when you're ready? I'm sure I'll have got my strength back by then.'

I decided that if the morning had been anything to go by, the Stables Café was going to be bursting at the seams come lunchtime, so once I'd packed Mark back to his office and arranged for his tour group to receive a discount on their bill, I set off up the back lane to help out. It was a challenge to walk along this short, private lane without being stopped multiple times by colleagues for a catch up, which was lovely, but meant I always needed to add at least ten minutes to any journey. Today was no exception, although I didn't mind too much. The Stables Café team wasn't actually expecting me; I would just be an extra pair of hands.

As I walked under the archway that led into the courtyard housing the café, I spotted a familiar face sitting at one of the outside tables. A young woman had a Jack Russell dog at her feet and a small child in a pushchair next to her. As I got closer, I recognised her as Carla – Elliot Forrester's girlfriend who had picked him up from work yesterday. I assumed the young girl was Isabella.

I looked around, but there was no sign of Elliot.

'Hi, Carla?'

'Yes?' She looked up from feeding the young girl carrot sticks, looking confused and clearly not recognising me. But then, why would she?

'I'm Sophie, I work here. I cross paths with the gardens team quite a lot, so I know Elliot.' I was stretching the truth so far it

THE CHARLETON HOUSE MYSTERIES

could snap at any point, but I needed her to relax. It seemed to work.

'Oh, hi. I don't think he's mentioned you, but I guess this place is so big.'

'It is. I've been here just over a year, but I still get lost on my way to meetings.'

Carla laughed. 'I know the feeling. I used to work here and I never went anywhere without a map. I thought I'd get my head around it, but I never did.'

'Do you miss it?'

Carla offered Isabella a small sandwich from a box she'd retrieved from under the pushchair.

'I do, but Elliot keeps me up to date on what's happening, and I still see old friends when I come and collect him.'

This was my chance. 'That must be nice. I've already made some great friends here. It's a wonderful community.' Carla nodded as I talked. 'You really see that at times like this – everyone's been so supportive.' I stopped and waited to see if she would react, but she didn't seem to pick up on what I was getting at, so I kept going. 'It was such a shock when that stallholder was murdered. Just awful, but everyone pulled together. Ben – that was his name. So sad.'

Carla went pale and stared down at her feet. She definitely knew him; there was no way she would have reacted like that if he had been a stranger.

'I'm sorry, was he a friend? I didn't mean to upset you. I didn't realise.'

'It's fine.' I waited for her to continue, but again she didn't say anything so I kept going.

'So many people have told me what a nice person he was. I only got to meet him briefly and he did seem really nice. No one's had a bad word to say about him.'

I watched as a smile started to form on her lips, but there was sadness in her eyes. 'He was very sweet.' She stroked Isabella's hair.

'So you knew him well?'

She nodded. 'Yes, I hadn't seen him much recently, but I used to know him.' Her gaze lingered on Isabella. The child was the classic blonde-haired blue-eyed cutie. It was easy to see why Elliot doted on her.

'Did Elliot know Ben?' I knew he had, but I wanted to give Carla a chance to explain before I bulldozed my way in. Her eyes dropped again; she started to pick at one of her fingernails.

'Sort of, but they weren't friends.'

'Did they not get on?'

She looked around the courtyard as though wanting to make sure she wasn't being watched. I assumed that she wanted to check Elliot wasn't around.

'Not really.' She stopped and I was sure that was as much as I was going to get. Carla didn't know me and she had no reason to tell me anything, but I was impatient.

'Carla, it's none of my business, but I know Elliot and Ben didn't get on. I witnessed Elliot laying into him the day before he was killed. He didn't hit him, but he looked like he really wanted to. This was in front of a lot of other people, so he didn't seem to care who was watching.'

'He didn't kill him, I swear!'

'I'm not saying he did, but what was he so angry about? Do you know?' Carla shook her head, but I knew she was lying. And I wasn't being entirely honest, either – Elliot was at the top of my suspect list. I just needed to understand why he'd wanted Ben dead.

As I watched Isabella eat a second little sandwich, I felt the cogs in my brain turn. Why on earth hadn't I realised it as soon as I'd heard the rumours about Carla's affair? Everyone thought that she'd slept with someone she worked with, but that was only hearsay. What if the affair part had been right, but the colleague part wrong? What if she'd had an affair with Ben, and Isabella was the outcome? What I didn't understand was why Elliot would want to kill Ben after all this time. Joyce had told me that Isabella was three years old now. Ben was local, and if Elliot was mad enough to want him dead, he'd had plenty of opportunity. Something must have set him off and triggered a renewed burst of fury, but what?

Carla looked at me. I knew she wanted me to leave well alone. Elliot clearly had a temper and I hoped that she was never on the receiving end of it, but there were no physical signs, and Joyce had talked about Elliot becoming happier again after Isabella's birth. Maybe fatherhood had calmed him down – with the exception of some recent Ben-related event.

'Sophie, sorry to disturb.' I looked away from Carla towards the member of staff who had come out to see me. 'We've got a customer who wants to talk to a manager and... well, I saw you out here. Would you mind?'

'Give me one minute.' The staff member walked away and I turned back to Carla. 'I'm just trying to understand why he was so cross. It might help.'

'It was nothing, I'm sure of it. You know what men can be like. They didn't see each other very often and Ben travelled a lot, so it was never a big deal that they just didn't get on.'

I knew I wasn't going to get anything else from her, and for her sake, I didn't want Elliot to find me questioning his girlfriend, so I said goodbye and went inside. Trying to figure out a murder was still new to me, but dealing with disgruntled customers – and I was sure that was going to be the case – was old hat. I took a deep breath and allowed a serene smile to spread across my face, determined to be the most charming version of myself. Kill 'em with kindness – it always worked.

. . .

In order to find Mark's office, it is necessary to step into the entrance lobby of one of the ladies' toilets that are available to the visitors. You then take a sharp right turn before venturing into the main area of the toilets – and if you are a man, being chased back out – and up a narrow flight of stairs marked 'Private'. Once you arrive, you find a large, bright and airy space that Mark shares with two others.

Despite the sharing aspect, Mark has still ended up with a space about four times the size of my office. Mind you, I wouldn't want to swap. The courtyard below is where school groups often gather and the noise is enough to prevent anyone from thinking. Then there is the occasional pipe blockage in the toilets below. The aroma when this happens is enough to force Mark and his colleagues out of their office and into the cafés to work. So, as much as I may be envious of the general airiness, that air could become the exact reason that I wouldn't want his office in a million years.

I knocked on the door frame and walked through the open door. Mark was chatting to a man wearing a long moss-green coat, matching breeches and cream stockings, sitting at the desk opposite him. His black shoes had a slight heel.

'Sophie, meet Lancelot Capability Brown. Ignore the smell, he's been dead for over two hundred years.'

Capability took his feet off the desk and stood. Removing his tri-cornered hat and revealing a grey wig with tight curls over the ears, he performed an exaggerated bow.

'Greetings. A pleasure to meet you.' He tossed the hat onto the desk and sat back down. 'Mark's just been filling me in on the adventure you have planned for this afternoon.' I scowled at Mark. We'd never actually said that we'd keep our activities quiet, but I had no idea who this man was or if he could be trusted.

Mark read my mind. 'It's fine, Capability and I go way back.'

'Besides which,' the man in the wig continued, 'I'm basically a ghost so no one will believe they've seen me, let alone what I've said.'

As I sat on the edge of a desk across the room from them both, I must have looked confused. Mark tried to clear things up for me.

'He's not actually a ghost, Sophie.' He threw a pen across the room and it hit the man in the chest. 'See? Solid.'

'Idiot,' was the only word I could think of to direct at my friend. I turned back to Capability. 'What are you up to today? Designing an addition to the garden?' As one of the country's most respected landscape architects of the eighteenth century, Lancelot 'Capability' Brown had worked at Charleton House and played a key role in the way the beautiful gardens looked today. I guessed he was going to be delivering a tour or performing somewhere outside, talking to visitors and telling them his story and plans in 'real time'.

'I'm thinking about a vine. We're possibly a little far north, but I've had great success installing a vine at Hampton Court Palace and I would like to try something similar here. Only instead of one large vine, I'm wondering about a small vineyard. I'm spending this afternoon considering the best location for it. There seem to be a lot of strange folk wandering around the garden in unusual garb and I'm finding their input most useful.'

'Give it a rest, Ed.' Mark sighed and stood up. 'Come on, Sherlock.'

I looked at Ed – or was it really Capability's ghost?

'Sorry to rush off, only I'm keen to follow up some information we found.'

'*I* found,' chipped in Mark, 'and I haven't forgotten that drink you owe me.'

We left the eighteenth-century gentleman at the computer, checking his emails. The longer I worked at Charleton House, the more I found my definition of 'odd' being redefined.

. . .

It was a thirty-minute drive to Chester Manning's antiques shop and we spent most of the journey going over what we knew about the various people in Ben's life. The good weather had yet to come to an end, the view across the Derbyshire hills was beautiful, and the further we went, the more I relaxed.

I drove us down a single-track lane that turned off the main road just as we hit the edge of Buxton. After waiting for a tractor to pass, I parked in front of a converted barn. The exterior wooden walls had been painted a gloss black, and with the burgundy red edging, it looked distinctly out of place. Far too grand and perfect for an old farm building. The sign for 'Manning Antiques' was just as showy. This wasn't going to be one of those places that looked like a junk shop and smelt of abandoned history and mothballs.

'So how are we going to play this?' Mark whispered as we walked in.

'We were passing and we're just browsing. Easy.'

'But exactly what are we looking for?'

'I have no idea. I guess we'll know it when we see it, or we'll just learn about his link with Guy. And before you ask, I have no idea how. Maybe it will come up in conversation.'

Mark didn't look at all convinced.

We stepped through the large double doors that were wedged wide open, and into the cold shadows of the barn. Just as I'd expected, the space was well laid out. The antiques had been displayed to resemble different rooms; it looked like a nineteenth-century IKEA store.

We wandered around a couple of the display rooms, running our hands over the furniture and making sounds of approval.

'Hmm, this is rather nice.'

'Superb quality, but not what we're looking for.'

'I'm sure my great-aunt Gertrude had a lamp just like this. Ah yes, this is hers. See that crack down the side? That's from the time she used it to hit my great-uncle after she discovered his affair with the scullery maid.'

Mark appeared to be relaxing into our charade and enjoying himself.

We wound our way through the leather armchairs and coffee tables. There was an enormous display of silverware and the collection of paintings seemed to exclusively depict scenes of Derbyshire. I couldn't imagine myself ever having any of the pieces in my own home, but there was no escaping the fact that Chester had taste and, judging by the price tags, his customers had the money to buy that taste.

'Can I help you?' I jumped as Chester appeared at my side. 'I'm so sorry, I didn't mean to startle you.'

I laughed awkwardly. 'It's fine. Err no, thank you. We were passing and thought we'd come and have a look. We're just browsing.'

'Well do shout if you need any assistance, I'm happy to help you with any spur-of-the-moment purchases.'

He smiled and made his way back to a desk just as the phone rang. I breathed a little more easily as his attention was focused on the caller. As he'd taken a seat and put his feet up on his desk, it looked as if it was going to be a long call. Or at least, I hoped so.

There was something familiar about him, and it wasn't just because I had seen him at the pub with Guy. Mind you, he wore the uniform of the upper class male and his outfit practically mirrored Malcolm's wardrobe: salmon pink trousers and a checked shirt. His brown leather belt was decorated with a weave of multi-coloured threads, he had the same ruddy complexion as Malcolm, and it was easy to imagine them sharing a sherry and discussing the stock market or how 'Tarquin was faring at Eton'.

I walked towards the back of the building and saw a couple of doors on the far wall. It seemed the building was actually split in two and there was a lot more that lay beyond the wall. I signalled to Mark and he made his way over to me.

'We need to go in there.'

'Why? What excuse are we going to give when he finds us rooting around?'

'We don't need an excuse. There are no "Staff only" or "Do not enter" signs; we'll say we just thought it was another area of the shop.'

'OK, you go in. It'll be obvious if we both suddenly disappear.'

He had a point. I checked that Chester was still distracted by the phone call and slipped in through one of the doors.

There were long shelves of vases, picture frames, snuff boxes – everything that you'd imagine looking at home in *Downton Abbey* could be found back here. Some items had tags on them that said 'reserved'; others looked as if they were waiting for a polish before they went out on display. The room was gloomy and I decided there was no way I was going to spot anything of any use, so I made my way back out into the showroom.

I caught Mark's eye and shook my head, pointing at the second door. He glanced at Chester and gave me the thumbs up.

This room was much brighter. There were large double doors pinned open on the far side, allowing the sunlight to come streaming in, but it was much less tidy than the first room I'd explored. A desk and a shelf full of files were in the far corner. An enormous table held remnants of bubble wrap and brown wrapping paper, and a pile of wooden crates was stacked up in the corner, waiting to be filled with delicate antiques and shipped out.

Next to the door was a stack of boxes, a couple of crates and some very well-padded envelopes. A look told me that they were all addressed, ready to go. As I took a step closer, I felt something crunch under my shoe, and then again under my other foot. I stepped back and looked down – whatever I had stood on was now brown powder.

There were more brown lumps scattered around. Stones? No, they were coffee beans. I picked one up and smelt it – I was right. I collected more until I had a handful of misshapen and small beans. There were a couple of Quakers: the under-ripe coffee seeds that had been picked too early. This wasn't good quality coffee; it hadn't been dried or milled carefully. This had been roasted by someone who was more interested in volume than quality – a company like the Northern Bean Company.

I followed a trail of beans on the floor and found more next to the large table. As I stood up to see if they were anywhere else, the name on one of the parcels caught my eye: 'Malcolm De Witt' and a Paris address. I took out my phone and snapped a picture of the box, grabbed a couple of the coffee beans and went to find Mark.

Mark was examining a painting close up – very close up. His nose was practically touching the canvas.

'Mark, look at this.' I opened up the photo on my phone, but he didn't turn towards me.

'No, look at this,' he said. 'I swear this farm hand looks just like you.'

'Mark, we don't have time. Stop it.'

I showed him the picture on the phone, but he wasn't impressed. 'So, Malcolm dropped by and did some shopping.'

'It's too much of a coincidence. Plus that box – it's the perfect size for the Duke's bowl. And I reckon the bowl would have been stored in a sack of coffee beans before it got here. *Silver Bullet* coffee beans.'

I gave Mark my best 'eureka' look. 'I still think she looks like you,' was his only response.

'Mark, for heaven's sake, take this seriously! I need you to stay here and make sure those parcels don't go anywhere. I'm going to call Joe and get him to meet you here.'

'And where are you going?'

'I need to have a chat with a certain coffee roaster. Also, I've remembered why Chester is so familiar looking. He went to university with both Malcolm and the Duke – all three of them are in a photo that's hanging in the Duke's office. None of this is a coincidence.'

Mark was paying attention now. 'How do I keep Chester occupied once he gets off the phone?'

'I have no idea. You could ask him for more information on that painting of me.'

I walked out of the barn as quickly as possible, nodding to Chester as I left. He gave a lazy wave – he could probably spot a time waster a mile off and I guessed he had put us in that category, so he was in no rush to get off the phone. I dialled Joe's number as I got in the car, then headed off to the pub.

CHAPTER 16

Four o'clock in the afternoon wasn't, by my reckoning, too early for a gin and tonic, but that wasn't why I was pulling into the Black Swan car park. When I'd given Joe a rundown of what I had found at the antiques shop and made sure he was on his way there, I'd neglected to tell him where I was heading, but only because I couldn't be sure that I'd find who I was looking for. That, and Joe would tell me to mind my own business, and I didn't want him to spoil my fun. I felt like a hound who had got the scent and I didn't want to be dragged away from it.

As I turned the engine off and got out of the car, the back door of the pub opened and Kyle walked out with a large bag over his shoulder. Bingo!

'Hi, Sophie, day off?'

'No, I was looking for you. Do you have a minute?'

'Not really, I've just checked out and need to get on the road.' He hadn't actually stopped to talk to me. Putting his bag in the boot of the car and opening the driver's side door, the keys already in his hand, he seemed very keen to get going.

'I really need to have a word, Kyle, it's important.' I stared at him. He could run and there was no way I could stop him, but he looked tired, like a man who'd had enough. He stood for a moment, staring beyond me, and then sighed, closed the car door and finally returned my gaze.

'Can I buy you a drink?'

I nodded and let him lead the way back into the pub.

Kyle bought us a couple of cokes and we went outside to a table in the far corner of the garden where no one could overhear us. Running his finger round the rim of his glass, a haunting chime emanating from it as he did so, he again refused to look me in the eye.

'Kyle, I have a theory, and the police are on their way to check it out. A valuable item – sentimentally valuable, not financially valuable – was stolen from Charleton House a week ago. Right now, I reckon it's sitting in a box at an antiques shop, waiting to be shipped out to Malcolm De Witt in Paris. That item, a beautiful ceramic bowl, has spent some time stored in a bag of coffee beans – Silver Bullet coffee beans. That means that someone who works for Silver Bullet knows how it got there. Am I right so far?'

Kyle nodded.

'I'm guessing that someone from Silver Bullet stole it during the drinks reception last Friday night after Malcolm told them where it was and how to get in, or Malcolm stole it and handed it over to one of you.'

I gave Kyle a chance to respond, but he didn't take it.

'Is this what you do? Steal when you're travelling the country for food festivals and events?'

'No!' He sounded horrified, then quietly continued, 'Or it wasn't. And it wasn't me. I know about it, but I'm not involved.'

Kyle looked and sounded like he was pleading with me, and I immediately believed him.

'Ben needed money and Guy caught him stealing from a stately home last summer. He threatened to tell the police, but then Ben offered him a cut of any money he got for the item in order to keep him quiet. Guy's all about the money, whatever we're doing, so he said yes and encouraged Ben to steal again. In fact, he started to plan it for him. After that, he made sure that Ben never stole from anywhere we were actually working, only before or after the event so that there was no link.'

'And you knew about it? Why didn't you go to the police?'

Kyle didn't respond and that gave me the few precious moments I needed to fit in another piece of the jigsaw.

'You didn't go to the police because if they investigated, they would likely discover your sham coffee business.' His eyes shot up to meet mine and I nodded. 'I've been to your offices, I know what you're doing: flogging Northern Bean Company coffee as your own and saving yourself all the production costs. I assume that was just a little project to increase your profits, and then it became the perfect cover for stealing artefacts as you travelled for events. Combine the two businesses and the overall profit must be huge.'

Kyle nodded. 'It was so easy. Most of these places have little or no security. Occasionally Guy and Ben would get something of little value, but sometimes they hit the jackpot. Ben was always up for it – he took any chance he could to make some extra money. I managed the coffee side of things to provide the cover and Guy was often down in London, working with Chester to sell whatever Ben managed to steal.'

'Why were you arguing with Guy the other day? It looked pretty nasty.'

'Things changed when Guy started taking orders off people.' I didn't know what he meant and I looked questioningly at him. 'Chester had a couple of clients who were looking for something in particular – an object or painting they knew the owner would never sell – so Chester would arrange a way to get hold of it for them.'

'And that "way" was Ben?' Kyle nodded again. 'The St Ives Bowl, did Malcolm put in a request for that?'

'Yeah, he was at university with the Duke, along with Chester. I reckon he had a chip on his shoulder. He'd made a lot of money, but it was new money. The way he used to talk about their university days made me think he was jealous.'

'And he took something that meant a lot to the Duke to get back at him.' I finished the story off for Kyle. 'So that's what you were fighting over – this was all getting far too serious for you. They'd gone from opportunist thefts to stealing to order and you weren't keen?' Kyle nodded once more. 'And Ben? Did he have a change of heart, threaten to tell the police?'

'Oh hell no, Ben was well up for it. If anything, he didn't think we were doing enough.'

'So why was he killed?'

Kyle shook his head and looked genuinely confused. 'I don't know. Really, I have no idea. Everything was going well. I was here at the pub with Guy the night of the reception and we got a text off Ben to say that he had the bowl and it had all been really easy. As planned, it was stashed in one of the sacks of coffee beans in the van. We figured no one would check there. We'd get it out once the festival was up and running and there were thousands of people to serve as a distraction, and no one would have a clue.'

'What about Guy?'

'What about him? Ben was making him money, so he wouldn't want him gone. And anyway, he was with Malcolm when Ben was killed. I met up with him just before Ben's body was found.'

Despite Kyle's certainty, I wasn't so sure anymore.

'Where's Guy now?'

'Heading back to London. He and Chester had put a couple of jobs on hold until Ben's murder all blew over, but he says he can't wait anymore. Plus I'm not sure Guy wants to get his hands dirty. He was happy leaving that to Ben, so he won't be taking any more orders for a while.'

I drained my glass of coke. 'Are you going to tell the police or am I?'

'What?'

'You can hand yourself in, tell them everything you know and there's a chance they'll look favourably on you. Or you could do a runner and make the whole thing worse.'

I knew he was going to call them; he really didn't seem like the fugitive type. Plus if he was telling the truth, then his involvement wasn't worth being on the run for. I stood up and thanked him for the drink.

'Where are you going?' he asked.

'I think I know what happened, but there's something I need to check out first. I've been barking up the wrong well-manicured tree.'

I sat in the car park at Charleton House and called Joe.

'Sophie, I'm here with your friend, Chester. It appears you've been ignoring my advice.'

'Uh?'

'Well, despite me telling you to keep your nose out, you're clearly still digging for information, so you may as well tell me what else you've got.' He'd made various comments about the need for me to let him do his job, but he'd never taken me aside and torn strips off me, so I figured he couldn't be that annoyed. Plus if what Mark had said about Joe having a thing for me was true, he was unlikely to. I didn't want him to have a thing for me and was trying to forget about it, but on the other hand, if it saved me from a telling off, it might have its uses.

I started to fill him in. 'You're going to have Kyle Rushton contacting you, or at least you should. He said he was going to call.'

'He beat you to it. I had a call on the way here, and he's at the station waiting to talk to me. I presume you know what it's about?'

'I do. You're going to have the thefts all wrapped up by the end of the day. The one thing I'm not so sure about is Ben's murder. I think I know who did it, but you're going to need the help of your Parisian colleagues.'

'I've already put a call in to them,' he responded.

'And Chester? Have you got anything useful from him?'

'He claims to know nothing about the contents of the parcel, that he was just doing someone a favour and shipping it out. He says he has no idea what it is or where it's from.'

'Do you believe him?'

'Of course not. Right now I have a couple of officers going through the other parcels and we've already found the painting from Berwick Hall.'

'And Malcolm?'

'Our Parisian friends will be on their way to apprehend him. Hopefully Chester won't find a way to give him a heads up, so he won't be expecting the knock on his door that's about to come.'

'OK, well, make sure they ask him exactly when Guy was with him. I'm not convinced that either he or Guy have been entirely honest about that morning. I think Guy in particular has a lot of explaining to do.'

'Sure thing, boss. Anything else while I'm at it, or can I go and get on with my job?' Oddly, that question wasn't laden with sarcasm, which slightly threw me off.

'Err, no, I don't think there's any more to tell.'

I could hear voices in the background and someone shouting for Joe. 'I have to go. That's DS Harnby, and if she knows I'm talking to you, she'll kill me. Give me two minutes, I'll call you back.' He hung up.

I'd quite liked Malcolm, he was pleasant company and had seemed harmless enough. But now it seemed he had quite an intense green streak running through him. On the plus side, the Duke would be getting his bowl back. I would be curious to see if it went back on display or if he decided to keep it out of sight; I wouldn't blame him if he did. It seemed his trusting nature had left him a little burnt.

I wasn't going to wait for Joe to call; there was an important conversation I needed to have. I'd got something very badly wrong and I needed to fix it.

I started to walk towards the gardeners' yard.

I found Elliot Forrester in one of the greenhouses. He was tidying up small pots and I was relieved to see that there weren't any sharp objects immediately visible.

He turned as I walked in. 'Oh for crying out loud.' He leant against one of the workbenches that ran along both sides of the narrow building and dropped his head as though he was gathering his energy. 'What do you want?'

I wasn't quite as worried about this conversation as I had been last time we'd spoken, as my motive was very different this time.

'I want you to be honest with me.'

'About what? It's none of your business. If you think I'm a killer, just say so, but you'd have a hard time proving it...'

'Because you didn't kill Ben,' I interrupted. That caught him off guard and he was silent long enough for me to say what I needed to get out. 'I don't believe you did it, but there's enough evidence to make people think you did. If you tell the truth it will be easier for everyone else to believe you too.'

'This isn't anyone's business.'

'But you've made it people's business by having a go at Ben in public. You've put the idea out there. Elliot, you must know you have a reputation for having a bit of a temper. It makes people wonder whether you could go further – or at least, it did after some of us saw you with Ben last week.'

He grunted in response, but I took it as some sort of acquiescence.

'It's private,' he said quietly. 'Private, that's all.'

Now I had a second man in front of me who appeared defeated. Elliot was such a big, muscular man that it seemed even more incongruous than it had with Kyle. He clearly had the strength to do some real harm – throw me over his shoulder and bury my body, but with his slouched shoulders and downcast eyes, he looked as if someone had found a nozzle and let the air out of him.

He looked up at me. 'I hated him, but I didn't want him dead. I just wanted him to clear off and leave us alone. I told him to time and time again, but he was always sending money. Lots of it. I'm a damned good father, I can provide for my family. I didn't need his help, but he wouldn't stop. It was embarrassing.'

I spoke softly; I didn't want to antagonise him. 'He's Isabella's father?'

'*I'm* her father,' he spat back. 'I've raised her, provided for her. I'm the one that she calls Dad, not him.'

'But he's her biological father?'

He stared hard at the floor, then slowly nodded. 'But that's all. He promised me he'd stay away, they both promised me they'd have nothing more to do with each other, and Carla and I would raise Isabella as our own. But he kept sending money; he told us he'd set up a savings account to send her to college. The idiot was getting into more and more debt doing it. It was as though he was trying to prove a point, make up for sleeping with Carla by throwing money at Isabella, but he was making it worse.

'Look, I'm not happy he's dead. I'm not heartless. I guess he loved his daughter, but I didn't want him round here. It turned out I had already shared Carla with him, I didn't want to share my daughter with him as well.'

'And then he arrived at the food festival. That must have been hard.'

'I couldn't believe it, I was furious. That was why I had a go at him. I know it was stupid, but you've no idea how hard it is. I'm not an idiot; I know a lot of people round here know about him and Carla and what they did, and I have to live with that every day that I come into work. But he was just rubbing my face in it. I lost it. It was stupid.'

'And the next morning? I know there was a period of time when Robin left you alone. There was time for you to go and kill him.'

'I know that now, but I don't know what I can do about it. I just stayed in the Rock Garden, working; I never left, I swear.'

For the first time, Elliot looked as if he needed something from me. He had a temper, but I felt sorry for him. Imagine knowing that everyone around you was aware of your private life and were all just playing along. There was a child-sized elephant in the room every day of his life. I knew that the last thing he wanted was pity, but that was what I felt.

'I believe you.'

His whole body relaxed and he lifted his face up to the roof. With his eyes closed, he asked, 'What do I need to do?'

'Nothing, Elliot, not right now. I think that while we've been talking, a few things have been sorting themselves out. I need to make a phone call. The police might still want to talk to you, confirm a few things, but if what I'm thinking is right, then you don't need to worry.'

He didn't respond. His eyes met mine again and I smiled. There was nothing left to say, so I turned and walked out of the greenhouse. I needed to get out into the fresh air; I'd spent a week believing that an innocent man had killed someone and I felt dreadful.

. . .

I took a long route through the gardens. There was no sign of the festival and its little white tents. All the cables had been packed away, the gravel raked over so there was no evidence of the cars and trucks that had removed all the stallholders and their goods from the site. The ducks were happily doing laps around the pond and the flowerbeds once again took pride of place. There was no indication that thousands of people had been enjoying pork pies or fudge, cider or freshly made lemonade right here just a few days ago.

There was also no sign that someone had been murdered here less than a week ago, twenty feet from where I was standing.

After giving myself time to take a few deep breaths, I walked back to the Library Café. I felt like I'd been neglecting my team over the last couple of days, and the least I could do was help them clear up and close for the day. I reached the entrance to the café and pushed the door open.

'Sophie?' I jumped, my hand flew to my chest and I stopped breathing for a moment. I felt like I'd returned to the first day of the festival when Guy had surprised me, spilling my coffee. At least this time I didn't have hot liquid in my hand.

'What the hell...'

Chelsea was standing immediately behind the door, chewing hard on a piece of gum and apparently waiting for me. She went bright red.

'Sorry, I thought you'd seen me.'

'Chelsea, what have I told you before?'

'Eh?'

'Chewing gum, Chelsea, get rid of it.'

She looked around and grabbed a napkin off a table, spitting the offending lump into it. 'You had a phone call. Bruce Keen, and he sounded desperate to talk to you. I told him you'd call him back.'

I took the slip of paper that Chelsea passed to me, Bruce's number scrawled on it, and put it in my pocket. He could wait until tomorrow morning. Right now, clearing dirty plates and wiping down tables seemed like the most normal thing I could possibly do, and I needed some normality back in my life.

CHAPTER 17

For the first time in weeks, there were grey clouds overhead and, if I'm honest, I was overjoyed. Like anyone else, I spend the British winter longing for spring to arrive, and then I start pining for summer to come, and with it the chance to leave the house without a coat (not without picking it up and putting it down a dozen times first, of course). But after the recent weeks of high temperatures, I was happy for some respite. My office was still unbearable – the thick old walls of Charleton House did a great job of holding in the heat, but at least it was now possible to sit in almost any seat in the cafés and not stick to the furniture.

I had decided that it was time for a change and so, at nine-thirty in the morning, before the visitors arrived on what promised to be a busy Saturday, Joe and Mark joined me for coffee in the Garden Café.

'I'm not sure whether I should be flattered or deeply suspicious,' Mark commented as he eyed me over the miniature glass flower vase and perfectly laid-out silver cutlery. 'I haven't been invited out anywhere with tablecloths since... ooh, since Bill was still trying to woo me, which was fifteen years ago.' He thought for a moment. 'I'm going to have words with him, he needs to step up his game. I'm quite a catch and he shouldn't forget it. I deserve a few more classy restaurants in my life.'

I sniggered, but straightened my face out as much as I could when he caught me. The glare that followed could have shattered the glass vase, if it hadn't been combined with Mark sticking his tongue out.

Joe was back in his motorcycle leathers and they creaked as he made himself comfortable. A server in a crisp white shirt with the Ravensbury ducal coronet embroidered on the pocket made his way over. He was carrying a tray with a large French press and three china cups. The cups were beautifully decorated with views of the estate. The server smiled at me as he placed one with a scene that included a herd of deer on it in front of me; it seemed my love of the beasts was becoming well known. Appallingly, I didn't know his name; I would have to change that and let his supervisor know I was impressed at the rather classy example of sucking up to the boss. I was also going to remind his supervisor that he should have been wearing a name badge: one hand giveth, the other taketh away, or something like that.

As Mark poured our coffees, I pulled out a notebook. I'd spent the previous night pulling together all my thoughts, trying to see if I could fill some of the gaps before Joe did, but as he had a couple of suspects in custody and the Paris gendarmerie had, I presumed, Malcolm in a cell on the other side of the Channel, I was sure to be less well-informed than he.

Joe turned to me. 'As you insist on getting involved, no matter what I say, you go first. I'll tell you if you stray off the path.'

'And don't miss anything out,' Mark added. 'I know you two have already spoken to one another, but I'm just as important a member of the three musketeers.'

I looked at Joe, who subtly raised his hands in a 'no idea' way. I decided not to comment.

'OK, so there are three things going on here. In the background there are the thefts from numerous historic houses around the country, all of which are open to the public. There's Ben's murder, and then there's the shady business dealings of Silver Bullet Coffee.'

Talking of coffee, I took a mouthful. It was far too bitter.

'Silver Bullet Coffee are selling themselves as a Derbyshire-based coffee-roasting company. They appear at a lot of the food festivals in the county and beyond, supply a few shops and have enough of a reputation that people recognise them, know them to talk to and view them as a legitimate business that roasts reasonably good coffee. They certainly started out that way, renting equipment at a roasting facility, probably because they were a start-up business and couldn't afford their own equipment.

'Ben, who I'll come to in detail later, was always trying to get more money, and on a whim stole something from one of the historical houses that was holding an event they were working at. Guy finds out and threatens to blow the whistle on him unless Ben gives him a cut of the profits, and thus a new business is born. Am I right so far?'

Joe nodded.

Our server made a perfectly timed return and placed a plate piled high with miniature pastries in front of us. They were fresh and still warm from the oven. I smiled at him and passed him the empty French press, hoping he'd realise that we needed it refilling. Joe took over the story while Mark inhaled a mini chocolate croissant.

'Guy is claiming he had no idea and it was all Ben...'

'You have Guy? Since when?'

'Since late last night. Sadly he was too far ahead for us to catch him down in London, but we made an educated guess that he'd try and make the most of his contact in Paris. He was identified on a boat from Dover and picked up by the gendarmerie when they docked in Calais. He claimed he had business in Paris.

What he didn't realise was that his "business" was in a Parisian police cell.'

'So you have Malcolm too?'

'We can function reasonably well without your help,' Joe replied.

I removed the apricot Danish pastry that he was holding from his fingers as a response and took an enormous bite before muttering, 'And?'

Joe playfully shook his head. 'And he's singing like a canary.'

That didn't surprise me; I didn't really imagine Malcolm having a backbone of steel.

'Can I finish?' Joe asked. I nodded and reached for another pastry, a chocolate twist this time.

'Ben approached Chester to sell on the first few antiques he'd stolen and got lucky. Chester has been involved in dodgy deals for years, but we've never been able to pin anything on him. He recognised an opportunity when he saw one and had enough contacts on the antiques black market that he could get rid of the items Ben took, while taking a percentage of the profits of course.'

I took over while Joe reached for another pastry. 'At this point, when Guy got involved and he and Ben started to make decent money – albeit in a criminal fashion – most coffee roasters would have invested in their own equipment. But not Silver Bullet. They started repackaging coffee roasted by the Northern Bean Company, saving themselves money, but also making life easy for themselves when the company became just a front. They didn't want to be making too much of an effort; coffee's not what they really cared about. It might have been in the beginning, but not now. Instead, Guy used one of his first big payments to buy the Airstream. It gave them an air of success and looked great, so they were invited to more and more events and they had more access to buildings with valuable treasures.'

This, of course, had added Bruce Keen into the mix.

'Did you talk to Bruce?' I asked Joe.

'I did, and I don't think I've met someone quite so nervous, despite being completely innocent. He was babbling like a schoolkid who was being wrongly accused of stealing someone's lunch money. It took me forever to get him to calm down enough for me to understand what he was saying.

'Like you, he was just passing the estate where Silver Bullet had its premises and dropped in to say hello and check out where they were based. He'd met the guys plenty of times before, but they'd always engineered things so any meetings were held away from their offices, understandably. But they hadn't planned on him dropping by unannounced. When he saw what they were doing, he was furious. He must have accidentally dropped his card while he was there. He got to Charleton House early on Saturday morning to confront them, and a friend who had one of the stalls got him in. He couldn't see any activity over at the Airstream so assumed no one was in there, and didn't get his chance to talk to Guy or Kyle before the body was found. He knew that he had motive and opportunity and has spent the week absolutely terrified.'

No wonder Bruce had been furious and wanted to rearrange our meeting on the Friday – he'd just discovered what the Silver Bullet lads were up to. I felt sorry for him, but not enough to stop me ditching his coffee. I had my standards.

'But why did they take the Duke's fruit bowl if it's of no financial value to anyone?' asked Mark as he topped up everyone's mugs from the newly returned French press.

'As you well know, that fruit bowl, as you call it, was handcrafted by one of the finest ceramicists of the twentieth century, who was also a very close friend of the Duke's mother, the late Dowager Duchess. It has no financial value, but the sentimental value is huge.'

Mark pretended to look apologetic, but then I had done my

finest impression of a well-spoken headmistress who was disappointed in his ignorance. I continued.

'Malcolm went to university with the Duke, and although they got on pretty well at the time and were part of the same social circle, Malcolm still ended up with an enormous chip on his shoulder. One that he carries with him to this day. The Duke was extremely wealthy, as were most of his friends, and Malcolm was from a regular working background and couldn't compete. He knew all about the bowl; in fact, there's every chance he met the artist. He was spending summers here at Charleton House around the same time that she became part of the Dowager Duchess's social scene.

'After running into the Duke at a university reunion a couple of months back, and having his chip deepened, Malcolm came up with a way of getting his own back. Chester had been a fellow student and was also at the reunion. I'm guessing that over a few too many glasses of port, Chester and Malcolm came up with a plan. Chester could put him in touch with Guy, who was by that point running the whole Silver Bullet artefacts stealing operation, and arrange for the bowl to be taken. In return, Malcolm, who isn't short of a penny or two – self-made, of course – could pay them good money. The reception last Friday night was the perfect opportunity. Malcolm could feed information to Ben, Ben could use that information to steal the bowl without being seen, and then...'

I looked at Joe. I had my suspicions as to what had happened next, but I hoped he and his colleagues, both here and in France, had been able to gather enough information to confirm my idea. I was about to share my theory when the empty chair next to me was scraped back and a cloud of mint green and lavender settled down. Joyce had joined us, resembling one of the beds in the garden. I half expected a swarm of bees to be following close behind.

'Good morning, how are we all?' She looked around the table. 'Am I interrupting something?'

'Sophie was just about to tell us who killed Ben,' chipped in Mark, allowing Joyce to catch up in record speed.

'Oh my God, poor Ben, you know who did it? I don't care what he got mixed up in, but the sweet young boy that I remember did not deserve to be killed.'

Our nameless server had returned with a cup for Joyce and poured her some coffee. I watched as Joyce picked up the cup; her nails had been painted in stripes that matched her outfit and were long enough to be used to stir in the lumps of sugar she'd added. I forced myself to focus as it looked as if everyone was waiting for me to carry on.

'It's not that complicated, I just got side-tracked by Elliot Forrester. His display of anger, his history with Ben, Isabella's paternity – it all made perfect sense that he might want to kill Ben in a fit of pique, and so I focused on him as the most likely killer. I'd accepted that as he was a friend of the Duke, Malcolm's alibi was going to be unquestionable, and as a result Guy had a rock-solid alibi too. But I was wrong, wasn't I?' I looked at Joe.

'As much as I hate to say it, Sophie, you were. Guy did join Malcolm, but not for as long as they claimed. Guy had gone to the Silver Bullet van on the Saturday morning to meet Ben and retrieve the bowl that had been safely hidden in one of the sacks of coffee beans. We worked this out from all the information you gathered, Sophie – thank you, by the way.' He placed his hand on mine briefly and I saw that Mark had spotted it. That was all I needed.

Joe continued, 'Ben was keen to save as much money as possible. Every chance to make any extra cash, he took it. When Guy turned up, they got into an argument about money. Ben wanted more – a lot more – and Guy wasn't having any of it. They got into a fight, and in the process, Guy grabbed the... you know, the coffee thing?'

'Portafilter.'

'Portafilter, and hit him with it. He didn't have to worry about fingerprints as he had good reason for them to be all over the van, so he tried to make it look like a burglary gone wrong, took some of the stock, and then called Malcolm who snuck him into his room. Once there, Guy made him agree to provide an alibi or he'd reveal Malcolm's plan to steal from the Duke. Guy's claiming that it was self-defence, that Ben got angry when he refused to increase his cut and Guy was afraid he was going to be killed.'

Joyce shook her head. 'All because he loved his daughter.'

'Who, the gardener? But he didn't do it.' Now Mark was looking confused, so I topped up his coffee. He clearly needed it. On the other hand, and despite having been at the table for only two minutes, Joyce had caught up and enlightened him.

'Mark, if you spent as much time listening to people as you spend sculpting your moustache, you'd know that I meant Ben. He made a huge mistake when he slept with Carla years ago and took a back seat in raising Isabella. But she was his daughter and his love for her, combined with a need to make up for his mistakes, led to him throwing money at her. That in due course led to him making some rather silly mistakes, which led to his death.'

'So what happens now?' I asked.

'We finish off the interviews, and the Art and Antiques Unit will come in to help us try and track all the objects that have been stolen over the last twelve months. There's also a chance that they'll be able to find evidence of more of Chester's black market dealings while they're at it.'

'It's Elliot I feel sorry for.' We all turned to face Mark, who seemed to be having a rare introspective moment. He looked up at the three of us. 'What? The poor guy's private life is already a non-secret round here. This will have blown it further out into the open. Everyone knows he was a suspect; he's been one of the water-cooler topics for days. I'm sure he just wants to put what Carla did behind him and get on with his life.'

'He won't need to worry about it for long,' said Joyce. 'I heard that he resigned first thing this morning. Came in at six o'clock, gave his month's notice and asked to be given duties that took him as far away from the house and the rest of the staff as possible.'

'What will he do?' Joe asked. Joyce shrugged.

'There's plenty of grand gardens that need staff in Derbyshire. Some are open to the public, some not, but either way he'll have no problem getting work. I was always surprised that he hadn't left before, but the gossip had died down and he just got on with his job. He never socialised with his colleagues, not after Carla... well, you know.'

'You could always transfer from retail to gardens and replace him,' Mark suggested.

'What?' Joyce responded, her voice dripping with incredulity.

'Well, you look the part. You could be a roving lavender display, attracting bees and wildlife to different parts of the garden.'

I put my head in my hands. Joyce's nails, or talons, could easily be used as weapons and Mark was sitting dangerously close to her. I worried for his safety.

'Young man, I like Sophie a great deal. For unknown reasons, she has become extremely fond of you, so for her sake alone I will suffer from a brief moment of partial deafness and assume that what I just heard was no more than a rather embarrassing bout of flatulence.' As I raised my head, she slowly brought her cup to her lips and stared at Mark as she took a long sip of coffee. Her eyes never left him, even as she placed her cup perfectly in the centre of the saucer. If I hadn't known Joyce any better, I would have been terrified.

'Well, I owe you all a great deal of thanks.' Joe raised his cup in the air. He spoke quickly and glanced in my direction, but I knew he was trying to save Mark from himself. In a battle of wits between him and Joyce, there was no guarantee that Mark would win. 'Sophie in particular. I've always known you had an unhealthy coffee addiction, but I would never have thought that it would help solve a case. You are a wonderful addition to the Charleton House clan.'

'Hear, hear,' chimed Joyce and Mark, their momentary clash forgotten.

'You know, she could be worse.' Mark had taken on a considered tone, which meant that he had entered tour guide mode and was about to enlighten us. 'Rumour has it that Beethoven counted out his coffee beans each morning to ensure that each cup of coffee was to his taste. He required precisely sixty beans.' He raised his eyebrows at us, then buried his face back in his cup. We were silent. It was a 'mic-drop' moment.

Joe broke the silence. 'She looks like a sixty-five bean girl to me.' He locked eyes with me over his coffee cup and I prayed that I wouldn't see any twinkling. I desperately tried to think of something to say, but ironically, I didn't seem to have had enough coffee to think that quickly.

'Well, if you've finished solving murders and identifying coffee scandals, I have places to be, tours to give, stories to tell.' Mark got up from the table. I could have hugged him for his timing. 'Sophie, I'll see you later for a celebratory gin in the Black Swan. Joe, I expect you to be there. Joyce,' – he paused briefly – 'you are a visual delight and I adore you. There will be a glass of prosecco with your name on it should you wish to grace us with your presence.' He kissed her on the cheek and walked away quickly enough that she couldn't have reached for him if she'd tried.

Joe and I sat in nervous silence.

'Oh, for heaven's sake!' Joyce exclaimed, taking in our anxious faces. 'He's a fool, but my life would be much less colourful without him in it.'

'I doubt it,' risked Joe, looking her dress up and down. All three of us laughed as Joyce put her cup down and picked up her handbag. It was large enough to constitute a sack and had an enormous image of a peacock feather printed on the side.

'Sophie, dear, I believe we are expected somewhere.'

She was right. I had come to an agreement with Signal Box Coffee that Lucy and Kathy would supply some of the coffee we used at the house. Sadly, they were unable to produce the quantities I needed to supply all our cafés, so we'd decided that theirs would be the special blend that was served in the Garden Café and at events. Joyce and I were off to meet with them and discuss selling bags of the same blend, and maybe a few others roasted especially for Charleton House, in the gift shops.

I'd been at Charleton House for just over twelve months and I was going to finally start putting my mark on the cafés. I had all sorts of plans to give them real personality and a solid connection with the house, its history and the stories that inhabited its walls. So long as there were no more murders for me to become distracted by, I could make a lot happen here.

Joyce looked over her shoulder. 'Come on, Sophie, chop-chop.'

'No more murders,' I said under my breath. Now there was a phrase I never thought I'd hear myself use.

A KILLER WEDDING

For Susan Stark,
who ensured this woman had a room of her own in which to write fiction.

CHAPTER 1

Father Craig Mortimer sat with his head in his hands. His face was pale and his hair hadn't seen a comb all morning. I placed a double espresso in front of him.

'You're an angel,' was mumbled from somewhere near his chest.

'You should know.' My response resulted in a hiccup and chuckle combination, followed by a groan.

'Don't make me laugh, it hurts.' He groaned again as the chair next to him was scraped back and a tall, gangly figure dropped into it. Mark, my friend and colleague who was normally the most well put-together man I knew, was slumped like the proverbial sack of potatoes and mirrored Craig as his head fell into his hands. Letting them sit in their own sickly silence, I made another espresso. I tried to repress the smile that was forming on my lips, but I can be as evil as the next person and failed.

I pushed the thick black liquid under Mark's nose. No response.

'Good night, lads?' I asked.

'It's Ma Greaves's fault,' was the response from under the mop of hair that covered Craig's eyes.

'Ma who?' I'd never heard of her. I lived over the road from the Black Swan, the pub they'd spent the previous night in, and regularly crossed its threshold, but I'd yet to meet a Ma Greaves.

'Ma Greaves. Her cook accidentally invented the Bakewell Pudding,' he clarified, not particularly helpfully. I knew that the Bakewell Pudding, a famous Derbyshire delicacy, had been invented in the 1800s, which meant that Craig was either still drunk or he was winding me up.

'Mark?' I was talking to the top of his head and had yet to see his eyes. 'Am I going to get any more sense out of you?'

He raised his head slowly. His usually perky moustache was in need of some attention and I had to resist the urge to lean across the table and curl the ends back into their glorious handlebar position.

'Ma Greaves,' he replied, 'is the name of a locally made raspberry and almond infused beer which, unfortunately, goes down as easily as a slice of the actual pudding.'

I decided I was going to stick with the pudding, especially after witnessing the state of these two this morning. 'But I thought there was still disagreement over who invented it.'

'There is.' Mark was a walking encyclopaedia of local knowledge, so the fact that he had opted not to elaborate on what I knew was a source of much contention in the area told me exactly how bad his hangover was. I felt like a mother desperately trying to get a coherent response out of her two teenage sons.

Martin, one of my young café assistants, came over with a plate of fresh chocolate croissants. Mark's obsession with them was well known amongst my staff. He placed them directly in front of the two lolling heads, smiled, raised his eyebrows at me and walked back to the kitchen. Good lad. As though they'd been hit by a dose of smelling salts, the two men raised their heads and signs of life could be seen in their eyes. I left them to devour the pastries and went to fetch them more coffee.

. . .

The bonus of being a café manager is that I have access to as much coffee as I need, and on days like this I could provide my hungover friends with as much as they needed to revert back to their human forms. We were starting the day in the Library Café. It is my favourite of the three cafés that I manage at Charleton House, a historic stately home that makes Downton Abbey look like a reasonably well-cared-for bungalow. We welcome over half a million visitors a year and I have to ensure they enjoy as much tea and cake as they can consume.

As I filled three mugs with coffee my two assistants for the day, Martin and Chelsea, beavered away in the background, filling fridges with freshly made sandwiches and displaying the trays of cakes that had been delivered from the large kitchen attached to the Garden Café, the most high end of our dining experiences. We also bake a range of pastries here in the more compact kitchen and I could hear Martin slotting more trays into the oven.

Martin was a calm, level-headed young man who I enjoyed having around. Chelsea, on the other hand, had a good heart, but needed to be prompted into action every five minutes otherwise she'd become distracted by her nails, hair or mobile phone.

'Chelsea,' I called across the room, 'put your phone away, please, we have half an hour until we open for visitors and the till hasn't been set up.'

'Bossy,' Mark shouted at me and winked at Chelsea.

'Don't encourage her or I'll return this coffee and send you to your office to actually get some work done.' I swapped their empty espresso cups for the mugs. 'Are you both going to be okay for tonight? You look like you need to take the weekend off.'

Craig, the resident chaplain at Charleton House, was beginning to look less green and was the first to respond.

'Nothing can be harder than delivering a Sunday service with a severe hangover; tonight's pre-wedding dinner will be a doddle in comparison. Besides which, the wine can serve as hair of the dog if necessary.'

I looked at Mark.

'I'll be fine. Once I get a bacon butty inside me and mainline a few more gallons of coffee, I'll be delivering the best tour of my career by three o'clock this afternoon. By this evening, I'll be the highlight of the dinner, even more so than the bride and groom.'

'That will be a challenge,' grunted Craig. 'Having spent quite a lot of time in their company over the last few months, I know the happy couple are capable of putting on quite a show.' He opened his eyes wide in mock horror before disappearing momentarily behind his coffee mug.

I wasn't going to let him get away with that. Tonight was a dinner for the close family and friends of a couple who would be getting married in the Charleton House chapel tomorrow afternoon. The evening would be a stylish, low-key affair for fifteen people before the much larger event with 150 guests the next day. In theory, it would be a simple event, but over my twenty-year restaurant and catering career, I've learnt that assuming that anything would be simple is a shortcut to disaster.

'Expand please, Father. I'm working tonight and would like to know if I should carry one of our well-polished bayonets along with my radio.'

He shook his head. 'It'll be fine, I'm sure, but I've never seen such an argumentative couple. Every conversation I've had with them has resulted in them having a full-blown argument; it was incredibly awkward at times. I'd have to find a reason to slip out of the room and leave them to it, returning when things quietened down.'

'Doesn't sound like a match made in heaven.'

Mark had said exactly what I was thinking.

'But that's just it – for all the raised voices, they always came to an agreement. They always left with smiles on their faces, and on more than one occasion I saw them... well, making up against the side of their car.'

'You don't mean... in the car park?' If Craig meant what I thought he meant, I was horrified.

'No, no, I didn't mean... I meant kissing... a lot... without stopping to breathe. That's all I meant.'

I let out a sigh of relief.

'I guess they're just incredibly passionate people,' Craig continued. 'I never once felt like this was one of those couples who would spend a fortune on a big, grand wedding and then get divorced within a couple of years. They seem to genuinely love one another, and they are clearly well suited. I wouldn't be surprised if there were fireworks tonight, but everyone will go home happy.'

'Good to know.' I looked over at Mark. 'You can have some particularly spectacular and attention-grabbing stories up your sleeve to distract everybody should things get a bit heated.'

Mark Boxer was a Charleton House tour guide and was used to adapting his tours and talks to cater for everyone, from gaggles of schoolchildren to visiting politicians and the occasional royalty. Tonight would be a breeze for him, if he could surface from the fog of his hangover.

Mark was about to respond when the doors to the café flew open and a woman wearing what looked like a tea cosy on her head and a badly crocheted cardigan stormed in.

'FATHER!' she screeched. I watched Mark clutch his head, and Craig winced. 'FATHER, we need you in the chapel NOW. If you don't do something immediately then I swear your next service will be a funeral. I can no longer be held responsible for my actions.' She glared at Craig, seemingly willing him to argue with her, spun on her heel and vanished.

'Who, in the name of all that is holy, was that?' Mark was still staring at the doors. 'And should we start hanging up bulbs of garlic?'

Craig giggled; it was an unusual sound coming from someone the size of an over-fed bear.

'I shouldn't laugh. She makes my life hell, but I do like your garlic suggestion. That is Harriet Smedley, my newest chapel volunteer. She's quickly become the most active and most vocal of the group. I often wonder what I did in a past life to deserve her, but in my position it's impossible to do anything other than trust in God and His mysterious ways. I'd better go and see what she wants; I've often felt that she's capable of murder.'

CHAPTER 2

I left Mark with his head resting on one hand, the other scribbling away in a notebook. The first customers of the day had arrived, all of them house staff with a great thirst who had come to pick up their morning coffee and take it back to their offices. A lot of them would be after our famous barms, or butties depending where in the country you come from, served with bacon from one of the farms on the 40,000 acre Charleton estate. The bacon's aroma had been known to tempt people from all over the house – no mean feat as this was a house with almost three hundred rooms across four floors.

'Sophie, phone.' Martin handed me the receiver and went back to serving customers. I stood in the corner of the kitchen and listened to Nick, my heart slowly sinking as he spoke. Nick was the supervisor of the third café I managed, the Stables Café, set within the stables courtyard outside the main house so visitors didn't need to pay in order to reach it. It was a firm favourite of local dog walkers, cyclists and others who loved to spend their free time roaming the rolling hills of the estate, and did a roaring trade in simple hearty foods like sausage rolls and soups. Even in the colder months, it was a honeypot for people wrapped up in scarves, warming themselves with a hot chocolate at one of the tables outside.

Nick had called to tell me he wouldn't be in work tomorrow. He'd come down with the flu and wouldn't be getting out of bed for a few days. Most weeks that would have been fine, but Tina, the supervisor of the Library Café and most definitely my 'right-hand woman', was on holiday in Cyprus. So, while I offered sympathy and told him to take all the time he needed, I cursed internally and tried to come up with solutions.

I looked across at Martin as he efficiently served a line of customers, answered questions, made coffee and gave Chelsea an encouraging nudge when she got distracted. Martin covered some of Tina's responsibilities in her absence, which allowed me to get on with my own work; I was reluctant to lose him from the Library Café, but it seemed I might have to.

He didn't know it yet, but Martin was about to save my bacon.

After I'd told Martin about his mini promotion, I packed him off to the Stables Café to learn the ropes in preparation for taking over the running of it. He carried with him a smile of pride stretching from ear to ear. My next couple of hours involved rescheduling some meetings, calling in another member of staff to support Chelsea, jiggling the rota and selling countless cups of tea.

Once things had calmed down, I joined Mark who was sitting in the same place I'd left him two hours earlier.

'You're going to have fun this week. I bet you're counting the days until Tina comes back now.'

'How do you know...?'

'I might look like the living dead, but I've been watching and listening. How do you think you're going to pull it off?'

I ignored his lack of an offer to help, not even an empty gesture made simply out of good manners, but I knew him better than that and wouldn't be holding my breath. Plus I knew that he could burn frozen pizza and the one cake he'd made had been inedible. I would have laughed if he'd offered to assist.

'It'll be fine. I won't have the time to do any baking, but I'm sure Ruth can fit in another hour or two a day once tomorrow's wedding is out of the way.'

Ruth Danforth was my pastry chef, and although I baked some of the less challenging cakes and biscuits, I wasn't trained and I only really did it to help out, and because I enjoyed it. Ruth, on the other hand, was a baking genius. She worked part time for me and spent the rest of her week self-employed, making spectacular cakes for special occasions. Tomorrow's wedding was a case in point and she'd been working long nights to get her latest creation finished in time. Fortunately she was married to Gregg, my head chef, so she had a very understanding partner.

'I'm lucky it's not the middle of the summer or I'd struggle, but at this time of year we can muddle through.'

'Well, good luck. You can count on me to be cheering you on.' Mark smiled and sat back in the chair, his arms folded.

'Oh thanks. You'd better be nice to me or I'll be putting an apron round your neck and you'll be washing dishes for me before you can say, "Another cup of coffee, please".'

'Since when have I said please?'

'Fair point. Look, while it's quiet, and while you're in the mood for being sweet and supportive, don't you think we should go and check that Craig is alright and Harriet isn't burying his, or someone else's, body under the chapel floor?'

Mark closed his notebook and gathered his belongings.

'I'd love to, but I have to deliver a tour in half an hour so I'd better go and clean up. I'm afraid you're on your own. But...'

He left me hanging for a moment, then grinned.

'Don't forget your garlic.'

. . .

I knew I had time to fit in a visit to see Craig before the lunchtime rush – once Chelsea returned from her break, and she was ten minutes late. Eventually she wandered back in, out of breath, stuffing her mobile phone in her coat pocket and attempting to tidy up the strands of hair that had escaped from her ponytail, but she only made things worse.

'Sorry, I got chattin' to someone and forgot the time, sorry.'

I gave her the once over as she busied herself with a group of schoolchildren who all wanted chocolate chip cookies and were discussing what they'd do if they had as much money as the Duke and Duchess. Chelsea's white shirt was no longer white and it was a size too tight, the gaps between the buttons showing off her bra. She also needed to give her shoes a good clean. I sighed, knowing that I couldn't hand the issue over to Tina, told Chelsea where I was going and set off to see Craig.

The chapel isn't too far from the Library Café, but even the short walk gives me an immense amount of pleasure and the feeling that I'm walking through history. The foundations of Charleton House had been laid in 1550 and the property had remained in the Fitzwilliam-Scott family ever since. Over the centuries it had become a glorious symbol of England's history, wealth and art. The family had participated at the heart of British politics, fought in some of Europe's most significant wars and socialised with celebrities. Alexander Fitzwilliam-Scott, the current Duke, is the 12th Duke of Ravensbury, and he and his wife Evelyn, the Duchess, welcome the tourists with open arms. They genuinely love sharing the house and its history with anyone who is interested, and it isn't uncommon to see them walking through the grounds and chatting to awestruck visitors.

Today I walked down a stone corridor and passed walls with bricks that dated back to the Tudors. I stepped into cloisters that remained much as they had been in the late 1500s, and then stood before a large wooden door from 1832. I didn't need Dr Who's Tardis; I just needed to walk 200 yards out of my office and look around. That's not to say it's always this easy. The building is vast and it could take years to be able to find your way around without ever getting lost. I'd long since learnt to leave for meetings ten minutes early to ensure that I could make multiple wrong turns, but still make it on time.

I pushed open one of the enormous wooden doors and stepped into the cool air of the chapel. I've never been particularly religious, but even I felt like I'd walked into a space that demanded my respect. The chapel has witnessed the christening and marriage of almost every member of the Fitzwilliam-Scott family since it was built, and now anyone who could be considered part of the congregation could be married there.

I watched as visitors slowly admired the space in reverent silence. Some sat on the pews that had been made from the wood of trees off the estate for a moment of quiet contemplation; others admired the alabaster altar or the stained-glass window that threw multi-coloured light across the marble floor. Gilded angels patiently watched the activity below, as did a member of staff who would tut if someone's mobile phone rang, or quietly step in if it looked as if someone was going to take a photograph.

'You can't have those in here, you'll need to leave.'

I turned to face Harriet Smedley, who was examining the takeout coffee cup and paper bag containing a slice of cake through half closed eyes.

'They're for Father Craig, I...'

'Food and drink is not allowed in the chapel, you'll need to leave immediately.' She was shorter than me, which bearing in mind I'm five foot nothing is saying something, and still wore the ridiculous looking tea-cosy hat, but I couldn't remember the last time I had felt quite so intimidated. She was clearly not a woman to be messed with.

'Harriet, it's quite alright.' Craig's soothing baritone voice flowed over my shoulder. I closed my eyes. *Thank you, God,* I muttered to myself; I might not be a believer, but I wasn't taking any chances.

'But, Father, you know the rules...'

'Yes, Harriet, I do, but Sophie has been kind enough to bring me refreshments and I will immediately escort her to my office and remove any risk to the chapel.'

'But visitors...'

'She's not a visitor, Harriet, this is Sophie Lockwood. She's the Head of Catering for the house.' He looked over at me, nodding slightly; I nodded in return, confirming my title.

I offered Harriet my hand; I figured it might go some way to placating her if I treated her like a colleague rather than a faintly irritating barrier between a hungover member of the clergy and his caffeine. She stared at my outstretched hand as if I'd offered her a wet fish, then looked up at Craig, her lips now a flat line.

'As you wish, Father.' She didn't move and I had to step around her in order to follow Craig up the aisle.

Once we were round the corner, he leaned over and whispered, 'I'm absolutely terrified of her.'

I followed him through a small wooden door and down a flight of concrete steps. I was a little concerned that we might end up in some haunted catacombs – not that I'd ever been told the chapel had any – but instead we stepped out of the stairwell and into a wide low-ceilinged corridor.

'This way,' Craig called over his shoulder. He stopped in front of an open door and spread an arm wide. 'Welcome to my humble abode.'

Bearing in mind it was a windowless space in the bowels of a chapel well over 400 years old, he'd done a decent job of making his office feel homely with a large green rug on the floor and an array of plastic plants that could survive without a drop of natural light. It was considerably bigger than my own matchbox-sized office, but other than that I'd yet to see anything that would make me want to swap. I made myself comfortable while he tore open the bag and started on the wedge of chocolate cake.

'What was the problem this morning? I thought Harriet was going to burst a blood vessel when she appeared in the café.'

Craig shook his head. 'She's a one-woman crusade against all of humankind. In her mind, no one is innocent, ever. I'll admit she's the hardest working volunteer I've ever had, but if she had her way, everyone who entered the chapel doors would be put in some sort of hazmat suit and made to levitate in order to prevent them coming into contact with *anything*. Great cake, by the way.'

'This morning?' I asked again.

'Oh yes, sorry. The photographer for tomorrow's wedding had been in. He knows he's not allowed to take pictures in the chapel, but he can take them through the door as the wedding party leaves at the end of the service, so he was outside, reminding himself of lighting and angles – that sort of thing. He hadn't set foot through the door, but Harriet read him the riot act.

'A little while later, he came into the chapel, just to look around. Unfortunately he had his camera slung over his shoulder so Harriet assumed the worst, tore strips off the poor guy, and then came to fetch me. He's returning tonight to shoot the pre-wedding dinner – that's if he's not too afraid to set foot anywhere near the building ever again. I'm almost tempted to offer to pay for any therapy he needs.'

Weddings at Charleton are usually a dream for photographers – and the couples, of course. Charleton House is a palatial sandstone jewel in the Derbyshire countryside. Catch it at the right time of day and the light can make the whole building gleam like an enormous bar of gold. It is a baroque dream fit for royalty, and every corner and every courtyard makes for the perfect wedding photo. The gardens too present the ideal backdrop: manicured lawns; streams cascading through rock gardens; magnificent water features; delicately formed topiary; exotic glass houses;

rose gardens... the list goes on and on. If anything about the grounds presents a problem for photographers, it's too much choice, and that's before they've even got inside the house and seen the lavish furnishings and artwork that could move you to tears with the beauty they have captured.

Craig took an enormous mouthful of coffee and sat back in his chair. The electric razor and comb on his desk explained his much improved appearance. He'd also changed his shirt since he'd crawled into the café this morning and the colour was returning to his cheeks – he looked like a respectable member of the clergy again.

He lives onsite in a small flat that forms part of the converted stable block, so he must have been late getting up if he hadn't had time to shave at home. He's a much-loved part of the Charleton community and carries out services in the house chapel and a local church on the estate. Although Church of England, he prefers to be called 'Father'; he views it as a healthy equaliser.

Suddenly there was the most horrendous noise, somewhere between a crash and a deep growl. I quickly clamped my hands to my ears and ducked; I could feel the vibrations through my seat. I looked at Craig, hoping he knew what was going on and could lead me to safety, and was confused when I saw the laughter etched on his face. He raised a finger as if to say 'Just a minute' and picked up his phone; he didn't say a word, but when the sound came to an abrupt stop, he was still laughing.

'I'm sorry, Sophie, that happens from time to time. This office is immediately below the church organ. The organist is in to practise for tomorrow's service. He sometimes forgets to check if I'm down here. My usual office has been out of commission for what feels like forever and this was the best we could come up with. I'm hoping to be back above ground by Christmas. Mind you,' he winked conspiratorially, 'every cloud has a silver lining. Harriet hates it down here.'

CHAPTER 3

I was flagging and knew I was going to be at work for the next couple of hours at least, so at five o'clock I made myself another mug of coffee without being afraid of a sleepless night. The pre-wedding dinner was being catered by Gregg, but I wanted to show my support and be there for a while. Having drunk my coffee, I pulled on my coat for a walk down the cloisters. Autumn had hit hard and despite it only being October, the temperature drop made it feel more like January.

I stepped out into the early evening air just as Joyce Brocklehurst walked past, her hands full of Charleton House gift bags from the shop.

'Perfect timing, here you go.' She thrust a handful of bags in my direction and I unknotted the handles from around her fingers.

Joyce was the retail manager for the gift shops at Charleton House. She was known for being fierce and I'd heard that some of her staff called her the dragon lady, but I'd spent enough time with her to know that it was largely a front – although I still wasn't prepared to risk getting on the wrong side of her. Joyce was also known for her mind-bending wardrobe and this evening she had opted for a bright green dress that flared out at the bottom, narrow black stripes giving it a crepe effect. The green continued down long sleeves and gave her the overall impression of a rather tall cactus, topped off with her trademark blonde bouffant, which was unlikely to make a single movement due to the large can of hairspray that I imagined her getting through each day.

I had no idea how she was coping without a coat; I shivered as I looked at her. The black leggings she wore underneath the dress ran down to black patent wedge heels that must have been at least four inches high. These, however, were a huge sacrifice on Joyce's part. She was known for her towering stilettos and refusal to wear anything else, except on the few occasions that she ventured out of her shops and into the main areas of the house. Inside the house there was a risk of her heels damaging the floors, and while the conservation team had long since accepted that controlling the footwear choice of visitors was an impossible task, staff were easier to influence. Joyce had largely avoided coming inside on a point of principle as a result, but she appeared to be softening in her old age (the amount of makeup she wore made it impossible to tell if she was in her sixties or eighties).

As we walked side by side, I tried to peer into the bags.

'Gifts for the guests,' Joyce said. 'The bride wants them displayed on a table for people to take when they leave. She's spent a fortune on some of our nicest items: everything from Christmas tree decorations to little bottles of liquor. There's earrings for the women and cufflinks for the men – some of those nice stag-antler cufflinks I started stocking this summer. Each bag is worth at least £150.' She raised her eyebrows and I whistled.

'No expense spared,' I observed.

'Not for these two. Personally I'd have a small do, but spend the money on the best champagne money can buy and a honeymoon fit for royalty, as is befitting my status and style.' Her eyebrows headed upwards again, a challenge to contradict her that she knew no one would ever take.

We were indoors now and I led the way through the Antler Room. More a corridor than a room, it had walls that were covered with magnificent antlers from stags, elks and antelopes. Some were from stags that had been hunted on the estate by previous Dukes and their guests, while others were gifts. One pair was so large it was impossible to comprehend the size of the animal it had once belonged to. The current Duke held no interest in hunting, but this was a fabulous display that had been added to over the centuries and each pair of antlers had its own story to tell.

One side of the room had been closed off with a ratty piece of rope; it was ugly, but prevented anyone from walking underneath the largest pair of antlers, which I knew had been deemed unsafe. It was still waiting for someone to come and secure it. In the meantime, everyone had to remain on the far side of the room as they passed through.

After turning a couple more corners and dodging the frantic serving staff who were setting up the table and the florists who were coming and going, we stepped into the State Dining Room. Usually a dark room with its Grinling Gibbons carvings around the doors and fireplace, and walls covered in tapestries and dark wooden panelling, it had been transformed into a warm, inviting and intimate space by cleverly placed lighting. In a room that could easily seat eighty for dinner, the small table for fifteen could have seemed like furniture from a dolls' house. But instead, it looked like a stage set that you were drawn to and wanted to play a part in. Clusters of pink and purple hydrangea ran along the centre of the table, and hanging amaranth spilled out in between, giving a mossy backdrop and the feel of a forest floor. Crystal glasses and polished silver cutlery sparkled, and the delicately embroidered ivory fabric that covered the tables and chairs glowed in the light. It was stunning.

'Pass them over,' Joyce called from the other side of the room where a table had been set up so she could display the bags.

'It's gorgeous,' I commented. Joyce looked over her shoulder, and then carried on laying the bags out.

'It's not bad; not a patch on what my own table looks like when I have people over.' I imagined leopard-print tablecloths and enormous gold candlesticks. I also imaged a lot of laughter and gallons of prosecco.

A familiar voice disturbed my thoughts.

'Thanks, Joyce, they look great. Hey, Sophie, doesn't the table look stunning? I really hope the bride is happy; she's been quite hard work. Now I just need the musicians and we're set.'

Yeshim was the events manager for Charleton House and I was beginning to wonder if she breathed through hidden gills as I rarely heard her take a breath. I often ended meetings with her feeling utterly exhausted. She was always perfectly turned out in a dark skirt suit and court shoes. Her jet-black hair was tied in a neat ponytail and her bright red nails added just a drop of glamour. I always felt scruffy next to her, no matter how hard I'd tried.

As Joyce finished her display and Yeshim had a quick peek into the bags, I heard footsteps behind us and turned to see Gregg, who stopped and smiled.

'When will we three meet again, in thunder, lightning or the State Dining Room? Evening, ladies.'

Joyce slowly turned to face him. 'Well I'm glad you ended on "ladies", Gregory, an improvement on calling us witches.'

'I wasn't calling you a witch. I was merely intimating,' he teased.

'Call, intimate, either way, watch yourself. I'll start calling you a cook next.' She wagged a finger playfully in his direction while Yeshim and I looked on.

I knew that Joyce had a soft spot for Gregg; it was hard not to. His long, messy fringe partially covered his eyes and his strong jawline matched his long noble nose. He was thin and angular in a way that I couldn't understand, bearing in mind how much I knew he could eat. Men and women couldn't help but track his movements around the room.

A loud crash and the sound of shattering glass had Gregg turning on his heels and dashing out of the door, shouting expletives. Yeshim went too. Joyce gave me a wave and mouthed 'See you tomorrow' before following them through the door. With the musicians now setting up in the corner, the scene was set.

I was staring out of the window when I heard footsteps behind me. I adjusted my sightline so that instead of looking out at the gardens, I was watching the reflection of the room. The photographer had arrived and was quietly taking photographs; his ability to come into the room with a minimum of fuss was a good sign if he was to capture people enjoying themselves throughout the evening and not rely on staged photos.

He took a few shots of the room, and close-ups of the table and its beautiful decorations, and then started looking around behind plant pots and curtains.

'Can I help you?' I offered.

'Yeah, maybe. I need to stash my bag; I don't want it in anyone's way, but I need to be able to access my stuff. I've not worked in this room before.'

'No problem, follow me.' I led him back the way I'd come and into the Antler Room. 'It'll be safe in here; a couple of staff use it for shortcuts, but no more than that. Put it in the corner and no one will even notice it's there.'

'Thanks. I'm Nathan Wallace, the wedding photographer, but I guess you knew that.' He glanced down at his camera and smiled. There was a confidence in the way he held himself and I guessed he could be a bit of a charmer.

'Sophie Lockwood, Head of Catering. Do you have everything you need?'

'Yes, I'm ready. All we need is our blushing bride and Prince Charming.'

'Are you here all night?' I asked as we walked back.

'No. I'll head outside and get some shots of them arriving, and then I'm only going to be inside for about half an hour. Make sure I get some shots of them at the table, and then I can go.'

'Sophie?' Yeshim stuck her head around the door. 'They've just pulled up.'

'Damn!' Nathan exclaimed. 'I should be out there.'

'Follow me.' Yeshim led the way and they both dashed out of the room.

Next to me, two servers holding trays with glasses of champagne took up position by the door. The musicians began to play and I stepped into the corridor so as not to spoil the initial view of the room in all its glory.

It was show time.

CHAPTER 4

The string quartet playing Vivaldi's *Four Seasons* could never have been loud enough to hide the ooohs and aaahs that came from the guests as they entered the State Dining Room. It was a common response, and another reminder that I should never get complacent about the extraordinary environment I got to work in every day. The guests explored the room with their glasses of champagne, admiring the tapestries and the delicate carvings around the door. I always took great pleasure in telling guests that you could tell whether or not the late seventeenth-century carver, Grinling Gibbons, had actually been paid by looking at the detail in his work. The story goes that he often incorporated a peapod into his carvings of fruit and flowers. If he had been paid for his work, the peapod was open; it would be closed if he had yet to receive his money.

I watched as the bride stood at the window, looking out into the gardens. It was pitch black except for the fountain in the Great Pond, which had been lit to show off the magnificent lions that prowled around its base. The light danced and sparkled within the bursts of water; from time to time, they'd rocket into the sky and vanish into the night.

I helped top up the occasional glass and Nathan captured the enjoyment of the guests within the warm glow of the space. The happy couple seemed just that: happy and composed. They were both beautiful and stylish and looked very at home surrounded by so many signs of wealth; it was easy to imagine that they were the residents and hadn't paid huge sums of money in order to hold their event here.

The bride, Amelia, ran her own makeup company and was on her way to making a fortune. She was a classic beauty, slim with long blonde hair and perfectly tanned skin. Her husband to be, Patrick, was a lawyer and equally good looking, but he didn't appear as relaxed as his fiancée. He had sharp features and looked as if he was continually overthinking something; I concluded that he was a man who found it hard to relax. He'd been born only a few miles outside the Charleton estate and his mother still lived in the same small village, which gave him the connection to the house that he had needed in order to get married in the Charleton House chapel.

I watched Patrick slip his arm around Amelia's waist. Nathan stepped over to take what looked like the perfect photograph: the beautiful couple admiring the view from within the magnificent State Dining Room, looking every inch the lord and lady of the manor. As Patrick turned and saw Nathan, his expression darkened.

'Do you have to?' he muttered, loud enough for both Nathan and me to hear. Nathan lowered his camera, apologised and backed off, although he didn't look sorry, more exasperated. I was surprised by Patrick's annoyance, but I knew that many people hated being in front of a camera, and as discreet as Nathan was managing to be, it was a large room with a small group of people in it, and limited places for him to secrete himself and remain out of sight, especially if he wanted to capture some intimate photos of the couple and their guests.

Eventually Yeshim called everyone to dinner and the group

took their places. They were seated at a large round table, which made it feel like an intimate family meal. Patrick and Amelia sat side by side, talking quietly, but now she didn't look quite so happy. She appeared to snap a remark at Patrick, then took a swig of champagne. Looking steadfastly across the table, she ignored whatever he was muttering through gritted teeth. It seemed Craig was right about them. I hoped that marriage would indeed introduce a little bliss into their lives.

Next to Amelia was her mother with a neat and tidy blonde bob. She was sitting with a round man in a dark suit who reminded me of Oliver Hardy, only without the bowler hat and toothbrush moustache. Beside him was Craig, who looked decidedly uncomfortable behind his forced smile. Amelia's mother was trying to get his attention and show him something on her phone, leaning across the rotund man as if he wasn't there. He didn't seem to mind and kept chatting across the table with a young brunette woman, who was laughing at all his jokes.

The brunette finished laughing at his latest comment and stood up, clinking a spoon against her champagne glass.

'Ladies and gentleman,' she clinked the glass again, 'ladies and gentleman.' Her voice was firm and clear; I guessed she was used to public speaking. The chatter turned into whispers, someone 'shushed' the table, and eventually silence settled. 'Welcome to glorious Charleton House, the perfect setting for the wedding of such a beautiful couple. Amelia, Patrick, it's wonderful to be able to spend this evening together, a much more intimate prelude to tomorrow's celebrations. I'm honoured to take on the perhaps unusual role of best woman for Patrick, and although I have prepared the obligatory embarrassing speech for tomorrow...' there were cheers and whoops from some of the guests '...I would like to say just a few words this evening...'

. . .

Everything seemed to be running like clockwork and I quietly stepped out of the room. I made my way down some back stairs to the kitchen where the smell of lamb made my mouth water. Gregg was serving the locally farmed lamb with a broad bean ragù, goats' cheese, pomme purée and lemon jam. I'd been lucky enough to experience it first hand when he'd been exploring ideas and trying things out months earlier.

I loved the cacophony of sound in a working kitchen; it was like being on the footplate of a steam train and just as exciting to me. Gregg's height and bearing made him the perfect engine driver and he delivered his instructions with clarity, and everyone who worked with him respected both his culinary and organisational skills. He wasn't one of those awful stereotypes of the angry chef; he was firm and in control, but respectful. It was very difficult to imagine him losing his temper.

Servers were collecting the prepared plates and heading upstairs.

'Do you want a hand?' I shouted over at Gregg.

'Sure, can you grab another basket of bread? Apparently they want more.'

I returned to the dining room and placed the bread on the table.

'What a beautiful blouse.'

I looked at my shirt. It was made from cream-coloured cotton with tiny stag heads dotted all over it. It was also five years old and fraying at the cuffs, but I loved it and hoped no one would notice the signs of wear and tear.

'Just perfect. In fact, your whole ensemble is really quite lovely.'

My 'ensemble' was, I knew, nothing special, and the owner of the slightly syrupy voice was clearly a lunatic. I looked at my admirer. He was the only person dressed in a dinner jacket and looked like a butler who had accidentally sat down for dinner.

From where I stood, I was able to look down onto his shiny bald patch.

'I'm going to assume, from your attire and bearing, that you're management, and I have to say everyone appears to be doing a splendid job, with few exceptions. I'm used to attending some rather fine dinners and this compares very favourably.' His eyes were fixed on mine and I could have sworn I saw him lick his lips, slowly.

'Umm, thanks,' I responded, unsure how else to reply to his condescendingly delivered remarks.

'Levi Moreland.' He offered me his hand, but I noticed he didn't bother standing. 'I was able to fit this wedding in between acting jobs; I've just completed a stint on the West End and am about to head off to LA. My agent has a number of auditions lined up for me – all just going through the motions, of course. There are numerous directors who have been trying to fit their filming schedules around my recent engagements. It seems my experience and talent at accents are very much in demand.'

The only thing I could imagine him being in demand for was the role of 'gruesomely murdered victim on a gurney', and even that would probably get cut in the edits. I smiled and nodded, not wanting to encourage him.

'I've taken a week off and am staying at a pub down the road. A lovely inn – The Grey Duck or something...'

'The Black Swan,' I interrupted.

'That's the one. You know, it would be marvellous to have a local guide to show me some of the highlights of the area; perhaps you have a day off and could show me around. I'm sure your knowledge of the house is second to none.'

'Thank you, but we have some very good tour guides who would be more than happy to take you around.' I could easily think of one it would be fun to inflict Mr Hollywood on.

'Oh, but I can't imagine they would be such delightful company.' He dug a business card out of his pocket. 'Please, call me anytime. I can have a bottle of Dom Pérignon put on ice in my room for when you've finished showing me around and you can tell me all about yourself.'

Making a show of inspecting his card and then tucking it in the waistband of my skirt, I attempted to smile sweetly, although I probably looked as if I had constipation, and backed away. On my way out of the room, I turned and saw him cast a lingering eye over the legs of a young female server.

I passed Mark as I returned to the kitchen. Between courses he would deliver witty talks about the history of the house, weaving in wedding themes here and there.

'Mark, there's a guy in a tuxedo. I'm sure he'd appreciate some of your time.'

'On it,' he replied. I chuckled to myself as I walked away.

Regardless of my desire to avoid the winner of the Oscar for most skin-crawling attempt at chatting me up, there really was no need for me to stay for the whole evening. I'd shown my face and Gregg had seen that his boss was interested in what was going on. The food looked and smelt wonderful, and the occasional mouthful that Gregg had passed my way had been superb.

When I made my way back up to the State Dining Room to say goodbye to Yeshim, happy that my team was – as ever – doing the department proud, I was surprised to see Joyce. I thought she had long since left the house. I leant over the table of gift bags to see what she was doing.

'I finished a pile of paperwork and was putting on my coat when I spotted a box of cufflinks on my desk. I must have been distracted. Now I need to find which blasted bag is missing a pair.' It was remarkable how, with nails like the blades on a Swiss army knife, she was able to untie the ribbons and fasten them back up again at such speed. 'Got it. Right, I'm going home.'

She let out a sigh of relief.

'Cookie?'

Until he spoke, I hadn't noticed an older gentleman watching

Joyce, his eyes practically out on stalks. Initially I put that down to her rather conspicuous outfit, but it wasn't just that. In fact, he didn't seem to be paying any attention to her outfit. His eyes were firmly set on her face.

'Cookie?' he asked again.

I looked at Joyce. Despite the solid layer of makeup that she wouldn't have been seen dead without, I could tell that she had gone pale. Frozen to the spot, she resembled the proverbial rabbit in the headlights, and after a few seconds I was starting to get worried. I'd never seen her speechless; I hadn't thought it possible.

I was about to rest a hand on her arm to try to stir her when she finally spoke.

'Harold? Harry? It can't be.' A smile spread across the man's face. 'But it's been almost forty years.'

'It's me, Cookie, and you're as beautiful as you were all those years ago.'

Now I was speechless.

CHAPTER 5

I pulled the duvet up higher and rolled onto my side; I would have sworn that every morning was colder than the last. Hearing a grumble from the bottom of the bed, I realised that Pumpkin, my oversized tabby, must be curled up by my feet. I could feel her weight shift as she stood, stretched, and then resettled herself in behind the crook of my knee.

She was out of luck if she thought I'd be in this position for long, especially as I'd caught a glimpse of the clock. As blind as I was without my glasses, I could see enough to know that I was two minutes away from my alarm going off. I reached out to turn it off and sat up. Pumpkin gave a tired meow and jumped off the bed.

'Sorry,' I shouted after her. 'Put the kettle on, will you?' I briefly considered taking a shower before I made my first coffee of the day, but reconsidered when I realised that might result in me drowning or flooding the flat. I shouldn't do anything without a cup of coffee in me, and that included making decisions about whether or not I need a cup of coffee.

. . .

I was grateful for the rich smell of my espresso. I'd spent the last few weeks painting my sitting room and the smell of fresh paint lingered, so coffee aromas were a welcome alternative. It had taken me well over a year to choose a colour, and a month to complete the job, which for such a small room was, I realised, ridiculous and a perfect illustration of how lazy I could be without a work-imposed deadline.

I held the cup to my nose and took a deep breath. Pumpkin was eating and purring simultaneously, and I had a couple of eggs in the pan. As far as I was concerned, breakfast was a distraction I could do without, but to my eternal frustration, I was not one of those people who could start the day on coffee alone.

My walk to work was a two-mile stroll through the rolling hills of the estate and I made the effort to do it far less often than I should. My path took me across fields and eventually along the banks of a river that passed in front of the house. The morning mist was still covering the tops of the trees. Sheep had their noses to the ground and were resolutely ignoring me. In the distance a herd of deer gathered under some trees, and just beyond them a stag stood alone, head up, antlers on full display.

I stopped to look at the house. It too was still shrouded in mist, looking eerily quiet as I was too far away to see any signs of life. I was used to seeing it through the eyes of many of our visitors; it was everything they'd be likely to expect from a historic British house, with the romantic characters and polished displays of wealth and generosity that go with that. Sometimes, however, I got a peek at the other side. At night, or on days like this, it wasn't difficult to turn my mind to the darker side of life at Charleton.

Throughout the centuries, the family had had their fair share of scandal and shady dealings. There were ancestors who had brought shame on the Fitzwilliam-Scott name, and others who had managed to keep their secrets locked away, but they were there. It was impossible that everything could be known from centuries of history. The current Duke was well known for being prepared to discuss every story, no matter how dark or disturbing. He often said that the best way to avoid scandal was to air your dirty linen before anyone had the chance to steal it from your laundry basket and air it for you.

And those stories were added to day by day, even now. In the short time I had worked there, there had been two murders, both of which I'd found myself caught up in investigating. For a while they had thrown confusion and sadness over the house, but now they were just the most recent additions building on the history of those who had gone before. They were a part of the lies and the intrigue, the gossip and the pain that a family of this kind could never avoid.

The house looked so calm, as if it was still sleeping, the past forgotten and the future not yet known. I was excited by the thought that I was now a part of its history, and although I wasn't a historian and my role had more to do with cupcakes than revealing the stories of the past, I was curious to know more. The sleeping house was a source of excitement and possibilities for me, although I knew that in reality today was going to be more about sore feet and paperwork piling up in the office as I hadn't been able to get all the staff I needed.

I turned towards the house, watching the pediments and urn-like finials on the roof slowly revealing themselves from within the mist. I could have been the only person around for miles. In the summer months, it was easy to find excuses to get out of the office and take a long route to meetings or explore the gardens with a coffee in my hand. In the winter, it was far too easy to stay indoors and forget that we had access to most of the estate. It didn't take much to remain at my desk or close to the ovens and stay warm and dry, and it became a hard habit to break out of as the months slid by. This morning I was determined to enjoy the chill that crept in under my jacket and breathe in the ice-cold air, knowing that I might not get out of the café for hours now that I was a supervisor down.

I was disturbed from my thoughts by the rustle of leaves and the snap of branches on the hillside above me. A runner was heading in my direction. They half ran, half slid, allowing the gathering momentum to propel them down, but with enough control to be able to come to a stop in front of me. The woman was familiar, although I couldn't be 100 per cent sure as her face was partly obscured by a baseball cap.

'Morning. On your way to work?' she asked as she took hold of her foot and brought it up under her bum, stretching out her toned thigh. She was barely out of breath.

'I am. I'm sorry, do I know you?'

'I was at the dinner last night; I'm Suzanne, the best woman. I made one of the speeches.' I nodded as I remembered. It wasn't the first time I'd known a groom choose a woman as his best person.

I looked down at her running shoes. 'I'm impressed. I'd love to be the kind of person who could get up early for a run, but somehow the snooze button always gets another hit.'

Suzanne laughed. 'My father was in the military and he extended the routine to home life. I can count on one hand the number of lie-ins I had as a teenager. Now it's so ingrained in me, I couldn't stay in bed if I wanted to.'

I laughed too, remembering the mornings I'd spent in bed in my youth, driving my parents crazy. 'Are you ready for this afternoon?' I asked.

'Absolutely. In fact, I'll probably be short of things to do today. I'm glad I'm responsible for Patrick; he's so easy to organise. We're very alike so everything's been finalised for days.' She started running on the spot. 'I might even fit in another run before the ceremony.'

Suzanne beamed a smile at me and set off down the hill, disappearing along a path that would take her up and around the back of the house into woodland. I shook my head in wonder and strode off, a little faster than before, inspired by her boundless energy.

Boundless energy was not what I had when I arrived in the Library Café. It was still dark and there was little natural light in the room at the best of times. I tossed my coat and bag onto one of the armchairs that sat in front of the fireplace, switched on the lights and illuminated the rows of books. Hundreds and hundreds of books around the walls recreated the feel of the Duke's library.

I fetched my favourite Kenyan coffee beans and started to prepare a mug of drip coffee. This was my quiet time – an opportunity to enjoy the café before staff and visitors arrived, and get my thoughts in order. I enjoyed watching the water soak through the coffee grounds, it was the closest I got to meditation.

I had spent my entire career working with the public and I wouldn't have it any other way, but I loved it when I had the place to myself. Before we opened or after we closed, it didn't matter; there was something soothing about a public space without the public in it. I took a mouthful of coffee and closed my eyes.

I heard the door to the café open. There was never any need to lock it; with the house not being open to the public for another couple of hours, the only people who could reach it were staff members. I opened my eyes and saw Joyce standing in front of me.

'Any chance you could make another of those?' She looked different, but I couldn't explain why. She also sounded a little flustered and her northern accent was more apparent than usual. When I worked in London and returned from a visit home, my colleagues would say they could immediately tell where I had been for the weekend as they could hear my Derbyshire accent coming through. I wondered if this was an early morning thing for Joyce and she just hadn't warmed up her faux upper-class speech patterns.

I pushed my mug over the table for her to finish off; I'd meant it as a joke, expecting her to be horrified, but she took a long drink while I got up to make another cup. I decided it would be easier just to get the big espresso machine going.

'I didn't think you were working today,' I mused over my shoulder.

'I'm not. Well, I wasn't, but I am now. I needed something to occupy myself.'

I had already guessed that this had something to do with Harry, the gentleman at last night's dinner, but I wanted to let Joyce tell me in her own time. I put two fresh mugs of coffee down in front of us.

'So come on then, Cookie, whassup?' I grinned as I attempted my best teenager speak. Okay, so I couldn't wait for her to tell me in her own time; I'm only human.

She stared at me and I wondered if her eyes were capable of burning holes through flesh. 'Call me that again and yours will be the third body you get involved with here.' But her face quickly softened, and instead she just looked confused and shook her head. She was clicking her nails one against the other. They were bright green, left over from yesterday's outfit I assumed, and stood out against the navy sweater she was wearing.

'A blast from the past, that's what's up. I still can't believe that it's all real. Harry and I dated years ago, and I mean years ago – over forty years. We both grew up just outside Sheffield and met on my twenty-first birthday in a club. We were love's young dream for three years, and then his parents moved to Australia. He went with them, saying that he would help his dad set up his business and then come back here, to me. Of course that never happened. We were young; we both met other people and got on with our lives. But he was always the one I compared the others to. Every time a relationship broke down, I wondered if it was because they just weren't Harry.'

She stopped and drank some more coffee, and then stared off into space. I wanted to hear more.

'Why's he back now? What's his link to the wedding?'

'He's the father of the groom,' she declared. Her northern accent vanished and she sounded like a shocked member of the Royal Family. She paused, and then carried on in a less dreamlike state than before. 'He met and married another British ex-pat and they had two children. Patrick is the elder. His wife, Lindy...' she shook her head as she said the name. I knew she wasn't keen on nicknames, not even – as it turned out – her own '...wanted to return here to raise the boys, which they did. Turns out they'd been living fifteen miles from me, but our paths never crossed. When the boys were teenagers, the marriage broke down and he returned to Australia, where he still lives. He's only here for the wedding.'

'Are you going to see him again? Catch up properly?'

'Well we spent most of last night together.'

'You didn't!' I exclaimed, trying hard not to think about Joyce in a passionate embrace. She looked horrified.

'I did not! I'm not that sort of lady and I would hope you knew that. No, he's staying at the Black Swan, so we met there for a drink when the dinner was over. We did end up in his room, but *only* to talk. Keep your mind out of the gutter.' She glared at me as the smirk stuck to my face.

'So, what next?'

'I have no idea. He's staying the week, so I imagine we'll spend more time together. It all seems a little pointless, though, if he's returning to Australia.'

'Fun, Joyce, that's the point. Have some fun and make some more memories.'

She grunted, stood up and collected our mugs, returning them to the counter. It gave me the chance to look at her properly. I noticed that her navy sweater was paired with a navy skirt and shoes. She looked smart, but very un-Joyce like. Where was the crazy splash of colour? Why was she still wearing yesterday's nail polish? Why was she not wearing an eye-catching necklace or headache-inducing scarf? It didn't matter how early it was, the Joyce I knew would have made sure her accessories matched, and right now, she wasn't wearing any. Harry really had thrown Joyce for a loop; she definitely wasn't herself this morning.

'I'm going to my office. I may as well do something useful, distract myself. And, Sophie, don't tell anyone about "Cookie" – I mean it.'

I nodded solemnly.

'Morning, Cookie,' Mark trilled as he burst in through the door. Damn! I'd messaged Mark last night and spilt the beans. If looks could kill, he'd have been dead on the floor. Instead, he was still standing and looking Joyce up and down.

'You alright, Cookie? Nice outfit, who died?'

Joyce turned and scowled at me, and then marched out of the door.

CHAPTER 6

If Chelsea hadn't been running thirty minutes late, I would have had time to tell Mark how much trouble he'd got me into and remind him that if I told him to keep quiet about something, I meant it. I just hoped Joyce would forgive me. But right now I needed to set up the café and worry about whether I'd have enough staff, so I sat him at a table in the corner of the room with a coffee and told him to keep out of trouble.

With Chelsea missing it was all hands on deck, but with the help of Leah, who worked part time for me and had come in to help out, we were ready to go with five minutes to spare. Of course, it was once we were ready that Chelsea walked in, flustered and pulling her hair into a ponytail.

'I'm so sorry, Sophie, I got caught up.' She dashed around the counter, almost pulling a display of chocolate over, and threw her bag and coat in a heap in my office. 'I'll work through my break,' she shouted across the kitchen.

I was about to pull her into my office when a couple of members of the Education team walked in, wanting bacon butties and lattes. There was a series of activities lined up for the day aimed at children under seven, so I threw in some complimentary chocolate brownies – they were going to need them. Then a few more staff members came in: a couple of gardeners, and one of Joyce's deputy managers for a round of coffees, so I sent Chelsea with her to help carry them. Of course Chelsea took twenty minutes to do a five-minute job. I asked whether she had got lost on the way back, but the joke was wasted on her so I pulled her aside and gave her a brief lecture on the importance of good timekeeping.

'How did it go?'

I placed a plate of apple and cinnamon muffins in front of Mark on his next visit to the café and sat down.

'Did you make Chelsea cry?'

'No!' I exclaimed loudly. 'I didn't. What do you take me for?'

'I thought you'd be getting out the thumbscrews and giving them a twist for every day that she's turned up late, half a twist for each time she's forgotten part of her uniform...'

'I'm not that bad. She has got to up her game, though, she's on thin ice. Slow down, you won't be able to taste them.'

He closed his eyes and mumbled what sounded like 'yum' through a mouthful of muffin. Once he'd swallowed with an over-dramatic gulp and 'aaaaaah', he looked at his watch.

'Isn't the wedding soon?'

He was right. We grabbed our drinks and cake and went through to the kitchen. The window that ran along the back of the Library Café kitchen afforded us a front-row view of everything that happened on the narrow back lane that ran beside the house. It was a secure area, only accessible to staff. Ticket holders for the house were blocked by a security barrier that could be raised for vehicles. Here deliveries were made, people attending meetings were signed in, and guests of the Fitzwilliam-Scott family entered.

It was also where Amelia the bride would be dropped off, and then accompanied through to the chapel.

The heavens had opened a couple of hours ago, but as if working to a schedule designed for the wedding, the rain had stopped and the grey clouds held no further threat. The lane was dotted with small puddles and the buildings shone in what little sunlight made it down to the ground. Mainly, though, the back lane was simply a grey tarmacked alley. Not the most auspicious start for a wedding, but once Amelia stepped into the chapel, every aspect of her day would be surrounded by opulence and grand decorative details that were sure to make her feel like the princess she no doubt aspired to be.

As Mark and I finished off our muffins, the security barrier was raised and a fancy car with cream ribbons fluttering on the door handles pulled in. Mark smiled.

'Ah, the Caribbean blue Rolls-Royce Silver Shadow II.' He nodded knowingly. I turned to face him.

'I didn't know you were a car buff. In fact, I know you're not, so how do you know that one?'

'There are only so many car hire firms around here that have supplied cars for weddings at one time or another, you start to recognise them after a while. I can also tell you that the driver is called Derek Veazie, and if he had a toothbrush moustache, he'd be a dead ringer for Oliver Hardy.' He smiled smugly. 'Fount of all knowledge, me.'

We watched as Derek got out of the car.

'I've seen him before, he was at the dinner last night.'

Mark nodded. 'He mentioned he'd be a guest at a wedding here when I last spoke to him. I didn't realise it would be this wedding until I saw him last night.'

'Why's he driving if he's a guest, though?'

Mark didn't answer.

Derek opened a door and Amelia stepped out, carefully lifting the edge of her dress to ensure it didn't get too wet, but Derek had done a good job of pulling up away from the worst of the puddles. A bridesmaid dashed round and started tidying up the edges of the full skirt; Amelia had the train gathered in her hands and she passed it to the bridesmaid, who kept it from touching the ground. The bodice, which appeared to have a delicate lace pattern, showed off Amelia's figure perfectly. She clutched her bouquet, a waterfall of pink orchids, and she looked beautiful.

Amelia spoke to one of the bridesmaids who dug into a clutch purse she was carrying and pulled out a packet of cigarettes. She lit one and handed it to Amelia, who took a long, hard drag, immediately destroying the image she had clearly worked hard to achieve.

'Here comes the bride, Fag-ash Lil,' commented Mark. 'I dread to think how much money she's spent on that dress, and now she ruins it all with *that*.' His lip curled as he spoke. 'Eugh!' He shook his body in exaggerated horror.

We watched as Craig appeared through a small wooden side door in the wall of the house, dressed in all his ceremonial finery. He wore a long black cassock under a white flowing vestment with big pointy sleeves. Around his neck was a long strip of white fabric rather like a scarf. Over all of that, he wore a white cloak. He looked incredibly smart – handsome, almost. It was quite a change from his daily outfit of a black shirt, clerical collar and blazer.

Despite the cigarette and the cloudy day, I still felt some excitement. I always did when I saw a wedding party making their way to the chapel. I was in no rush to marry, but I enjoyed seeing others on their happy day and was quickly sucked into the atmosphere of anticipation.

Craig made his way over, chatted to the bride, and then returned inside. It was a minute to three; this bride had no desire to be fashionably late, which I knew would please Craig immensely. Derek had removed his chauffeur's hat and gloves and now looked like any male guest at a wedding. He offered

Amelia his arm and, looking every inch the proud father, walked her towards the side door to the house. As they set off, Mark jumped to his feet, put his hand on his heart and started whistling the tune of 'Here Comes the Bride' – loudly.

'Stop it, you idiot, she'll hear you.'

'No she won't, she's in her own world,' he responded. But he had changed it to a much less ear-piercing hum by the time she'd disappeared into the building.

'Where's Gregg?' asked Ruth. She was delivering the wedding cake with less than an hour to spare.

'In the Garden Café kitchens, I think, getting ready for the dinner.'

'Okay, so long as he stays there.' There were five large white boxes in the boot of her car, one for each tier of the cake. I'd seen her arrive through the window and had brought out a trolley to help ferry the cake to the display table in the café.

I checked my watch. 'The ceremony will be over in half an hour, you're cutting it a bit fine.' I attempted to keep my tone light; I wasn't having a go at her. She smiled knowingly.

'Ah, it's all part of the plan. After Gregg once destroyed a cake with less than twenty-four hours to go before the wedding, I swore I wouldn't bring them in any earlier than necessary, and that Gregg was to go nowhere near them.'

'Oh my God, what happened?'

'The loon thought he was superman and decided he would try and move the cake singlehandedly when some of the furniture needed to be rearranged. It was eight o'clock the evening before the wedding. It took half an hour for him to convince me he wasn't kidding.'

'What did you do?'

'Made another one overnight. I was exhausted and didn't speak to Gregg for a week.'

'Do you want me to give him a heads up that you're coming?'

'No need, he knows the routine by now. Plus I sent him a message to say I was on the way in, so he's probably too terrified to leave the kitchen. I reckon he'd stay in there even if the house was on fire.' She laughed as she pushed the trolley down the lane to an entrance at the far end, dodging puddles and potholes as she went.

I had half an hour until the house was closed to the public; it was time to go back and help Chelsea and Leah before chaining myself to the computer. It didn't matter that it was a Saturday, it was just another working day to me.

CHAPTER 7

'Come on!'
 I hadn't heard Mark come into my office and nearly leapt out of my seat.

'Where? I want to get these reports done.'

'They'll wait. Come on, I want to see how the Garden Room looks, and I know you do too.'

He wasn't wrong, but I would usually wait until a little later when everyone was in the swing of things. I hated to get under Yeshim's feet, and I knew Gregg would have everything under control. I had nothing to do with this event so would be a mere spectator, something they didn't really need.

'Two minutes.'

Mark let out a dramatic sigh. Then another. He leant against the doorframe, crossed his arms and sighed again.

'Oh, for crying out loud, Mark, I give up. I'm coming.'

I left everything as it was. There was no point shutting my computer down; I'd have to come back and finish off. I reached up and grabbed Mark's shoulders, spun him round and pushed him out of the doorway.

'I didn't take you for such a romantic, or are you getting soft in your old age and wishing that you and Bill had thrown a huge event?' Mark and his husband Bill had held a quiet wedding in a registry office, and then an intimate dinner for immediate family and friends. They had always talked about throwing a huge party, but five years later it had never happened.

'God no, I just want to poke fun at the hats, and maybe get a free glass of wine in the kitchen.'

I gave him a gentle shove, and then tucked my arm through his. I wasn't sure if the wedding party would have finished with the photos yet; we might even pass the bride and groom with Nathan. The guests would certainly be waiting with champagne in hand, some regretting that they hadn't eaten more for lunch and counting down the minutes until dinner would be served.

We followed the route I'd taken with Joyce the previous evening and passed through the Antler Gallery, only now there were a couple of orange cones on the floor and some yellow and black tape wrapped around the tops connecting them to one another, creating a rather ugly low barrier.

'That'll annoy Visitor Services,' Mark commented. 'They hate it when people don't use our proper safety barriers. It's a mess.'

'It's better than it was last night. Are the guests coming this way? Do we need to tidy it up?' I asked. Mark shook his head.

'No, they'll be led the long way round via the colonnade. It gives them a much better view of the house, gets a few more gasps of amazement from them, and it's covered so there's no problem if it's raining.'

The rain had failed to return, but it was cold so I was glad we could take the indoor shortcut. We passed the turning to the State Dining Room where the dinner had been held the night before, passed the kitchen and followed the murmur of voices. We peered into the Garden Café, although 'café' seemed such an inappropriate word now.

It had previously been an orangery, and even on a grey day like today, the light streamed in from the ceiling-high windows that ran the length of the room. All the usual furniture had been removed and in the middle of the long space were two tables that stretched the length of the room. Along the centre of the tables ran umbrellas of cascading willow, orchids and ivy. Beneath them were masses of hydrangea with orchids pooling out from them, the pinks and purples of the orchids and hydrangea reflecting those at the dinner the night before. But this was so much more dramatic, the grandeur matching the sweeping view through the windows, the sparking crystal on the tables and the servers in their neatly pressed shirts. If you'd told me that royalty was attending, I wouldn't have been surprised.

Some of the guests had braved the chill to gather on the patio under propane heaters and enjoy the view. Others milled around inside, admiring the floral decorations that continued with the same theme around the room and no doubt dissecting the ceremony they had just witnessed, perhaps reminiscing over their own weddings or dreaming of those yet to happen. Everyone held a glass of champagne and from time to time there was the sound of them clinking over mini toasts between friends.

Mark and I had stepped into the room and were standing by the door. Servers whizzed past us, carrying more trays of drinks and bottles to top up glasses. One stopped and offered us a glass of champagne. I shook my head and batted Mark's hand away when he reached for a glass.

'Oi, we're not on the guest list.'

'They won't notice one.'

'Have one out of sight when we leave.'

'Yes, ma'am.'

Yeshim sidled up next to us. She looked as smart as ever in a navy suit and a pink blouse that matched one of the shades of the orchids that decorated the tables. Her beautiful jet-black hair was now hanging in a perfect plait down her back. We must have made quite a pair, her sleek elegance next to my spiky grey hair that looked as if someone had come up behind me and ruffled it.

The irony was my look probably took twice as long to achieve as hers.

'How do you think it looks?' she asked as she scanned the room.

'I'm blown away, it's stunning,' I replied.

Yeshim nodded, a look of satisfaction on her face. 'The florist did a good job, although I thought we'd lose them at one point. This must be the tenth design that they put together. The couple disagreed on every single design that came through. They only agreed on this one when Patrick finally said he no longer cared and he'd just accept whatever Amelia chose.'

'They sound like hard work.'

She shook her head. 'I'm considering training as a marriage guidance counsellor, I've got enough experience.' The radio that was clipped onto the waistband of her skirt must have crackled into life, as Yeshim suddenly reached up and pressed the earpiece that was tucked over her ear closer to her head. She took hold of a small microphone and responded.

'Received, I'm in the café standing by.' She looked at us both. 'Photos are over, the bride and groom are on their way back. They'll come across the lawns so everyone can welcome them on the patio; I'll just get someone ready with champagne for them.'

I watched as she whispered in a server's ear and then made her way outside, deciding that she must have the patience of a saint. After ten rounds of flower designs, I'd have told the couple to pick some up from the nearest supermarket on the way here and I'd leave a few vases out for them.

It was clear I should never consider a career move into wedding planning.

We watched as the bride and groom arrived. A huge round of applause and shouts of congratulations echoed around the room. Amelia and Patrick beamed at their friends and one another, and glasses of champagne quickly made their way into their hands. Everyone wanted a chance to congratulate the happy couple and they disappeared into a scrum of kisses and handshakes.

I turned to tell Mark that I was heading back to my office, having seen what I'd come for, but he'd gone. Turning towards the door, I saw him retrieving a glass of champagne from a server's tray, and then sneaking out of sight.

Well, if you can't beat 'em, join 'em, I thought.

'Hello again.' I recognised the voice, took a deep breath and pulled my mouth into a smile.

'Levi, lovely to see you. You look very smart.' The tuxedo had been swapped for an olive-green three-piece woollen suit. A deep purple silk handkerchief had been tucked into his breast pocket and matched the purple shirt he'd chosen. I had to admit he had chosen well for an October wedding. Despite his good taste in clothing though, he still exuded an overconfidence that was off-putting.

'Thank you. I have an expansive wardrobe to choose from, so it's rare I have to wear anything more than two or three times. It's important to keep on top of the latest fashion.' There was little about him that seemed up to date, especially when it came to his approach to chatting up women. 'I was thinking, we really ought to get to know one another better. I have an instinctive feeling that we are going to get on very well. How about a drink tonight? I can slip out of this event a little early and we could get acquainted in front of the roaring fire at the Black Swan.'

GOD NO! I screamed inside my head. *I'm sure I need to amputate my own foot tonight so I'm afraid I just can't make it.*

But my response came out as, 'That's a lovely idea, Levi, but I'm afraid I'll be working late tonight and I just can't see myself being able to escape early.'

'That's such a shame, but how about breakfast? They do a marvellous full English breakfast. I don't think you could have a more perfect start to your day.'

He was clearly not going to give up. As I looked across the room and saw Amelia vanish into a group hug with some screaming women, it gave me an idea.

'The thing is, Levi, as wonderful as that sounds – and I have no doubt you would make the most charming companion – the fact is, I'm engaged and my fiancé would never allow me to join another man for breakfast. Well any meal, for that matter, not without him present.'

I expected to see more of a response in his face, but it didn't change.

'That's a shame, but not an insurmountable problem, Sophie.' He winked and I could feel all my internal organs start to curl up. 'Who is the lucky man? Does he work here?'

Out of the corner of my eye, I saw Mark making his way back across the room.

'He does... MARK!' I called out. 'Come and meet Levi, he's an actor.'

Mark came across. He shook Levi's hand.

'Good to see you again.'

'This is Mark, my fiancé.' I looped my arm through Mark's and watched the confusion appear on his face. It was an expression I'd never seen before, somewhere between shock and complete incomprehension; it was rather sweet. 'We're lucky enough to work together, so we are aware of each other's every move. Isn't that right, darling?'

Mark didn't reply; there was a glassy look in his eyes and I could have sworn I heard the cogs turn in his brain as he tried to figure out what on earth was going on. I tugged him roughly and pulled him tighter, hoping I could wake him from his stupor.

'Aren't we lucky, darling?'

'What? Yes, absolutely. Lucky, very lucky.'

Levi was looking down at my hand where it rested on Mark's forearm.

'What, no engagement ring? I would have thought you were

deserving of diamonds. What are you thinking, Mark? You should be treating this woman like royalty.'

'Oh, he is. It's... it's... at the jewellers. A family heirloom that belonged to Mark's grandmother; it was a little too large, wasn't it, dear?'

'Too large, yes, yes,' Mark stuttered as I gave another tug on his arm.

'Well, we must be off. We both have work to get back to. It's been lovely to meet you, Levi.'

I spun Mark round and marched us towards the door before either of the men could say anything. Mark grabbed a glass of champagne off a server's tray as we went. Once through the door, he stepped to one side out of sight of the wedding party, and chugged half the champagne down in one mouthful, then looked me in the eye.

'You do know I'm gay, don't you?'

'And my heart breaks every day at the thought,' I cried out dramatically and stole the champagne from his hands. 'I owe you.' I winked at him and emptied the glass. 'Come on, let me do at least an hour's more work, and then we can come back and you can have a giggle at the tipsy guests, and I can get to see how the room looks when they're all sitting down for dinner.'

An hour later and I was standing in the corner of the Garden Café with Yeshim. The guests were beginning to sit down.

'So far, so good. I haven't witnessed a single argument between the bride and groom, although the best woman has looked a little tense – nervous about her speech, I'm guessing.'

I watched as Mark chatted with a couple of guests as they looked out over the gardens. They were clearly enraptured by whatever historical nugget he was sharing with them. For all his witty and occasionally barbed humour, there was no doubting that he was a knowledgeable and charismatic guide. After a few minutes, he ambled over.

'That guy used to work as a gardener at Blenheim Palace, we had a lovely chat about historic landscaping. I think I'm done – shall we go?'

I nodded.

'Take another drink,' Yeshim said. 'This lot aren't as thirsty as other wedding parties.' She signalled over a server and we followed him in the direction of a champagne bottle.

Armed with our glasses, we stopped outside the Antler Room and Mark's hand reached for the door handle.

'No!' I stopped him and raised my glass at him. 'We can't go through there with these, we need to go out and via the lane.'

Mark stepped backwards, letting go of the door handle. As soon as his hand had left the brass knob, the door opened slowly inwards. Gregg was standing before us, his kitchen whites matching the ghostly pallor of his face.

'Gregg, are you okay?'

He looked straight through me and nodded over his shoulder. I sidled past him.

The first thing to catch my eye was a big space on the wall where the loose pair of antlers had once hung. Two ragged holes now replaced it. It was heart-breaking damage to such a historic building and someone was going to be in serious trouble for not repairing it, instead letting it get so bad that this could occur, but I wasn't sure why Gregg would appear so shocked.

'Sophie.' Mark rested his hand on my arm. 'Not up there, down here.'

I followed the wall down, expecting to see the antlers smashed to pieces, but they were in one piece. It was just that they were sticking out of the stomach of Nathan, the photographer.

CHAPTER 8

'Sophie, meet Detective Sergeant Colette Harnby. This is Sophie Lockwood, she manages all the visitor cafés here, amongst other things.'

DS Harnby reached over and gave me a bone-crushing handshake.

'Sophie. Your name has cropped up a lot recently, it's time we met.' She had the accent of someone brought up in Manchester, and the steely look of a woman who was taking me in and adding all the information to her mental filing cabinet. DS Harnby was Detective Constable Joe Greene's boss. Joe was Mark's brother-in-law and a regular recipient of free coffee and cake whenever he dropped by the house, which was often. He was also someone I considered a good friend. Until now I'd done a good job of avoiding DS Harnby.

Joe looked at me with a wry smile. This was the third murder at Charleton House he'd had to question me about.

'You found the body?' he asked.

'No, that was Gregg.'

'Where's Gregg now?" asked DS Harnby as she made notes. I pointed to the kitchen just a couple of yards away where he was standing with Yeshim, discussing how to deal with the dinner that had yet to be served. He looked a lot better than he had earlier and the colour had returned to his face.

The problem they were dealing with was quickly solved when Patrick approached.

'Yeshim, I've spoken to Amelia and a few of the others. We know things are going to be disrupted for a while, so we've decided that once the police have finished with us, we'll decamp to the pub down the road. Some of the guests want to go home anyway, and there's no way you can serve a full dinner now.'

'I'm so sorry, Patrick, this is just awful. We can move to another room in the house and serve more canapé style food, make sure people still get plenty to eat. The drinks are easy enough to move.'

'Thank you, but I don't think many of us are feeling particularly hungry now. We'll do something else when all this is over. If you'll excuse me, I should be with my wife.'

'That makes life easier,' Harnby commented as she and Joe started to walk over to the kitchen. I watched as Gregg was taken aside by the two detectives. After a brief chat, they left him to his work and Joe made his way back to me.

'What is it about you, Lockwood? Dead bodies have been popping up all over the place since you arrived.'

'I don't know, maybe they can't resist my chocolate muffins? So what happens next?' I looked around the room. Some guests had remained at the long dining tables and servers were bringing them drinks and canapés. Others were standing in groups, talking quietly; some had ventured outside into the cold to have a cigarette. No one looked as if they were at a wedding. Some looked shocked; others looked awkward, like they were unsure how to behave when the body of someone they didn't know had been found. It wasn't like they could burst into a display of grief, but then carrying on as normal didn't seem quite right either.

Police officers were questioning the guests, who were slowly filtering out after handing over their details and answering a few questions. Men had loosened their ties or removed them completely. Jackets were slung over chairs. Women had kicked off their shoes, and those who had attempted to appear at home in the splendour of Charleton by delicately sipping their wine were now taking great big gulps and numbing the shock. None of them had seen Nathan's body, we'd made sure of that, but it hadn't taken long for word to get around that he'd been gored by a particularly terrifying set of disembodied antlers.

Amelia's mother was helping her tidy up her makeup; she'd clearly been crying. Derek was standing close by, holding what I assumed to be his wife's handbag, a look of concern on his face. Mark had told me that Derek was Amelia's stepfather, her own father having died years ago, which explained why he had looked ready to walk her down the aisle. That was exactly what he had been about to do when we'd seen him outside.

'We'll talk to the guests and put together a picture of Nathan's last movements, and then they can go,' Joe told me. 'We'll have their details in case we need to talk to them again, but there's no reason to keep them all here beyond that. Right now Nathan's death looks like a really unfortunate accident, no more than that. Did you know him?'

'No, I'd never seen him before yesterday evening. Mark says he's done a fair few weddings here, but I've never seen him around.'

'Okay, well I should be going. I know DI Flynn wants to be the one to brief the Duke and Duchess so Harnby will be going to talk to him and I'll oversee the uniformed officers here for a while. You may as well go, there's nothing more you can do. Why don't you and Mark go and have a drink? You probably need it.' He smiled, a gentle look of concern on his face. I suddenly felt very tired, but I wasn't ready to go home yet. Despite the champagne I'd already drunk, I decided a drink in the Black Swan would do me the world of good and give me a chance to wind down before I tried to get some sleep. I'd expected there to be some drama at this wedding, but nothing like this.

As I left, I spotted a server who was in tears and being consoled by a colleague. It was the young woman whose figure had attracted Levi's attention at the dinner the night before. There was no sign of Levi, which was a relief; the last thing she needed was him sniffing around at a time like this.

I rounded up Mark, who didn't need much convincing to accompany me to the pub. As we'd both had a couple of glasses of champagne, I booked a taxi to take us the two miles to the Black Swan Pub that lay just within the boundaries of the Charleton House estate. We were walking across the house car park towards our taxi when we spotted a Norman knight climb out of an estate car. I wondered if I was succumbing to tiredness and had fallen asleep, only to dream of medieval battles. But no, there was actually a Norman knight before me. He had a helmet under one arm and a laptop under the other. His chainmail rattled as he walked across the car park. As he got closer, I recognised him as Anthony Leggett, our Health and Safety Manager.

Mark and I looked at each other.

'Say one word, Mark Boxer, and I will make you rewrite every risk assessment for every tour you have ever or will ever deliver.'

Mark raised his hands in the air and gave a look of hurt surprise. 'I was going to say how handsome you look, if a little overdressed for the occasion. The antlers aren't actually attached to a stag so the risk is minimal.' I was amazed at the lack of a smirk on his face; Mark was doing a reasonable job of controlling himself.

'I did warn you, Boxer.' He turned to me. 'So it's true, then, it was an antler?' I nodded. 'Well someone's in deep trouble. That loose pair of antlers was reported to me days ago. I can't believe nothing was done about it, the room should have been closed off.'

'Technically it was,' I told him. 'Some of us used it as a shortcut, it hadn't been locked and...' I paused, immediately feeling guilty, 'I suggested Nathan keep his bag in there, but it was tucked away in a corner, and there was safety tape to keep people away from the area immediately underneath the antlers. I guess that must have been moved, or he stepped over it for some reason.'

Anthony shook his head. 'I'm going to be in meetings all week about this. There's nothing I can do now of course, but I figured I'd come in and fetch all the paperwork from my office. I'll spend Sunday preparing my response.' He paused. 'Poor guy. I'm not sure it's how you'd want to be remembered, gored by an antler that wasn't actually attached to a beast. At least that would have been dramatic and possibly a little heroic if he'd tried to fight it off.'

'Talking of heroic,' Mark sounded tentative as he wiggled his forefinger at Anthony's outfit, 'are we going to get an explanation?'

'You're not the only one with a passion for history. I might be the grey-suited health and safety geek that people moan about, but I have a life outside work too. I was at combat training at Cote Heath Park with a Norman knights re-enactment group. We've won more awards than you've had hot dinners.' Mark looked impressed; I guessed that Anthony had gone up in his estimation. 'Well, the sooner I get in there, the sooner I can go home and start work, so I'll see you both on Monday. I'll be wanting to hear your side of things, seeing as you were there.' He nodded at us, tightened his grip on his laptop and helmet, and strode across the car park, his chainmail rattling again as it swung against his legs. Mark laughed, and I quickly shushed him.

'Don't let him hear you, I doubt he was kidding about the risk assessments.'

The pub was already filling up with wedding guests. I found a table in a corner close to the large stone fireplace while Mark fetched our drinks. Steve, the landlord, already had a fire going and the room had a wonderful welcoming glow to it.

This was as traditional an English country pub as you could find and it was a huge hit with the tourists that were drawn to Derbyshire throughout the summer. Black and white photos on the walls showed the pub throughout the ages; bent and sun-worn farmers lined up with pints in their hands for the rare occasions that someone with a camera had come into the village. There were paintings of Charleton House and framed newspaper clippings of when royalty had visited, or film crews had taken over for a blockbuster Hollywood film. The gnarled tables and chairs looked as old as the building itself, but they were well cared for and had been polished smooth. A number of the wedding guests had taken over many of the tables, looking like they were starting to relax now they were away from Nathan's body.

I watched Mark return with two glasses of champagne.

'Well, I never got to finish mine once we found Nathan, and anyway, I felt like we should toast him. Cheers.'

'May he rest in peace,' I replied. Thinking briefly about the young man I'd seen lying on the floor below the antlers, I shook my head. 'Unbelievable, talk about bad luck.' I paused and peered at Mark over my glass. 'Do you think it was an accident?'

Mark laughed. 'I wondered how long that would take, Sherlock. Well, Joe said it looked like an accident and there was nothing to suggest foul play, so I guess it was. Unless a ghost pulled it off the wall and launched it at him, which might be the story that I add to the upcoming ghost tour season.'

'You wouldn't? I thought all the stories you told on the tours were true, or at least people really believed that they had seen things, not completely made up by you.'

'They are, I'm kidding. You can guarantee I'll get questions about it, though. I wonder how long it will be until some terrified member of staff comes running to me having seen the ghost of Nathan in the Antler Room.'

'What ghost of Nathan? Is he haunting the house already?' Joyce appeared as quickly as a ghostly apparition between Mark and me, and pulled up a chair. Her perfect blonde bouffant wobbled slightly as she sat down. She must have left home in a rush – that thing is normally covered with enough hairspray to withstand a 7.0 magnitude earthquake.

'What are you doing here?' I asked as she took a swig of my champagne, the little diamonds stuck on each of her fingernails glinting in the firelight. She seemed much more like her old self. Her dark green chiffon blouse had speckles of gold thread and the light bounced off them, although it was the impressive cleavage and the edge of a lacy black bra that caught my eye. Her wrists were covered with gold bangles and the noise as they moved would have given Anthony's chainmail a run for its money.

'Harold called and told me what happened and I said I'd meet him here for a drink.'

'It's a very exciting time, our good lady Joyce has a man in her life,' Mark commented.

'Calm down, I don't have a man in my life. Well not exactly – he's sort of back in my life. Oh, I don't know. I need a drink.'

As if on cue, Harold arrived with a glass of prosecco for Joyce and what appeared to be a whisky for himself.

'Here you are, Cookie.' He smiled at her. I noticed that Joyce gave him the slightest of glares, but it was momentary and she quickly returned to looking like a love-struck teenager. I moved my chair so he could sit between Joyce and me. Mark smirked.

'Finally we meet the man who has got our lovely Cookie in a bit of a tizz.'

'Harold, I'd like you to meet my friends. This is Sophie, she manages all the cafés up at the house and keeps my caffeine levels topped up, and this gormless looking nitwit is Mark, tour guide and general fount of all knowledge.' Mark opened his mouth to comment, but shut it again and shook Harold's hand. 'Darling,' Joyce looked at Harold, 'please remember, it's "Joyce" at work.'

'No it's bloody not, not anymore!' exclaimed Mark. 'So, Harold, how do you know our delightful Aphrodite here?' He was leaning over his drink, Nathan's death long forgotten. Harold smiled and looked across at Joyce.

'She was my first true love. We dated for a couple of blissful years and then I moved to Australia. It was only meant to be temporary, but life got in the way and, well, that was that. I never stopped thinking about her, though.' There was no denying that Harold was a good-looking man. He must have been in his late sixties, with tidy silver hair and the complexion of someone who lives in a country known for its stinking hot summers, although there was little evidence of an Australian accent. He was wearing a pale purple waistcoat, the same as all the other men in the groom's party. His shirt was undone at the neck and there was no sign of his tie or jacket.

'And what brings you back into the arms of Cookie?' Mark asked, ignoring the long fingernail that Joyce stuck in his arm as he used her nickname. 'How are you connected to the wedding?'

'I'm the father of the groom, Patrick.'

'And the mother of the groom?' Mark wasn't yet satisfied.

'My ex-wife. We met in Australia through friends who thought we should meet because we both grew up here in Derbyshire. I never imagined my son would get married back here at Charleton. There he is.' Harold turned as Patrick, Amelia and another man walked in.

'Who's he?' I asked.

'Kristian, Amelia's older brother. Nice guy, very protective of her. Took Patrick forever to convince him that he wasn't just after her money. It didn't seem to matter to Kristian that Patrick had plenty of money of his own; he's a very successful solicitor. But I guess that's big brothers for you; I don't think anyone would have been good enough for his baby sister. I like him.'

'How are they doing? This is meant to be one of the biggest days of their lives, and instead they're in a pub and all anyone can talk about is a dead body.'

Harold sighed and looked over at the bride and groom again.

'Patrick's okay, seems to be taking it in his stride. Amelia was pretty upset, said she'd come here for one drink to see everyone then she wants to go back to the cottage they're staying in. Her mum has to keep reapplying her makeup every time she cries. She knew him – Nathan – so it's no wonder she's upset, the poor thing.'

'How?' My curiosity had been piqued. 'How did she know him?'

Harold took a sip of his drink.

'He was her boyfriend when Patrick came on the scene.'

I looked over at Mark, wide eyed. He grinned at me and raised his glass.

'Oh yes, Sherlock is back in town.'

CHAPTER 9

'Oh come on, he was the bride's ex-boyfriend. Of course it's suspicious.'

'You've no evidence of that, Sophie, I think you're getting ahead of yourself here.'

After a quiet Sunday at home with only the company of my cat, Pumpkin, and a recipe book, Monday had come around too soon. Chelsea had arrived half an hour late in a world of her own and had been neither use nor ornament, so I'd done most of the setting up of the Library Café on my own. I'd asked Martin if I could borrow one of his team for the first hour of the day, and then I'd finally made myself a coffee when Mark had walked in demanding something with a high sugar content. I sat where I could watch Chelsea and leap in to help if I saw she was struggling.

'I'm sure you're right. I guess it just seems like too much of a coincidence and I had far too much time to think yesterday.'

'Are you sure it's not the excuse to spend time with Joe that's making you think this way?' Mark had got it into his head that Joe was interested in being more than just my friend. I thought

Mark was out of his mind, and at any rate, I didn't want or need a man in my life right now. As much as I liked Joe, we were friends and I wanted it to stay that way. I ignored his comment.

'I spoke to Yeshim this morning, everywhere is back open. The Antler Room remains off limits to everyone except the police right now, but other than that you wouldn't know anything had happened. Well, the press are sniffing around, but security have put a couple of extra staff on the main gate to try and stop them getting in, and an officer is outside the Antler Room to make extra sure. Otherwise, life goes on as normal.'

'Have you heard from the love birds?'

'No. In fact, I heard that Joyce had taken the day off work. Shall we guess who she's with?' I attempted to wink, but only succeeded in screwing up half my face.

'You okay, Sophie? Got something in your eye?' Joe sounded concerned. He'd picked quite the moment to walk in. Mind you, maybe seeing me mid wink, he'd find me less appealing.

'Oh, morning. No, I'm fine. Coffee?'

'Please.'

I left him with Mark for a moment. After getting Chelsea to tie up her apron which was hanging loose, helping her correct a mistake she'd made on the till and amending the order she'd mixed up for a couple of visitors, I returned with a large mug of coffee and a chocolate twist.

Mark was smiling at me in a slightly unnerving way.

'Joe has some news for us. Top-secret hot-off-the-press kind of news.'

'How can it be top secret if it's hot off the press?' I asked, wondering if maybe I'd made his coffee a little too weak this morning. I could see him thinking.

'Oh yeah. Never mind, you're going to love this, Sherlock.'

I looked at Joe.

'Focus on the top secret bit, we've not released this information yet, although it'll be public in a couple of hours.'

'What? Will one of you tell me what you're on about?'

Joe lowered his voice, despite there being no one close enough to hear us.

'It was murder, Nathan was killed.'

He filled us in through mouthfuls of pastry and gulps of coffee.

'We got the coroner's report back early this morning. It seems that the antlers did fall and hit Nathan, piercing his stomach. If that was all that had happened, he would have been fine. Gregg would have found him in time to call an ambulance and he'd have survived. But, it looks like someone else found him injured, and then gave the antler an extra shove. It hit his abdominal aorta and that was fatal. Nathan didn't stand a chance.'

'Dear God,' Mark muttered, looking horrified. 'I assume there are fingerprints on the antlers?'

'No, they're completely clean. The rest of the room is covered in dozens of prints, including – I would guess – yours, as you both took a shortcut through there. There's nothing that's going to help us.'

'Well that means there's someone with a very particular motive.' I was thinking aloud. 'It's not accidental, or mistaken identity. He was lying there in a well-lit room. Someone really wanted him dead; it wasn't enough to take pleasure in his injuries.'

'Correct on all counts, Soph.' Joe pushed his chair back and stood up. 'Right, I'm due to meet DS Harnby. Thanks for the coffee. Do me a favour, though: can you actually leave this one for us to solve? I'm not sure that the boss has come to any kind of conclusion about you yet, and when she does I'd like it to be favourable, so don't get under her feet.'

I scowled at him. 'Would I ever?'

'Yes, all the blooming time.' But he smiled warmly as he said it, and then turned on his heels and walked out of the door.

Mark and I walked towards the counter. Chelsea seemed to

have things more under control and we both wanted another coffee.

'Blimey, someone is going to be in trouble for not securing those antlers.' I could see that Mark had been taken aback by Joe's news; it sounded like he was trying to think about something other than the details. He was right, though; if there was a chance Nathan's death could have been avoided, then the proverbial heads would roll.

I thought about it for a minute.

'Fortunately, that's not our problem. Unfortunately, our problem is much bigger.' Mark look confused. 'The murder,' I clarified in a whisper, not wanting Chelsea to hear.

'Why on earth is that our problem? That's Joe's job and he's already told you to stay out of it.'

'I must have missed that comment.' I avoided his gaze. 'Alright, yes he did, but come on – you enjoyed the puzzle solving the last couple of times, right?'

'I don't recall ever expressing any enjoyment as you sniffed around after dead bodies. I'm in this for the cake and the coffee, you're the one who started dragging corpses into our relationship.'

'Ah, so you are *in this*.'

'I'm not *in* anything.'

'You know, Sherlock Holmes never got this attitude from Watson, and Watson didn't get an endless supply of coffee and chocolate croissants. Here...' I returned his fresh, steaming coffee. 'Use this to get your cogs turning and earn the aforementioned croissant that's in the oven.'

Mark paused, stared into his mug then over at the oven and sighed.

'Okay, fine, I'm in. But first we might want to focus on why Joyce is dressed like she walked into her wardrobe blindfolded.'

I followed his eye line. He was right. Joyce, whose wardrobe choices caught the eye at the best of times, looked as if she was moments away from being the entertainment at a children's party.

CHAPTER 10

I dashed across the room, took hold of Joyce's arm and steered her to a table; she looked like a rabbit caught in headlights. A rainbow-covered rabbit caught in headlights.

'Get off me, girl, I'm fine.'

'Joyce, have you looked in a mirror this morning? You are not fine, and I thought you were taking the day off.'

Joyce had paired a very smart, if a little too tight, pair of red trousers with yellow stilettos and a leopard-print blouse. What really stood out, though, was that her nails hadn't been redecorated to match her outfit. She had managed to style her hair and apply her makeup with absolute precision, so the clown comparison had to stop there. Well, that was depending on your view of her makeup choices on a normal day.

Joyce sat down and stared at me. 'What are you talking about? It took me over an hour to decide what to wear today, I've lost track of how many outfits I tried on.'

'So you decided to choose all of them?' Mark asked bravely as he joined us with a mug of coffee for Joyce. 'What's with Chelsea?' he whispered to me. 'She asked me to bring this over, didn't want to come near Joyce. I think she's terrified of her.'

'Who's terrified of me?' Joyce asked before shouting across the room, 'GIRL, I need some sugar.'

Chelsea froze, and then slowly carried a bowl of sugar across the room. Approaching from the far side of the table so she didn't have to get too close to Joyce, she then scurried back.

'Joyce, you really do need to be a little nicer sometimes. Perhaps add a please.'

'They need to toughen up. It's good for them, especially her, dizzy blonde.'

Mark coughed and I saw him eye the mound of blonde hair balanced on Joyce's head. Staff across Charleton House were terrified of Joyce and I understood why, but fortunately she'd taken a shine to me and I had quickly been introduced to the warmer side of her. I was now incredibly fond of the woman, but she could be her own worst enemy. Having said that, she did normally add a please and thank you. Something was definitely off today.

'So, are you going to tell us what's happened?' I asked as I spooned sugar into Joyce's mug.

'What makes you think anything has happened? I'm just not quite myself this morning, happens to the best of us.'

I decided not to respond; Mark and I just sat and waited. After a painful couple of minutes, Joyce let out an enormous sigh.

'Harold and I spent the day together yesterday. It was like old times. We didn't stop talking from dawn till dusk. It was wonderful.' She paused and looked across the table at us both. 'He wants me to go back to Australia with him, permanently.'

Joyce's announcement left us in stunned silence. I knew it was selfish, but my first thought was *no, you can't leave us*. My friends at Charleton House were becoming increasingly like family to me, and Joyce was an essential part of that. But Joyce, who had been unlucky in love, deserved to be happy, and that was of course what I wanted for her. I did my best to reshape the expression on my face to one of happy surprise rather than horror.

Mark's first response was utterly in character. 'You can't leave, you know where all the bodies are buried. Mainly because you buried them.'

She glared at him. 'Too damn right, and I'll make sure yours is amongst them before I go anywhere… What am I meant to do now? I have a house, a job. But he's the same man I fell in love with all those years ago.'

'And the same man who ditched you to go to Australia and never return,' Mark added. I kicked him under the table.

'When you reach my age, you'll understand how life just happens sometimes. My life moved forward too. It moved three husbands forward, to be precise. I can hardly judge.' I knew that Joyce had also been the 'other woman' so she definitely couldn't judge. 'You know, the idea of Christmas on a beach is very appealing. I could have a fabulous collection of sun hats, and…' she paused for a moment and a smile curled the corners of her lips, 'and my sweet Harry.'

'And he'd have his sweet Cookie.' Joyce turned to Mark and gave him a look that could have sunk ships. I was still trying to move past the sense of loss I was already feeling. After all, she hadn't said she was going yet, so I was being daft. As she kept talking, she jumped from excitement to nervousness and fear, and then back again.

'Well at least they drive on the left and speak the same language,' said Mark encouragingly. 'Although I'm not sure your stilettos will fare so well on Bondi Beach.'

'Well I'm not going to resolve this now, and Harold is meeting me for lunch. I'm sure you've got work to do. Well, you do.' She looked over at me. 'You, on the other hand…' She turned her attention to Mark and shook her head. Mark put his hand on his chest in mock horror, but I knew from the glint in her eye that she was teasing him. As much as she would pretend to find Mark deeply irritating, she was extremely fond of him.

I watched her walk out of the café, wondering what she would decide to do and hoping she had some spare clothes back in her office.

The morning had started slowly and seemed to be continuing in that vein. I'd taken the opportunity to place an order with my friends and regular suppliers at Signal Box Coffee and hear about some new blends they were working on. Then I'd had another cup of coffee and a chocolate twist, not because I was hungry, but because it was there. It's one of my biggest failings: I have no willpower, not an ounce. Finally I dragged myself out of my office. Chelsea was making a pattern out of a pile of napkins, so I went to clear the one table that had a single cup on it.

'Here comes the bride.' A dreadfully out-of-tune male voice was attempting to sing behind me. It was Levi Moreland.

'What are you doing here?' A daft question, as anyone could buy a ticket to tour the house and grounds, but still, I was surprised to see him.

'A visit round the old pile was overdue, plus it's rather wet out there. I wasn't expecting to run into my ray of sunshine.'

I thought I tasted blood as I bit my tongue; I wasn't *his* anything.

'You know, I was thinking. I would have made sure your ring fitted you perfectly, none of this sending it off to be resized. If your fiancé had really put his mind to it, he could have found out what size you needed and had the work done first. You deserve a man who puts that kind of effort in, every day.'

I wasn't entirely sure what he was talking about, and then I remembered he was under the illusion that I was engaged to Mark Boxer, the gayest man to ever walk the corridors of Charleton House.

'I bet there was no real effort put into the proposal either – a swift down on one knee here in the café? I would have scattered rose petals on the ground, had champagne on ice and a string quartet ready to serenade you. You deserve only the best.'

I felt like I was going to be sick.

'Levi, you really should be exploring the house. There's a lot to see and it can take a whole day.'

He looked around the café. I sensed a slight disapproval, but it didn't seem to put him off.

'I was thinking it might be time for a cup of tea, perhaps a scone. Please tell me you'll join me?' He smiled and revealed a mouthful of gleaming white tombstones. Was nothing about this man genuine?

'It's a lovely thought, but I have a meeting to attend. Chelsea will take care of you.'

With that I ran – actually ran – out of the door and didn't look back. He made my skin crawl and I wasn't sure how much longer I could remain polite. There was a very serious risk of yet another murder being committed and I was having more fun solving them from this side of a prison door.

After spending most of the rest of the day hiding in other people's offices and taking ridiculously long routes in order to avoid the public areas, thus dodging my own nauseating version of Romeo, I was heading home to get ready for a night out. A little gallery in the nearby town of Bakewell, home of the Bakewell Pudding, was launching a new exhibition of artists, and had got together with one of my favourite local gin distillers who would be providing the drinks. It sounded like my perfect night, and as the gallery owner, Connie Cropper, had said, everyone needs something fun to do on a Monday night in October to make it a bit more bearable.

It had been a cold grey day and by five o'clock, when I drove through the estate, it was starting to rain. But even the low cloud and muted colours couldn't stop me enjoying the drive. Charleton House was located in a beautiful estate of rolling hills and woodland, and despite the weather, the landscape was showing itself off in all its autumnal glory. This was the time of year that families would come to spend an afternoon in their wellies, hunting for conkers against a firework display of colour. The yellows and oranges of larches shone against the gently glowing oranges and reds of the beech trees that were giving the American oaks a run for their money as they still displayed greens and yellows.

My parents used to bring me here every autumn to kick my way through piles of leaves. We'd always finish off with a hot chocolate at the Stables Café. It was funny to think that I was now in charge of making sure the children that came here today were able to wrap their hands around a cup of hot chocolate and watch the steam rise in the cold air before diving into the thick layer of whipped cream, dotted with marshmallows. This would be my second autumn here at Charleton House, and with every month that passed I felt more and more at home.

I glanced over at the house as I drove along the estate road. 'That's my office,' I muttered to myself and shook my head in wonder. Up on the hill on the other side of the road a herd of deer were standing, surveying the estate. Off to one side was a stag. This was the time of year that the stags would start to rut and the testosterone would course through their veins as they went, quite literally, head to head with one another. Their magnificent antlers could do a huge amount of damage, and I knew that the gamekeeper would sometimes have to tell overeager amateur photographers to move further away. A decent photograph was not worth getting gored for.

Of course, Nathan had experienced that without having to set foot outside the building. The next thing I knew I was picturing him, propped against the wall, a massive pair of antlers on top of him. I shook my head in an attempt to remove the image; it only partially worked. The antler that had killed him was considerably bigger than anything you'd find here on the estate once the deer had shed them.

I slowed the car and stopped as the deer made their way down the hill towards the road. They were such graceful animals, and yet the stags were capable of displays of great violence as they fought for dominance. Rather like one of the wedding guests, it seemed, who despite the surroundings of great beauty had taken an opportunity to kill Nathan rather than help him.

The thought sent a shiver through my body.

CHAPTER 11

Cropper's Collectables was a small art gallery tucked between a bank and a bakery. With only one room, it didn't need much to start feeling crowded. Mark and I headed straight for the drinks table. There, Chris Bailey-Jones of Twenty Trees Gin was mixing small gin and tonics and talking to people about his choice of ingredients and favourite cocktails. I gave him a little wave as I retrieved a glass each for Mark and me. I'd chat to Chris later.

Mark and I toured the walls; I was half on the lookout for something to go in my newly decorated sitting room. So long as the prices didn't make my eyes water.

'Check this out,' he whispered to me as he stared at swirls of colour on a glass panel, 'and look at the price. I could do better than that after a couple of these.' He took a sip of his drink.

My attention was drawn to a beautiful watercolour of Kinder Downfall, an impressive waterfall on the edge of Kinder Scout, a moorland plateau that was the highest hill in the area. The downfall was famous for the water being blown back up in high winds and could be incredibly dramatic. I was starting to picture it hanging above my fireplace when Mark pulled on my sleeve like an attention-seeking child.

'Over here, look, they're really creepy.' He led me to a series of five black and white photographs. They were eerie images taken around garden sculptures and landscaping. Swirls of mist created a timeless otherworldly quality. In each photograph was a figure in a long black cloak and a mask – the mask of the plague doctor.

In past centuries, doctors who were treating those with the bubonic plague would wear a mask with what appeared to be a long beak. This they would stuff with herbs and spices in the hope that it would protect them from unclean air. It must have been terrifying to be at death's door and be approached by someone dressed in such a frightening way.

Something about the photographs was familiar, and as I looked closer I realised they had all been taken in the gardens of Charleton House. I wasn't surprised; the house and its grounds were popular with local artists and you would often find one or two with their easels set up or carrying expensive-looking camera equipment. It took me no time at all to decide that these would never find their way onto the walls of my home. I'd have nightmares.

'Sophie, wonderful to see you. Mark, you too. I'm so glad you could make it.' Connie had glided across the room towards us, or so it seemed as her feet were invisible beneath a long flowing skirt that appeared to be made from off-cuts of 1970s curtains. 'They're so atmospheric, aren't they? They really show off the potential for darkness behind the spacious beauty of the gardens that we think we are so familiar with. They must particularly resonate with you, knowing the house and gardens so well?'

Mark and I grunted in agreement while looking at each photo with exaggerated quizzical expressions, stopping suddenly as Connie turned to face us. She took Mark's free hand and held it tightly.

'There is a painting you must see. The moment I saw it, I thought of you – you will love it.'

Mark looked slightly terrified, and as Connie led him away, he looked over his shoulder and mouthed, 'Help'.

Left alone, I decided that art could take a back seat for a while and walked across to Chris. He had just finished pouring drinks for a couple of guests as I approached him and I waited until they had gone, admiring his waistcoat, one of many in bright colours that had become his trademark.

'Could I possibly get a top-up?'

'Sophie, of course. How do you like it?' He had a voice that bounced with enthusiasm and energy.

'I have two bottles at home. Well, one and about an eighth. It's currently my go to.'

'Currently?' he questioned. 'Hope it stays that way. How do you fancy a sneak peek of our latest?' He reached into a cardboard box under the table and pulled out an unlabelled bottle. 'We don't launch this for another couple of weeks, but I brought some so I could allow a few people to taste it. This is our autumn special.'

As he poured a tiny measure into a glass, he listed the ingredients. 'I use sweet orange peel, cardamom, cubeb berries, allspice and, of course, juniper, Angelica and orris root. Before distillation, I also add apple cider from a local orchard. I wanted to capture autumn in a bottle. Let me know what you think.'

I closed my eyes and took a sip, letting the liquid rest on my tongue for a few moments before swallowing. The scent of smoked applewood pulled me in, the orange and cardamom immediately popped on my tongue, and the allspice and juniper added depth. This was a gin I could drink on the rocks without any mixers.

I opened my eyes to find him keenly waiting.

'So?' he asked.

'I hope you have a bottle with my name on it.'

'Yesssss.' He raised a fist in celebration. 'Consider it done.'

'I'm pretty sure this is something the Duchess would like too. She's been talking to the gardeners about some autumn-coloured flower arrangements for the dining room and library. I think she might like this for some of her smaller events.'

'Do you really think so? How would I get it to her to try?'

'Get me a bottle and I'll take it to her. I'm happy to pay and use mine once I have it.'

'Cheers. It would be wonderful to have some kind of royal seal of approval.'

'Well she's not royal, but I know what you mean.'

I felt someone nudge my arm. 'Am I going to need to carry you out of here?' Mark commented, looking at the glass in my hand.

'You better give him some,' I said to Chris, 'before he feels left out and starts sulking.' While Chris retrieved the bottle, Mark rubbed his eyes in a mock display of tiredness.

'I've just been regaled with stories about an artist who Connie feels reflects my aura in his work. I think she means he's gay, but is trying to find a more ethereal way of saying it.'

'Which one?' I was curious to see which piece of art he meant. I was hoping it would be awful so I could spend the next couple of days teasing him about it.

'Over there, that tall bloke is standing in front of it.'

'Everyone's tall to me, be a bit more specific.' I spent most of my time in other people's shadows, and tonight was no exception.

'The one with a cream blazer and dark brown cords, Mr Mediocrity.'

Mr Mediocrity, as Mark rather cattily called him, was completely blocking the view, but Mark was distracted by the glass of gin Chris had just given him. He took a drink.

'Well, there's no way that artwork is making its way into my house, but I'll have a bottle of this any day of the week.'

Chris smiled at him. 'I'll drop you off a bottle with Sophie's.'

If we were entirely honest, the gin was why we had come this evening, not the artwork. So with that item on the list ticked off, we were both ready to go. We grabbed our coats and sneaked out the door. We didn't mean to be rude by not saying goodbye to Connie, but with her it always turned into one of those painful hour-long goodbyes as she tried to introduce us to everyone we 'just had to meet', and then attempted to sell us a piece of work. I gave Chris another little wave as we slipped out the door and into the welcome night air.

We had both parked our cars at the end of the high street so we ambled along, arm in arm. The rain had dried up and it had turned into a lovely evening. I stopped suddenly, jolting Mark as he attempted to keep walking.

'Look, it's Nathan's studio.' The small shopfront was in darkness. 'Nathan Wallace, Photographic Studio' was painted above the window in beautiful script. The window itself displayed large prints of happy couples on their wedding day and beaming families in studio portraits. Even in the gloom I could see they were well shot.

I tried to look into the building, but I couldn't make anything out. It looked like a business where the owner would be back in the morning rather than one that was now closed, forever. I wondered if someone would come and take it over, buy it all, lock stock and barrel, or if it would just get cleared out and before long it would be like Nathan had never existed. Right now, he was a murder victim in a case without a suspect or a motive, just a rather unusual weapon and a cast of hundreds with the opportunity.

'Come on, it's cold.' Mark tugged at my arm. 'I have a warm man waiting at home for me, which is much more preferable to dwelling on a dead one.'

He had a point, but tomorrow I was determined to start putting some energy into finding out why Nathan was dead.

CHAPTER 12

I had spent the night tossing and turning. It hadn't been helped by the howling gale that had kicked off halfway through the night, causing the windows in my little home to rattle like all the ghosts of Charleton House were trying to get in. I'd then been joined by Pumpkin, who had decided she wanted to snuggle in under the duvet. She must have tried at least four different spots before settling into the small of my back.

The morning had brought further rain and I'd hit snooze three times before slowly forcing myself up and down the stairs. Pumpkin had decided to stay put; she had the right idea. I ground some coffee beans through half closed eyes and somehow managed to make an espresso without scalding myself. A piece of chocolate cake I'd brought home from work would suffice as breakfast.

I sat at the kitchen table, running through what I could remember of the wedding day that might be useful. If I did this while I was still half asleep, then maybe my subconscious would kick into action and I might be able to pull something from the depths of my mind, but all I succeeded in doing was stabbing myself in the lip with my fork.

After a while Pumpkin made her way downstairs and loudly reminded me that I hadn't refilled her bowl. 'You'll stuff yourself with cake first thing in the morning, but me – me you'll let starve,' was my interpretation of the look on her face. I poured the dried food into her bowl and wondered what Gregg would have on the menu for lunch today. At this time of year it was mainly warming stews or hearty pies. He made a particularly nice lamb stew with chicken and raisins.

Gregg – he'd been the first to find the body, which meant he'd spent time alone with Nathan. Could Gregg have killed him? They were both local and their paths would have crossed at a number of weddings at the house. They would definitely have known each other. I could feel my stomach churn at the prospect of Gregg being involved. I was his manager, but we behaved more like equals. He got on with his job and I largely gave him free rein; I trusted him to make the right decisions and he had yet to make me regret that approach. He and his wife Ruth were dedicated to Charleton House; it was a huge part of their lives and I had a really hard time imagining him putting that at risk.

On the other hand, I knew very little about him. We were always focusing so heavily on the menu or event at hand when we got together that I had never really given much thought to who he was outside of the kitchen. I ground a second handful of beans and started to think about what I did know about him. He was a bit of a mystery.

I was just about to put a layer of cream cheese frosting on a tray of pumpkin and cinnamon cupcakes when there was a tap on the kitchen window. Yeshim, as immaculately dressed as ever, was on the other side. She put a finger in the air and mouthed 'Got a minute?' I nodded and she disappeared out of view.

I finished the last cupcake and carried the tray through to

Chelsea to put on display. Wiping my sticky fingers clean, I made Yeshim and myself a mug of coffee.

She was sitting at a table using her phone when I carried the mugs over. She didn't look up as I placed them in front of her.

'Look at this.' She handed her phone over to me; she had been looking at Nathan's account on Instagram. I flicked through the photos. There was everything from traditional weddings in churches to a bride and groom dressed as Harry Potter and Hermione.

I returned it to Yeshim. 'What am I looking for?'

'It's the comments, look.'

She returned the phone, having focused on one. *'Fraud,'* it said. *'This is not his work.'* And another one, *'It's amazing what Photoshop can do. Don't use this photographer, only 1 or 2 photos will be any good.'*

'There're more on dozens of photos and all written by the same person. They call themselves darkraven24. We have a list of photographers we recommend to clients who book their weddings here so I use this as one way of looking at their work and how they present themselves. If they're already on our books like Nathan then I occasionally look at what they've been up to. Do you think it's related? Should I tell Joe?'

'I'd tell Joe, but you know what the internet is like. This sort of thing happens all the time. It's probably just a jealous rival who'd do this anonymously, but was too cowardly to confront Nathan face to face.'

'Probably,' she agreed.

'Is any of it true, do you think?'

Yeshim shook her head. 'No, I've known Nathan for a couple of years and he's had nothing but satisfied customers. Plus it's ridiculous to claim the photos weren't his. I was there when he took a lot of the shots at Charleton, there weren't any other photographers around. I agree with you, it's probably just someone stirring up trouble. I know that Nathan made a few enemies along the way. He was a savvy businessman as well as an artist; he wouldn't let anyone take advantage of him and could be a bit direct in his approach if he didn't like something that was going on. Wouldn't take any prisoners, that sort of thing. But the bottom line is that he was good, very good. He didn't undercut people, he wasn't underhand in his methods. He was the best in the business and that's something that less talented people just can't compete with.'

'Well he met his match with Harriet Smedley, that's for sure.'

Yeshim laughed. 'See, he was human like the rest of us. Maybe she killed him and planned to bury him under the chapel floor, I wouldn't put it past her.'

'Maybe who killed him? Have you solved the case for me?' Joe smiled down at us. 'Morning, ladies, can I feel my ears burning?'

'You certainly can. Yeshim has something to show you; I'll get you a drink.'

I left them to talk and watched them as I poured Joe a coffee. I could have sworn he had lost weight. Joe had always been on the 'cuddly' side, but it looked as if DS Harnby was keeping him on his toes.

As I returned, Yeshim was getting up to leave. 'Joe's going to take a look,' she told me. 'See you later.'

'Is it anything?' I asked him.

'Maybe. I'll get the tech team to see if they can identify darkraven24, but it isn't unusual on social media and they're not threatening, just trying to discredit him.'

'Are you getting anywhere with the case?'

Joe shrugged. 'Not really, and I need things to start moving. DS Harnby is getting jumpy. She's still trying to prove herself and every time something happens here, she goes into overdrive. Having a murder in the most high-profile building on your patch is never good, everyone is watching you.'

'Hope she's not taking it out on you.'

'Not yet, but I'm treading carefully just in case.' He took a gulp of coffee. 'You know, I've heard that coffee goes really well with…'

Before he had a chance to finish, I stood up, rolling my eyes so far into my head I'd have been surprised if he didn't hear them clang as they landed somewhere near the back of my neck. I returned a minute later with a pumpkin and cinnamon cupcake. He grinned at me like a kid who had just been given the Christmas present he'd written to Santa requesting.

With his mouth full of cake, he mumbled, 'I have a question.' Fortunately he waited until he had swallowed before continuing; I didn't fancy being covered in a spray of crumbs. 'When you were about to head out through the Antler Room, did you see Kristian in the area?'

'Amelia's brother?' I thought for a moment. 'No, I don't recall seeing him since the dinner the night before. Well, not until he walked into the pub after the murder. Why, is he a suspect?'

Joe was licking the cream off his fingers. 'Possibly. It turns out that he was in a fight with Nathan about fifteen years ago, we found it on file. No charges were pressed, but he did receive a warning. He claims that it was a drunken thing after Nathan and Amelia split up. It was her idea to split and Nathan spent the next six months trying to get her back. He turned up drunk at a party she was attending with Patrick, got a bit mouthy and Kristian stepped in. Apparently that was the end of it and the two men hadn't seen each other since.'

'Harold didn't mention that to me.'

'What?'

'The fight. He said they'd been a couple, but didn't let on that it was anything other than an amicable split, although I didn't ask for details.'

Joe was looking at me through unblinking eyes. 'Why were you discussing Nathan? You've not reopened the Sophie Lockwood Private Detective Agency again, have you? I did tell you not to get involved.'

'We were talking about him in the pub after the wedding – what else do you think we were going to talk about? It had been a pretty memorable day.'

'Okay, I'll take that, but no probing.' I pretended to salute. 'That's my job, and I have something else to run by you. We're trying to track down Nathan's third camera. One was over his shoulder and trapped underneath him, a second was near his hand, but I've been told he always had a spare in his camera bag. The bag was open and near him, so it looks like he was disturbed when he went to get something. Did you see it anywhere?'

'No I didn't, so I'd say it was either stolen before he was killed, or it was taken by the killer. But why would they take it? It can't be the reason for the murder, unless they were really stupid. It's a risky place to kill just for a camera.'

Joe nodded. 'Agreed. We don't think it was the motive, unless there was something on the camera the killer wanted to conceal; it was most likely panic. But then they've got to get rid of it, and no one has reported seeing someone acting suspiciously with a camera. In fact there's no reports of anyone acting suspiciously anywhere in the house. No one was seen in an area they weren't supposed to be in. Your security team has confirmed there were no unusual activities on CCTV in the house or any of the outside areas. It's like someone was spirited into the Antler Gallery and out again.'

'But it was a busy area: servers coming and going with food, people like Mark and me taking a shortcut. There was lots of opportunity for someone to go in there, kill Nathan and leave.'

Joe sat back in his chair, looking deflated. 'And that's the problem, there was a lot of activity. We've spoken to the catering team – it's made up of people who work together regularly and they all recognised their colleagues. The wedding guests are accounted for, as much as that's possible, and the house was closed to the public by that point. There is one thing, though: how well do you know Gregg?'

'Chef Gregg? Professionally, very well. I wondered if he would be a suspect – are you looking at him because he was the first to find the body?'

'No. Well partly. One of the servers says she saw him arguing with Nathan not long before he found the body. Don't most chefs have a temper?'

It seemed my earlier thoughts hadn't been wrong, and that worried me.

'Stereotypically yes, if you spend all your time watching cooking shows on TV or those behind the scenes in failing restaurants documentaries. They're in a high-stress role, but Gregg isn't like that. He's never lost control.'

'You can't think of any reason why he and Nathan could have argued? They were both local, might they have known each other?'

I thought back to my conversations with Gregg, but nothing came to mind. 'Possibly, but he's never mentioned him to me. I've never seen Gregg really lose his temper; he's had the occasional argument and raised his voice, but nothing serious.'

'Okay, well we'll have to chat to him. The server was pretty adamant it was him and she's worked events here for the last year, so it's not a case of mistaken identity. She knows very well who Gregg is.'

'Well, putting Gregg aside for one moment, as I don't believe he'd do it, we're looking for someone who knew the house or was part of the wedding party. That's a lot of people. Is there anything else on file for Nathan? Anyone else annoyed at him enough to kill him?'

'No, nothing. Hang on, what's this "we're looking for"?'

'Sorry, slip of the tongue, nothing more.'

He eyed me suspiciously. 'I hope so. Just make sure that if you have another one, Harnby is nowhere to be seen.'

I could have sworn he winked, but maybe he just had something in his eye.

I was still smiling to myself about Joe and his departing wink when I looked over at the door and my heart sank. Harriet Smedley, wearing a burgundy red tea-cosy hat, bustled in and straight to the counter.

'One English breakfast tea, and a tea cake please. Which I will consume *in* the café.' If she hadn't made it clear that she wasn't returning to the chapel, I would have offered her a takeout cup just to see the response.

'Of course,' I replied. 'I hope you didn't experience any more issues with the wedding party.'

'No, no. It seems that everyone followed the rules accordingly. The... incident... was of course very sad. I hope the young man is at peace.'

There followed an uncomfortable silence as I prepared her order.

'I was disappointed by one of your staff, however.'

I paused, wondering what was coming next.

'I was round the corner from the Garden Café before the unfortunate incident. I saw the photographer talking to one of your servers. She didn't have her hair tied up, her shirt was untucked, and those trousers – they might be *in fashion,* but as far as I'm concerned, they were far too tight. She's not in a fashion show. You really should keep an eye on that sort of thing, it's not appropriate for somewhere as distinguished as Charleton House.'

And your choice of headwear is? I thought as she carried her tray to a table. It didn't surprise me that she had been sniffing around the wedding on the off chance that someone had stepped out of line and she'd have something else to complain about. Reluctantly, I made a mental note to keep an eye on the servers at the next catering event. The last thing I needed was to give the delightful Harriet Smedley any more ammunition.

. . .

Despite Joe's insistence that I leave the investigative work to the police, I was going to do no such thing. I was curious; more than that, I was fascinated. I wasn't prepared to accept Gregg as a suspect, so that threw the field wide open and left us with an impossible situation. How had the impossible become possible? How could someone who was completely out of place go unnoticed in such a busy part of the house while a wedding was on? Everyone who works in Charleton House knows to be on the lookout for suspicious behaviour. The house is full of incredibly valuable objects and we are always checking that staff have their badges or passes on display and that no one has wandered into areas that are off limits. You even need a special pass to go behind the ropes that serve as a barrier between the public and some of the more precious objects and furniture. Charleton doesn't have the most high-tech security set up, but what it does have is a lot of eyes on the ground, and on this day the eyes hadn't seen anything unusual. I wanted to find out more.

I decided to start with Patrick and Amelia, the bride and groom. It seemed really odd that they would have Nathan as their wedding photographer. Not only was he Amelia's ex-boyfriend, but he was someone who had caused enough of a problem that Kristian had stepped in and punched him. The newlyweds were staying in a cottage on the Charleton Estate, one of four cottages dotted about the grounds that could be hired by the public for holidays. They were beautifully renovated and their decor had been chosen by the Duchess herself. Amelia and Patrick were staying in Pheasant Cottage, which was along a gravel track about fifteen minutes' drive from the house.

I waited until after lunch, and then with a large gift basket containing two portions of beef stew, a bottle of red wine and two enormous pieces of chocolate cake, I set off. It was a cold grey day and I turned the heating on full blast when I first got in the car. I had to hold myself back; I was keen to hear what they could tell me, but knew I had to keep to the speed limit. The last thing I needed was an ear bashing from security if they saw me shoot out of the car park at forty mph.

The track ran along the edge of a small valley, and at the end, with a wonderful view over one half of the estate and the river that wound its way along the bottom of the valley, sat the old worker's cottage. The stone work had been cleaned and the window frames painted a pale green. I could see smoke coming out of the chimney and lights on inside.

I parked up and carried the basket to the door. Balancing it awkwardly on my hip, I used the brass door knocker that took the shape of a pheasant's head. Amelia opened the door in jeans and a pale pink sweater, her blonde hair tied back, and as far as I could tell she wasn't wearing any makeup, but she still looked beautiful and perfectly at home framed in the doorway of the cottage.

She looked momentarily confused, and then seemed to recognise me.

'Oh, hello, you're from the house, aren't you?'

'I'm Sophie, the catering manager. I thought I'd bring you this; I can't imagine you're in much of a mood to cook at the moment and it might help.'

She looked at the basket. 'Thank you, come in. We've just got back from a walk and are warming up by the fire, come through.'

She led me into the small but cosy and stylishly decorated room. The furniture was all cream and had faux fur throws to curl up under. A large sheepskin rug lay in front of the fire, and minimalist artwork displayed views of the estate. A particularly impressive sketch of a stag was hanging over the fireplace.

Patrick sat by the fire, adding a piece of wood. He stood up as we walked in.

'I remember you; you found Nathan's body.'

'Not really,' I corrected him. 'That was Gregg, my chef, but I was one of the first on the scene. I brought you this.' I handed the basket over to him and he placed it on a coffee table, and together he and Amelia had a look through.

'Thank you. We just opened a bottle of wine, can I get you a glass?'

I sat down and accepted a small glass of red wine. I felt like I was encroaching on a romantic afternoon, but I wasn't going to stay any longer than I needed to.

'How are you both? This isn't the relaxing week you were hoping for, I'm sure.'

'No.' Amelia sat on the floor by the fire, leaning against Patrick's legs as he sat in the armchair behind her. 'We had booked the week here so we could spend time with family and friends before going on our honeymoon next weekend, make it a group holiday for everyone. Most of the cottages on site are being used by family members, but one or two have gone home early. We're just trying to make the most of our time here.'

'I have to say you seem remarkably calm. A lot of brides I've come across wouldn't handle it so well.' I was surprised; there was no sign of the bickering couple that I'd heard so much about and glimpsed at the dinner. Maybe this experience had calmed them down a bit, made them think about the important things in life.

Amelia looked up at Patrick and smiled. 'I wasn't so calm the last couple of days, I guess I've rather run out of energy.'

I watched Patrick stroke the back of his wife's head. At least they seemed to have genuine affection for one another.

'Had you seen Nathan much before the wedding?'

There was a second or two's silence.

'No.' Amelia was looking down at the carpet and seemed to be picking at the threads. I noticed that Patrick had removed his hand from her hair. 'He was a last-minute booking so we never actually met face to face until the night of the dinner, and after that we just left him to get on with the job.'

I sensed a change in the atmosphere. Not much, but enough to be discernible.

'It's handy that he was available on such short notice. Did your original photographer cancel?' That was a complete guess on my part, but I couldn't imagine a wedding of this size not having a photographer booked months in advance.

'He did. He broke his leg mountain biking, but he recommended Nathan and, well, I knew he was good, so I called him.'

'So you didn't look for Nathan?'

'No.' Patrick sounded annoyed. 'Of course we didn't. Why would we want to? We hadn't see him for years, and when we last saw him, well, let's just say we didn't part on good terms. But we needed someone fast and he was available, end of story.' He emptied his wine glass. 'It's very nice of you to bring the food, Sophie, but we really need a quiet afternoon after everything that's happened. I'm sure you understand.'

My cue to leave couldn't have been clearer. Patrick shook my hand and left Amelia to walk me out.

'Everyone at the house has been so kind, we're really very grateful,' she commented as she opened the door. 'Thank you again for the gifts, it was really very sweet.'

She closed the door behind me. As I walked to the car, I thought about how all I'd managed to do was confirm that they knew Nathan and get a slight acknowledgement of the fight years ago, which the police were already aware of.

I was about to climb into the car when I heard the door to the cottage open. Amelia slipped out.

'Sophie.' As she got closer, she dropped her voice. 'Sophie, I'm worried people might have got the wrong idea of Patrick.' I was confused and my face must have shown it. 'The argument we had before the dinner on Friday, I know people saw and heard us.' I didn't know anything about it, but I decided to pretend otherwise.

'Yes, I did wonder. I'm afraid I heard most of it and it doesn't look good, especially now. Why don't you tell me what really happened?'

Amelia glanced over at the door. She pulled a packet of cigarettes out of her back pocket and lit one, taking a long drag. I stepped back, wanting to avoid the ghastly smelling smoke.

'I told Patrick I wanted to ask your advice about local places to eat so I can't be out here long.' She took another drag. 'Nathan was a last-minute booking, but we had about two weeks' notice so although I was limited in choice, I could have probably got someone else if I'd really tried. But Patrick and I had just had a huge row. I knew Nathan worked weddings here, so I decided to see if he was free. I figured that would be my way of getting back at Patrick. By the time I'd calmed down and realised how stupid it was, I'd already signed the contract. I told Patrick just before the dinner, before he saw Nathan, and that was why he was so angry and didn't like having his picture taken that night. I don't blame him, it was a stupid thing to do. Fortunately he was okay the next day. I know that he said some awful things about Nathan,' I nodded as if I'd heard them, 'but he's not a violent man. I promise.'

'But you used your wedding day to get back at your husband.'

'I know, it was stupid.'

'If anyone says anything, I'll shut it down.' In reality no one had said a peep, and most gossip made its way to the café eventually. None of the staff had been talking about Amelia and Patrick; their constant bickering had been well and truly overshadowed.

'Thanks.' Amelia looked relieved as she dropped the cigarette and ground it under her shoe before running back into the house. I stared at it, horrified, and picked it up.

So Patrick had had no idea Nathan was going to be there – an ex-boyfriend of Amelia's who had done something bad enough to make Kristian punch him. As far as I was concerned, there were now two suspects on the list, no matter what Amelia said.

. . .

I drove carefully back down the gravel road, avoiding puddles that as far as I knew could be a foot deep. A herd of deer sheltered from the cold wind under nearby trees, and sheep minded their own business as they kept the grass short. The rain had started to pick up and big drops landed on my windscreen. Charleton House was beginning to vanish behind a wall of grey weather.

A lone figure came into view as I turned a corner. Suzanne was on another of her runs. I would have thought her crazy, but then it would have been dry when she set off. I wound my window down as I slowed next to her.

'Do you want a lift?'

She hesitated, and then jumped in. 'Thanks, even I have my limit and that rain is really coming down.' Her hair was plastered to the side of her face and her clothes clung to her athletic physique.

'I'm impressed you set off at all, it's a miserable day.'

'I needed to get out, clear my head. Running really helps. Where have you been?'

'I went to see Amelia and Patrick; I thought they'd appreciate some home cooking, save them the trouble. I can't imagine they're in the mood for anything other than shoving something in a microwave.'

'That was good of you. Maybe they'll be left alone long enough to enjoy it.' There was a sarcastic edge to her voice.

'Have there been problems?'

'Not at all, unless you count the press and the police. Both have been hounding them. It was nothing to do with them, they're victims too. Their wedding was ruined, their week here has so far been spent hiding in the cottage to stay clear of journalists and photographers. They're finding it really hard.'

'Why are the police interested?' I looked over at her. Her face was set hard and she stared straight ahead. For a moment I thought she wasn't going to respond.

'Patrick and Nathan were seen arguing a couple of times, but it's hardly surprising. You find an ex-boyfriend of your wife is going to be your wedding photographer and I'm sure most people would be livid. I know Patrick can have a temper, but it's nothing serious. I've known him since I was eighteen and he wouldn't hurt anyone. He's a nice guy, he just raises his voice, like a lot of people. He should be left alone.' It sounded like a demand, not a wish.

'How well did you know Nathan?'

'Well enough to know that he got what he deserved.'

'Really?' Distracted, I drove us through a pothole that caused us both to leave our seats. 'Sorry, what do you mean?'

'Nothing, I just meant… he was a complete jerk about Amelia leaving him for Patrick.' She had softened her tone a little.

As I drove slowly down a straight stretch of road, I considered the woman next to me. She was extremely fit and the line of muscle definition in her arms showed how much strength she possessed. Had I just seen a glimpse of someone who could become angry enough to kill?

CHAPTER 13

Charleton House could be divided into three parts. A third was open to the public, a third formed the business operation and had been turned into offices and storerooms, and the final third was the private quarters of the Fitzwilliam-Scott family. I was fortunate enough to have reason to make regular visits to those private quarters for meetings with the Duke and Duchess, or to help prepare for private events.

Today was one of those days as the Duchess was hosting a private lunch for the Mayor of Sheffield, a nearby city with a history embedded in the industrial revolution. The Mayor, Kathleen Carsdale, was one of only three female mayors in the whole of the UK, and she and the Duchess had become firm friends.

The two of them were framed by a window as I entered the dining room. Their backs were towards me and I paused briefly. Even though the light meant I was looking at two silhouettes, it was impossible not to see the strong, confident postures and perfectly fitting clothes. They were both the kind of women that I admired, but far from being imposing characters who could intimidate, they were warm and friendly and made me feel like the most important person in the room when they spoke to me.

'Sophie, you've met Kathleen, haven't you?' Together the women crossed the room and I could make out their faces and the detail of their outfits. The Duchess, casually dressed in jeans and a navy polo neck, was only missing riding boots and a wax jacket and she'd look like the off-duty country lady she was. The Mayor, who I assumed was here between engagements, was much more smartly dressed in a pale blue skirt suit and a simple set of pearls round her neck, her neat blonde hair in a perfect bun. She reminded me a lot of Joyce, if Joyce had ever been inclined to wear pastels and refrain from applying an inch of makeup and an entire can of hairspray.

'Lovely to see you, Sophie, I do hope this weather isn't stopping people heading to your cafés.'

'It is a lot quieter than usual,' I acknowledged, 'but no more so than we'd expect at this time of year. Our figures are still healthy.'

'I'm very glad to hear it.'

Behind me, Gregg was pouring two glasses of white wine, having laid out two plates of salad. The ingredients were all beautiful autumnal colours, many of them from our own kitchen gardens. There was butternut squash and beets, figs that I knew were perfectly soft and juicy, because I'd stolen one as Gregg had worked earlier, and freshly made bread, brought up straight from the oven and served with butter from a farm on the estate. I knew there was a warm cardamom and apple tart to follow. The thinly sliced apple, laid out like tightly packed rose petals, created a stunning effect that you almost didn't want to spoil by slicing into it. I had helped Gregg bring everything up. To be honest, he probably could have managed with a catering cart, but I was always after an excuse to venture into the private apartments and insisted he needed my help!

'Is there any news on the investigation?' asked the Duchess. 'I do hope the police are close to solving it, there have been too many deaths here in recent months. I'm starting to wonder if I need to be continuously looking over my shoulder. Have you any thoughts on the matter, Sophie?' She was referring to my involvement in solving the two previous murders at the house. I was already starting to get a bit of reputation, and whether it was good or bad depended on who you asked.

'I think it's proving rather challenging, but I'm sure they'll have a breakthrough soon.'

'I heard about that, so unfortunate,' said the Mayor. 'I met Nathan Wallace last year. He was working on a photographic project for the council. I recall him being extremely talented, but he could rub people up the wrong way.'

That got my attention. 'In what way?'

She thought for a moment. 'He had a good sense of humour, only he didn't always know when he was crossing a line and could take a joke too far, or not realise when someone was tired of being teased, that sort of thing. He'd still find whatever he was saying amusing while everyone else was starting to get a bit tired of it – does that make sense?'

'It does.' That was interesting.

As I left the room, I heard the Duchess toast her friend. 'Happy birthday, my dear Kathleen, you really don't look a day over twenty-one.' The tinkle of laughter followed me down the stairs while I thought about what I'd just learnt.

Gregg and I returned to the Duke and Duchess's kitchen to tidy up. It was a modern, light room, full of marble and stainless steel, and the best stove and appliances money could buy – a sharp contrast to the ornate rooms full of antiques that surrounded it.

'Any leftovers?' Derek Veazie had stuck his head around the door. Gregg laughed.

'You're out of luck, Derek. You not had lunch?'

'Of course, but you know I'll never pass up the chance to eat anything you've made.'

'What are you doing here?' I asked as Derek sat on a stool and watched us work.

'I'm driving the Mayor, I fill in sometimes when her driver is on holiday. My sister works in the Mayor's offices and gets me the occasional job. I've just been upstairs with Gloria, she has some work for me next month.'

Gloria was the Duchess's PA, and she was fearsomely protective of her boss's diary. She was fearsome in many other ways too, but I'd managed to tame her by organising an afternoon tea fit for royalty for her mother's ninetieth birthday. I'd made sure the red carpet had been rolled out in every possible way and Gloria had been a fan ever since – a relationship that I made sure prospered by leaving the occasional plate of warm cookies on her desk.

'What've you done 'em for afters?'

'Cardamom and apple tart, and no there won't be any left. The Duke hoovers up any desserts the Duchess doesn't finish, he has a real sweet tooth.'

'Damn, I liked the sound of that. Well I should be off, I've got time to get some shopping in before I need to be back to pick the Mayor up.'

Derek vanished as quickly as he had appeared.

'I notice he didn't offer to help,' Gregg complained goodnaturedly. 'Next time I'll shove a cloth in his hand and he can pay me back for all the free food he's had over the years.'

In order to get to the Library Café, I had to walk through the security reception and show my staff pass, before getting onto the back lane and then walking through a side door into the main body of the house. Next door to reception was the security office, home to a bank of monitors, where an officer would watch all the comings and goings on the CCTV cameras. This was where I was heading. It was, strictly speaking, off limits to me, but that was a rule I was starting to break on a regular basis.

I peered through the window and saw that Roger, a jovial

grey-haired man who was partial to my baking, was on duty. He was leaning back in his chair, feet on the desk in front of the monitors and talking on the phone. Rapping my knuckles on the glass and making him jump, I grinned at him and waved. A moment later the door was opened.

'Come on in, Soph, quick, mind. Grab a seat in that corner then no one will see you if they look in.'

'Am I right in thinking you were working the dinner on Friday night?'

'You are, love. I'd done the day shift, but stayed to do a couple of hours' overtime. Nice easy gig it was. I was on the gate as the guests arrived, then we locked up and I spent the rest of my shift in here. I was back home by the time it was all finished. Why you asking?'

'I was wondering if you overheard an argument between the bride and groom? Apparently they had a bit of a set to.'

Roger had his hands on his stomach and they moved up and down as he laughed. He would have made a great Santa Claus if his beard had been a bit longer and his uniform red instead of navy blue.

'I'd have been surprised if they hadn't heard it over in Sheffield, right humdinger it was. They seemed right enough when they arrived, but that photographer appeared to take pictures of them. The main entrance had been lit up and looked really special, so he wanted to capture them walking in like they owned the place. Well as soon as the groom saw him, he hit the roof. His missus, well missus-to-be, was trying to calm him down.'

'Did Nathan get involved?'

'No, he stopped taking photos and stood well back. Didn't seem to want any part in it. He – the groom – calmed down after a couple of minutes of ranting. Looked like he'd got it all out of his system.'

'Did you hear anything that Patrick was saying?'

'Oh aye, but it was all the same sort of thing: "Don't want you here, not my idea, stay out of my way", that kind of thing. Nothing too bad. I stepped out of the doorway to let them all know I was there, which seemed to calm them down. Good job too. I didn't want to have to get involved, not when they were the ones getting married, but he seemed to get the point when I made myself known.'

Nathan's presence had certainly caused a reaction in Patrick, but one he seemed able to control. That didn't seem like a man who would get angry enough to kill, but he certainly had a temper and I wondered if the outcome would have been different if the two men had been alone.

'Thanks, Roger, I was just curious.

'Just curious? Is that what you call it? I've heard about the help you gave our Joe Greene last time, are you sniffing around again?'

'No, no, just… well, you know.' I didn't know how to finish. I hated to lie to Roger, but he saved me the need. He tapped his finger on the side of his nose.

'I won't say a word. Anyway, I won't be able to if I'm eating one of your cookies.' That made me laugh and I promised I'd drop by later with a fresh batch.

I stepped out of the office and nearly walked into Oliver Hardy, or rather his lookalike, Derek the chauffeur.

'Oops, sorry.' I stumbled as I backed away and he took my arm.

'Steady there. Hello, Sophie, dashing around a bit today? Got lots on?'

'No, just not looking where I'm going.' I looked at his car; it had been polished until you could see your face in it.

'How is everyone here after Saturday night?' he asked. 'That was quite a shock. Unlike any wedding I've been to before.'

'Other than the press hanging around and the police coming and going, you'd never know it had happened. Did you know him well? Nathan? You must have worked a few weddings together.'

'We did. I didn't have all that much to do with him. He was polite, businesslike, his focus was always on the bride and groom unless they wanted a shot with the car, and I got used to what Nathan wanted, so I was never with him for all that long.'

'What about at family events? Didn't Amelia ever bring him along when they were together?'

Derek shook his head. 'She and Nathan split up a long time before her mum and I first met. Anyway, we prefer family only, small dinners, that sort of thing. We don't get to spend a lot of time with the kids, so when we do it's precious and we want to focus on them, not their friends. Of course, when Patrick proposed to Amelia, he became part of the family too. They did mention Nathan from time to time, though.'

I nodded, storing this information in my mind. 'When you worked with him, did he ever mention that he'd had a run in with anyone, or been threatened?'

'Ha, to me? Never. It wasn't that kind of relationship. We barely said hello.' Derek's phone beeped and he pulled it out of his back pocket to read the message.

'Did anyone else in the wedding business talk about him?'

'Sorry, I need to get ready. That's the Mayor, she's almost done. I've never heard anything about him. I do cross paths with different drivers, photographers, event managers, that sort of thing, and we help each other out from time to time. But Nathan kept to himself. A dedicated businessman, I guess you'd call him. See you around.'

He tipped his hat, pulled on his leather gloves and climbed in the car. I watched him drive up the lane so he was closer to the side door. He was clearly a man who knew his way around the house.

Perhaps Derek Veazie was deserving of a bit more thought.

CHAPTER 14

Mark's office was up a narrow flight of stairs above the visitors' toilets. I opened the door to a wall of stuffy heat that made me cough, but each of the four desks in the office was unoccupied. The room was eerily quiet.

The silence was soon broken by the sound of visitors entering into the courtyard below. I opened a window and breathed in the fresh air, watching the school group gather just below me. They looked to be in their teens and were being spoken to by a young man who was wearing a Victorian outfit. He had on close-cut plaid trousers and a long frock coat. In one hand he held a top hat and the other a cane with a gold top.

He was one of the live interpreters who gave talks and tours while acting the role of someone associated with the history of the house. They were incredibly knowledgeable and spent a lot of time researching the people they would play and the events in their lives. I perched on the windowsill and listened as the gentleman explained to his young audience that he was a friend of George Aloysius Fitzwilliam-Scott, the 7th Duke of Ravensbury. He had been charged by the Duke's mother with the task of helping him find a wife. It appeared the Duke's mother was greatly concerned that he had not yet married and produced an heir. The Duke, on the other hand, was more interested in politics.

'My mother is a dear friend of hers, you see, so I felt obliged to assist. I know the Duke reasonably well, but not enough to speak directly to him about this matter. I can invite a variety of eligible ladies to dinner, but I cannot force him to take a fancy to them. Now I'm running out of options – I've asked all my own single female friends, and their friends, and even some of their friends, but to no avail.'

He scanned the group of teenagers before him. One or two were chatting, but most of them were enjoying the performance.

'Have you seen any attractive young women around the house today? Anyone who looks like they might make a suitable Duchess? To be honest with you, I'm not sure the Duke is that fussy, so she doesn't have to be all that attractive.'

'Why don't you marry him?' one of the youngsters called out. This was going to get interesting. The live interpreters were brilliant at thinking on their feet and dealing with all sorts of situations without slipping out of character. The 'Duke's friend' looked momentarily confused, and then laughed.

'But, young man, that's simply not possible. Two men cannot marry.'

'Yes, they can.' The second teenager was at the front of the crowd and I could see him clearly. He wasn't laughing or nudging his friends; instead, he rolled his eyes as he spoke, like he was dealing with an idiot. I realised he was being deadly serious, and no one was contradicting him.

'Don't jump.'

I turned to see Mark closing the door behind him. I stood up and pushed the window to, leaving it open a crack so I didn't suffocate in the heat of the office.

'What are you doing?'

'I'm watching the Victorians being schooled in gay rights.' I told Mark what I'd just witnessed and he laughed.

'Well that gives you hope. If anyone had tried that when I was a teenager, they'd have had their head forced down the toilet before you could say Elton John.'

'How were your VIPs?' I asked as I settled in a chair next to his desk.

'So silent I'm not sure they spoke English. I think some people come here just to tick a box. Not to worry – the house coffers get their pieces of silver, I get to stretch my legs and the VIPs get to spend a few hours out of the rain. Not a bad use of ninety minutes. What are you doing here, anyway, missing my company?'

'Always, dear,' I replied sarcastically. 'No, I wanted to run something past you, but I don't like what I'm about to say.'

Mark kicked his shoes off, and then turned his attention to me.

'I've been thinking about Saturday and how Gregg found Nathan's body. Well, couldn't it be the case that the reason Gregg was leaving the Antler Gallery was because he was the one who killed Nathan?' I screwed up my face like there was a bad smell. I felt truly awful thinking it, and even worse saying it out loud.

Mark opened his eyes wide and leaned back in his chair, putting his feet on the desk.

'I'll be honest with you, Sherlock, it had crossed my mind, but I didn't even want to go there. Just the thought of it makes me feel sick. But the police must have already thought of that, and if he was in any way involved, Joe would have carted him off by now. Is Gregg still at work?'

'Yes, he's currently in the kitchens preparing menus for the next couple of months.'

'There you go then. The police must be happy that he's innocent.'

'Or they just don't have enough evidence,' I added.

'Either way, he's not locked up.'

'You're right. I just needed to say it out loud and get some reassurance.' I stood up and walked over to the window; there was no sign of the group of teens. I did, however, spot Harriet Smedley walking across the courtyard so I quickly stepped out of sight. I didn't know what it was about that woman, but I automatically felt like I was in trouble whenever I saw her.

'Well consider yourself reassured.'

I left Mark to it, but I was still feeling uneasy.

I walked across the courtyard where the Victorian gentleman had sought the help of the school group, and out of the main entrance. Visitors drove slowly past me as they made their way out of the car park; a golf buggy with members of the gardening team trundled past and they all gave me a wave. Behind them was a silver saloon car, which I vaguely recognised. Gregg was in the back seat, staring out of the window, but he didn't see me.

Then I realised why I knew the car: it was an unmarked police car that I had seen Joe drive a couple of times. It looked as if Gregg was of interest to the police after all. I ran round the corner of the building, through reception without bothering to show my pass, dodging staff and visitors until I made it to the Library Café kitchen. I wanted to phone Ruth, but I turned the corner to see her walk into my office.

'Ruth, what's going on?'

She looked pale and tired, unusual for someone who was usually rosy-cheeked and full of energy – something I put down to her permanently inhaling sugar.

'The police want to question him further. It's ridiculous, he had nothing to do with Nathan's death. He's not been sleeping since he found the body, he was horrified.' She sat on the edge of my desk. 'He didn't know Nathan well, he has no motive, and anyway he was in the middle of dinner prep. He didn't have time to leave the kitchen, not until he realised he'd left his phone in the car and had to go and get it as there were a couple of notes on it he needed. That was when he found Nathan.'

'But he was seen arguing with Nathan outside the Antler Room. Do you know anything about that?'

'No, nothing. He told me he was in the kitchen the whole time. You know him – he can get irritated, like anyone, and he's had the odd argument, but he doesn't lose his temper. He's always in control. Is it okay if I leave? I need to go down to the station and wait for him.'

'Of course, go now. Keep me posted.'

'Thanks, Sophie.'

I watched her walk through the kitchen, still not wanting to believe that Gregg had anything to do with Nathan's murder, but his being taken in for questioning made me think that the police were starting to seriously view him as a suspect. I looked around my matchbox-sized office, which felt particularly claustrophobic right now. I needed to get out. I needed fresh air.

CHAPTER 15

J was starting to wonder when I'd get any work done, but seeing as I was in charge, I didn't have to worry about getting into trouble. It was time that I showed the Stables Café team some support, so I used that as an excuse to get some air.

I wasn't surprised to be quizzed by them on the events of the previous weekend. Their heads were full of gossip about Nathan, and whether it was true that he'd been killed by the bride's mother, the bride's father, the best woman or the gamekeeper. I put the last suggestion down simply to the fact that a set of antlers had been involved; what other reason a gamekeeper would have to be at the wedding, I really didn't know. I wouldn't have been surprised if gossip had included the Duke's two black Labradors as possible killers.

Apparently, one or two members of the press were still combing the area, looking for employees they could bribe to get them into the house. I was actually pleased to hear that as it meant that the security officers were doing a good job of spotting them at the main entrance and sending them packing. Here at the Stables, Martin also appeared to be doing a great job, and as I left, one of his team even asked if he was going to keep the job on a permanent basis. I gave a noncommittal comment in reply and made a mental note to tell Martin what had been said. It was a great reflection on his work.

I was about to leave when I saw the server who had been the object of Levi's wandering eyes and whom I had seen crying after Nathan's body had been found. I pulled her aside, away from the visitors, and asked how she was doing.

'I'm okay, thanks, it was just the shock. I've never experienced a death before, not even in my family, and now it's murder.'

I hadn't talked to her very often; she'd been hired by the supervisors at the start of the summer, along with a number of other temporary staff, but they'd clearly liked her enough to keep her on over the winter. I hated to admit it, but I couldn't remember her name. Thank goodness for name badges, they'd got me out of many a sticky situation. Hers said her name was Olivia and she seemed young, maybe eighteen. She was playing with a ring on her finger, spinning it around and around.

'Is everything okay?'

'Yes. No. I don't know.' She swapped the ring to another finger. 'When the police questioned me, I didn't tell them everything. I think I might have been the reason that photographer was killed.'

'What on earth makes you think that?' She looked around. 'Do you want to go to my office? We can talk in private.'

'No, it's fine. It was that actor…'

'Levi?'

She nodded. 'At the dinner on Friday, he started chatting me up, wouldn't leave me alone. Well, the photographer, he was leaving and saw what was happening. I was stuck in a corner and couldn't get away. Levi wouldn't move, he just kept trying to get me to go out with him, wouldn't take no for an answer. The photographer grabbed Levi and told him to leave me alone. I thought they were going to have a fight, Levi was so angry he went bright red.'

I gave her a moment to carry on, but she seemed to have finished.

'So why would you be the reason Nathan was killed?'

'Maybe Levi was so angry, he killed him. Because of me. Because Nathan was protecting me.'

'Even if that was why he was killed, and I don't think it was, it's not your fault. Levi was harassing you. He was in the wrong. I mean it, Olivia.' She nodded unconvincingly. 'Look, how about I talk to Joe, one of the detectives on the case? He's a friend of mine. He will probably want to talk to you again, but I promise you are not in any trouble.'

'What about me not telling them everything in the beginning?'

'You'll be fine, I promise.'

'Okay.'

'Go back to work, it will all be okay.' I gave her what I hoped would be a reassuring smile and watched her help a young boy choose a cake. Levi was a real slimeball and I loved the idea of Joe giving him a hard time; it was the least he deserved.

I left the café and stepped outside. Joe was hovering in the courtyard.

'Are you following me?' I asked him with a smile as I joined him.

'Well, yes, actually I am. Fancy a walk?'

'One minute.' I ducked back into the café and got Olivia to make Joe a coffee. I decided to break the habit of a lifetime and had a hot chocolate, but only because I wanted lashings of squirty cream and marshmallows. The grin on Joe's face when I returned outside told me I'd made the right decision.

'Ahhh, cheers. I was up at the crack of dawn going through Nathan's phone records and bank statements.'

We walked up the hill and around a wall that brought us to an open gate. In the summer months, we charged people to get into the gardens without a ticket to the house, but in the winter anyone could come in. We were miles from any town, and there was limited public transport which meant that we never had any trouble. The worst you'd get is a couple of harmless drunk teenagers on a summer's night trying to climb the walls. At this time of year, it was cold and wet enough that you had to really want to be here.

After walking through the stone archway, we followed the wall of the house all the way to the patio outside the Garden Café and sat on a bench. It was dry, but the cold seeped through my coat.

'This is a much darker place than I ever realised,' Joe said as he looked out across the valley.

'It probably always has been; it's just that many of the stories get hidden from us in order to protect the family's reputation.'

'I thought the Duke was pretty laid back about people discovering the stories of the Fitzwilliam-Scott family?'

'He is,' I confirmed, 'but that doesn't mean his ancestors were. I'm sure there's a lot we don't know, that the Duke doesn't know. Clearly the stories are still stacking up.'

'How has the Duke taken it?'

'I've barely seen him since it happened, not to talk to.' I took the lid off my takeout cup and fished out some of the melting marshmallows with a finger. I turned to see Joe watching me with a bemused look on his face. 'What? I might work for a Duke and Duchess, but I've never claimed to be a lady myself.'

Joe put his hands up in surrender. 'I never said a word.'

'You didn't need to.' Next I scooped out some cream. I was about to put it in my mouth when it fell off and landed on the front of my coat. Joe burst out laughing.

'That'll teach you.'

I shook my head; it was a good job I wasn't trying to seduce him.

'Who's that?' Joe was looking out in the direction of the rock garden. A couple were walking away from us. 'They look familiar.'

'Familiar? Who else would be going for a walk on a gravel path in lime green stilettos paired with a bright orange coat?'

'Joyce?'

'Full marks.'

As we watched, the tall grey-haired man put his arm around Joyce's shoulders and pulled her tightly against his side. She slipped her arm around his waist.

'That must be Harold. They're rather sweet together.'

'Harry and Cookie.' He smirked as he said it. 'Mark told me.' I elbowed him.

'Hey, it's cute. I'm pleased for them, especially now. It must be quite upsetting for all the family and it's nice for Harold to have her support, especially if his son is a suspect.'

'Who said anything about Patrick being a suspect?' Joe had quickly gone from sneering teenager to serious police detective.

'No one. But he clearly wasn't happy to have Nathan here and they do have history,' I explained.

'It's fifteen years since Amelia and Nathan were dating.'

'Some people carry grudges for longer than that, and he flipped when he saw Nathan for the first time.' I looked up at Joe. 'He's not who you're focusing on, is he?'

'No, and I can't tell you any more.'

'Who just got you a coffee, which means you'll be able to keep on working until late tonight?'

'It'll take more than a coffee for me to achieve that.'

'So how's it looking for Kristian? He punched Nathan fifteen years ago – has he finally taken the opportunity to finish him off?'

'That's what we're trying to figure out. It's hard to believe that he would kill him after so long if Nathan hadn't done something to provoke him, so we're trying to track both their movements in the run up to the wedding. It might be that they met up and had an argument that kicked it all off again; maybe they ran into each other accidentally. Kristian denies it, of course, but we want to be sure.'

'Well I've got someone else to throw into the mix for you.'

Joe did an exaggerated eye roll. 'Of course you have. Go on.'

As I told him about Olivia and Levi, his expression changed to one of distaste.

'What a creep. I'll make sure Harnby knows. He's definitely worth talking to, and if you see Olivia again, tell her not to worry. We will need to talk to her, but we won't give her a hard time about not telling us in the first place. That's not what matters now.' He drank his coffee and seemed to disappear into his thoughts, but I had a question for him.

'I was wondering… what about Gregg?' I was still feeling uncomfortable about this, despite Mark's reassurance.

'What about him?'

'I watched him being driven off. He's a suspect, isn't he?'

'Look, Sophie, I know this is hard, he's part of your team, but we have to explore every avenue.'

'I know you do, but come on, Gregg? What evidence do you have?'

'This is an investigation, Soph. If we're given information that raises questions, we investigate. It's what we do.'

He wasn't going to put me off that easily. 'What information? That he argued with Nathan? That doesn't make him a killer. Besides which, I find it hard to believe he had time to leave the kitchen. Who claims to have seen them?'

'Soph, give it a rest. I've already told you more than I should.'

'I know, and I know you could get in a lot of trouble, but I've been able to help so far, haven't I?'

He pretended to glare at me, but he couldn't sustain it. 'No more questions, okay? Talking of which, DS Harnby is starting to ask questions about you, so I suggest you don't give her any reason to worry.'

I nodded, but I was already rolling a few more ideas around my head and I wasn't going to let on to Joe.

There was a roaring fire burning in the large stone fireplace that dominated one end of the Black Swan pub, and the welcome glow made my shoulders immediately soften and relax. I heard my group before I saw them. Joyce's cackling laughter guided me to a large round table at the far side of the fireplace. Mark was holding court, and Harold and Joyce were laughing their way through the story he was regaling them with.

'What can I get you, Sophie?' Craig suddenly appeared next to me. 'I'm getting an order in at the bar, so what are you drinking?'

'Gin and tonic, please, Father.'

'You'll have to narrow it down for me, they have over seventy.'

'Close your eyes and point.' He looked confused. 'I'm not joking. Close your eyes and point at the list of gins; it's how I do it if I can't decide.'

He still looked bemused as he walked back to the bar.

'Sophie dear, you made it.' Joyce stared at her male companions. 'At least make a pretence of being gentlemen and make some room for her.' Mark and Harold shuffled round and made space for me, Mark muttering something under his breath about me never having been a lady so he didn't know why he should be a gentleman.

'I heard that, Mark Boxer, just do as you're told,' Joyce responded. I peeled off my coat and could feel the heat of the fire on my back.

Craig arrived at the table and distributed the drinks.

'Cheers, mate... er, Father,' was Harold's response, and it was the first time I'd heard evidence of an Australian accent sneaking out.

'I followed your instructions, Sophie, and you've got Dragon's Back gin. I hope that will suffice.'

'It's gin, it'll suffice,' commented Mark as he reached for his pint of beer. 'How goes it, padre, are your flock behaving themselves?'

Craig scratched the stubble on his chin. 'Most of them. Two of them are crossing the line, though.' We waited for him to continue. 'I had a couple in today, planning their spring wedding. It was all going really well – lovely couple. Plans are a little unusual, but nothing that would raise alarm bells, until they revealed that they are having a pirate-themed party and asked if I would dress as Long John Silver.'

'Ha!' Mark threw his head back. 'Priceless. Are you going for it? Please say you are, you'd look great with an eye patch.'

Craig just shook his head. 'The eye patch isn't a problem, it's the wooden leg. You can guarantee I'd go head over heels as I walked down the aisle, and can you imagine what Harriet would say?'

'She could be your parrot.'

I immediately imagined Harriet Smedley dressed as a pirate – I couldn't stretch as far as a parrot – and desperately wished that Craig would agree to the wedding.

'Tell us you'll do it,' I said with a sense of glee. He shook his head.

'It's just not right for Charleton House, doesn't fit the dignity of the place or the family. I don't mind that sort of thing in general, just not here.'

It made sense, and when he put it like that, I couldn't disagree. Charleton House wasn't a theme park, it was a family home with a significant history. The talk of weddings brought me back to our recent drama and I looked over at Harold.

'How are Patrick and Amelia?'

'Okay, surprisingly. I think it's all gradually sinking in and now they're just trying to enjoy the last couple of days before they head off on their proper honeymoon. I think the time alone after all the stress of planning the wedding in the first place will be good for them.'

'I went to see them yesterday. I saw Suzanne afterwards. She seemed to think the whole thing was incredibly stressful for them and they might be struggling.'

Harold swirled his drink and the ice cubes rattled in the glass.

'I'd take what she says with a pinch of salt. She's a good girl, but very over-protective of Patrick. She does seem to view herself as his personal bodyguard. They've known each other since university and I can't think of a significant event in his life that she hasn't been involved in. That's why he asked her to be the best woman. She's been his one consistent friend since he was eighteen. They've always been very close.'

'Why didn't Patrick marry her then?' Mark's question was a reasonable one.

'I just don't think he was attracted to her. I vaguely recall that they dated a little at university, but it never amounted to much. Patrick had other girlfriends over the years, and then met Amelia. Suzanne was always there, just not romantically.'

'Do you think she wanted more?' Joyce asked. Harold shook his head.

'She's never shown any signs of that.'

'Amelia must have found it a little odd,' I said, imagining that a lot of women would have struggled with the situation.

'Not really. In fact, Suzanne is as protective of her as she is of Patrick. She's a good friend to both of them.'

I wondered if she was protective enough to be able to kill someone if she felt the couple were at risk in some way. It was worthy of more thought. I zoned back in to the conversation just as Mark was telling the group about his own wedding. He looked over at me, oblivious to the fact that I hadn't really been paying attention.

'What about you? Do you imagine a wedding in your future, or is your engagement to me the closest you plan on getting? I wouldn't blame you if it was – no man will ever match the high standards I've set.'

I was still only half aware of what he was saying and so replied with my mind partially elsewhere.

'After I broke my engagement off, I just put the idea of getting married out of my mind.'

It was the bang of Mark's glass landing heavily on the table that made me focus on the conversation and what I had just said. I looked across at my friends. Joyce was holding her glass in mid-air and staring at me so hard I thought she was going to burst a blood vessel. Mark was still holding on to his glass, and I felt like his eyes were drilling a hole through my head and out the other side. Craig had a wry little smile on his face and a look of curious surprise, and Harold was looking at the other three, clearly not quite sure what had just happened.

Bugger! That was information I hadn't planned on sharing, and it would teach me to pay attention in future. I knew that the haunting tableau that had formed in front of me wasn't going to change unless I filled them in, so I started to talk about a part of my recent past that I had confined to history. Anyway, it was long overdue that I shared that part of my life with the people who had become my closest friends.

When I left London, I left behind an engagement ring and a man who had proved to possess a dark side. Moving to Charleton had been a chance to put all that behind me. When I first arrived, I didn't know anyone here well enough to confide in them, and then gradually I had moved on and my new life had been enough to keep me busy, and the drama of what seemed like a past life had started to slide into the shadows.

In the shadows was where it turned out my fiancé had been living. I'd fallen in love with my restaurant manager – well, I say love, but looking back I'm not convinced it was quite that. I'd eventually discovered that not only was he sleeping with a waitress half my age, but he was also skimming money from the profits of the restaurant. I hadn't seen him since the day he was driven off in the back of a police car. A part of me felt insanely foolish for not spotting what had been going on, in both the restaurant and the bedroom.

After I'd finished telling my companions the ins and outs of my disastrous and mini-series worthy engagement, I sat back and looked around the group. They had listened quietly and respectfully, which was a miracle in itself. There was a softness in Joyce's eyes. She was terrifying and took no prisoners, but I'd always known she had a heart the size of a house, and I had been proven right.

Mark was the first to speak.

'Is there anything else you have neglected to tell me?' he said calmly. 'I don't want to marry a stranger.'

'Is this why you've been paying attention to the crimes that have been taking place at the house?' Craig asked. 'You were in the dark last time and you don't want to be in that position again?'

It was a good question and his theory made sense. I hadn't thought of it that way, but he was right.

'Well, whatever the reason,' stated Mark, 'you will always have my support, through murder and theft, sickness and in health. Just promise me one thing: you don't have any other secrets up your sleeve. We're not going to have someone bursting into the ceremony claiming that he has "just cause and impediment" and cannot hold his peace?'

Joyce closed her eyes, slowly opening them and turning to face Mark.

'Mark, you're ridiculous. It's your turn to get a round in, now scoot. The barman awaits.'

Mark stood, and as he walked behind me he gave my shoulder a squeeze. I was glad I'd told them. A weight that I didn't even know I had been carrying had lifted. Charleton was feeling more like home with every passing day.

CHAPTER 16

I woke as Pumpkin settled on my chest. We were practically nose to nose and her big brown eyes stared into mine. I couldn't be sure if what I saw in them was affection or a threat. Either way, I stroked her head and she purred like a lawnmower; I could feel the vibrations through my breastbone. She was only a pound or two from leaving me unable to breathe, but it was still a lovely way to start the day.

I'd slept fitfully, remembering the slip-up I'd made in the pub, revealing some of my past. I really hadn't been actively hiding my engagement from my new friends; it had been either not the right time to tell them or, mainly, utterly irrelevant. Although I did now feel a little guilty, I really hoped that none of them had interpreted it as me feeling that I couldn't trust them.

CRACK!

The sound sent Pumpkin running and I sat up in bed. It had come from the window and sounded like someone had thrown something at the glass. I stood to one side so I was out of the way of anything that might be flung at me and whipped the curtain back.

There was a white shadow on the glass, the outline of a large bird. Some poor creature had come flying straight into the window hard enough that its image remained, like a frozen ghost. I looked down, but couldn't see anything lying dazed and confused on the ground; wherever it was now, the poor bird must have a dreadful headache.

Pumpkin was peering at me from the other side of the bed, only her eyes and ears visible above the duvet.

'For heaven's sake, you're meant to be a terrifying bird-chasing killer cat, not hiding from our feathered friends. Birds are meant to be afraid of you, not the other way round.' I looked back at the outline of the bird. It was remarkable – in some places, I could see the marks left by individual feathers. There was a deep white line down the centre of its head where its beak had come into contact with the glass, which gave it a creepy, evil look.

I sat on the edge of the bed and stared at it. Pumpkin joined me and rubbed the side of her face against my shoulder. Beaks. Beaks that looked dark and evil; why was that image now dancing around my head?

The artwork at the gallery, the plague beak mask – that was what it reminded me of. The morning mist beyond the glass blocked my view of the scenery that normally greeted me and added to the creepy reminder of the photos taken in the gardens of Charleton House.

It was going to be a cold and damp day, and I decided to start it with a long, hot shower. But before I could even turn the water on, my brain went into overdrive – an uncoordinated form of overdrive that came from a lack of caffeine. Beaks, ravens, dark raven, darkraven24. The social media account that had been trolling Nathan had been called darkraven24; the plague mask in the photos resembled a raven. I hadn't paid attention to the name of the photographer when we'd been at the gallery on Monday night; I was more interested in the gin. It seemed a far-fetched link, but I wanted to put my mind at rest. As Craig had said last night, I didn't like being in the dark.

The high street was still quiet as I walked towards the gallery; the closed sign was visible, but I could see a light on inside. As I got closer, I could hear music and peered in through the window in the door. Connie was in the back of the gallery, dancing, and every now and again she would stop what she was doing and pretend to sing into a microphone. It was quite funny to watch and I was hesitant to interrupt her.

That turned out to be difficult to do anyway and it took some pretty hard banging on the door to get her attention. She looked a little embarrassed to have been spotted, and skipped towards the door.

'Sophie, sorry, you caught me. Come in, let's keep the cold air out.' She quickly closed the door behind me and looked hopeful. 'Did you see something on Monday that you just have to have?'

'Sorry, no, but I do have a question about some of the art.' I led the way towards the photographs that had got under my skin, or at least been sitting at the back of my brain for the last couple of days without me realising it. 'Who are these by?'

'Atmospheric, aren't they? I knew they'd catch your eye. The photographer goes by the name of Dark Raven.' She attempted to add some spookiness to her voice. 'I wondered if the Duke and Duchess might be interested in displaying them somewhere. Perhaps in your cafés – they'd work wonderfully there, especially in November. He has more.'

I wondered how the old dears who arrived by bus, keen to catch a glimpse of the Duchess and eat scones, would react to the dark, haunting photos if I displayed them.

'I'm not sure they'd sit right with the demographic, especially at this time of year.' *Dear God, no,* was what I really wanted to say, *they'd give me nightmares, let alone Enid and Betty and their pensioner pals.* 'What's his real name? Is he local?'

'He's local, I can tell you that much, but he likes to remain behind a cloak of mystery. It's a little pretentious, to be honest, but he insists that his true identity remains a secret. Except when it comes to writing cheques after a sale, of course.'

'It's really important I find out who he is, Connie, please.'

She looked down at the floor. 'I'm sorry, Sophie, I promised him. Do you want me to pass on a message?'

Did you kill Nathan? I thought. 'I think there might be a link between him and Nathan's murder up at the house. It might be nothing, but I at least need to rule him out.'

I thought Connie's eyes were going to bulge out of her head. Her life revolved around paintings and sculptures in this tiny art gallery in a small Derbyshire town; she was surrounded by other people's interpretations of reality. I would imagine that little of the real world entered into her life if she chose to keep it at bay, but the idea of there being a link between a murder and the world she had made for herself seemed to make her feel differently about Dark Raven's identity.

'Okay, but please don't let him know I told you. I promised him.'

'I won't say a word.'

'Ralph Veazie. He has a photography studio at the far end of the high street.'

The name rang a bell. 'Does he do weddings?' Maybe this was a case of professional jealousy.

'He does, but not as many as I think he'd like. He wants to sell some of his work here, help him pay the bills. He was hoping to be able to move into this kind of work full time as he was struggling to compete with Nathan. You must have seen Nathan's studio, it's immaculate. He's – was – clearly bringing in the money; Ralph wasn't keeping up.'

She stopped talking and looked intently at me.

'You don't think he did this, do you? He doesn't seem the type.'

I was curious about whom she considered to be the murdering type, but I wanted to go and talk to Ralph, find out if the evil-looking photos were the only source of darkness in his life.

From the outside, Ralph's studio was considerably more cramped than Nathan's. The wedding photos that formed a display in the window looked faded. As I walked in, a bell above the door rang.

Inside was much smarter and it looked as if Ralph was making more of an effort. A modern grey sofa sat at one side of the room, next to a white desk. On the opposite side of the room, a large white fabric screen ran the length and height of the wall and down onto the floor a couple of metres. I guessed it was the backdrop for portrait sessions.

'Hi there, how can I help?'

I turned and immediately recognised him. 'You were at the wedding.' He looked confused. 'Charleton House, Patrick and Amelia.'

'Ah yes, wasn't that quite the event? None of us are going to forget that in a hurry.'

'How do you know the bride and groom?'

'My dad, Derek, he's been married to Amelia's mum for a couple of years. I don't know either of them well, I've hardly seen them since Dad's wedding.'

That was why the name was familiar. The more I looked at him, the more I could see the family resemblance. He wasn't very tall, maybe five foot six, and stocky; it was easy to imagine him developing a rotund figure down the line just like his father's. An Oliver Hardy junior.

'I can't imagine you're here to talk about the wedding, so how can I help? Are you looking for a portrait session?'

'But I do want to talk about the wedding. Well, Nathan actually. How well did you know him?' I took a seat on the sofa, hoping it would encourage Ralph to sit too, get comfortable and start talking. He perched on the edge of the desk.

'As well as I know any of my competition. Well enough to say hi in the street.'

'So you were on speaking terms?'

'I might not go that far.'

'You didn't get on then?'

'What's with all the questions?' He folded his arms. I paused for a moment, wondering what would be the best approach, then decided to drop the preamble and just focus on my recent discovery. But I'd try a little flattery, and lying, first.

'I love your photographs. Really atmospheric, and the Charleton Gardens are the perfect setting.'

He looked quite pleased, and then I watched as a wave of realisation crossed his face.

'How did you know? Who told you?' He looked out of the window in the direction of the gallery. 'Was it Connie? I'll kill her; I told her to keep it to herself.'

'It wasn't Connie,' I lied, 'it just wasn't difficult to work out.' Now he'd confirmed it, I could dig a bit deeper. 'Tell me more about Nathan. You both have studios here on the high street, you must have known him better than most of your competition?'

'We weren't friends if that's what you mean.'

'Enemies?' I suggested.

'That's a bit simplistic, isn't it? Good guys and bad guys. Well if you want to take that kind of route, then Nathan was one of the bad guys. He'd do anything he could to get business; he could be pretty cutthroat, even though he'd reached the point where he didn't need to do that anymore. He was well established and usually at the top of the list when people wanted a wedding photographer, which left people like me floundering in his wake, picking at whatever scraps he left behind. And they were scraps, hardly enough to survive.'

I looked around the shop. It was a bit scruffy on the outside, but it was okay in here.

'You look like you're doing alright,' I offered.

'For now. I haven't been able to afford the rent for months.'

'So how come you're still open?'

'My dad. He's been helping me out, giving me money, trying to find me work. He's got me bits and pieces by recommending me to his clients as he's driving them around – the ones that want to talk while they're in his car, anyway. But in most cases, he's driving people on their way to an event that already has a photographer and it's far too late.'

'He sounds like a great dad.'

'He is, he'd do anything for me.'

Kill? I wondered. 'How long have you been trolling Nathan?'

'What? Christ, you're crossing a line.' He was holding the edge of the desk and I could have sworn his knuckles were going white. 'I don't use social media, it does more harm than good.'

'It does when people are using it to bully others, threaten them, try and wreck their business.'

'I never threatened him.' He froze, and then gave up. 'Okay, I needed some way to let off steam. Can you blame me? My business was dwindling to nothing, my dad was having to bankroll me, and there he was swanning around with the best camera equipment money can buy and wearing tailor-made suits. It was all talk, though, I'd never... wait, are you thinking I killed him? That's crazy.'

His voice went up an octave as he realised exactly what I was thinking. But instead of making him sound surprised, it made him sound slightly deranged.

'There were plenty of days that I hated him. I wanted to get my own back, but I'd never have said anything to his face. I just wanted him to get a taste of his own medicine.' He sounded panicked now, but I couldn't tell if it was out of genuine horror at the thought of being accused of murder, or because I was onto him. He stood up and opened a drawer in the desk, pulling out a set of keys. They jangled as he walked towards me.

'I don't like where this is going; you need to leave now. I have to lock up.'

It was the middle of the morning and apparently he didn't have much in the way of work, so I knew he was just trying to get rid of me. He was right, though. I didn't have any evidence and I'd got what I'd come for – an admission that he was Dark Raven – so I was happy to be shown the door, even if it was slammed behind me.

CHAPTER 17

I'd left my car parked outside the gallery so I walked up the street, wondering if Ralph seemed like the kind of man who would kill a competitor. He had plenty of motive: his business was failing and he'd had to swallow his pride and have his dad keep him afloat for the last couple of months. That sort of thing had certainly driven people to murder in the past.

The town was starting to get busy now, and although it was no longer tourist season, there were plenty of locals going about their business. I unlocked my car and got in. As I looked up the road, I saw a familiar face.

Chelsea was on the opposite side of the road, walking towards me, although she didn't show any signs of having seen me. I wasn't surprised; it was her day off and I knew she only lived a couple of streets back from the shops. She wasn't alone, though; she was pushing an older man in a wheelchair. He was grey-haired and slim, and she chatted to him as they made their way along. Occasionally he laughed and seemed to comment on whatever she had just said. There was something easy-going about their interaction. Chelsea looked tired, but happy. It was unusual to see her just going about her business, rather than dashing around late or looking confused or distracted.

I watched as they turned into a café. Chelsea pushed the man's wheelchair to a table near the window and helped him remove his coat. Her movements were gentle and considerate. Once he was settled, she walked over to the counter to place an order. I realised just how little I knew about her; there was a whole side of her life that was a complete blank to me, and it was my own fault. It was time for another chat with her, only this time I would approach it very differently.

I took the long route back to the house; I wanted time to think. I followed the narrow country lanes, the grass beyond them a flat muted green in the drizzle. The grey cloud sat heavily above me, and there was no sign of the sky at all. I cursed as my windscreen wipers squeaked with each wipe. I'd need to get those fixed or they'd drive me crazy, and if there was one thing I could be sure of, it was that they'd get a lot of use over the coming months.

I turned onto the estate road that led to the house just behind a smart black car that had come from the opposite direction. It was immaculate. I wondered for a moment if the Duke or Duchess were in it, but I knew they preferred to drive themselves in their Land Rover, unless it was a very special event. I followed the car along the road towards the visitors' car park, and then watched as it turned towards the barrier that prevented the public from heading down the lane at the side of the house. The barrier slowly raised – the security team must have been familiar with the driver.

As the car rolled past, I watched Joe walk into the security office. I went to park in the main car park, and then got ready to run back towards the dry of my office. My mid-morning coffee was long overdue.

Ruth was sitting at a table in the corner of the café, a notebook and sketches spread out before her. She was chewing on a pencil and didn't look as though she was paying much attention to the work in front of her. I decided that my coffee wasn't that important and sat down across from her.

'Ruth, how are you doing? How's Gregg?'

She sighed. 'He's okay. They let him go, but he's on a short leash. He's at home working on some menus. He didn't want to face the team after being driven off in a police car like that. He'll be fine tomorrow, it's just a bit raw.'

'And you?'

'Mad as hell. Do you know who claims to have seen him arguing with Nathan?' I shook my head; I genuinely had no clue. 'Leah.'

'Our Leah?'

Ruth nodded. Leah didn't have a set contract, but would work when the catering team needed an extra set of hands and often came in for evening events. She was competent and got on with everyone, but her erratic hours meant I didn't know her well.

'She's stirring up trouble. She's had a crush on Gregg since she started here. She flutters her eyelashes at him and finds excuses to be in the kitchen more than she should. She tried asking him out once, claimed she hadn't known he was married. There was also one time, after we'd opened a couple of bottles of wine following a particularly demanding event to say thanks to the team, she had a few too many and cornered him, tried to kiss him.'

'Why didn't you tell me?'

'Because Gregg can handle it. He didn't mince his words and she seemed to have got the message. We thought that was that, but I guess she bears a grudge a little more than we realised.'

'But to try and get someone on a murder charge? That's ridiculous.'

'You'd think so, but that's what she seems to be doing. She's also dragging up some minor arguments the two of them had.'

'Who, Gregg and Leah?'

'No, Gregg and Nathan.'

'Were they serious?' I asked.

'No, not at all, but add them together and mix in Leah's story – and that's what it is, a story – then it looks worse than it is.'

'Does Joe know all this?'

'Gregg told the police yesterday and they said they'd check it out, but I have no idea if they've spoken to her. They really ought to take her down to the station, it would be safer for her. If I get my hands on her…'

'Which you won't, because you'll take a deep breath and walk away. You don't want to make this worse.'

'I know, I know, I'm just—' She seemed to have run out of steam. 'I'll be fine; we'll be fine.'

I squeezed her shoulder and left her to it. Nothing I could say would improve things for her.

I heard Mark before I could see him.

'We are in great peril,' he declared in a loud, dramatic voice as he marched through the kitchen door like he owned the place. 'The future of our nation will be in the sweaty palms of a generation who have been utterly passed by when it came to the distribution of that great, yet admittedly rare, quality – common sense.'

I didn't look up from the pastry I was rolling as I replied.

'A school group?' I asked, knowing full well that was what Mark was talking about. I'd heard similar declarations before.

'I'd just finished telling a group about the painstaking work that goes into cleaning and protecting the books in the music room. As soon as my back was turned and I was heading for the door, I heard a squeal, like someone had stood on a guinea pig. A lanky teenage boy had leapt over the ropes and decided to pull out one of the aforementioned books while his mate took a photo, no doubt capturing his muppetry in order to share it with his equally irritating friends.'

I stopped rolling out pastry. 'Don't tell me we have another dead body on our hands?'

'Not quite, although I might have traumatised him.'

'Where was the teacher?'

'In the next room on her mobile phone. She'd slipped out while I was talking; she didn't look much older than some of the kids. I called the Education Department and they're liaising with Conservation who came down to check on the books. The boy did look suitably guilty when he watched Ellie pull on a pair of gloves and handle the books like they were newborn babies.'

I briefly looked up from the pie crust that I was gradually forming to see the black car I had followed into the estate drive past.

'Do you know who that was?'

'Derek, I imagine. He uses the Rolls Royce for weddings and a black Jag for more day-to-day work.'

'What were you saying?'

'When?'

'Just then.' Something he'd said had struck a chord, but I wasn't sure what.

'About Derek, or the school group and Conservation? Were you not paying attention?'

'Ellie, you said Ellie came down.'

'And checked the books, yes. She can be surprisingly delicate for a woman who plays rugby on the weekends. I've watched her play, she doesn't half get stuck in. She's caused a few nose bleeds in her time, and always comes off looking like she's walking off a battlefield, all mud and fresh blood. You know, it's oddly attractive, which is saying something from me, seeing as I lick the other side of the stamp, so to speak.'

I ignored his ramblings. 'Is Joe still in the security office?'

'I've no idea, why?'

'Back in a minute.'

I dropped the rolling pin and dashed through the café, almost knocking over Anthony, the Health and Safety manager, and narrowly missing an old lady with a tray of sandwiches.

Joe was sitting in front of a bank of screens with Roger beside him. They both had enormous mugs of the darkest tea I'd ever seen in front of them.

'Soph, nice to see you. You brought any cookies to go with our tea?' Roger was a sweet man who was soon to become a grandfather; he talked of little else, unless it was food.

'Sorry, not this time. I just wanted a quick word with Joe.'

'No problem, love, can I make you a cuppa?'

I looked again at the mugs on the desk, half expecting the creature from the black lagoon to stick its head out. Joe widened his eyes at me in a look of horror.

'I'm okay, thanks, I've just had one.'

'No problem. Well, I'll leave you to it and go and put my feet up for ten minutes. Joe, give me a shout when you're done. I'll leave the CCTV in your trusty hands.'

Joe spun round. 'You can't, I—' but Roger had disappeared. 'He shouldn't do that. These monitors should be watched all the time, and not by me.' Joe sighed and rolled his eyes simultaneously. 'I'm amazed that there aren't more problems here, the security team is a little distracted. But I didn't say that. How can I help?'

'I was thinking about Nathan and how there weren't any fingerprints on the antlers. That means either someone wore gloves, or... well, I don't know, but they didn't leave any evidence. Who do we know who wears gloves as part of their job? Who do we know was at the wedding and knows their way round the house? Plus, has a motive?'

He stared back at me. 'If we knew that, we'd have our man, or woman. And if you've figured it out, I'm phoning my resignation straight into the station. I'm still trying to be sure of everyone's movements in the run up to the wedding and rooting out connections between the key players. If you've cracked it, I'm done.'

I decided to ignore him. 'Derek Veazie, the driver. He was a guest at the wedding. He knows his way around behind the scenes and he wears a very smart pair of leather gloves when he's driving.'

Joe sat upright. 'And his motive?'

'His son's photography business is on its knees. Derek has been bankrolling it for months.'

'How the hell do you know this?'

I shrugged and tried to look innocent. 'A little birdie told me. Well, a raven to be precise.'

Joe looked confused, and then went over to the door. 'ROGER!' he bellowed.

'Yes, boss?' Roger's cheery face appeared at the door.

'I'm going to need to see the CCTV from the day of the wedding again. Can you set it up for me?'

'Sure thing.' Roger sat down in front of the monitors, focused on one screen and started hunting through a series of computer files. 'Which camera do you want to look at?'

'Let's start here on the lane. I'm looking for Derek Veazie after he dropped off the bride.'

'Well I can tell you what he was doing.' Roger turned to face Joe. 'I chatted to him after the ceremony, he came back out to the car.'

Joe looked confused. 'But we went through the footage. We asked all of you about anything that seemed unusual on the day.'

Roger either didn't pick up on the slight annoyance in Joe's voice or was choosing to ignore it.

'That's right, and there's nothin' unusual about Derek being in the lane. He's often here, comes and goes during events, joins us for a cup of tea, occasionally wanders into the kitchens if he knows the events manager and gets some free grub. Nice chap.

He'll sometimes bring what food he's been given over to us to share, but he's always around.'

'But he was the father of the bride, did you not think it odd that he came back out to the car?' Joe asked.

'No, not really. He could have been fetching something for his missus or the bride. Maybe he had a gift in there.'

'Find him on the footage for me, will you?' Joe pulled up a chair and Roger started fast-forwarding through the images of the lane. It was funny to watch. People walking quickly look really odd; they wave their arms like robots who have had a malfunction. Cars zoomed over a short distance, came to sudden stops and manoeuvred in jerky movements. The garden team's cat did a jaunty speed walk down the lane, and I watched as Harriet Smedley, in her trademark tea-cosy hat, walked down the centre of the lane like a wooden mannequin that had been given life and consumed far too much caffeine.

'There, stop.' Joe pointed at the screen. 'Go back.' Roger pressed rewind, and then paused the tape. Derek was walking out of a side door. He looked just as he did when he had dropped off Amelia. He wasn't wearing gloves, but he did have something in one of his hands. He opened the boot of his car and dropped the object in.

Joe ran his finger across the top of the screen and checked the time; it was around the time that Nathan had been murdered. He spun round on his chair to face me.

'Well it looks like we've found the missing camera. The question is did he take anything else, like Nathan's life?'

'That's not all.'

'What do you mean? What else do you know, Sophie?'

It was time to tell Joe everything else I knew about Ralph and what he'd been up to. By my reckoning, both father and son had motive, and possibly opportunity. But by the look on Joe's face, there was now also the risk of another murder.

I shifted uncomfortably in my seat.

'Roger, would you mind leaving Sophie and me alone for a couple of minutes?'

Roger rose silently; he gave my shoulder a squeeze as he walked behind my chair.

'Good luck,' he whispered.

CHAPTER 18

After being told off by Joe for interfering and apparently being incapable of listening to advice that was for my own good, I needed distracting, and I knew just the person to do it.

'Where the hell have you been, Madame Mystère? I've spent most of my day going to and from your café trying to catch you. Come on, I need more information. Follow me.'

Joyce signalled to a member of her staff that she was leaving the shop floor and led the way into her office. It wasn't much bigger than mine, but you could at least make your way to either of the chairs without having to climb over any of the furniture. The shelves were overflowing with books, mugs, children's toys, jewellery boxes and other possible shop stock that had been sent by suppliers and was under consideration. Packaging spilled out of empty boxes in each corner of the room, a full suit of armour was tucked behind the door, and I couldn't help but notice a pile of Joyce's vibrantly coloured shoes under the desk. It seemed her wardrobe extended into her office.

Joyce sat back in her office chair and crossed her legs, revealing a rather shapely thigh. However, my eye was drawn to the leopard-print stilettos, one of which was now dangling off a toe as Joyce rocked her foot up and down.

'I'd offer you coffee, but I'd rather have expected you to bring that with you. At the very least, you'd better be ready to tell me more about your engagement, which you slyly kept from us.'

'There's nothing more to tell, really. As soon as I found out what my ex was up to, I filled a black bag with all the stuff he'd ever left in my flat and dumped it on his front doorstep. He tried to call me in the early days, but I blocked his calls. If he did serve time I would guess that he's out by now, and there's no reason for him to know where I am.'

'Would it worry you if he did?'

'No, not at all. He was never threatening or abusive, just a liar and a cheat.'

'And you've never spoken since?'

'Never,' I confirmed.

'Good girl, wash your hands of him. Now, we need to get you a good man. Is there anyone here that makes your heart beat a little faster? A certain detective, by any chance? We could do with a Charleton House wedding, it's been a while.'

'Talking of Charleton House weddings,' I wanted to change the topic, quickly, 'is there going to be an antipodean wedding?'

Joyce's head fell dramatically backwards and she stared at the ceiling. 'Heaven only knows. It's all been rather a whirlwind.' She sat up straight again and gestured towards an enormous bouquet of roses that was sitting on the top of a filing cabinet. 'He's sent me one of those every day this week, my house is starting to look like Kew Gardens.'

'Most women would kill to be treated like that.'

'Interesting choice of words, but yes, I realise I am rather lucky. But what if it's just a holiday romance to him and he goes home and returns to his senses? In the meantime, I've quit my job, sold almost everything I own and bought a one-way ticket. I'm just not sure I can risk that.'

I didn't know what to say. My love life was full of car wrecks and I was turning into the proverbial spinster, along with the obligatory cat that I had full-blown conversations with and treated like a very spoilt child. I was in no position to advise others.

'What would you say to me if our roles were reversed?'

'Don't be such an idiot, book a ticket and follow your heart!' she exclaimed without a moment's hesitation. 'But I realise it's a little different when I'm the one taking such a risk, and as much as it pains me to admit it, I am a little older than you.'

That was the closest I'd ever heard Joyce come to admitting she was over twenty-one.

By the time Joyce had finished running through a list of possible suitors for me, and avoided all future attempts to have the conversation turned back on herself, it was time to go home. We hadn't even noticed that her team had closed the shop and left us to navigate the aisles in semi darkness. Neither of us was in the mood to begin any more work, and instead we called it quits and walked towards the car park together.

As we made our way towards the security gate, I spotted a familiar figure talking to Roger.

'Give me strength,' I sighed.

'What?' Joyce followed my eye line. 'Someone you know?'

'It's my not-so-secret admirer. Just so you know, I'm engaged to marry Mark.' I left Joyce standing with her mouth open, held my head high and walked swiftly towards the two men.

'Goodnight, Roger, see you tomorrow.' I gave him a big smile and tried to ignore Levi, but the reality is I'm far too polite and found being quite so consciously rude a challenge. 'Levi.' There, that was the best he was getting.

'Sophie, my dear.' He started walking behind me. 'I was hoping I'd catch up with you before you left. I've come to say goodbye. I leave for LA tomorrow so I'm heading down to Heathrow. I'll spend the night in a hotel there – unless, of course, I have a reason to delay my flight.'

I came to a sudden halt; the man had absolutely no self-awareness at all, and I couldn't understand why he was being allowed to leave the country if he was a possible murder suspect. Or at least, he was in my mind.

I was trying to figure out how to respond in as firm a way as possible without losing my job – I was, after all, still on the Charleton House estate, and a manager – when Joyce butted in.

'My dear man,' she said, sounding like an irate headmistress, 'I have no doubt that this delightful young lady would rather pass a kidney stone than spend an evening in your company. Now I suggest you make your way to Heathrow as quickly as possible or I might have to introduce you to my considerably less subtle twin.'

Levi looked confused, but not offended. I wondered briefly if he was going to turn his attentions to Joyce; I didn't think it was beyond him to mistake her directness for attraction, he was that thick-skinned.

Joyce threw an arm around my shoulders and frogmarched me towards my car. 'Dear God, if that man had a brain cell it would be lonely. You really do attract them, don't you; you definitely need my help in the romance department. No wonder you've found yourself engaged to Mark, you must have been desperate. Now, you've had a long day. Go home, light some candles, run a hot bubble-filled bath and pour yourself a glass of fizz. Revel in your singledom. I on the other hand will go home and try to decide, while consuming a whole bottle of champagne, if I should completely turn my life on its head. I'm bound to find the answer at the bottom of that bottle.' She kissed me on the cheek and strode across the car park looking like a woman on a mission.

I decided that I would put my own twist on Joyce's advice.

Instead of a hot bath and candles, I made a roaring fire in my sitting room. Instead of sparkling wine, I made myself an autumnal cocktail of Twenty Trees Gin, fresh apple cider, ginger simple syrup and thyme sprigs. Making fresh cocktails from scratch might seem like a bit of a faff, but I find it's worth the trouble. Especially when I sink into an armchair, the heat from the fire warming my legs, a cat curled up in front of the flames and the gentle warmth of ginger on my tongue.

I closed my eyes and rested my head against the back of the chair. I'd yet to have the chance to calmly consider all the evidence around Nathan's death; I'd been too busy running the Library Café without a supervisor, fending off Levi and worrying about whether or not I would soon be losing Joyce. Add to that the lack of evidence around any of the suspects – or, at least, as far as I could tell there was a lack of evidence. Joe could be hours away from solving the case, especially now he had Derek on CCTV taking something back to his car.

I realised that I found the thought of that slightly disappointing. Much as I wanted to see Joe succeed, maybe part of me was more competitive than I'd realised, and if I was honest, I wanted to get there first. I ran down the list of people who had possible motive: Amelia's brother Kristian, Derek, his son Ralph, Patrick, Levi. All could have followed Nathan into the Antler Gallery; all had reason to dislike him, either personally or professionally. There was also a distinct lack of evidence to tie anyone else to the location of Nathan's murder, and despite what Leah claimed to have seen, I refused to believe that Gregg was involved.

Pumpkin stirred in front of the fire, her ears straight up. The doorbell rang and she shot up, beating me to the door and standing on the mat, ready to greet her guests.

'You'll need to move or I can't open it.'

She just stared back at me as if to say, 'That's your problem. Solve it, and if that door touches me, you're in trouble.'

'Oh, for heaven's sake, Pumpkin, MOVE.' I gave her gentle

push with my toe and she sulked behind me. I opened the door to Joe's smiling face.

'I was just passing, thought you might like an update.'

I stepped aside. 'Go through, make yourself at home. Can I get you a drink?'

'Please, but one with distinctly less alcohol than I'm guessing yours contains. Tea would be great.'

I handed Joe his mug of tea and he held it out to one side. Pumpkin had made herself at home on his lap and was now nuzzling his chin and purring loudly.

'Push her off if she's in the way, she can be a bit of a tart.'

Joe rubbed the top of her head. 'She's fine. I've spent most of the day being shouted at so this is a nice change.'

'Anyone I know?'

He nodded. 'Well, after Ruth had spent some time laying into me, I caught up with Derek. First he denied he'd been anywhere near his car during the wedding, then realised it had "slipped his mind". Like the security team, he views his wandering around the house and going back to his car as normal behaviour. It's what he does all the time. He certainly knows his way around well and wouldn't have had a problem following Nathan, or going in search of him if he wanted to. He also claims he had a perfectly civil relationship with Nathan, said that he didn't like the guy, but knew they had to get on professionally.'

'What about Ralph? Derek has been propping up his business for a while now and Ralph claims it's Nathan's fault that he's been struggling so much.'

'Derek says he was only doing what any supportive father would. He knew Ralph was finding it tough, but he didn't have any opinion on why that would be other than the difficult early days of running your own business.' Joe was stroking Pumpkin who had finally settled down on his lap. She normally spent a good fifteen minutes kneading my legs with her paws – and sharp claws – before she settled down. I was envious of how quickly she'd gone to sleep on him. It amused me to think of how differently she behaved with Mark, whom she treated like some kind of mortal enemy. I wondered whether Mark and Pumpkin were busy plotting to convince me that Joe was the ideal man – love me, love my cat kind of thing.

The sound of a car passing outside the window brought me out of my thoughts and prompted me to ask, 'What about Derek's car? Any sign of what he'd put in there?'

'No, nothing, apart from a bag containing a clean shirt and shoe polish. Whatever it was is long gone. There was something that didn't seem quite right about him, though; he was almost too angry about my questioning. What was it Shakespeare said? "The lady doth protest too much"? Well Derek was certainly protesting too much.'

'So he's still a potential suspect?'

'Hmm, that might be taking it too far, but I feel like there's something he's not telling us.'

'Maybe he's protecting someone?'

'Possibly. I quizzed him on what he saw when he was heading out to the car. If he is innocent, then maybe he saw something that could help.'

'And did he?'

'No, nothing that we didn't know before.'

'What about Levi, did you know he plans on leaving the country?'

Joe nodded. 'He seems to be nothing more than a creep who can't take no for an answer. There's no evidence he went anywhere near Nathan on the day of the wedding itself. We asked Olivia if she wanted to press charges for harassment, but she said no. Keep an eye on her, will you? She says she's okay, but just make sure.'

'Of course.' I was disappointed. I quite liked the idea of Levi being taken off in handcuffs for anything, not necessarily murder, just to see his ego take a beating.

My glass was empty so I went to top it up. I'd made a double quantity for precisely this moment.

'Are you sure you don't want anything stronger?' I called. 'I'll split this with you.'

'No thanks.'

'Have you spoken to Leah yet?' I asked him.

'Who?'

'Leah, the woman who was mad at Gregg for spurning her advances.'

'Is there anything you don't know about? Maybe we should relocate our team of detectives to your café, it seems that all the relevant information ends up making its way there eventually.'

'I just keep my ear to the ground, and I guess I have one of those faces that makes people feel like they can talk to me.'

'You mean you bribe them with coffee and cake. Yes, we have spoken to Leah, and she's sticking to her story. There's no one to back her up where the argument with Nathan on Saturday is concerned, but there are witnesses for some of the previous arguments they've had. Leah does seem pretty convincing, but I admit Gregg doesn't have any motive that we know about.'

'He doesn't have one because he didn't kill him.'

I knew I was sounding a bit exasperated and Joe gave me a look that seemed to say, 'Calm down before you hack me off', so I changed the subject.

'What about Kristian? The last time we talked you were trawling through his phone records.'

'He did call Nathan the morning of the wedding, apparently to warn him to behave, but based on Nathan's behaviour at the dinner, that was unnecessary. I think Kristian was genuinely just being the protective brother and he didn't do any more than that. Beyond the fight years ago, he has a squeaky clean record and a really good reputation.'

Something about that didn't make sense to me. 'But there was a fight, so they were both capable of violence at one time in their lives. Could that not remain the case, and was there a repeat of the incident when they next saw each other all these years later?'

'Not impossible, but think about all the young lads I've stopped fighting on a Friday night after they've had a skinful. Alcohol, emotion, youth – it can be a dangerous combination, but in most cases it's something they grow out of. Bill and I have swapped a couple of blows in our time. Now the worst I'd do is call him a plonker or ignore his calls for a day.'

'What's your next move?'

'I quit before I'm fired! I'm kidding. Fortunately DS Harnby is as frustrated as the rest of us and knows this is a devil of a case, so she's not started screaming at us yet, but I can feel it coming. We're going to go re-interview some of the kitchen staff tomorrow. One of them must have seen something, and if that something helps Gregg, then all the better. After the incident with Derek, we also need to reassess what is actually unusual up at the house. What's normal to you lot might be important to us.'

That made me laugh. 'Working there has certainly made me reassess what is normal. Last week I made a buffet lunch for Mary, Queen of Scots and her entourage.'

'Precisely my point.' He chuckled. 'Now come on, Pumpkin, it's time for me to go. I've warmed the seat for you.'

In a demonstration of docility I'd never seen before, Pumpkin allowed herself to be relocated into Joe's seat. She looked at him through half-closed eyes, and then went back to sleep. She really was in love.

CHAPTER 19

'Oi, I want a word with you. Don't ignore me. YES, YOU!'

With a red face and slightly out of breath, Derek resembled a tomato in a black suit. I'd only just arrived at work and was hoping for a stress-free end to the week, but it seemed my Friday was already getting off to a bad start.

'I know it was you that spoke to the police about me, and I know you've been sniffing around asking questions of my Ralph. I've 'eard you think you're some kind of Miss Marple. Well you're on the wrong track here, lady.'

I could feel my heart beating and wondered if Derek could see my body shake with the reverberations. The blood was pounding in my ears as I tried desperately to look calm and composed. I'd had enough customers shout at me in my time, but this felt different.

Behind Derek, I saw Roger stick his head out of the security office door. He folded his arms and leaned against the window frame. I didn't think that Derek would do any more than rant, but it was good to know Roger was watching just in case.

I tried to keep my voice steady as I replied. 'You know your way around this place as well as I do. Probably better. You might have seen something important.'

'Rubbish! You thought I'd done it. I know what Ralph told you, and he did something stupid putting those comments online, but that's all it was: stupid. Neither of us are killers. Nathan wasn't worth the effort.'

He started to walk slowly towards me and I watched as Roger uncrossed his arms and stood up straight, but Derek stopped a couple of feet in front of me.

'I've worked damned hard to set up this business and I'm well respected. I won't let anyone destroy it.' He was talking softly now, but I actually found that more threatening. Straightening his jacket and tie, he removed a handkerchief from his pocket, wiping his forehead. At no point did he take his eyes off me; it was quite sinister. He certainly looked like a man who could lose his temper and do something more than stupid.

I watched him walk away with an angry swagger. Outbursts seemed to come naturally to him. Roger signalled Derek over and the appearance of anger and threat left him; instead, his swagger resembled that of a schoolboy who was about to get his wrists slapped, but didn't want to lose face. He had seemed like such a friendly, almost cuddly chap; it was easy to imagine why people liked having him as a driver, but he'd left me slightly shaken and I didn't like the idea of ever being in a car on my own with him.

I had one thing I needed to do before I went to my office and started my day properly. As I'd arrived, I'd seen Gregg's car in the car park; he must have felt up to facing his colleagues today. I found him in the Garden Café kitchen and knocked on the frame of the door to let him know I was there. The last thing I wanted was to startle someone who was holding an enormous knife, no matter how gentle a character I knew them to be – or had thought them to be.

'Figured I'd come and see how you are.'

'Fine. I didn't get much sleep, but I'm okay.' There was silence. 'I didn't do it.'

'I know.'

'Really? They have a so-called witness.'

'I know about Leah. I also know she's been giving you a hard time, making advances. You should have told me.' I walked around and stood by him, leaning with my back to the counter. He put the knife down and joined me; we didn't look at each other.

'I thought I could handle it. Didn't think it would come to this.'

'What about the other times you were seen fighting with Nathan? There are more witnesses to those events, which you have to admit makes Leah's story more credible.'

'We weren't fighting. He'd taken to coming into the kitchens from time to time. Said he wanted to get some action shots of us all at work, but he just got under our feet. I put up with it for a while, made a few comments, but he never took the hint. Eventually I lost my rag with him, more than once. It's dangerous in a kitchen and I snapped.' His voice was flat and tired.

'It makes it look like a pattern, a sour relationship.'

'I can't help how it looks, that's the truth. Maybe if I talk to Leah.'

I turned to face him. 'You'll do no such thing, it'll only make things look worse. I know it's frustrating, but you need to let the investigation run its course. I'm doing what I can to find out more; I want this resolved too. I don't think you did it, but if I didn't know you, you'd be very high on my list of suspects. Keep your head down.'

He nodded and I squeezed his arm, then left him to his thoughts.

After my dramatic start to the day with Derek and my heart - to - heart with Gregg, I needed a very large mug of coffee. I also couldn't resist a fresh sausage roll that looked too good to turn down, despite it being eight o'clock in the morning and sausage rolls not being normal breakfast food. Still unsettled by my encounter with Derek, I couldn't focus on any of the paperwork in my office. I had enough staff in the Stables and Library Cafés that they could take care of themselves, so I decided I needed a change of scenery, and I wanted to limit the chances of running into Derek again.

There was also someone I wanted to talk to, someone I hadn't spoken to at all yet: Kristian, Amelia's brother. He had history with Nathan: a fight that had something to do with Amelia leaving Nathan and starting to date Patrick. In some ways, Kristian was an obvious suspect – the reigniting of old angers that flared when his path unexpectedly crossed with Nathan's, but Joe hadn't been able to find any evidence that tied Kristian to Nathan's death. Perhaps he knew something else or had seen something else that could help. Even if I couldn't find out anything useful from him, it didn't feel right not to have spoken to him myself and ticked him off my mental checklist.

Kristian was staying at the Black Swan in one of the guest rooms upstairs. I knew the place well, probably too well, but that's what came of living over the road from one of the loveliest pubs I'd ever come across with the most extensive gin list I'd ever had the pleasure of working my way through. This all meant I had a good relationship with the landlord, Steve. As a result, I also knew which door would be unlocked at nine o'clock in the morning.

Steve was behind the bar, pouring a glass of orange juice.

'Sophie, bit early for a gin and tonic, isn't it?'

'It's always cocktail hour somewhere in the world, Steve, but that's not why I'm here. You've got a Kristian Nipper staying here?'

Steve nodded in the direction of the window. A man I recognised sat in the window seat, a newspaper spread out before him and a knife and fork in his hands. I had personal experience of the traditional English breakfasts that Steve served his overnight guests; they were superb. Everything on the plate was locally sourced and packed with flavour. I hated the idea of disturbing Kristian while he ate something so enjoyable, but it was important.

'Can you take this over to him?' Steve handed me the orange juice. Well at least it would give me a way in.

I placed the glass on the table.

'Thanks,' Kristian muttered without looking up. 'Great bacon.'

'It is, isn't it. They get it from a farm on the Charleton estate.'

Kristian looked up, surprised. 'Sorry, I didn't mean to be rude.' He put the newspaper down and stared at me. 'I recognise you from somewhere.'

'I work at Charleton House, I'm the Head of Catering.'

'You work here too?' He sounded even more surprised than he'd looked. 'How does that work then?'

'No, no, I wanted to talk to you. Do you mind if I join you?'

He folded up his newspaper and tucked it by his side. 'Please. I decided I'd enjoy a leisurely start to the day so I'm no rush. How can I help?'

I could tell he was a northerner, but his was a softened, gentle version of the Derbyshire accent.

'I want to find out more about the fight you had with Nathan years ago. Would you mind telling me about it?'

He looked confused by my interest, but not annoyed. I sensed no change in atmosphere or frustration at my raising the subject. He cut off a piece of sausage and ate it while I waited. After a mouthful of juice, he looked me in the eye.

'It's amazing what comes back to haunt you. It seemed like such a minor incident and I'd largely forgotten about it until Amelia told me that she'd booked Nathan for the wedding. I was as mad as hell when she told me what she'd done; she's her own worst enemy sometimes. She's inherited our mother's temper. I was pretty hot headed in those days too, plus Amelia is my sister and we've always been close. I'd have done anything to protect her, still would. It was stupid of me, but someone had badmouthed our lass and I wasn't going to stand by and do nothing.'

'How did the fight start?'

He looked over my shoulder and started talking like he was watching it play out in the corner of the room. 'It was a house party, nothing special. Amelia had left Nathan for Patrick six months earlier, and although Nathan had been pretty hurt, we thought it had all calmed down, so none of us were worried when he showed up at the party.'

'Who was with you?'

'Just the four of us: Amelia, Patrick, Suzanne and me. Suzanne and I were never a couple, but we were both single and would often be each other's date for parties. We were all enjoying ourselves – dancing, drinking, usual stuff – when I heard shouting at the top of the stairs and recognised Nathan's voice, so went to check it out. He was having a go at Suzanne. She was giving as good as she got, though, and didn't seem to need any help from me, but then Amelia appeared from behind them and Nathan had a go at her too. That's when I went up and tried to calm him down. He wasn't having any of it and starting having a go at Amelia again, so I decked him. Thought I'd broken my hand at first. Someone at the party called the police and that was it, the fun was over.'

'What was the original argument about?'

'No idea. Like I say, I came across Nathan and Suzanne laying into one another. Next thing, he targeted Amelia. I just assumed that it was the alcohol talking; we'd all had a bit to drink. Nathan and I were taken down the station and kept in the cells for a couple of hours, then after a ticking off from the police, allowed to go home. That was that. I never saw Nathan again until last weekend.'

It sounded like the typical alcohol-fuelled overflowing of

testosterone to me. 'How did you feel when you saw Nathan last Friday?'

'Amelia gave me the heads up in a text message when I was in the taxi on my way to the dinner, so it wasn't a surprise. She'd been pretty stupid to book him, but like I say, she has our mother's flair for the dramatic. I didn't say two words to him on the Friday or Saturday. Do you reckon the police are close to figuring out who did it?'

'I know they're throwing a lot of energy at it and there are a couple of possibilities, but I'm not sure if they're much further than that.'

Kristian nodded. 'It'll be nice to get home. I only stayed because Amelia and Patrick were determined to make the best of the week, try and salvage some happy memories. There were meant to be group hikes and pub lunches, that kind of thing, but a lot of people left. I'll be glad when they're off on their honeymoon, then it'll really feel like we can put all this behind us. What about you? Why are you so interested in it all?'

I didn't want to go into the full story behind my knack for getting involved in murder enquiries, so told a little white lie.

'Someone I know ended up on the list of suspects when all this happened and I knew they hadn't done it, so I decided to dig around. After that I got rather sucked in.'

'Have you proved they didn't do it?'

I thought of Gregg and how worried Ruth had been. I nodded. 'Sort of. He's no longer a suspect, anyway.'

'I'm glad.' He smiled and I felt a brief stab of regret that he would be leaving soon.

After I'd parked my car, I decided to take a long route back to the house through the gardens and think about what Kristian had told me. There had clearly been enough anger around to result in quite a fight all those years ago, but I was still struggling to understand why any of it would linger now. A lot of time had passed; everyone involved seemed to have moved on with their lives. Even Nathan, who had found himself in a difficult situation when it turned out that Patrick had no idea he was going to be there, had remained calm and professional. There was a lot of anger and grudges floating around this wedding, but none of it seemed intense enough to spill over into murder. Everyone just seemed very annoyed, and it was becoming rather annoying!

'Hello there, Sophie, going for a walk?' The Duchess strode towards me. She had a remarkably straight posture that always made me feel like a hunchback.

'I'm just heading back to the office after getting some fresh air.'

'I don't blame you, it must get awfully hot in your kitchens. You must crave fresh cool air now and again. I'm just off to the kitchen garden. The team is doing some splendid work and it's time to harvest some medlars. They're unusual things; they're rotten before they're actually ripe – rather a metaphor for ageing, I feel – and only then can you make them into jam or jelly or whatnot. You pop them in sawdust or bran from the stables and you leave them until they're almost rotten, and that's when you use them for cooking. Delicious. They're my favourite. I'll bring you a jar of jam when I've finished. Look, I'm glad I caught you; I believe that unfortunate couple are leaving tomorrow, is that right?'

'As far as I know, yes, they're heading home before going abroad for a proper honeymoon.'

'I bet they can't wait to get away. I was thinking, I'd like them to be able to take something with them other than rather gloomy memories. Do you have any ideas?'

'I took them a basket of food during the week to save them cooking. Perhaps something along those lines?'

'Yes, what a marvellous idea. We could get some champagne and chocolates; lots of lovely Charleton House goodies from the shop. Could you arrange that for me? Don't worry about the expense; tell the shop to talk to Gloria and she'll transfer the money between budgets.'

'Absolutely. I can also drop it off, if you'd like.' That would give me an excuse to visit Amelia and Patrick again.

'Oh thank you, Sophie, that's very kind. I do appreciate it. Now if you'll excuse me, my medlars await.'

I watched her walk off, turning so I could continue to track her route along the path. When I was around her, I felt like a kid who wanted to impress her favourite teacher. I was one step away from leaving an apple on her desk.

I took a shortcut through a walled garden that would lead me to the back lane. The flowerbeds had been turned over and left bare for the winter. A familiar figure appeared in the arched gateway and walked towards me.

'Sophie, I've just left your office. I was going to pick up my pay slip for last month.'

It was Leah, Gregg's accuser. Bright and cheerful, she clearly had no idea that I knew of the conversations she'd been having with the police.

'You can come back with me, it's on my desk.'

'It's okay, I'll get it when I'm next in. It's not urgent. See ya.'

She walked past me.

'Leah.'

'Yep?'

'Why are you lying about Gregg? You could destroy his career, his life.'

'I don't know what you mean.' She turned away and I wondered if she would walk off, but she stayed where she was. 'I'm not lying. He argued with Nathan, we've all seen it.'

'I don't mean in the kitchen, I mean just before Nathan was killed. Why did you say you saw them outside the Antler Gallery?'

'Because I did.'

I shook my head. 'We've all had our hearts broken, Leah. We've all fallen for the wrong people, but we move on and meet someone else.'

She looked momentarily disgusted, her lip curling. 'What are you talking about? You don't know anything.'

'I know more than you think. He's a good man. You need to tell the truth, or you'll destroy your own reputation too when this gets out, but you've time to put it right.'

'I did see him arguing with Nathan, though, in the kitchens.'

'I know, he's not disputing that and there were other witnesses, but he didn't kill Nathan. He didn't even fight with him on Saturday.'

She pulled her chin into the collar of her jacket, looking like a child.

'I just... I just said it. I didn't think, and then I was mad at him.'

I felt sorry for her. I knew what it was like to be attracted to someone and yet not stand a chance. She looked lost.

'You need to talk to Joe. He'll just be grateful that you're being honest, then the police can focus their investigation elsewhere. He'll be cross if you keep wasting his time.'

'Will I be arrested for lying?'

'I doubt it, but the longer you leave it, the more likely that becomes.' She nodded slowly. 'Will you talk to him?'

'Yes.'

She turned and walked away. I hoped that this time, she was telling the truth.

I sat in my office, staring at my computer screen. I was tired of getting nowhere with this murder, tired of the lack of evidence, and dreaded to think how Joe was currently feeling. Admittedly the police could be on the verge of a breakthrough and I'd never know, but if they were still stumped, he'd be pulling his hair out. This was his job; it was more of a hobby for me.

Actually, it was more than that; it was an itch that wouldn't go away, no matter how hard I scratched. I had once compared trying to solve a murder with working on a recipe: putting all the clues, or ingredients, together, figuring out quantities and new flavours, and working out what I could make with them. Well, right now I didn't have enough ingredients to make a basic sponge cake and it was driving me up the wall.

As I ran through the possible suspects in my head, it was still Derek and Ralph who stood out. They both had motive, and each had the other to help protect them. They were a team in many aspects and I wondered if murder had been added to their list of activities. If I was right, then Nathan must have done something to tip them over the edge.

Oddly, Nathan was the one person involved in this crime I knew least about, and I needed to change that. I picked up my phone and called Mark's office.

'Mark's Mortuary. You stab 'em, we slab 'em.'

I looked at my handset; he had to be kidding.

'You muppet, good job we have caller ID.'

'I'm hardly going to answer a call from the Duke like that. Mind you, I could have some fun.'

'Don't you dare. What are you doing tonight? Fancy doing some breaking and entering with me?'

'Sounds interesting. As far as I know, Bill has chicken wrapped in bacon and roasted broccoli planned for me, but your offer sounds much more racy. What do you want to drag me into now?'

'Wear something dark, bring gloves and meet me outside Nathan's studio in Bakewell at eight pm tonight. I want to do some digging.'

'Then shouldn't I bring a spade?'

I hung up on him.

Before I'd had a chance to pull on my coat, the phone rang again. It was an outside number.

'Sophie Lockwood, Charleton House Head of Catering, can I help?'

'I hope so,' replied Joe.

'It's unlike you not to do this in person, get a free coffee while you're at it.'

'Are you calling me a freeloader?'

'Absolutely, but you brighten my day in the process.'

'That's okay then. Look, there's a serious reason for my call. I believe you provided some of the serving staff for the wedding party.'

'Yes, but not many. Three, I think. Most staff were from an agency we use regularly so they all know what they're doing and the various rules we have to put in place, but our café staff are given the chance to work some overtime as well.'

'Were they all female, and what colour was their hair?'

I thought for a moment, and then nodded my head as though he was in the room with me.

'Yes, one blonde, one redhead, and Leah, who's also a blonde. Why?'

'Double and triple checking all staff were accounted for around the time of the murder. We're going over everything again with a fine-tooth comb. Thanks, Soph.'

The line went dead. He must be under pressure.

CHAPTER 20

The street lamps gave off an orange glow and the tarmac glistened after the most recent rainfall. Mark and I had pulled up within seconds of each other and parked as far away from the high street as possible.

'So what's the plan, Stan?' Mark asked as he drank from an insulated mug.

'I hope that's coffee. I want to know more about Nathan. If someone hated him enough to kill him, then chances are that he might have been threatened in ways other than just on social media. I want to get in his studio and have a root around, see if there are any threatening letters or other objects that might have been missed.'

'Isn't his studio a crime scene?'

'Not any more, it will have been signed off a couple of days ago. We can go round the alley at the back; there's bound to be a window we can crawl through.'

'So you're serious, then? You actually want to break into a dead man's studio?' Mark looked a little surprised.

'Why else did I drag you out here in the freezing cold?'

'I didn't think you'd actually want to go through with it. I figured you'd apologise for making me leave my cosy home, we'd go to the pub for a drink – which you'd be paying for – and then I'd be back in front of the TV watching *Agatha Raisin* before the clock struck ten.'

'Oh ye of little faith.' I shoved a torch into his hand, locked my car and strode off across the car park towards Nathan's studio. I was on a mission.

A narrow alley ran along the back of the studio. It was mainly used for people to store their bins and boxes of recycling before putting them out for collection once a week. The cobbled stones were wet and weeds grew between them, so I had to tread carefully. I knew that many of the properties had flats above them so the chances were that people would be inside – something I'd reminded the still disbelieving Mark of before we'd rounded the corner.

I counted the doors until I came to one that I was certain led into Nathan's studio. There was a small window and I peered in. To one side I could see an open door, and beyond that a toilet. A glance in the other direction revealed piles of cardboard boxes and what looked like a couple of tripods leaning in a corner. I started to look for chemicals that would be used in a darkroom before I remembered that he would have done everything digitally; I needed to be sure that I had the right place.

'What are you waiting for?' asked Mark.

'I don't want to break into the wrong building,' I whispered.

Mark removed the lid of the nearest bin and pulled out an empty envelope. He shone his torch on the address revealing Nathan's name.

'I think we're safe.'

I rattled the window frame, hoping the catch would be loose, but it was solid. There were glass panels in the door, but they were narrow and there was no way either of us could fit through them, not even Mark who could vanish from view if he turned sideways. Then I felt my foot dislodge something and looked down to see half a brick. My luck was in.

I raised the stone over my shoulder and got ready to throw it through the window.

'Stop!' hissed Mark. 'What if there's an alarm, or someone hears us?'

'Get ready to run,' I advised. I threw the brick and cringed as the window smashed. We ducked down and perched on our heels in silence, waiting for activity from above or the wailing sound of an alarm.

Nothing.

I knocked the remaining glass out of the way, and then pulled myself up. The window was shoulder height so it didn't take too much effort.

'Give me a shove.'

There was a couple of seconds' pause, during which I imagined Mark trying to figure out where he could safely put his hands without facing a sexual harassment case, or having his sexuality questioned. In the end he wrapped his arms around my knees and hoisted me up. I landed in a heap on a pile of opened boxes, rolled over onto my back and opened my eyes. Mark was standing over me, staring down with a look of smug satisfaction.

'Alright down there? Need a hand?'

'What the…?'

'The door was unlocked.' He looked at me like it was the most obvious thing in the world.

'Why the hell did you let me break in?'

'It was funny.'

'You're an evil man, Mark Boxer. Help me up.'

We spent the next twenty minutes in darkness, rooting through drawers and searching through bags. I checked inside books in case anything had been hidden. I knew there was no point in even trying to look at Nathan's computer; the police would have combed through every email and its entire web history. Fortunately, Nathan's filing cabinets were unlocked so Mark searched through those. Every time a car drove past, we dived out of sight.

'Won't the police have done this already?' Mark asked, starting to sound a bit bored.

'Yes, but they're only human. They might have missed something. Even if we don't find anything that shows he was being threatened, we might find out something else useful about the man.'

'Well so far I can tell you he spent more on one suit than I spend on my entire wardrobe over the course of a year. He also owned at least one pair of shoes that would fund the cost of my next holiday...'

'What was that?'

I stood stock-still; Mark froze. There were voices coming from the door where we'd entered – well, where Mark had entered, at any rate. Mark waved in my direction and pointed towards the tiny walk-in wardrobe in the corner of the room that he'd been focusing his search on. We scrambled in and pulled the door shut behind us.

'Maybe we'll find Narnia,' he whispered in my ear.

I held my breath. Someone had entered the room and was going through the drawers, just as we had been. They finally settled on the filing cabinet opposite the wardrobe as I cracked open the door and peeped out. I'd given up holding my breath and now felt like I was breathing so loudly, they could have heard me inhale and exhale back at Charleton House.

I peered through the darkness until the intruder moved out of the shadows. It was Ralph Veazie. There was a clatter behind me and I froze as a number of coat hangers hit the floor. Mark muttered 'Bugger' in a rare moment of understatement. Ralph spun round and I stepped out. There was no point hiding anymore.

'What the hell?' he exclaimed.

'We could say the same thing,' Mark replied calmly, pushing past me and grabbing the handle of the filing cabinet. He yanked it open and reached in with his gloved hand, pulling out a large professional camera. There was no lens attached. 'This wasn't in here a moment ago, and I'm sure I remember something about Nathan having a third camera that went missing. Want to fill us in, Ralph? I'm sure you've some excuse you can regale us with!'

Ralph looked back and forth between the two of us. He seemed to be struggling for words.

'I just took the chance… I saw it and…'

'Saw what? The chance to get back at someone who was destroying your career?' Mark was doing a great impression of 'bad cop'. His height and strong voice made him quite an imposing figure. Unfortunately he'd rested one hand on his hip, which was eroding some of the impact, but he seemed to be enjoying himself. 'So when did you just "take the chance"? After you'd killed Nathan? Was this a souvenir? Something you planned to carry with you as a little reminder when you got all his wedding gigs?'

'Dear God, no! I didn't kill him, I swear.'

'I don't believe you.' Mark was edging closer to the terrified Ralph and I started to feel sorry for him. Mark was one of the least threatening people I knew, or so I'd thought, but throw in some atmospheric lighting and a costume of sorts, and he appeared to be in his element.

'What are you doing in there? Come on.' The second voice we'd heard earlier was shouting through the door. 'Just dump it somewhere and let's go.'

Ralph looked at us and started to smile.

CHAPTER 21

We listened as footsteps made their way closer and we were joined by Derek. So this was a father-and-son evening out. Derek looked at me and forced a smile; it made him look particularly creepy in the orange gloom.

'You again. Making a habit of breaking into other people's property now, are you? I'm already aware you love to stick your nose in where it doesn't belong.'

The four of us were facing off. We were all in the wrong, being in Nathan's studio, but when it came to gathering further information, Mark and I had succeeded in a way we hadn't expected. But we weren't murderers, nor had we ever been under suspicion, so I felt like we were the ones who had the upper hand. I also knew that Derek was incredibly supportive of his son, so decided to use that as a point of weakness.

'Why are you returning the camera, Ralph, if not to avoid being caught by the police and having your even bigger crime discovered? Not many people knew where Nathan's spare camera was – how did you find it...?'

'You don't have to say anything,' Derek interrupted.

'It's fine, Dad, I've got this. Everyone knew where it was, we saw him leave his bag. It was just waiting for someone to take something, so I took a chance, spur of the moment...'

'Ralph.' Derek tried again to interrupt his son, but Ralph just waved his hand in his direction to silence him. I knew Ralph was lying. The wedding guests had no reason to go anywhere near the Antler Gallery and they'd have had no idea where Nathan had stashed his camera bag. Even Ralph wouldn't have known, unless Derek had shown him.

'How do you think it looks, Ralph? Someone you have a history of discrediting online is killed and you're found trying to return his property. The only reason you'd do that is you had something major to hide.'

'Okay, I stole his camera. He's been trying to destroy my business for years. I saw an opportunity to get my own back, and I took it. How was I to know someone was going to kill him?'

'Call the police, Mark,' I ordered without looking away from Ralph. I wasn't serious at this point, but I hoped he'd think I was. I heard Mark step towards the phone on the desk.

'Stop this, Ralph, you don't have to do this.'

'Shut up, Dad, I told you I'd take care of it.'

'I screwed up, son. I won't have you take the blame.'

'Dad, please.'

It seemed like once again we were dealing with family members who couldn't help but argue. First it was a newly married husband and wife, now it was a father and son. What had happened to just getting along? Being nice to one another, or at least not airing your laundry in public, and particularly not killing people?

'If you hadn't stuck your nose in, no one would have known,' Derek snarled at me.

'Known what? That you killed Nathan because he was destroying your son's business and sending your investment down the drain? Only he wasn't; he was just incredibly talented and you couldn't compete.' I was looking at Ralph now and could have sworn I saw his eyes glow with rage. 'Jealousy, a common motive for murder.' I saw Ralph flinch and thought he was going to come flying across the room at me, but Derek stepped in front of him, blocking his path.

'He had nothing to do with this. ENOUGH, RALPH! Back off, it's over.' With a steely anger spreading across his face, Derek stepped forward. 'This is nothing to do with Ralph, but think about it.' He looked around the room. 'I don't think your mate Joe would be happy to know you broke into a murder victim's premises. No one needs to know any of us were here, do they?' He grimaced, but I guessed it was meant to be a smile. He was giving me an opportunity to do a deal.

'Too late for that,' chimed Mark. We all turned towards him with the synchronised motion of curious meerkats. To the side of Mark and on the other side of the window was a man and his dog. The man had his phone out and was, I assumed, interrupting his evening stroll with a call to the police.

'Joe's going to kill us,' Mark muttered. 'This will go down as well as a horse's head birthday cake at a child's party.'

Mark and I watched as Derek and Ralph were loaded into the back of a police car. Derek had alternated between 'This is all a misunderstanding, officer' and a furious 'I have friends in very high places, your job is in jeopardy'. Neither tactic had worked their magic, and father and son were now on their way to the police station, Derek facing a murder charge. Derek had always seemed like a possibility, but his reputation and genuine reasons for being able to wander freely around the house meant he'd kept ducking below the radar. Not anymore, though.

Sadly, Mark and I had also found ourselves on a different kind of radar.

'I can't keep covering for you, Sophie, and this time – well, there's nothing I can do. Harnby is on her way here and she's probably going to have you arrested and throw away the key.' Joe shook his head in weary exasperation. 'Breaking and entering? What were you thinking?'

'We didn't break in,' Mark pleaded. 'The back door was open. You can check, it's not been forced.'

'Then how did the window get broken?'

Mark put his hands up in mock defeat. 'No idea, but why would we do that if the door was unlocked?'

I decided to stare at my shoes for a moment.

'I'll try and prevent Harnby from pushing through charges. We'd never have known about Ralph and Derek if you hadn't been in here playing hide and seek, but she might not see it that way.'

Mark bowed as if to an appreciative audience. Joe flicked him a look and Mark stopped messing around.

'Don't push your luck. Family or not, you're still a living nightmare for me right now.'

'This can't be good for Derek,' I commented, trying to swing the conversation away from Mark and me. I didn't like lying to Joe, but I wasn't going to argue with Mark, and the door had been unlocked so we were only half lying.

'No.' Joe smiled. 'Derek knows his way round the house like a full-time member of staff, so getting to the Antler Room wouldn't have been a problem for him. He wears gloves for his job and he'd driven Amelia to the wedding, so chances are he still had his gloves on him. We have multiple pieces of evidence that tie him to the camera and therefore the studio. Not that any of that is quite so important now he's admitted to stealing the camera.'

'Which you'd never have been able to prove had we not been in the right place at the right time,' added Mark.

Joe hesitated. 'Alright, I'll give you that, but don't let it go to your head. You're still in trouble.'

'Plus he had motive,' I continued.

'What about a lack of fingerprints, or is there anything else tying him to the Antler Room?' Mark was starting to take more of an interest.

'We should have enough evidence to mean that's not a problem. Hopefully we can get hold of the suit that Derek wore on the day and there might be some blood on it. Even if it's been dry cleaned, there's a chance that some evidence remained. Then there are his gloves which will also be seized for forensic examination. But even without that, we're building a pretty strong case now.'

I started to think about how easy Derek had had it. Talk about being presented with the ideal opportunity.

'The wedding was the perfect backdrop,' I mused out loud. 'They're the kind of events where if you're not with someone, they just assume you're mingling with others. No one misses each other, no one is suspicious of someone's absence. He could have been gone for an hour, and so long as he was back in time to sit down for dinner, no one would have noticed.'

'Apart from the photos,' Mark added. 'You'd be missing from the usual group shots.'

'Agreed,' replied Joe, 'only they'd already been done. Everyone was mingling before the meal was served, so everyone was distracted.'

'This is going to open the field up for local chauffeur companies. Derek did a lot of work at the house,' Mark said.

I thought about the Mayor, and how Derek sometimes drove the Duke and Duchess if they were in a tight spot. 'It's rather sad. A lot of people treated him like a member of Charleton staff. He had a lot of friends in the security team.' I looked at Mark. He was scruffier than usual in black jeans and an old waterproof jacket, but he was usually perfectly attired in a suit with a waistcoat and tie. It was easy to picture him with a chauffeur's hat, his neatly groomed moustache the ideal finishing touch. 'You could embark on a new career, Mark.'

'What do you mean?'

'Well Derek's business will probably be up for sale once he's been sentenced. You could offer tours of Derbyshire from the warmth of the Rolls. You'd also make the perfect driver for people heading to the house – you could fill them in on its history before they arrived...'

'Stop right there,' Joe interrupted. 'Have you been in a car with him? He'd be hitting deer like they were bowling pins and knocking over old ladies. We'd be scraping tourists off the bonnet.'

'Oi, what happened to family loyalties? And there's nothing wrong with my driving...'

'Oh hell!' Joe exclaimed, cutting Mark off and looking at us like we were troublesome teenagers. 'Harnby is here. Please go home, both of you, and stay out of trouble. I'll talk to you in the morning.'

We had a quick glance in the direction of the police car that had just pulled up and watched as DS Harnby got out. Before she had a chance to spot us, I grabbed Mark and pulled him in the direction of our cars. It was time to go home. Joe had his man, and without us there, there was a chance Harnby would focus on that, rather than our own foray into a life of crime.

CHAPTER 22

I didn't work every Saturday and today was one of those blissful weekends when I didn't need to be anywhere near Charleton House, but I had promised the Duchess I would deliver a gift basket to Amelia and Patrick before they left, so I stirred my tired joints and rolled out of bed. I was only in my mid-forties, but I had already started groaning whenever I attempted to get out of a low sofa or armchair. I'd also taken to sitting on the edge of the bed for a second, gathering the strength I needed before standing. I was turning into an old woman.

Bleary-eyed, I made my bed and pulled the duvet over Pumpkin. She didn't stir. We had reached the time when the bed officially became hers, and as a result I wasn't worthy of any kind of acknowledgment. It was a timeshare arrangement. By eight o'clock in the morning, the bed became Pumpkin's property, and I'd quickly learnt that she wasn't keen to negotiate the time of handover. It was amazing how she could be sweet and happy to be cuddled at 7.59am, but if I didn't leave her alone at eight, she'd look at me out of the corner of a half-closed eye and emit a low growl. I knew my place.

Last night's dinner had been pork and apple sausages, so this morning's breakfast was... cold pork and apple sausages! As I munched my way through them, I ground some coffee beans, and then made myself a mug of coffee so large it would have been better described as a jug. I had opted for jeans and a cosy Fair Isle sweater that had been a gift from a favourite aunt many years ago. Wearing it meant I had finally succumbed to autumn and given up all hope of a final blast of heat before we rolled into winter.

My hiking boots were next to the front door, along with the basket that Joyce had helped me fill. It was overflowing with Charleton House goodies: bags of coffee, boxes of chocolates, three bottles of wine that had been made exclusively for sale in our shops by a friend of the Duke. There was jam and chutney, biscuits, sweet and savoury, and my favourite honey that came from beehives on the estate. It weighed a ton and I had been pleased to hear that Amelia and Patrick were going to his mother's for the night rather than heading straight to the airport, so at least they could leave it there and enjoy it on their return.

I sat at the kitchen table with my feet up on the chair in front of me. I didn't have a sense of victory or even mild satisfaction after Derek and Ralph had been picked up by the police last night. It was clear that Derek in particular had motive and more opportunity than anyone in the house; the means had just fallen into his lap, so to speak. But I felt sorry for everyone who had trusted him over the years. He had spent time alone with the Duke and Duchess, and he was able to wander the house more freely than many Charleton House staff because he had been trusted and liked. Yet he was capable of the kind of anger and spur-of-the-moment action that saw him take advantage of someone's moment of weakness, and instead of helping Nathan, he had killed him. It was sad, but with hindsight, incredibly simple.

I transferred my coffee into a thermal travel mug, pulled on my coat and shouted a goodbye up the stairs to Pumpkin. I was nothing if not entirely under her non-opposable thumb.

The weather had cleared overnight, and although it was still cold, there were signs of blue trying to break through the cloud. The road that wound its way through the estate had plenty of cars on it, most likely locals making the most of the improvement in the weather and wanting to get out for some fresh air after such a wet and grey week. The Stables Café would be busy, but I knew the team could cope and decided not to worry about work. They had my phone number if they needed me.

I took the turning onto the gravel track that led to Pheasant Cottage and swerved my way around pot holes, making a mental note to remind the maintenance team that the road needed a bit of work for the sake of future cottage guests and the suspension on their cars. Up ahead, the cottage looked like something that belonged on the front of a box of shortbread. There were a number of cars parked outside, including one that I recognised as Joyce's. It confused me momentarily, until I realised that she must have accompanied Harold as he said goodbye to his son and new daughter-in-law. I guessed he would be returning to Australia before they got back from their honeymoon, but I still didn't know if he'd be returning with a brightly dressed woman on his arm. I felt my heart sink slightly as I once again considered life here without Joyce to brighten my day, literally and metaphorically.

The door to the cottage was ajar so I pushed it open with my shoulder, my hands gripping the sides of the basket of goodies.

'Hellooo!' I called out towards the sounds of chatter that came from the sitting room. 'I come bearing gifts.'

The small room felt packed with so many people in it. Amelia and Patrick were standing in front of the fireplace, laughing at something Harold had said.

'The Duchess asked me to bring this to you. She hopes that

you have some fond memories of your time here and that you'll return soon.'

'That's so nice of her,' said Amelia as Patrick took the loaded basked from me. Everyone crowded in as they went through the contents.

'I assume you've heard the news?' Harold asked. 'It's such a relief to think that it's all over now. But Derek, how could he? He wasn't exactly family, but still. How's your mother?' he asked Amelia.

She let out a quiet sigh. 'Still in shock, I think, doesn't believe he did it. We offered to delay the honeymoon and stay here with her, but she refused. I think she's convinced that it's all a big mistake and will blow over in a couple of days. I hope she's right, but I'm not so sure.'

'Did you know Derek well?' I asked.

'No, I only met him a couple of times before he married Mum, and I've been so busy with the business since then, I've only been home a handful of times so I haven't got to know him.'

'You'll be glad to get back to normal, I imagine?' Suzanne asked me. She was perched on the arm of the sofa, next to Patrick. I smiled.

'There's no such thing as normal here.'

Joyce laughed at my comment. 'You're right there, girl, and we wouldn't have it any other way. We're a colourful crowd and life here is marvellously unpredictable.' I shot a glance at Harold. He looked a little concerned as she described life here in such positive terms.

There was a knock at the door and a male voice shouted hello down the corridor. Suzanne ran out to see who it was and everyone started to gather their coats and bags.

'It was the dry cleaners,' Suzanne declared to Amelia as she came back into the room. 'I sent Patrick's wedding outfit off to be cleaned along with mine, one less thing for you both to think about after the honeymoon.'

Patrick reached for the coat hanger, the transparent bag showing his black suit and pressed white shirt. Suzanne put hers over her shoulder and led the way out of the room. I followed her outside. There was something familiar about the neatly pressed outfit she carried. I had of course seen her in it, looking incredibly stylish – sort of Greta Garbo, or Marlene Dietrich without the top hat. If I'd worn the same outfit, I would have resembled a dumpy waitress without an ounce of grace.

I watched as the various family members said their goodbyes. There were hugs and kisses, wishes for a wonderful honeymoon and promises to send lots of photos. I felt a little awkward; I didn't really belong there as the family said goodbye after such an emotional week, but I'd been unable to find an appropriate moment to make my escape.

But there was something else that left me feeling uncomfortable. While everyone else was clearly relieved that Nathan's killer had been identified, I felt no such relief. Something was niggling; something I'd seen recently, but I couldn't think what it was. It was as though I had forgotten someone's name and it was on the tip of my tongue.

I thought of something Joe had said to me. He'd asked me a question. Stepping away from the group, I stood next to my car and phoned Joe, willing him to pick up.

'Sophie, I was just thinking of you. I need a coffee and that always makes you come to mind.' I could hear the smile in his voice. He was probably still enjoying the feeling of having caught Nathan's killer, and I hated the thought of being the one to burst his bubble.

'Yesterday you asked me the hair colour of the female waiting staff for the wedding. Why was that?'

As I listened, I watched Patrick load bags into the boot of the newlyweds' car. There followed another round of hugs, then everyone waved them off and started to get in their own cars.

Joyce waved at me, mimed making a phone call and I gave her a thumbs up. We'd chat later.

Suzanne got into her car after laying her dry cleaning out on the back seat. When Joe had finished talking, I took a deep breath and told him that I thought the police had arrested the wrong person. Derek hadn't killed Nathan, but I was sure I knew who had.

CHAPTER 23

'Joe's furious!' Mark was the first to arrive and walked into the house looking down the hallway, checking for Pumpkin. They didn't get on. 'Not at you; at himself, the rest of his team. Mind you, I doubt DS Harnby is going to become your best friend anytime soon.'

There was a loud bang as he placed a shopping bag on the counter. It contained multiple bottles of wine, a selection of cheese and two enormous baguettes. I'd invited everyone round to mine for the evening, with instructions to 'bring whatever you've got in your fridge'. I knew that they'd do no such thing and we'd end up with a massive amount of delicious food, made or bought expressly for the evening; I already had a butternut squash soup bubbling away on the stove and an apple pie in the oven.

Mark reached for wine glasses, and then yelped, 'Where the hell did you come from?' He was talking to Pumpkin who had head-butted his leg with a force that made me question whether or not there wasn't just a little bit of goat in her DNA. She had a wicked look in her eye, and after staring at Mark long enough to unnerve him, she sauntered off towards her food bowl.

'I can't imagine I made his day,' I replied. 'I had to be the one to tell him that Derek didn't kill Nathan.'

Mark slowly turned his head towards me, and then tilted it. I half expected him to spin his head all the way round; he was already doing a fine impression of an owl.

'But Derek had every opportunity.'

'He did, but his anger hadn't been festering long enough to make him want to actually kill Nathan. I'll fill you in when the others are here; that way I only have to explain once.'

Mark had included a bottle of sparkling rosé in his bag and he popped the cork.

'This is for Joyce, but I reckon we can make a start on it.' The bubbles looked refreshing and I mentally willed him to hurry up. 'I was at work today,' he continued. 'A private tour for a couple's twenty-fifth wedding anniversary. Lovely people – hopefully we'll still be so happy after twenty-five years of marriage.' I laughed, but it came out as a snort. 'Anyway, I took them to the café afterwards and Chelsea was working. Now, I don't say this lightly, but she delivered the most incredible service. She was gracious, switched on, helpful, funny. She was a different person. Her hair was tied back and I swear her uniform actually appeared to fit her. Have you hired her more engaging identical twin?'

That really did make me smile, and I felt a warmth of pride flow through me.

'No, I didn't hire her twin. I actually got my act together and behaved like a decent manager. I talked to her and I listened. Remember I told you I'd seen her out with an older man in a wheelchair?' Mark nodded. 'Well, she was becoming so unreliable, there was a risk I would have to discipline her, but when I saw the two of them together, I realised how little I knew about her. So, I sat her down and insisted she come clean. Her mother died years ago, before Chelsea became a teenager, so it's just been her and her dad. A couple of years back, he was diagnosed with multiple sclerosis, and ever since she's been his sole carer. She wasn't a dizzy blonde, or bad at her job; she was struggling to cope. That's why she was always running late – she had to get him ready before she left for work. She was always on her phone because she was worried about him and sorting out the usual household issues like dishwasher repairmen, or paying bills. Often she just didn't have the time to wash her uniform before work.

'So, we made a few changes. She starts later in the morning, we've swapped her days off so they work better for her, and I've promised we can be flexible about that so she can take her dad to his doctor's appointments. She also knows that she can talk to me if things get too much, or we need to make more changes. It's only been a couple of days, but she already seems so much happier and more relaxed, which in turn means she can focus properly on her job.'

'Well it's working, she's like a different person. Tina isn't going to recognise her when she comes back off holiday.'

'True. I'm also going to spend some time with Tina, make sure there isn't anyone else falling through the cracks. I have a fantastic team, but I don't think I've been the best boss.'

'Rubbish.' Mark squeezed my arm affectionately. 'Here.' He passed me a glass. 'To Chelsea.'

I raised my glass and savoured the bubbles on my tongue. Our moment of calm was shattered by a loud banging on the door and shouts of 'Trick or treat'. Mark rolled his eyes and put his glass down.

'I'll let the children in.' I heard him open the door and welcome Joyce and Craig. 'You muppets. You're a few days early for one thing. Your costumes are great, though, you look terrifying. OW! Muuuuuum!' he shouted down the hallway. 'Joyce punched me.'

'Good,' I shouted back. 'Now get in here and pour the poor woman a drink.'

A grinning Joyce entered the kitchen. She wore a fluffy pink sweater with a pair of extremely tight cream jeans; so tight I could see how skimpy her knickers were. Her pink stilettos and bright pink nail polish finished off the outfit. Her hair looked a little higher than usual and she had opted to wear a pair of black-rimmed Harry Potter style spectacles; she looked as if she managed the children's section in a library. By her usual standards, it was a relatively low-key ensemble.

As I passed her a glass, I took a closer look. I was sure her makeup was hiding evidence of tears. She winked at me and raised her glass, but didn't say anything. I wasn't used to sensing sadness around Joyce, but this evening it was clearly there.

Everyone bustled around the kitchen, laying out their food, putting drinks in the fridge and paying varying degrees of attention to Pumpkin, who quickly tired of all the fuss and sauntered off to the bedroom. We then loaded up our plates and made ourselves at home in the sitting room. I'd made a fire and – miraculously, as it was something I'd never fully mastered – it was now crackling away happily and would have made the perfect backdrop for a Christmas card.

'Christ, Sophie, I need to take you shopping.' Joyce was standing in the middle of the room, inspecting my decor. 'You've been here well over a year, but this looks like a doctor's waiting room. There are more colours on the palette than white, off white and sort of white, you know.' She sank into the armchair closest to the fire and almost vanished. Mark grabbed her wine glass from her before she dropped it. Somehow managing to keep her plate of food straight, she used her now empty hand to pull herself into a more upright position. 'Does this chair even know what a spring is? That's it, you and I are going furniture shopping, and we'll get you some pictures while we're at it. You need some cheerful colours, some animal print cushions. You need to bring this place to life.'

'Errr, I quite like minimal,' I offered nervously.

'Minimal is another word for lazy. Matching colours and

experimenting with shapes and fabrics takes time and effort, but it's something I've perfected over the years. Think of it as my early Christmas present for you – I will be your interior decorator.'

She shovelled an enormous piece of cheese into her mouth on a chunk of bread. The discussion, it seemed, was over. Mark looked at me, eyes wide open, mouth clamped shut. I could see he was trying not to laugh out loud. Craig on the other hand mimed the sign of the cross and looked upwards. That was all we needed and the three of us burst into laughter, hiccupping wine and grabbing our napkins just to be on the safe side.

'Ungrateful,' was Joyce's simple response.

There was another knock at the door and Craig got up. I heard Joe's voice and took a deep breath. I hadn't seen him since I'd called him the day before to tell him I wasn't convinced the police had arrested the right person for Nathan's murder, and I wasn't sure what to expect.

He creaked as he walked in; he was dressed head to toe in motorcycle leathers, and closely followed by his brother Bill. Joe put his helmet on the floor, peeled off his jacket and sat down next to Mark on the sofa. Bill gave me a kiss on the cheek, winked and sat on the floor in front of his husband. He had the bulk of his rugby playing past, but clearly kept fit and got down on the floor with the ease of a child. Craig handed the two men a beer that he had fetched from the fridge. Joe was about to say something, but Craig cut him off.

'It's alcohol-free, don't worry.'

Joe looked at me, then took a swig of beer.

'Part of me wants to be mad as hell at you. You're forever ignoring my instructions to stay out of police business. But, thanks to you, we didn't arrest an innocent man for murder.' He took another drink and the rest of us sat in silence and waited. 'Thank you, Sherlock.' The small group erupted into cheers and more toasts, and I breathed an enormous sigh of relief.

Joyce was the first to speak. 'What gave it away, Sophie? I was with you up at the cottage and I don't remember anyone saying anything in particular.'

'It wasn't anything anyone said. Not at that point, anyway. It was what got delivered. Patrick and Suzanne's outfits were dropped off by the dry cleaners, and in the bag they both just looked like waiters' outfits. Joe had asked me the hair colour of the servers I'd provided for the wedding meal. If Joe was asking, then he was clearly looking for one particular hair colour. And none of the servers that night were brunettes. I realised that if she took off her suit jacket, Suzanne – a brunette – could have been mistaken for a server if she'd left the party and gone out towards the kitchens. No one would have looked twice at her.'

'Which gave her opportunity,' Mark said, quite rightly, 'but what was her motive?'

I looked over at Joe. He took another swig of beer, and then waved his bottle at me, indicating that I should go on.

'Harold told us that Suzanne and Patrick had been friends for years. They'd been a couple for a brief while, but split up and remained close. So close that Patrick made her his "best woman" for the wedding. Every time I spoke to her about Patrick, she was extremely protective of him. She might well have become friends with Amelia, but I guess that was only so she was able to keep Patrick close – something is better than nothing, kind of thing. So I was convinced she still had feelings for him.

'The other day, I talked to Kristian, who said that the fight that he and Nathan had had all those years ago actually started because Suzanne was having a row with Nathan. It was nothing to do with Amelia. Suzanne was the reason things got heated. She's the one who had a history of anger towards Nathan. Not Patrick or Amelia, or Kristian, not really.

'When Amelia decided to ask Nathan to do the wedding photos out of spite, he could have been any ex-boyfriend. The fact that it was Nathan was neither here nor there to her, or

Patrick. He was angry not because of any particular history he had with Nathan, but because Amelia had surprised him in a rather unkind way. Joe, you've got Suzanne in custody. Has she talked about what happened on the wedding day?'

'Absolutely. Once I told her that we had her shoes and were certain that there was blood on them, she started to confess.'

'And is there blood on the shoes?' Craig asked.

'Almost definitely. She'd made getting her outfit dry-cleaned a priority. I don't think there was much on there – maybe some blood hidden on the black fabric of the trousers – otherwise she wouldn't have hung around for so long after the wedding. She'd have wanted to get cleaned up. But she didn't give much thought to her shoes. Any blood on them wasn't obvious, and she was probably going to ditch them as soon as she was heading home, leave the evidence miles away from Charleton.

'It seems that Nathan had worked out that Suzanne still had feelings for Patrick. That's why they were fighting years ago: he was threatening to tell Patrick. Suzanne was terrified that if he found out, then Amelia, or maybe even Patrick himself, would say it was too difficult for them to remain friends, and Suzanne didn't want that. Like you said, Sophie, she still wanted him in her life, even if she couldn't be his wife.

'That was it for a long time, then Nathan appeared at the dinner on the Friday night. He started making comments to Suzanne, little digs about how she was probably wishing she would be the one in the white dress, how it should have been her day. Comments about how she wouldn't get to have kids with Patrick, but maybe they'd let her be godmother. Nathan just kept going and wouldn't stop. It seems he had a bit of a mean streak.

'He continued on the wedding day, making comments every time he walked past her or took photos of her. She was getting more and more wound up and followed him back to the Antler Gallery during an argument. As Sophie said, no one really paid her any attention. She was just someone else in a black and white outfit surrounded by servers wearing black and white…'

'Hang on,' I butted in, 'I've just had a thought. Suzanne must have been the "server" that Harriet Smedley saw, and then complained to me about being scruffy. Her hair was down, her trousers were fashionably tight – or just plain tight to Harriet – and her shirt wasn't tucked in like the other servers'. So to Harriet and her nit-picking mind, she did stand out. To everyone else who was so busy, she blended right in. They just saw someone in black and white.'

Joe pulled his phone out of his pocket and started typing. 'I'll make sure we talk to this Harriet, there's no harm in having another witness. Well remembered, Soph. Anyway, Suzanne and Nathan were in the gallery and, so she claims, they had a fight. She slammed him against the wall, which is easy to imagine as she's pretty fit, and the antlers fell and hit him. They were already loose and it didn't take much for the screws that remained to shake out. She could have helped him – the antlers had caused him a lot of damage, but he would have survived. Instead she, well, used her foot and gave them an extra shove, killing him in the process. She was then able to leave, once again being mistaken for a server, and rejoin the wedding party.'

'Luckily for her,' I continued, 'Derek had already been in the gallery and stolen Nathan's spare camera from his bag. Derek wanted to get back at Nathan as he felt he was sabotaging his son's business, which he wasn't. Little did he know that Nathan would later be killed and there would be plenty to point suspicion in his direction. All the while, Suzanne – a committed, loyal, loving friend to both Patrick and Amelia, who seemed so calm and level headed, the ideal best person at a wedding – was playing the part of being the perfect support in the aftermath of traumatic events on what was meant to be the best day of their lives. No one suspected that she had been harbouring pretty intense feelings towards Nathan. Feelings that were close enough to the surface to erupt in such a violent way.'

'So much love and pain on one day,' Craig observed. 'While Patrick and Amelia declared their love, Suzanne was devastated and ended up taking someone's life. It's all very Shakespearean. Talking of Shakespeare, although perhaps more comedy than tragedy,' he looked across at Mark, and then in my direction, 'have you chosen a date?'

'Father,' I moaned. Mark leaned over to where I was sitting on the floor and took my hand.

'Sophie, sweet Sophie, I have something I need to tell you.'

'Don't worry, darling, I guessed a long time ago,' I replied. 'I'm not your type.'

'As gorgeous as you are, no, you're not. I'm rather fond of ex-rugby players, and I've got my eye on one called Bill. Maybe he'll marry me.'

Everyone laughed as I pretended briefly to be hurt.

'Really, you think your luck's in, do you, Mark?' Bill responded with a grin. 'Don't give up hope, Sophie, I've not made me mind up yet.'

'Bit late for that,' laughed Mark as he wiggled his ring finger in the air and displayed his wedding ring.

After the laughter had died down, we all went quiet and finished our drinks, each of us in our own little world. Eventually, Craig returned to the kitchen and came back with another bottle of wine. As he topped up our glasses, I watched Mark take Joyce's hand. In a quiet voice, and with a sincere look on his face, he asked her what we had all been afraid to.

'So, sweet Cookie, do we get to keep you?'

I thought for a moment that she would snap at him for calling her Cookie, Harold's pet name for her. But instead she seemed to hold his hand a little tighter.

'Yes, I'm staying right here. I have a life, a home, a job I love and good friends. Too much time has passed. I don't belong on the other side of the world.'

With our glasses refilled, we gave a final toast and a chorus of 'To Joyce' echoed around my tiny living room. I realised that Joyce's sadness was accompanied by some relief; it must have been a difficult and heart-breaking decision. If I was honest, I too was relieved, but for entirely selfish reasons.

'But, Mark Boxer,' Joyce's face had taken on a stern look, 'if you ever call me "Cookie" again, you won't be heading down under, you'll be six feet under. Understood?'

'Please don't,' Joe begged. 'Or at least if you do kill him, write a confession and leave it with the body. That way I stand a chance of figuring out who did it before Sophie.'

Joe turned to look at me and winked. It seemed I had been forgiven.

SLEEP LIKE THE DEAD

*For Joshua,
welcome to a family of bookworms.*

CHAPTER 1

'Well you wouldn't catch me sleeping in here, not for love nor money. I can't believe people are paying to spend a night tossing and turning on these cold wooden floors. It's like a military camp. You're not even giving them beds.'

Joyce tutted before striding across the room and peering closely at a portrait of a young child from the 17th century. 'Dear God, I pity that child's parents, having to stare at that creepy mug all day.'

She had a point, it wasn't the most flattering portrait of the toddler, dressed strangely from head to toe in a smock and bonnet. Its protruding eyes and lips made it look as if someone was attempting to pump air into the child to see if it would pop. It was the kind of portrait that belonged in the attic.

'Just think of how much money they'll spend in the shop,' I offered. Joyce Brocklehurst managed all the gift shops at Charleton House, so I hoped that idea would cheer her up.

'They better had, we're opening early tomorrow morning and I have overtime costs to cover.' She strode off down the room, checking out more paintings as she went. I watched, fascinated by the pile of blonde hair on her head, her trademark bouffant as steady as a Roman column, not a wobble in sight. She turned slowly and steadily on her four-inch wedge heels, and surveyed the scene.

'Barmy, every one of them – £150 to spend the night sleeping on the floor of a creaky, draughty 500-year-old building.' She made her way back along the length of the room and rolled her eyes as she walked past me. 'Rather you than me, Sophie,' was her parting shot as she disappeared through the door.

I was left alone in the Long Gallery, the silence unnerving. Against the maroon velvet flocked wallpaper, portraits of the Fitzwilliam-Scott family members stared out at me, each one seemingly assessing my respectability and suitability to be gracing the hallowed halls of their palatial home. I half expected one of them to come alive and shout for a guard to escort me out.

But I very much belonged here at Charleton House, the home of one of England's most significant aristocratic families. The current Duke and Duchess resided on the floor above; the rest of the house was open to the public, and this evening sixty of them would experience a night in the splendid baroque building. Admittedly, as Joyce had observed, they were having to sleep on the wooden floor of the rather chilly gallery, but on the other hand, they would get to do what usually only family members and their personal guests got to experience: sleep amongst the art and antiques of one of the country's most outstanding historic houses.

These sleepovers occurred very infrequently and the tickets were much sought after. The evening's guests would be taken on tours and told tales that hadn't previously been shared with the public, hearing secrets and becoming acquainted with scandals that had occurred in the very rooms they were exploring. They would be entertained by characters from centuries past, and dine on food that my chef had researched and ensured fitted in with the theme for the evening.

Fortunately, I wasn't responsible for the whole shindig; that daunting role lay in the hands of Yeshim Scrimshaw, the events manager. I only really had to worry about the food, and as the Head of Catering, I'd worked with my chef to make sure we would offer a fun and interesting menu. One of the three cafés I managed would become a dining room for the night, and we would ensure our guests had constant access to hot drinks and, more importantly, a supply of biscuits. This wasn't the first of these events we'd run, and if there was one thing we had learnt, it was that biscuits could fix every problem, calm frayed nerves and ease the frustration of a sleepless night.

'So, tonight is your lucky night.'

I hadn't heard Mark Boxer enter the room so I jumped as he drawled his words into my ear, sounding like a medallion-wearing, chest-hair-revealing lothario. I turned to face my friend, who had a smirk on his face, and looked at him blankly, hoping he would explain. I'd always considered it a great honour to work in such a magnificent building, but tonight was going to be a lot of hard work, and he made it sound like I'd won the lottery.

'I bet you never thought you'd get to spend the night with me. We can create special moments throughout the evening, and then in the morning…'

'You can go home to your husband,' I interrupted.

'I was going to say that I'd do my best to be gentle while leaving you with a broken heart and unbeatable memories, but have it your way.'

I laughed as Mark feigned hurt and dramatically straightened his tie. Not that it needed straightening. Just like the rest of him, it was impeccable. The knot was perfectly tied, his waistcoat had the bottom button undone, as had been the convention from at least the Victorian period up to the present day; his handlebar moustache was waxed and curled, his suit spotless, and his shoes reflected the light from the chandeliers.

'Are you really staying the whole night?' I asked.

'No, not really. I figured I'd deliver my tour, stay for the rest of the entertainment, and then head home before the clock strikes twelve and I turn into a pumpkin. You?'

I shook my head. As loyal as I was to Charleton House, I drew the line at sleeping on a wooden floor. I checked my watch and swore – I had work to do.

Mark was fiddling with a watch he'd pulled out of a small pocket in his waistcoat. The gold chain matched his tie clip.

'Nice – new?'

He nodded. 'Early birthday present from Bill, he thought I might like to have it for this evening.' Mark gently wiped the glass.

'It's your birthday this week?' I asked in mock surprise. 'I had no idea.'

Mark raised an eyebrow as he put his present away. 'Really? Then I guess that carrot cake I saw cooling on a rack this morning must be for someone else.'

Damn, he'd seen it. I was hoping to keep it a surprise. I had yet to finish it, but in theory I had plenty of time before the get-together that Bill, Mark's husband, was hosting for him on Monday, his actual birthday.

'Come on, old man.' I took his arm and turned him to face the door. 'I have work to be getting on with, and if you've nothing better to do than creep up on unsuspecting women, you can give me a hand.'

Mark allowed himself to be led out. We were about to take our first steps down an ornately carved wooden staircase when a scream made us jump. It was followed by the shattering of glass and a tirade of shouting. I grabbed Mark, who steadied himself on the banister, and by some miracle neither of us fell. I had known this would be an eventful night full of drama, but hopefully of the entertaining kind.

I let go of Mark's arm and ran down two steps at a time. It seemed that the curtain was already up and the show had begun.

. . .

Yeshim Scrimshaw was standing in the middle of a sparkling sea of broken glass. Anger was etched on her face and she was glaring at a young blond-haired man in a small, partly concealed doorway. He was trying to hold back laughter.

Yeshim has an almost superhuman ability to remain calm, and we were getting a world-class display of her skills. For all his sniggering and nonchalance, the young man still hadn't moved. I guessed he was just a little afraid of the outcome if he did.

With a coldness that matched the sharp edges of the glass that lay around her, Yeshim spoke slowly, never once taking her eyes off the object of her measured wrath. After she'd finished telling him what she would do with him if he ever tried to surprise her like that again, she turned her attention to me.

'Sophie, I do apologise. Thanks to this buffoon's attempt at humour, I'll need you to fetch another thirty champagne flutes. I was transferring them through to the Gilded Hall so we could set up for the welcome drinks. That plan has, however, been thwarted.'

I stepped off the bottom stair and reached for the empty tray that hung by her side.

'No problem, Yeshim, I'm on it. I'll call housekeeping and ask them to come and clear this up. Mark, why don't you take our young friend here and put him out of harm's way?'

I looked over my shoulder before leaving and saw Mark rest a hand on the young man's shoulder and steer him out of another door. Yeshim gave her head a little shake and a smile returned, if a little mechanically. Clapping her hands, she sent everyone on their way. The first mishap of the evening had been dealt with.

'He's called Douglas Popplewell. He worked in the ticket office for a couple of years, and then started as a tour guide about three months ago, although he's been guiding in other buildings in Derbyshire as a volunteer for a few years. He could be worse. A bit overenthusiastic and more of a showman than I like, but that will calm down with time.'

Mark was filling me in on the young man who had jumped out at Yeshim. Apparently he'd thought it would be funny, but he hadn't spotted the tray of glasses in her hands.

'He's trying to play it cool, but you can tell it's an act. He thinks he can charm everyone, but it doesn't work on Yeshim – she can see straight through him.'

We were lining up sixty flutes, ready to be filled with champagne and handed to the evening's guests as they arrived. Yeshim was in a corner on her hands and knees, fiddling with a plug socket. The budget for this event wouldn't stretch to live music, so small modern speakers were concealed at the bottom of the grand marble staircase.

I nearly dropped a glass and added to the evening's tally of breakages when a burst of ABBA at full volume echoed around the room.

'Sorry,' shouted Yeshim as she turned it down. 'Wrong playlist.'

The more calming notes of Mendelssohn drifted out as we polished the glassware and Mark continued to tell me about his newest tour-guiding colleague.

'He can keep a crowd's attention, it's quite impressive really. But he needs to put more time in behind the scenes. He doesn't always get his facts right. The public generally don't notice if he's a year or two out on his timelines, or gets the Duke's great-great-uncle's cousin's name wrong, but it's unprofessional and drives me barmy.'

Mark continued to talk as my mind wandered. I was always slightly in awe of the imposing marble staircase that dominated the room and the gilded balcony that ran around all four sides, giving the space its name. We were being watched over by gods and goddesses who inhabited the fresco on the high ceiling.

'Are we ready?' Yeshim had composed herself and her calm, cheery voice was back. 'Where's the Duke and Duchess? They need to be here to greet everyone. What about the servers? They should have the champagne on trays.'

'Coming, I'm here, I'm here.' Betsy Kemp, or rather Henrietta Fitzwilliam-Scott, the 8th Duchess of Ravensbury, came flying down the stairs two at a time. The crinoline that puffed her dress out around and behind her made it drag on the carpet and was in danger of sending her tumbling as she ran.

'Where's the Duke? He's late,' Yeshim called as the Duchess jumped the last few steps and landed in front of her.

'He's struggling with his necktie, but he's right behind me.' Betsy was out of breath. The calm stately demeanour of a 19th century Duchess was nowhere to be seen; instead, she was red-faced and panting. Her hands planted firmly on her hips, eyes closed, she turned her head up to the ceiling. 'I really need to get fitter.'

'Or set off on time,' Mark muttered to me. 'Betsy's always doing this, the others are really good at adlibbing her late arrival for every scene she's in.'

'Time,' I shouted. 'Time, Betsy, you've still got your watch on.'

Betsy glanced down at her wrist.

'Bugger. Thanks, er...'

'Sophie.'

'Sophie, right, here.' She ripped the watch off her wrist and tossed it across the room at me. Fortunately, my schoolgirl rounders skills didn't let me down and I caught it, shoving it in my pocket.

Yeshim started organising things again.

'Where's the Duke?' she repeated. 'The guests are arriving. I want everyone in place when they walk in.'

I'd heard the chatter over the radios and knew that some of our overnight guests had already arrived. They were being taken first to the Long Gallery to drop off their belongings and claim a spot on the floor with their sleeping bags. Once they were ready they would be escorted, many of them in costume, here to the drinks reception, the first event of their packed schedule. I looked out of a window onto a courtyard and could spot a few of them being escorted by the warders on duty that night.

The warders' regular work was during the day when they would be in the house, talking to the public, sharing stories with them and making sure they didn't climb on furniture or touch the delicate and extremely valuable objects on display. At night, they helped out on events, and this evening a small team was staying over to support Yeshim and her staff.

The sound of someone running along the gilded balcony caused our heads to swivel and we watched as Harvey Graves, dressed as James Fitzwilliam-Scott, the 8th Duke of Ravensbury, came thundering around the corner towards the top of the stairs.

'DON'T RUN!' bellowed Mark. 'The Conservation Department will do their nut if they see you pounding along the balcony.'

'Sorry, sorry,' Harvey replied breathlessly. He too jumped the last few steps and landed next to his 'wife'. Between deep breaths, he leaned over to her.

'That bloody woman is here, I've just seen her arrive. She's all petticoats and cleavage.'

'Conrad was wondering if she'd turn up,' replied Betsy. 'I hope Lycia controls herself and we don't add fireworks to the evening's itinerary.'

They grinned at each other, and after straightening themselves out, they looked just like the portrait of the couple painted in 1865 – the year in which this evening's events were set – that hung in the Long Gallery, a reference that some of the guests might spot, if they hadn't consumed too much alcohol.

'Who are they talking about?' I asked Mark. He shook his head and let out a long sigh.

'If it's who I think it is, then we're going to have our hands full. Philippa Clough, blogger, Dickens addict, and subject of previous scandals.'

CHAPTER 2

Mark and I stood back and watched as the guests started to arrive. Some had clearly popped to their local costume shop and wore cheap 'historic' dress that didn't really fit any era. Modern shoes peeked out from under their hems, watches were on their wrists, and there was a century-leaping display of jewellery. They entered laughing, their excitability ramping up as they took in their surroundings and helped themselves to a glass of champagne.

Others were clearly obsessives who had spent days and probably weeks bent over sewing machines, surrounded by dress patterns and determined to get every detail right. The room was quickly filling with top hats and bonnets, and many of the women wore gloves that reached their elbows. Heavy silk mingled with velvet in a variety of hues, from sombre greens and blues to bright reds and pinks, with a few stripes thrown in for good measure. A couple of women had even poured themselves into corsets; it was going to be interesting to see how they fared in those, especially after the hearty meal that I knew Gregg Danforth, my chef, was cooking up for them. There were more women than men, whose costume contributions ranged from a reluctantly donned top hat and cane, to full evening attire with fitted waistcoat and tailcoat. It looked like a cross between a film set and a steampunk party.

This was a million miles away from my previous jobs, running cafés and restaurants in London. There I usually only dealt with city types in dull suits, talking about the stock market. This couldn't have been more different and it was wonderful. I looked down at my navy blue suit. I'd brightened it up with a vivid orange silk shirt, but I still felt dowdy compared to the peacock-like display before me.

'He doesn't look too happy.' I nodded in the direction of a middle-aged man who wore an oversized tailcoat over a pair of jeans.

'He'll be fine once Dr Alcohol has loosened him up. Which might be sooner than you think,' Mark commented. We watched him grab a second glass whilst simultaneously emptying his first.

Some of those who had made less effort looked a little crestfallen as they took in the works of art that others wore and, in some cases, had probably cost hundreds of pounds. They in turn looked snootily down their noses, no doubt viewing themselves as the true aficionados who in a parallel world would have lived somewhere as beautiful as Charleton House. The 8th Duke and Duchess circulated in all their finery, making their way to every guest as they arrived, complimenting them on their outfit, no matter how much effort they had made, or not. They asked them about their journey, if their horses were tired or if their coach driver had found a room in the local inn.

Betsy and Harvey were experienced members of the live interpretation team. They weren't just actors, they were passionate educators who carried out research and inhabited a role, taking pride in their ability to remain in character no matter what bizarre questions the public tried to flummox them with. I watched the Duke discuss the unusual fabric and design of someone's trainers as though he'd never laid eyes on them before in his life, wondering if they had travelled from the Orient or Americas and commenting that he was sure they would never catch on in England.

'There she is.' Mark was discreetly pointing to a large-bosomed woman in a straw-yellow silk dress. Despite having been one of the first to arrive at the house, Philippa Clough had engineered a grand entrance as the last to arrive at the reception. Her dress projected out, keeping people at arm's length, flounces of material making it appear large enough to house a small family. The low-cut neckline was trimmed with lace, drawing my eye down to her cleavage, which was indeed quite startling – you'd have to be blind, or dead, not to notice.

'She doesn't have to open her mouth and she's the loudest in the room,' Mark observed. 'Ah, there's her little coterie.' He nodded towards a couple that Philippa had spotted and was dramatically sweeping towards across the room in their direction. Giving them both exaggerated kisses and twirling in front of them, she laughed as she clutched her corset. 'Thomas and Annie Hattersley. Annie always comes to events with Philippa, but is a mouse in comparison. Hard to be anything else in her company. Thomas has been to one or two evenings – doesn't like to get too involved, but he knows his history.'

Silence slowly fell across the room as a young man dressed as a footman stood part way up the stairs. Looking wonderful in his double-breasted waistcoat, breeches and silk stockings, he cleared his throat and introduced the Duke and Duchess in a commanding voice.

Out of the corner of my eye, I spotted Joyce at the back of the room. She had clearly slipped in to watch. Joyce was known as a formidable woman who took no prisoners; there were colleagues who had wondered out loud whether or not she had ripped out her own heart with her talon-like fingernails, but those who got to know her discovered a pussycat behind the fearsome exterior, and she was as proud of the work of her colleagues as anyone at Charleton House.

The footman stepped back and the 8th Duke came forward to speak.

'Lords, ladies and gentlemen, the Duchess and I are delighted to welcome you to our home for what promises to be a most enjoyable evening. We always gain such pleasure from sharing our family's treasures with our guests, and tonight is no exception. It has been a little challenging to accommodate so many of you, but I feel we have been able to find you rooms which befit your status,' the Duke paused as the audience laughed, 'and we hope you have a restful night's sleep. Before that, however, our chef has prepared a magnificent feast for us to enjoy before you embark on a range of tours and activities. We also have a very special guest, Mr Charles Dickens, who will be entertaining us before the night is drawn to a close.'

There were whoops and whistles at the mention of the famous author.

'So please, take a moment or two to finish your drinks, and then our staff will direct you to the dining room.'

A polite round of applause followed and the Duke took his wife's arm, leading her back into the crowd. I watched as they approached Thomas and Annie Hattersley. Annie gave an awkward little curtsy, and then appeared to hang on every word the Duchess said. Thomas took a step back and avoided getting drawn in.

I was about to head into the kitchen and check on Gregg when we were joined by Douglas Popplewell, who along with Mark would be leading tours during the evening. He had a scowl etched on his face.

'I hope she ends up in your group, I don't want to be anywhere near that woman.'

Mark offered him some advice. 'I'll see what I can do, but don't let it get to you. It might have been the first time, but it won't be the last. Leading tours is like herding cats – some are easily pleased and will hypnotically listen to and believe every word, and some will hiss at you as soon as you put a syllable out of place. Just do your homework and be prepared for anything.'

Douglas huffed and walked off, plucking the sole remaining glass of champagne off a table. Mark shook his head.

'Like that's going to help.'

'What happened? Why's he so mad?' I asked.

'Our delightful Miss Clough writes a history blog. As well as articles about particular people or places, she reviews the attractions she visits, their customer service, cafés, and tours. Last month she came here for our new tour on the current Duke's modern art collection. Douglas was leading it and she tore him to shreds in her review. It was quite painful to read. We'll need to be especially careful tonight – she's a Charles Dickens nut and will be looking for inaccuracies.'

'Was the poor review of Douglas deserved?'

'Some of it, yes. The review was a bit over the top, but that's her style. She once described me as an extremely knowledgeable maypole whose main fascination is the sound of my own voice.'

'That's so unfair, you're the epitome of shy and retiring.'

'Exactly. If I had my way, I'd tuck myself in the corner of a library and have as little contact as possible with my fellow man.'

I laughed out loud. As ludicrous statements went, that one rated pretty highly.

Dinner was to be served in the Library Café. As the name suggests, it resembles a library fit for a family as significant as the Fitzwilliam-Scotts. The walls are lined with books; during the day, leather wing-backed armchairs are scattered about, with a few of them gathered around a surprisingly realistic fake log fire. Tables and chairs of various shapes and sizes, all in dark wood, fill the rest of the space, giving visitors a warm, cosy room in which to enjoy tea and scones or a sandwich as they recharge their batteries before heading off to explore more of the house.

Tonight, however, we had turned it into a dining room appropriate for guests of the 8th Duke and Duchess of Ravensbury. Three long tables filled the space, each decorated with candelabras and autumnal-themed foliage from the gardens. Ivy had been draped along the centre of the tables, red rosehip berries glistened amongst the leaves. The coffee and antique pink shades of dried hydrangeas gathered beneath the candles. Box, yew and fir gave a nod to Christmas that lay just around the corner. An array of cutlery had been laid out, although it was silver plated, rather than the antique silver that the current Duke and Duchess used when entertaining. The log fire was roaring and the faux candles flickered along the tables. It was a wonderful warm haven from the cold November night beyond the walls of the house.

Tina, my Library Café supervisor, was double-checking the tables and putting the chairs in place. Chelsea, one of my young and enthusiastic assistants, was laying out a set of cards in each place. They were both dressed in black shirts and long black skirts, a long white apron and white maidservant's cap finishing off the outfit. I realised just how strange it was to see them in anything other than modern dress.

I picked up a couple of the cards that Chelsea had laid out and took a look. Gregg had asked for little recipe cards so that the guests could recreate their meals at home, but there were a few extras that I knew we weren't serving: a large pork pie, and chestnut and apple mince pies. There was also a recipe for a gin punch, something that Gregg had told me was a favourite of Charles Dickens, but we'd decided there was already enough alcohol available this evening and we didn't want to find ourselves protecting the contents of the house from a bunch of inebriated partygoers who wanted to clamber over furniture to take the perfect selfie. The guests would also receive a decorated copy of the full menu as a souvenir, which contained extra information about Victorian dining at Charleton House.

I could hear a low murmur from beyond the door; it gradually got louder and was joined by footsteps and laughter. The guests were on their way, and I had yet to see Gregg.

'All set?' I asked Tina.

'Of course,' she replied confidently before shouting, 'Gregg, they're here.'

Gregg stuck his head out of the kitchen door.

'Hi, Sophie, I'm ready. I'll just change my outfit. Are you three okay to seat them? The wine is on the side and ready to be poured.' Chelsea had a wine bottle in her hand before he had finished speaking.

The doors flew open. The footman and an identically dressed colleague held them and the crowd poured in. The cacophony of sound increased in the confined space of the café as people debated where they were going to sit. Chelsea and Tina started to make their way around, offering red or white wine; menu cards were read and discussed; guests called to one another across the room; laughter bounced off the walls. This was a lively crowd, and we were going to have to make use of our very best skills of persuasion.

CHAPTER 3

Gregg emerged from the kitchen. And looked around the room nervously. It had taken me a while to convince him to say a few words to the group about the menu and I wondered how on earth he was going to cope with the excited chatter. He wasn't exactly shy, but he certainly didn't seek out the limelight and I knew he'd much rather be tucked out of sight in the kitchen.

His outfit was a little different to usual and I recognised it from old photos I had seen of kitchen staff at work in the 1860s. He wore the recognisable double-breasted white jacket of a chef. An apron was tied around his waist and he wore black trousers. On his head he had a white cap, a sort of loose bonnet that reminded me of a Scottish tam o' shanter. He didn't look wildly different from the chefs that could be seen on TV today, but his clothing was different enough to make you look twice at him. He was thin and angular, and his outfit seemed a little too large, like most of his day-to-day clothing.

'Ladies and gentlemen... Ladies and gentlemen, welcome...' Gregg's voice drifted off as he realised he was getting nowhere.

'LADIES AND GENTLEMEN!' bellowed Mark. He was

clearly well practised at getting the attention of large groups; the noise quickly dropped and people started shushing one another. 'Pray silence for Gregg Danforth. As well as preparing this evening's meal, he regularly cooks for the Duke and Duchess – the current Duke and Duchess, that is – and the variety of celebrities and dignitaries who join them in their beautiful home.'

Mark stepped back against the wall and Gregg was welcomed with a smattering of applause.

'Thank you so much for joining us this evening. I've had a great deal of fun poring through old recipe books and researching the dining habits of our Victorian forebears. In the end, I decided to take my inspiration from Charles Dickens, who will be reading to you later. Many of the dishes you'll enjoy are taken from or influenced by the food that appears in his works. For example, in *The Old Curiosity Shop*, Nell and her fellow travellers enjoy a stew. Don't worry, I've made a few changes and you won't be getting tripe.' There were sighs of relief from the room. 'Scrooge sees French plums in a greengrocer's window...'

As Gregg continued to speak, Mark sidled up to me.

'Motley crew,' he observed.

'Don't be so harsh, they've made a real effort. Well, some of them have.'

'I'm kidding. They seem pretty enthusiastic. We'll have our work cut out trying to exhaust them so they'll go to sleep at a sensible hour.'

Gregg had moved on to describing the intricacies of dinner service and its change from *à la Française*, where diners helped themselves from large serving dishes laid out on the table, to *à la Russe* where the courses were served separately and brought to each diner at the table by servers. The change had occurred during the reign of Queen Victoria, who was herself a huge fan of Charles Dickens.

'Why were Harvey and Betsy so concerned about Philippa and possible fireworks?' I whispered to Mark.

'Ah, come with me.' Mark led me out of the café and into the stone corridor immediately outside. I shivered. 'We don't have to watch the hordes attack their food. Not long before you arrived here, there was a bit of a scandal, depending on how much you really cared. Our delightful Philippa Clough had an affair with Conrad Brett. You'll see him later, he's playing Dickens. Once news got out, his wife Lycia hit the roof.

'Somehow, Lycia managed to resist wringing her husband's neck, and after about six months of living apart, she seemed to have forgiven him and they've been giving the marriage another go. To all intents and purposes, they seem quite happy. Although she does work with him a lot, probably keeping an eye on him. There were a few tricky moments in the early days. Philippa still visits the house on a regular basis and is often at the events that Conrad and Lycia are working, but there haven't been any serious incidents. Yeshim's team know to keep an eye on Philippa, but it's something we're all aware of.'

From inside the café there was a round of applause.

'Come on,' I instructed Mark. 'He's finished, I need to go help.'

As we returned, Chelsea, Tina and Gregg were distributing plates of a steaming, rich oxtail stew with root vegetables. I gave them a hand and left Mark to wander round the tables, engaging people in conversation, sharing a joke with them and no doubt passing on some of his remarkable knowledge of the house and its inhabitants.

With the main course underway, I paused and surveyed the room. I watched as Philippa and her friends tucked in, Philippa and Annie chatting away while Thomas silently worked his way through his meal. He didn't join in with the conversation nor, as far as I could tell, was he invited to. He picked up one of the menu cards and read it, shook his head as he laid it on the table and looked vaguely incredulous. I could only assume he didn't like or agree with what he had read.

'They all seem happy.' Tina had a wine bottle in each hand. 'They're thirsty, too.'

'Well, let's make sure they don't overdo it.'

There was a shriek of laughter from Philippa, and Tina winced. 'I'll never get used to that.'

'You know her?'

'My brother does, she lives on the same street as him. I've been to a couple of barbecues and Christmas parties that she's attended. She's good fun, but loud.' She spotted someone waving his empty glass in the air at her. 'Excuse me.'

A couple of the women in the room were starting to look a little uncomfortable. They were the ones who had opted to go all out in their costumes and were now finding that their corsets were not conducive to eating a large, heavy winter meal. Two women were loosening the ribbons on the back of each other's dresses. It was a wise move; there was still a lot of food left to come.

Mark nudged me. 'It drives me nuts when they assume that corsets have to be cripplingly tight. There were some daft fashion victims back then, just like now, who suffered in the name of a so-called perfect figure, but most didn't. How on earth do they think Victorian women danced, played tennis, sang opera, even climbed bloody mountains? They haven't done their homework.'

I spotted movement at the door and looked over to see two of our security officers, Pat and Roger. Roger looked at his watch and whispered something to Pat before they backed out and disappeared. I knew I'd see them again later, looking for leftovers.

An hour later and dinner was over. A dessert of stewed French plums with Italian cream and Gregg's melt-in-the-mouth shortbread biscuits had been welcomed enthusiastically, and many had taken the option of coffee, presumably with the intention of staying awake as long as possible and not missing a moment of their time in the house to the inconvenience of sleep. Mark once again flexed his vocal cords and called for everyone's attention.

'Everyone on this table, and the first half of this table – as far as you, sir – you'll be with me for this evening's tour. Everyone else will be with my colleague, Douglas.' Douglas waved at the guests from the far side of the room, no doubt relieved that Mark had split the group so that he had Philippa and Douglas had a slightly easier ride as a result. 'And don't worry, we'll make a comfort stop before we get going on the tour. Now, please gather your petticoats, don your top hats and follow me. Let's push through our need for a post-dinner nap and explore one of the country's finest buildings. Tales of scandal and salacious gossip await you, and if you're lucky, we'll bump into the odd ghost or two. Follow me please.'

He gave his handlebar moustache a quick twirl between his fingers, spun on his heels and dramatically marched out of the door, a gaggle of red-faced, overfed, but still enthusiastic and excitable guests behind him.

With the lights back on, the full glare made the carnage of dinner look even worse than I'd thought it would. Squint and the room resembled the scene of a food fight. As Tina and Chelsea set to work getting the room ready for breakfast in the morning, I joined Gregg in the kitchen. He was plating up a couple of meals for the live interpretation team so they could eat them in the privacy of their breakroom.

'They've asked for light meals only as they're going to be doing the dance scene in an hour or so and they don't want to be too full, so there's salad, but I've put a couple of dishes of stew aside just in case. They can always reheat them later, they have a microwave up there. Do you need a hand?'

I shook my head. 'I'll be fine, I can take my time.'

I was about to leave, but my way through the door was

blocked by Pat and Roger, who had returned and were surveying the scene.

'Bloody hell, no one said this was a party for toddlers. Don't these people know how to eat?'

'It's not that bad,' I replied. Pat, who was overweight and permanently red-faced, was known for his dislike of events that he considered 'modern'. His uniform stretched tightly over his stomach and he leaned slightly back, like he was trying to counterbalance the extra weight he carried. His colleague Roger was a favourite of mine. He wasn't exactly skinny either and he clearly enjoyed his wife's home-baked cakes, and he'd never turned down one of the warm cookies I occasionally dropped into the security office, but he looked like an athlete when in Pat's shadow.

He winked at me. 'I think it smells amazing in here, Soph, I bet you all did a grand job. Now, we were wonderin', any chance of some leftovers? It's a cold night and we've got our work cut out keepin' an eye on you lot.'

He smiled, and I couldn't resist. We'd have sent them some food over anyway, but I was a sucker for Roger; he was like an uncle everyone was fond of. Pat, on the other hand, was still looking around with a slight curl on his lip.

'It's a bleeding nightmare, we're expected to carry out all our usual duties and we've got, what, sixty crazies in costume that could sneak off anywhere to keep an eye on. We should be paid extra for these sleepovers.'

'Oh, it'll be fine, Pat. Won't it, Soph? It'll go without a hitch with you around.'

That was it – Roger was getting cookies delivered to his desk this week.

'Gregg's in the kitchen, he'll sort you out.' I smiled at Roger, but made sure it had left my face when I turned to Pat.

. . .

I set off down a stone corridor and round the side of a courtyard. Light from windows above cast shadows onto the cobbles that filled the space, my footsteps echoing as I walked along a colonnade. I passed doorways hidden in the darkness of the November night and jumped as a mouse ran alongside a wall. Stopping, I collected myself; the last thing I wanted was to drop a tray of food.

A sudden movement caught my eye and I watched as Romeo, the garden team's adopted cat, followed on after the mouse, disappearing into the shadows silently. At the end of the colonnade there was a waist-high black metal gate with a 'No Entry' sign hanging off it. I pushed it open with my hip and started up the narrow wooden stairs beyond it. It felt like the stairs went on forever, my legs telling me that I needed to take more exercise.

Back stairs like these, which were off limits to the public, fascinated me. Even as a child, whenever I was taken to a museum or gallery, my attention was always drawn to the doors that said 'Staff Only' or 'Private'. I would watch as members of staff let themselves in, wondering what fascinating job they had. I longed to know what lay beyond, what exciting project they were involved with. Now I got to pass through those doors, although I had to remind myself not to take it for granted and hold on to that sense of wonder.

On the second floor, beyond a white wooden door, was the breakroom. I backed in holding the tray to find the 8th Duke lying with his feet on a sofa, mobile phone in hand. Seeing someone in Victorian clothing using modern technology no longer surprised me, but it remained a source of amusement.

Against the wall behind him was an empty rail that earlier in the evening would have held the costumes that had been prepared for the live interpretation team. A tall bookcase contained dozens of history books, biographies, magazines and files labelled 'research'. A narrow tower of lockers for valuables had an ironing board propped up against it with a rather ancient looking iron next to it on the floor. The 'Duchess' was sitting at a small desk with her back to me. She was flicking through a magazine.

'Ah, perfect.' Harvey spun his legs off the sofa and got up, taking the tray from me and putting it on a coffee table. 'Betsy, grub's up.'

'I'm not hungry,' she replied, turning to face me. 'Thank you, I'll heat some up later when we've finished. Harvey, here.' She tossed a bundle of white fabric at him, which he unfolded. It was an apron and he put it over his costume. 'Get gravy on you and you'll be in trouble, I don't think any of us have keys to the wardrobe tonight if we need clean spares. And don't overdo it, you'll get indigestion.'

'Yes, Mum,' he mumbled as he took a mouthful of bread dipped in stew.

'How's it going?' Betsy asked me. 'They seem like a lively crowd, the dancing should be fun.'

I was about to reply, but Harvey spoke before I had the chance. 'Hopefully they didn't have too much wine with dinner, otherwise it'll just be carnage.' He shook his head and looked at me. 'Some of the ladies can get a little handsy.'

'Where are the others?' I asked. 'Do they want any food saving?'

'On their way,' Harvey replied. 'They'll be here in about twenty minutes.'

Betsy looked concerned. 'That's cutting it fine. How do you know anyway?'

'Lycia messaged me.' He paused. 'She was checking how it was going so far.'

'Did she want to know if *she* was here?'

'Nope, didn't mention her. I don't think she cares anymore.' I knew they were talking about Philippa, who was sounding more and more like the star of the show.

'Well, she better behave herself.'

'Philippa or Lycia?' Harvey asked, sounding a little irritated.

'Both of them.'

'None of it was Lycia's fault. How did you expect her to react when she discovered her husband was sleeping with Philippa?'

'Slept,' Betsy corrected him, 'it was just the once, not that that excuses it. It's really none of my business.'

It was none of my business either and I was starting to feel like a spare part.

'I should go, but there's plenty of food left if anyone does want more. Yeshim will know where to find me if I'm not around.'

'Thank you,' they both chimed. I was quite pleased to get out of there. Betsy didn't seem too bothered by Conrad's affair, but Harvey had shown signs of having a pretty firm opinion. It seemed that drama was more than just the day job for some of the team.

CHAPTER 4

I ran into Yeshim as I made my way back to the Library Café.

'I'm going to wait for the tour groups up in the Great Chamber, want to join me?'

I followed her through half-lit corridors, listening to her radio crackle from its position on her belt. It was business as usual elsewhere in the house and we could hear the security team locking up the parts of the building we wouldn't be using. Yeshim seemed to have fully recovered from the earlier shock of Douglas's childish games. I asked her whether that was characteristic.

'Sort of, he certainly likes attention. I heard that when Edward Flanders left, he applied for his job, and not just for the experience of applying; he really thought he could get it. It was a remarkable display of arrogance.'

Dr Edward Flanders had been a curator at the house and a minor TV celebrity, until he had been charged with the murder of a colleague. Shockwaves from the event had been felt deep within the Fitzwilliam-Scott family, as he was married to the Duke's younger sister.

'Douglas has no relevant experience; he loves history, but that's not enough. If I'm honest, I think he was attracted by Edward's TV work, that's what he really wants. Did you know about his book?'

'No, I don't know anything about him, except what I'm learning tonight.'

We had arrived in the Great Chamber. It was a large room with a dark-wood floor. The walls were covered in oak panelling and ornately carved lime wood displaying animals and plants that appeared to be tumbling down, so rich were they in number and detail. The large marble fireplace, normally filled with ornate vases, stood empty; the conservation staff had been concerned about potential damage and moved them for safekeeping like nervous parents before their teenager's first house party.

Yeshim and I sat on one of the large, low windowsills, our backs to the view of the courtyard I had walked around earlier. The windowsill was made of a light grey polished Derbyshire limestone revealing hundreds of fossils captive within it. It was cold to sit on and I regretted our choice, but Yeshim didn't show signs of noticing. I assumed this was where the next part of the evening's entertainment would take place. The room was more than big enough to hold a dance for sixty people.

I removed my glasses and gave them a polish on my shirt while I listened to Yeshim.

'I have no idea how he got a publishing deal, I can only assume he played on the name of the house. I can't quite pin him down on what the book's about, he's a bit evasive.'

We were interrupted by the arrival of Mark. Followed by his half of the group, he looked like the Pied Piper of Hamelin.

'We're almost at the end, ladies and gentlemen, and then you can have a quick comfort break before we head into the next part of the evening's schedule, but first I want to show you something that very few visitors know about. They certainly don't spot it unless one of us points it out to them.'

He made sure the guests had all come into the room, and then gathered them into a group just in front of the door, pointing to a piece of artwork above the frame.

'This shows the *Flaying of Marsyas*, a satyr, or nature spirit, who challenged the god Apollo to a musical contest. It was painted in the early 1700s. Marsyas is the one tied to a tree with his right hand above his head. Now, look closely. Can any of you see anything out of place?'

There was silence as the group peered at the painting. A few pointed at it, whispering to the person next to them.

A man in the group shouted out his answer. 'The watch! He's wearing a watch.' The group peered again.

'Where?' someone called out. Smiling, Mark stepped forward.

'Well done, yes. The right wrist of Marsyas. Can you all see it? Where there should be a rope binding is actually a wristwatch.'

The group members started to chatter to one another

'Ooh yes… There it is… I see it… Can you see it…? Where? Oh yes… Why…? Is the painting a fake?'

Mark started to talk again and the group quietened down to listen.

'Well, the theory is that it's a joke added by a cheeky restorer in the 1950s. Now you can point it out when you visit the house with friends, they'll be very impressed.'

A strident voice rang out from Mark's group. 'Appalling, why were they allowed to get away with it? It's not something to be made light of.'

Mark chose to ignore Philippa's remarks. 'If any of you would like to make use of the bathrooms, they are through this door. If you can then return to this room, we will await the other half of the party.'

Some of the group headed through the door, which led to a short corridor with a dead end. Other than to the toilets, they couldn't go anywhere, so we could relax.

Mark came over and joined us.

'How did it go, maestro?' I asked.

'Good. They laughed at my jokes; no one set any alarms off; I finished with the same number of people I started with.'

'Did they really laugh at *all* your jokes?' Yeshim asked with an exaggerated raise of her eyebrows. 'Really?'

'They did. Well, alright, almost all of them, but I blame the wine. It dulled their senses.'

'Is Douglas behind you?' I asked.

'You really don't know him, do you?' Mark replied. 'He's always running late, loves the sound of his own voice too much. What do you reckon, Yeshim, fancy a bit of a wager? I reckon he'll be fifteen minutes late.'

She appeared to be thinking. 'My money's on ten, but once we hit the five-minute mark I'll go and stand behind his group and make impatient faces at him. We're on a tight schedule.'

'I'll go,' I offered. 'I'd like to see him at work, plus he's bound to be telling them something I don't know and I want to keep learning.'

Mark stood up with me. 'I'll join you.'

'Won't that distract him?' I asked.

'If my presence distracts him then he's not much of a guide. We've attended each other's tours in the past and I trained him to deliver the Intro to Charleton House tour, so he's used to having me around. Come on, let's go find him and rescue his group.'

We found them in a wide corridor. Douglas was standing in front of a large window, his group had formed a semi-circle around him, and he was in the middle of a dramatic recreation of a duel that had occurred in the gardens over 200 years earlier. Unusually it had taken place between two women and was referred to as the Charleton Petticoat Duel.

I loved the story, a display of 18th century girl power. The elder sister of the 5th Duke had taken offence at a comment that a cousin had made about her age, claiming she was over sixty, when in fact she was not yet thirty. Both women fired their pistols, but neither had been hit. Next, they decided to resort to swords and moved to the courtyard below the room we were standing in. The cousin received a minor wound to her hand, but it had the desired effect and she agreed to write a letter of apology. It's said the swords used are somewhere in the Charleton House collections, but no one knows where exactly.

It was a story I had heard before, or I thought I had. As Douglas told it, two of the Duke's sisters were quarrelling and one lost a finger. I looked at Mark, a little confused. He turned to face me and grimaced.

'See what I mean?' he whispered. 'I bet even you could get that story right – you remember what I told you?'

I nodded. 'Cousins?'

'Yep. But he doesn't listen and I would guarantee he doesn't refresh his memory before delivering a tour. I'll have a word tomorrow.'

I looked over at Thomas Hattersley, who hadn't seemed worried about being in a different group to Annie and Philippa. He was shaking his head, sighing and glancing out of the window as though he had somewhere better to be. Something told me that Mark and I weren't the only ones to have spotted the inaccuracy in Douglas's retelling of history.

Douglas wrapped up his story and we stepped back as he led his guests through to the Great Chamber to join the rest of the group. He grinned at us as he walked past and gave us a thumbs up. Mark offered him the most exaggerated, cheesy thumbs up I had ever seen in response. I kicked his foot, but Douglas didn't seem to notice the obvious sarcasm.

By the time we arrived back in the Great Chamber, the 8th Duke and Duchess were once again mingling with the group. This time, they had been joined by a couple of 'friends': two more live interpreters we had yet to see during the evening. One was dressed as a handsome nobleman in a close-fitting maroon waistcoat and long black tailcoat. By his side was a young woman with blonde hair in a beautiful maroon dress that perfectly matched the waistcoat. The dress had a line of bows running down the back of the fabric that projected out behind her. They made an eye-catching couple.

This time, the Duchess addressed the group. She was excitable, unable to keep still, and clasped her hands together, giving a little clap from time to time.

'No event is complete without music and dancing, it's my favourite part of any evening. Now, I'm sure that many of you attend such dances on a regular basis – you are, after all, some of the finest members of society we've ever had the pleasure of welcoming here at Charleton. However, a little reminder does no harm. So, my husband and I, along with our good friends,' she indicated the couple in maroon outfits, 'the Marquess of Chelmorton and his wife, Lady Catherine, will guide you through some rather simple steps. We also have other friends here this evening who will assist.'

A couple stepped out from the crowd. They were beautifully dressed and wouldn't have looked out of place on a film set.

'Plants?' I asked Yeshim.

'Not exactly, they're paying guests like all the others, but they're friends of Betsy's and they know what they're doing.'

'My dear,' the Duchess turned to the Duke, 'would you be so kind as to ask the musicians to begin?'

There were, of course, no musicians; rather, another set of speakers was tucked out of sight, and Yeshim held a discreet remote control. The audience laughed as the Duke stuck his head out of the door and called to the 'musicians' to strike up.

A space was cleared and the six dancers took their places,

looking ready to start when a door burst open and a bearded Victorian gentleman with a book under his arm rushed in.

'Wait for me, please wait. I heard you were about to start dancing and you know how much I enjoy a quadrille. Please let me join you.'

Charles Dickens had arrived.

CHAPTER 5

'My dear Charles, you're early.' The Duke and Duchess rushed over and welcomed him warmly, the crowd responding with sounds of recognition, some laughter and a little gentle applause. The Duchess held Charles's arm firmly and walked him over to the group.

Like many of the men in the room, he wore a black tailcoat, beneath it a rather cheerful waistcoat with broad purple stripes, and his trademark straggly beard. Mark had taken great pleasure in showing off his facial hair knowledge, telling me it was a grown out door knocker beard, and ever since then I had imagined Dickens's face attached to my front door. His cheeks and jaw were clean shaven, his hair slightly long and wavy at the sides. Conrad Brett clearly went to great personal lengths to ensure that he looked the part, although he appeared to be in his mid-forties, about ten years off the age Dickens would have been at the time tonight's event represented.

'Ladies and gentlemen, it is my honour to introduce you to our good friend, Mr Charles Dickens.' The group applauded and Dickens made a small bow. 'We were just about to remind our friends here of the steps to the Sir Roger de Coverley. Would you assist and join our little demonstration?'

'Of course, of course. Nothing would give me more pleasure. Would you mind if my companion joins us? She's a marvellous dancer.' He turned back towards the door where a young woman was waiting. She walked towards the group. 'Your Grace, please meet Miss Ellen Ternan.'

This was the first time we'd been introduced to this character, who I knew was Dickens's mistress towards the end of his life, and the woman playing her had to be Lycia Brett, wife of Conrad. Lycia looked about ten years younger than her husband, which still made her fifteen years too old to play Dickens's mistress.

The Duchess approached her. 'You're most welcome, please, do join us. We were about give a little demonstration of the Sir Roger de Coverley. Shall we?'

She stepped out into the middle of the room once more and the small group of experienced dancers followed. Charles handed his top hat to a member of the audience and joined the others as they formed two lines of four, facing one another, and the music began. They moved with well-practised ease to the sound of the flute, violin and piano, and as the wider group merged into the background of my vision, it started to feel as if I was getting a glimpse of the past. I knew that the real Charles Dickens had visited Charleton House and had performed a reading of some of his books. He had become friends with the Duke, who was a keen supporter of the arts, and they'd had a number of friends in common.

As the dancers smiled and laughed and threw themselves into the movements, the group clapped along. Some were intently studying the feet of the dancers and moving their own very slightly in an attempt to recreate what they were watching, while others started to look nervous. Some edged closer to the front, chomping at the bit to take part. I noticed a couple of the men who had shown signs of attending reluctantly slip towards the back of the crowd. There was no way we would get them up and dancing.

'That looks exhausting.' I jumped; I hadn't seen Joyce come in.

'You're here late,' I noted.

'I decided I'd stay to catch up on some work.'

'You brought your dancing shoes, Joyce?' Mark had wandered over to join us.

'Don't be ridiculous, you won't find me throwing myself around a room, and most definitely not if there is an audience.'

'Come on, don't be such a spoilsport. I admit you might be better off removing those shoes, but you'd look very dainty whirling around on your tippy toes.' Joyce's leopard-print shoes matched her skirt and scarf. The gold sweater she had paired them with made her a definite contender should any vacancies arise at a zoo. She looked ready to party, just not at this party. 'Or are you afraid we'll discover the true extent of your two left feet? Is the Lady Joyce worried about dropping down a peg or two in our estimation?'

Joyce let out a puff of air. 'I'll have you know that my mother was a Tiller Girl. I can high kick with the best of them.'

Mark looked as stunned as I felt. I immediately pictured Joyce in a glittery leotard, with tall feathers on her head, her legs going, well, all the way up. I could tell Mark was doing the same. Joyce looked between the two of us as we stood in silence, a faraway look in Mark's eyes that mine no doubt reflected.

'Stop it, both of you, I know what you're doing. And for the record, I would still look incredible in shimmer tights and a feather boa.'

'I hope you'd wear more than that,' Mark replied, a little shocked. 'Come on, give us a demo. I'm sure Roger de Coverley wouldn't mind you adding a modern touch to his moves. Pleeease,' he begged.

Joyce was saved as a round of applause refocused our attention and we watched the Duke and Duchess split the large group into lines. They knew better than to ask the men skulking at the back more than once. A couple of women sat it out too, taking a seat on the windowsills. The rest of the group milled around, finding their places until they were lined up in a number of rows, ready to start taking instructions. Yeshim had joined the Duke as controlling the music was going to take a bit more focus.

'So...' Mark was edging round a subject, '...are you going to tell us why you didn't end up strutting your stuff on the stage of the Folies Bergère or the London Palladium? Can you imagine how high my gay street cred would have rocketed if it was known that I was friends with a Tiller Girl?' He looked playfully disappointed.

'I am sorry for shattering your dreams and sending you into social status poverty. If I have the chance to do it all over again, I'll ensure you are at the forefront of my decision making.'

'Thank you, Joyce,' he replied, 'I would appreciate it.'

'I was far too interested in boys,' she continued. 'Sadly I was too young to know just how much work was required for so little return when it came to the opposite sex.'

I wasn't sure Joyce had ever learnt that. Three ex-husbands and a number of failed affairs hadn't dimmed her enthusiasm for finding Mr Right, even in her... well, none of us are sure which decade Joyce is in, but I'd guess at least her sixth.

As I turned my attention back to the dancing, I watched as Douglas was persuaded to join in. He pretended to resist, and then succumb to the charms of the Duchess. He was positioned opposite Philippa Clough and his expression travelled from laughter, to surprise and recognition, and then to deep annoyance. A hard look set on his face, and his bow to her appeared to be delivered with deep reluctance. Philippa smirked, and then threw herself into the music. Her over-the-top enthusiasm served her well and made Douglas look like a miserable, sulking teenager.

'I can almost feel his pain,' Mark commented as he watched. 'I bet he's convinced his skin will burn every time he has to touch her hand.'

'Is that the blog woman?' Joyce asked. 'I heard about her dalliance with the charming Mr Dickens.' Her eyes were now following Charles Dickens around the room. 'I can't blame her, he is rather good looking.'

'And rather married,' I added. Joyce had been involved with a married man before, and it looked as if it wasn't necessarily off the table for the future either.

'Not happily if he's playing the field.' Her eyes hadn't left him.

'If the rumours are correct, they patched it all up,' Mark added, 'so allow your wandering eyes to wander elsewhere.'

'Are you telling me how to conduct my love life, Mark Boxer?'

'Oh God, she's used my full name,' he muttered. 'I wouldn't dare. Married men, men who live thousands of miles away, men who live in burrows, men who dance naked at the summer solstice – I will fully support your relationship choices, no matter where you cast your leopard-print net.'

'Good. How Bill puts up with you, I will never know. He deserves a sainthood.'

'He was rewarded this side of the grave when I married him.'

'I've had enough,' Joyce huffed. 'Sophie, keep an eye on him; he needs round-the-clock supervision and the baton has been passed to you this evening.'

I laughed as she tottered out of the room on her wedges while Mark screwed up his eyebrows and pouted.

'Bloody woman,' he muttered. 'Still, I'd give anything to see her as a Tiller Girl. The Grim Reaper could take me after that and I wouldn't mind.'

The dance was in full flow and most of the group had picked up the steps needed to muddle their way through. When someone stumbled or headed in the wrong direction, they were met with laughter and good-humoured shouts to get them back on track. Philippa's energy knew no bounds and she had moved on to resembling an overeager horse attempting to dance on ice. She was having a blast; those who received an enthusiastic tug or twirl from her, less so. Charles was met with the awe of a living celebrity each time he came into contact with a guest, although I noticed the smile briefly vanish from his face when the dance moves brought him close to Philippa. She seemed to remain utterly oblivious to her impact on those around her.

'This is a good way of exhausting them,' observed Mark. 'There's less chance of any of them rising at sparrows' fart and needing entertaining.'

'Sparrows' what?' I was getting used to Mark's odd expressions, but this one was new to me.

'Fart, sparrows' fart. Dawn. How did you not know that? Anyway, tire them out, give them some hot cocoa, smother the snorers in their sleep and you might get a nap yourself.'

'What makes you think I'm staying the night? I'm going to head home and snuggle up with Pumpkin before returning to make this merry lot breakfast.'

'You and that cat.' Mark shook his head. 'There'll never be room for a man in your life with her around, she's got you under her non-opposable thumb.'

Pumpkin, my overweight, domineering tabby cat was, if I was honest, the love of my life. She and Mark had a love-hate relationship that had got stuck on the side of hate. I was sure she'd welcome a man into our home, just so long as that man wasn't Mark.

'Excuse me.' I stepped away from Mark, having seen some movement through the doorway, and made my way onto the landing. The movement had been shadows and I looked over the balustrade. At the bottom of the stairs, the comedy pairing of Pat and Roger were dancing to the strains of music that floated out of the door. Roger seemed to be rather enjoying himself as he pretended to tango. Pat, on the other hand, seemed to be poking fun at the activity upstairs, doing an exaggerated effeminate walk and twirl before turning and repeating the move, his nose in the air and the curl of his lip still firmly in place. He stopped after only a few minutes, clearly having exhausted the limited amounts of energy he possessed.

'Bloody idiots,' I heard him mutter. 'Come on, Rog, let's leave them to it.'

Pat put an arm round Roger's shoulder as they walked towards the door.

'It's rather nice,' I heard Roger comment. 'I should take my missus dancing one of these days.'

As they left, I heard a mobile phone ring and watched as Roger answered it before they disappeared out of sight. I went back to Mark, questioning just how secure our crack security team would keep us if there was a problem during the night, and making a note never to deliver any more cookies to the security office if Pat was on duty.

Half an hour later and the dancing came to an end, the dancers looking particularly bedraggled. Ties were undone, corsets had been loosened and a few shoes had been discarded. No one could say that they hadn't thrown themselves into it with gusto. Those who had sat it out were starting to look bored; the timing was perfect to give them all a break and let the dancers get their breath back.

Bottles of water and plates of biscuits were waiting for the guests in a room off the Long Gallery; we needed to get them out of the way so we could set the room up for the next event of the evening. Warders escorted them out, and Mark and I watched as they wearily wandered, and in some cases staggered, in the direction they were led. Tired laughter echoed through the room and down the stairs.

Douglas accompanied a group of women who were hanging on his every word. 'I had a magazine article published last week, and my book will be released next year,' he was telling them. 'The manuscript is almost finished and I've been told that a TV deal will follow shortly. Of course I'm not interested in all the attention, I just want to be able to bring my love of history to as many people as possible.'

The women oohed and aahed like they were in the presence of a rock star. It seemed that Douglas had found some fans who were as impressed with him as he was himself. I was glad Mark had stepped away and not been privy to Douglas's comments; I didn't think his eyes could withstand rolling that far back in his head.

'Darling, you have got to be kidding.'

I turned and saw that the only people remaining in the room were Charles Dickens – Conrad – and his wife Lycia. Conrad was reluctantly defending himself.

'I only danced with her because that was the way the turns went. Betsy was placing everyone, not me. You know I can't stand the woman.'

'I'd hoped we'd put all this behind us.' Lycia stalked from the room. She didn't seem to have enjoyed the event quite as much as the others.

'We have, *I* have,' he called after her. As he followed his wife out of the room, I couldn't help but wonder if the sticking plaster holding their marriage together was becoming unstuck.

CHAPTER 6

I needed coffee. It was 10.30 and I was starting to flag. I could have gone home, I wasn't really needed anymore, but I wanted to stay for the reading.

I knew that Dickens would be reading from a number of his books, including *A Christmas Carol* and *Oliver Twist*. Both of them were books that I had loved growing up after my father had read them to me when I was a child. My father had passed away a couple of years ago, so I was expecting to find it emotional, but I wouldn't have missed it for the world.

I didn't want to fall asleep during the reading, so I needed an injection of caffeine. I left the group to it and headed to my office, just off the Library Café kitchen. Once down the stairs, I took a shortcut back across the courtyard, round a few corners, and then into the stone corridor that led to the café. It was dark, the only glow coming from the kitchen where Gregg had left a light on, so I was able to navigate my way round and through to my office.

The tables were all laid for breakfast and the kitchen was cloaked in the smell of freshly baked bread. Gregg and I had agreed to bring the group back into the 21st century with a modern breakfast menu that gave a nod to Dickens. In *Barnaby Rudge,* a breakfast included Yorkshire cakes, similar to brioche, and we would fill the bread rolls with bacon. Another option would be *Oliver Twist* inspired gruel, or oatmeal with lots of additional fruit and nuts that guests could add as they wished.

Helping myself to a Yorkshire cake, I trusted that Gregg had made plenty extra, and then prepared myself a coffee. I took the slow option, making a drip coffee and enjoying some silence as the water travelled through the grounds. I freely admit to being an out-and-out coffee addict, finding the perfect bean close to a religious quest, although right now I was more interested in its ability to keep my eyes pinned firmly open.

Coffee is one of my favourite aromas in the world and I took a deep breath, closing my eyes at the same time. I opened them quickly at the sound of coughing. Peering through the window onto the lane that ran along the back of the house, I could see the outline of a slim male in evening dress, at the end of one arm the glow of a cigarette.

On closer inspection, I could see that Charles Dickens was having a quick smoke before his performance. It was surreal, watching the famous author pace back and forth outside my window. It didn't matter how well I knew the circumstances, it looked very odd.

I cooled my steaming mug of coffee with an indulgent drop of cream and enjoyed a few mouthfuls, burning my tongue in the process, then poured the rest into a travel mug. I wasn't allowed to take coffee into the main rooms of the house, but I decided to take my chances and break the rules.

With my mug in my hand, I retraced my steps through the shadows of the courtyard and along the colonnade. Half way along, there's a deep doorway that always unnerves me; its thick black shadows have the potential to hide a number of people, and I always pick up my pace as I pass it, just to be on the safe side. Ridiculous, I know, but I do it every time.

Tonight was no different, apart from the fact I could have sworn I heard whispers and the rustle of fabric coming from within. My pace quickened even more than usual and I practically leapt the last few feet towards my destination. But as I reached the bottom of the staircase I was aiming for, I stopped. It hadn't been my imagination. It's always been ghostly quiet along the colonnade – no breeze, no paper blowing along the ground. Nothing that would naturally create the noises I could have sworn I'd heard.

Too afraid to get up close and investigate, I found my own shadowy corner and waited. After all, if the sources of the noises were anything to do with this evening's sleepover, they would have to reveal themselves soon; the reading was due to start at any moment.

It didn't take long before a man and a woman in Victorian dress stepped out into the half-light. From a distance, they could have been any of the guests, but as they walked closer, I could see the high quality of their outfits. As they were about to turn into the stairwell, the man took the woman's hand, raised it to his mouth, kissed it, and then let her run on ahead. She was Lycia Brett, and the man wasn't her husband, Conrad; it was Harvey Graves, better known this evening as the 8th Duke of Ravensbury.

The Great Chamber had been reset while everyone was getting refreshments. Chairs had been lined up for the audience, and at the head of the room was a superb copy of the reading desk that Dickens would take with him on his travels. I had seen the Charleton Estate carpenter hard at work on it the previous week and he had done himself proud. It looked just like the one I'd spotted in photos as I read up on Dickens in preparation for the sleepover.

It was different to any podium I had seen. The desk looked like a tall box without side walls so the audience could see the movement of Dickens's entire body. He had been an extremely physical performer and it was important to him that he wasn't hidden. On top of the desk was a small, solid box, giving Dickens something to lean on to rest his arm during the two-hour readings he commonly gave. A little fringe of scarlet fabric decorated the top of the desk. Behind the desk had been hung a background of swathes of red fabric, matching the fringe. Dickens had been a showman, passionate about the theatre. It was said that if he hadn't been a novelist, he would have become an actor, and an excellent one at that.

The audience had taken their seats, the Duke and Duchess on the front row, Ellen Ternan towards the back. After a brief introduction from the Duke, Charles Dickens strode into the room. Dressed much as he had been before, he now sported a red geranium in his buttonhole, and he clasped a leather-bound book.

He took his place behind the desk, and all the photos and illustrations I had ever seen of Charles Dickens came to life before me. He spoke earnestly about the similarities between the work of a novelist and that of a performer on the stage. Then he started.

He began with the opening of *A Christmas Carol*. A mean and miserly Scrooge, he would screw his face up in dramatic exaggeration. The voices of the characters, each one different, were introduced to us, and it wasn't long before his body was as involved in the reading as his voice. He had huge energy, and over the course of the twenty-minute reading of select scenes, he took us from misery and crankiness to humour and joy. His audience laughed one minute and were terrified the next as a new ghost entered the scene.

The Duke and Duchess played their part, their exaggerated shock and surprise, laughter and delight encouraging everyone around them. At the back, Ellen's face was a picture of pride in the Victorian equivalent of a rock star who had chosen her as his mistress. I was brought to tears more than once during the event, and I spotted others pulling out a handkerchief.

Next he moved on to *Oliver Twist* and I knew we were heading for the murder of Nancy by Bill Sykes, always a favourite at Dickens readings. I found it hard to imagine that there was a single guest in the room who believed that the person before them on the stage was anyone other than Charles Dickens himself.

He was delivering the final scene when I glanced out of the window and saw one of the male guests in the courtyard, on his phone. He paced back and forth in the cold night air, his breath creating great clouds before him. I recognised him as Thomas Hattersley, who didn't seem too worried about missing the reading.

Douglas appeared behind me. Out of breath and flustered, he had just come up the stairs, although I hadn't heard him running. He didn't look happy and I wondered if he'd received some negative feedback about his tour, although his group had seemed more than happy earlier in the evening, except for the overcritical Mr Hattersley who wasn't really entering into the spirit of the evening at all. I wasn't sure why Douglas was still here; his responsibilities were over once his tour had finished. Mind you, Mark tended to hang around with me at events, so perhaps it wasn't unusual for Douglas still to be here too.

Yeshim gently took hold of my arm. 'They'll be done in a couple of minutes,' she whispered. 'Are the refreshments set up?'

I nodded. 'I'll come down.' Leaving Charles to the rapturous applause of his audience and about to begin a short question and answer session, during which I knew Conrad would never break character, Yeshim and I left the room.

A cold stone kitchen that would have been the domain of servants had been set up for evening drinks. Before leaving,

Gregg had prepared an enormous urn of hot chocolate. We had a jar of marshmallows, chocolate sprinkles and lots of whipped cream ready for people to make their drinks as indulgent as they liked. For those without a sweet tooth, there were all sorts of herbal teas and decaffeinated coffee. We didn't want anyone waking too early, or at sparrows' fart as Mark would say.

'Harvey must have been squirming.' Yeshim was talking as she spread freshly made cookies out on a wooden board. They didn't look bad; my afternoon spent baking 200 of the things had been time well spent.

'Why?' I wondered.

'He has started to be more vocal about wanting to play Dickens. Conrad has made quite a reputation for himself as one of the finest performers of Dickens in the country. He doesn't just work here; he spends a lot of time on the road, and Harvey wants a piece of that success.'

'Won't Harvey be given a chance?'

'Maybe. It depends on the event, and whether or not Conrad is available. Something like this, where the guests have paid a lot of money, we want to make sure that what we offer them is the highest quality, and that's Conrad. He always does Christmas here too, and that's a really important event for us. There's no way I'd let Harvey get his hands on that; he needs to go off and do more on his own, build up a portfolio, get experience. Right now, he's just grumbling.'

'What about Ellen Ternan? Having Lycia play her was stretching the imagination a bit. From what I read, Ellen was in her very early twenties around now.'

Yeshim gave a wry lopsided smile.

'Ah, well that's part of Conrad's penance.'

'His what?'

'After he slept with Philippa, and after all the fireworks were over, he and Lycia decided to give it another go. However, one of her demands was that she'd always work with him when he was on tour, and closer to home if there was even the slightest chance of Philippa showing up. That can sometimes result in a bit of imaginative casting in order to crowbar her into an event.'

'But couldn't she have played the Duchess this evening? Surely she was closer to Lycia's age.' It didn't make sense to me.

'True, but Betsy is playing the Duchess at a number of events over the next two weeks and we needed continuity. Plus there's only so far I'll go to accommodate the whims of a jealous wife. Having Ellen in the scene is a nice edgy touch, but most of the guests won't know who she is. It should impress those who are real Dickens aficionados as she's not often added to live interpretation events, so I was happy to go with it.'

'They're on their way.' Mark had stuck his head round the door. 'Prepare for the hordes and the quickest consumption of a plate of biscuits in living memory. Oh and, Yeshim, you'd better head to the Long Gallery. I think there's a problem.'

CHAPTER 7

The Long Gallery looked like a war zone. Sleeping bags, camp beds, blow-up mattresses – the floor was covered in them. A couple of people were milling around, fetching toothbrushes and seeing if they could get an optimum spot near one of the heaters. Some clearly didn't care and had tossed their bags in a corner, happy to grab whatever bit of floor space was still available when the time came to go to sleep. A couple were standing near the door, bags in their hands, looking tired.

'We knew that the accommodation would be basic, but we didn't expect this. We thought we could cope with it, but we really need a good night's sleep. We were thinking we could stay somewhere else and come back for breakfast.'

Yeshim looked at me.

'Black Swan?' I suggested. The pub was my local and only a couple of miles from the house. 'You could give Steve, the landlord, a call, see if he has any rooms free and if he'll wait up for them.'

Yeshim pulled out her mobile phone and took herself off to a corner to make the call, returning a couple of minutes later with a smile on her face.

'You're booked in. One of my team will walk you out and give you directions. Breakfast is at eight. I hope you get a good night's sleep.'

'They'll be the only ones who do,' muttered Mark. 'Apart from the snorers, of course, who will keep everyone else awake, but sleep like babies themselves.'

Philippa chose that moment to walk past, toothbrush in hand, and indicate towards the couple as they gathered up their belongings.

'They couldn't take it, eh? What did they expect, silk sheets and breakfast in bed? Some people...'

She walked out of the room with a look of disgust on her face.

Full of hot chocolate and biscuits, which had no doubt been devoured as if a plague of locusts had appeared, more guests were starting to arrive in the Long Gallery to get ready for bed. Some had chosen particularly outlandish pyjamas which they happily wandered around the room in. Others dashed from the bathrooms to their sleeping bags and pulled eye masks on, quickly blocking out the world around them. Toothbrushes were lost and found, toothpaste shared between strangers as people discovered they'd forgotten to pack any. One couple were still taking in the paintings, although most people were now too tired to care what hung on the walls above their heads. Yeshim spotted someone take a sip from a poorly concealed hipflask and went to have a word, and then reminded everyone that only water was allowed in the room overnight.

With a warder sitting at the door, a desk lamp next to him so he could kill time with a book, the lights were dimmed and we called out goodnight. The guests would have resembled an extremely large, poverty-stricken Victorian family in one of Dickens's books, if it hadn't been for the lavish paintings surrounding them, and the expensive sleeping bags keeping them warm. The three of us made our way downstairs, acknowledging the warder at the bottom. Along with his colleague upstairs, he would make sure any night-time wanderers found their way to the bathroom and nowhere else. The last thing we needed was for the current Duke and Duchess to be disturbed by sleepwalkers.

'I'm off,' declared Mark. 'I might just make it home before the clock strikes twelve.'

'Me too,' I replied. 'Where are you sleeping, Yeshim?'

'The Duke and Duchess have given me access to one of their guest rooms, so while this lot toss and turn on the wooden floor, I'll get a couple of hours' gentle sleep in an antique four-poster bed. Don't let them know that, though, there'll be a riot. Thanks for your help tonight, you've both been brilliant.'

I gave Yeshim a hug and turned to Mark. 'Come on, I'll walk you to your car.' I linked arms with him and we stepped out into the cold night.

'That went well,' I offered. Mark shook his head.

'I'm deeply disappointed, and although they don't know it, every one of our visitors could have had a much more memorable night.'

I was confused; I thought it had been a fun, smoothly run event.

'If it's the last thing I do,' he continued, 'I will see Joyce high kick her way through the can-can in a leotard and tights that have more glitter on them than any piece in Liberace's wardrobe. How did we not know this about her?'

I laughed. 'She's a remarkable woman, and I reckon there's plenty more revelations where that came from. Chances are she was a member of the Résistance during the Second World War and carried out more missions than any man alive.'

'That would make her more than ninety years old,' he stated with a furrowed brow.

'Correct. Do any of us really know how old she is? There's also the chance that she was part of a youth preservation experiment and is now well into three digits, yet has the physical function of a woman in her thirties.'

He laughed. 'I wouldn't put it past her.'

We'd reached the back lane. Roger was standing at the security gate, bundled up in an enormous coat, his nose poking out from above a scarf.

'You're off?' He didn't sound very happy, which was unlike the ever-cheerful Roger, but I put it down to the cold and late hour. 'I wouldn't want to be sleepin' on that floor. But if they're prepared to pay good money to…'

Before he could say anything else, his radio crackled into life. He listened, and then responded.

'Okay, I'll call Yeshim and she'll be right with you.'

'Don't do that,' I butted in. 'Let her sleep, she'll be up early with that lot as it is. I'll go.'

'It was the warder in the Long Gallery, apparently one of the guests needs to talk to a manager.'

I kissed Mark on the cheek and sent him home.

I reached the top of the stairs where the warder was waiting for me with a rather tired-looking man in checked pyjamas. Before the warder had a chance to speak, the man stepped forward. He was clearly on a mission.

'It's ridiculous!' he fumed at me. 'How the hell are any of us meant to sleep with that kind of racket going on?'

'I'm sorry, sir, but I'm not aware of the nature of the problem.' The door to the Gallery was closed and I couldn't hear anything.

'It's inconsiderate and shouldn't be allowed.'

'Sorry, sir, but I don't…'

'Snoring! Snoring like a freight train. There's two of them, one in each corner of the room. What are you going to do about it?'

It took all my self-control not to laugh. What did he think I was going to do? Smother them in their sleep?

'There's nothing I can do, sir. I know that everyone was advised to bring earplugs if they were light sleepers. They're entitled to sleep, and this is one of the risks when you spend the night in a room with a large group of people.'

'Well, I won't be sleeping. I have to work tomorrow and... and...'

He trailed off mid bluster, turned and stomped back into the room, the warder running behind him. I winced as the guest attempted to slam the heavy wooden door shut, but the warder caught it just in time.

I figured that while I was here, I'd go and check that everything, other than the noise volume, was okay. Creeping through the door, I smiled at the warder as he made himself comfortable back on the stool and picked up his book. I could see the man getting back in his sleeping bag, huffing and puffing as he did so, no doubt trying to make a point and ensure a few others suffered at the same time.

Everyone lay peacefully underneath the watching eyes of Fitzwilliam-Scott family members, who were wide awake on the walls around them. Then I heard it. I couldn't help but smile. The guest was right – they sounded like warthogs stuck in treacle. Two of them, competing from opposite sides of the room. I stifled a giggle and let myself out. It was time for me to get some sleep to the soundtrack of a snoring tabby cat.

The moon was casting shadows through the colonnade and I thought about my warm bed. Midnight had been and gone and I yawned, then jumped.

Something had moved. I'd yet to encounter a ghost, although I had been told there were plenty around, and tonight was not the night I wanted to do so.

There it was again. It was the black-and-white cat, Romeo, on another prowl. It seemed this was one of his favourite night-time haunts. I watched him dart in and out of shadows, and then vanish up a staircase.

Looking up, I saw a light on in the room above: the Fitzwilliam-Scott private library. It was part of the house that the public never got to see. If the lights were on, there was a chance someone was in there, and if the door had been left open, which was something the Duke was prone to doing, then Romeo might get in and give them a furry surprise.

As quietly as I could, I crept up the stairs. Romeo was nowhere to be seen. The door was closed, so I turned the handle, wanting to check it was locked. To my dismay, the door popped open, and almost immediately, Romeo snaked round my legs and vanished inside.

Damn, I wasn't going home any time soon.

The room was empty, the dimmed lights giving it a cosy feel. The walls were covered floor to ceiling in books; a sliding ladder that would run along the shelves was parked in a corner. Three well-used leather sofas surrounded a fireplace; a coffee table in front of them had books scattered across it. A beautiful wooden desk and matching chair were in front of the window that looked out onto the courtyard, family photos on display around the base of a Tiffany lamp.

The room had a masculine feel to it and I could picture the Duke in here on a cold evening, a glass of whisky in one hand and a leather-bound book in the other. I could easily imagine Dukes before him writing letters with a quill and ink, and hosting their male friends after dinner, while wives and daughters chatted elsewhere.

I scanned the shelves; I would love to spend a rainy day in here, the fire roaring, exploring the thousands of books. Sitting on one of the sofas, sinking into its soft, well-worn leather, I closed my eyes and rested my head back, imagining a gin and tonic in my hand...

CHAPTER 8

'Sophie... Sophie...'

Feeling a hand gently squeezing my arm, I opened my eyes and found myself looking into the face of the Duke – the current Duke. It didn't seem right. I couldn't understand why he was there, waking me up.

'Sophie, you fell asleep.'

Then it hit me. Startled, I sat up and looked around. I was still in the library. My lap felt warm and I looked down at the black-and-white cat curled up there, fast asleep.

'Oh, I'm sorry, I'm so sorry.'

A smile crept across the Duke's face, and then he started to laugh. 'Don't worry. You must have been working late last night.'

'I was, it's the sleepover. I followed the cat and the library was open, he ran in and...'

'It's fine. Really, don't worry. It was actually the dogs that found you. Well, Romeo.' I looked over at the door where two well-trained black Labradors were patiently waiting for their master. 'They smelt Romeo and pulled me in here as we walked past.'

I was going to have to have words with Roger. The security

team knew the Duke was forever leaving that door unlocked and were usually pretty good about checking it on their rounds.

'They didn't want to chase him?' I imagined them both leaping on me in an attempt to get to the cat.

'No, they know him. He finds his way into the house from time to time. Before now, I've found all three of them curled up in one of the dog beds. He's part of the family, especially in colder weather.'

One of the dogs let out a quiet whimper and Romeo opened an eye. I stroked his head as he woke up, then watched as he leapt down, wandering over to say hello to his pals. He rubbed the side of his head against them and they sniffed him.

'Well, I should take them for their walk, and you... well, will you go home, or have you work to do?'

I was confused. Work?

'What time is it?' I asked him.

'It's 5.30. I like getting an early start on the day.'

'Oh God, oh, I'm sorry. Work, the sleepover. I should go. Thank you.'

He laughed again. 'Can I suggest that before you do anything, you make yourself a strong cup of coffee, and please, stop apologising. You've started my day with a smile. I just wish I'd found you earlier, I'd have directed you to one of our guest rooms.' He offered me his hand, I accepted and he pulled me to my feet. Face to face with him, I dreaded to think how I looked. Oh no, had I been snoring? Drooling?

'What should I do about Romeo?'

'Nothing, I imagine he'll come with us for a little while. Now, go and get that coffee.'

He gave me a warm smile and made his way over to the dogs and cat, the four of them looking quite the sight as they left the room. I stretched. My neck was painful after sleeping with my head back against the sofa for so long. My skirt was wrinkled and covered in cat fur. I made a conscious decision not to look in one of the large gilt mirrors on the wall as I walked towards the door. I didn't want to know what state the Duke had seen me in. Not yet, anyway.

The Duke was right, I needed coffee. Only I didn't need a cup, I needed a bucket of the stuff. I would head to the café, but first I decided I'd go up to the breakroom. I remembered I had taken dinner to the live interpreters the night before, but I'd never been back to collect their plates. It would save me a journey.

Sluggishly I pulled myself down and up various staircases and along corridors as though I was in some kind of dream state. I could barely function without my morning coffee. It was a good job I was already dressed, as that was something I couldn't be sure to achieve successfully without some caffeine coursing through my veins. I'd probably head to work looking like a clown, or Joyce!

I almost knocked on the door, imagining that there might be a half-dressed butler or 17th century Duchess in her underwear within. You never could be sure what, or who, you'd come across in this room. Then I remembered how early it was and just let myself in.

'Oh, sorry.' I had been wrong – someone was there. 'I just wanted to...'

In the dim light of a single lamp in a corner of the room, Charles Dickens was sitting at a small desk, his back to me, a top hat next to him. Still wearing the black tailcoat, his scarlet red necktie just visible over the top of the collar, he was slumped forward, his forehead resting on the leather-bound book he had read from the night before.

Stepping further into the room, not wanting to startle him awake – there had been enough of that this morning – I stood on the red geranium he had worn to the reading that now lay on the floor. It felt wrong; the whole scene felt wrong. His neck tie had never been scarlet. It had been crisp white, something the fashion-conscious Dickens would have insisted on. Now it was scarlet red with blood, the knife that I had brought up the day before on the dinner tray sticking out of his neck.

'Charles... Charles? Conrad?'

Silence. I backed out of the room and took my mobile phone out of my pocket to call security.

Charles Dickens was dead.

CHAPTER 9

*P*at and Roger had reluctantly made their way out of the security office, where I imagined at least one of them had been snoozing at his desk, Pat telling me over the phone that I was making no sense at all and to wait for them. On seeing the body, they were suddenly very much awake.

'Don't get any closer,' instructed Pat, taking on an almost comical tone of authority as he flattened the already battered geranium under one of his boat-sized boots. 'Rog, get the police here. Sophie, we should leave Charles... I mean... well, we should leave him to it, and I don't want anyone stepping in that blood. Nothing's going to wake him.'

I closed the door carefully and quietly behind us. Charles might not be about to wake up, but it seemed the respectful thing to do.

Sundays are usually busy at Charleton House. Today was no exception, but not because we had visitors pouring in through the door. There had been no choice but to close the house; the police were buzzing all over the place and wouldn't be finished with their essential work until the end of the day, probably later.

After I'd found the body of Charles Dickens, or rather Conrad Brett, Roger and Pat had crawled into action. It was almost the end of their shift, but any hopes they'd had of getting off home to bed had been dashed, and the look on Pat's face had made it clear that I wouldn't be forgiven for some time. Roger just looked resigned to it.

Poor Yeshim had thought she was having a bad dream when I crept into her room after being quizzed by the first police officers to arrive onsite and woke her with the news. After asking if it was part of the live interpretation and if Charles Dickens was playing a trick on his hosts, she had leapt out of bed and within minutes was in a well-pressed suit, her hair in a tidy bun, and she was as alert as ever. How she did it without coffee, I had no idea, and it made me love and hate her in equal measure. She went off to talk to the police, and then find the best words to break the news to the roomful of sleeping guests, and I went to start preparing breakfast for everyone.

Gregg was already in the kitchen when I arrived.

'Up to your usual tricks, then.' He smiled, his eyes twinkling from beneath his long fringe before he tucked it neatly under a white baseball cap.

'I know, I know, Sophie's around so there's bound to be a dead body somewhere.'

He laughed. 'At least the local constabulary is unlikely to get its police numbers cut with you here, so you're actually helping with jobs. Then there's the undertaker, florists, caterers – you're a one-woman employment campaign.'

'There must be better ways to keep people busy,' I sighed, 'but I'll go with the positive spin. Now, how are we going to keep sixty hungry, sleepy, shocked people happy? We can't do the sit-down breakfast we'd planned.'

'Already sorted, boss. I figured we could do a huge pile of

bacon butties – that way if people just want to leave, they can take them with them. I'll have takeout containers ready for the gruel. I'll also do extra for the police and any staff that are onsite and involved. Can I leave the coffee in your hands?' He peered at me. 'Have you had any coffee? You haven't, have you? Don't move, I'm not letting you near boiling water until you've had coffee.'

I pulled a face at him. 'Hey, what do you think I do at home?'

'What risks you take in your home are up to you. We have one dead body already, I don't want to add a badly scalded one – yours or anyone else's – to the casualty list. Now sit down.'

I did as I was told and watched as he made me a coffee. Willing him to hurry up, I noticed Gregg was eyeing me up and down.

'What?' I looked for a stain on my skirt. 'What is it?'

'Did you sleep in that?'

I groaned. 'Is it that obvious?'

'You did? I was only joking, but I must introduce you to my friend Mr Iron, and what's with all the fur?'

As Gregg handed me my mug of coffee, I told him where I'd spent the night. He howled with laughter.

'That's priceless. No wonder you look like you've been dragged through a hedge backwards.' He kept laughing as he started preparing the Yorkshire cakes, handing me half of one covered with a thick layer of butter.

'Come on, let's get coffee to the masses before you get dragged away for more questioning and I have to do this on my own.'

After helping Gregg take three huge urns of coffee over to the stone kitchen that we'd used the night before, I returned to the Library Café and dismantled the long tables we had set up. People were going to be coming and going, so there was no point having it set up for a formal meal. As I quickly turned it back into the cosy café, made sure the faux fire was roaring away and put the leather armchairs in place, I had a quick flashback to falling asleep in the Duke's library and grinned. I wasn't going to be allowed to forget that for a long time, especially once Mark and Joyce found out.

The Library Café back to normal, I put on an apron and helped Gregg with the mountain of food that was starting to grow. Looking out onto the back lane from the kitchen window, we had a prime spot for watching all the police activity. Forensic teams in white overalls fetched a case from the back of a van, and I watched as Detective Sergeant Colette Harnby walked past, focused intensely on a phone conversation. I had yet to see my friend Detective Constable Joe Greene, but I guessed he would be interviewing the guests.

Gregg carried a platter of bacon butties out into the café as I heard the door open and Yeshim announce to the small group with her that they could help themselves and stay in the café as long as they wanted. A warder was with them and I knew he would escort people out when they were ready to leave.

Yeshim came over to me. 'A handful have been interviewed and have left already, some are being interviewed and others are on their way. Just keep the food coming. How are you?'

'Me? Fine, why?'

'You found the body. I know it's not your first time, but still...'

'Honestly, I'm fine. I didn't get up close. Has Lycia been contacted?' Despite the problems in their marriage, it would still be an awful shock when she found out her husband had been killed.

Yeshim shook her head. 'No, the police can't contact her. Her phone seems to be switched off. They've sent a couple of officers to their house. She's also due at work today so she'll turn up of her own accord at some point. We'll keep an eye out for her.' Her phone rang. 'It's DS Harnby, I should go.'

Back in the kitchen, Gregg was almost done. I stood at the window, watching Pat chat to a colleague and then walk towards the gate. The police must have finished with him and he was heading home.

A couple of minutes later, I watched as a tall, slim man in a dark suit strode along the lane. He looked out of place in a Victorian gentleman's tailcoat, his cream necktie undone and flapping in the breeze. There was a confused look on his face and he glanced about him as he walked.

'Oh my God,' I gasped.

'What?' Gregg dashed over. 'Have you cut yourself?'

'No, no, it's Charles. Look, it's Charles Dickens.'

Looking like an extra in a movie, Conrad Brett was walking down the lane. He definitely wasn't dead.

Joe picked up his mobile phone on the first ring.

'Good morning, Grim Reaper.' There was a lightness in his voice. 'I appreciate you keeping us busy, but can you do it on a weekday? I was planning on getting the motorbike out today, it's finally stopped raining. Will you put the kettle on? I'll be over in a minute to ask you some questions.'

'Joe, stop talking. He's not dead, I was wrong. It's not Dickens. Charles Dickens isn't dead.'

'Umm, I thought he died 150 years ago. People tend to die when you're around, not come back from the dead.'

'Shut up, Joe! The body – I said it was Charles, I mean Conrad, but I was wrong.'

There was silence on the end of the line.

'One minute, Sophie.' I heard mumbled voices; one of them sounded like Yeshim. 'Looks like we've just reached the same conclusion. They were about to move the body and Yeshim was asked to double-check his identity. It seems Dickens lives to write another day.'

'So who is it?' I realised then that it could have been one of a dozen men at the event. While the women could vary their costumes wildly with different colours, width of skirts, frills and hats, it was easy enough for the men to find a black tailcoat and a top hat and all look pretty similar.

'Thomas Hattersley. Yeshim has gone to find his wife with one of our officers. Apparently she's here and wondering where her husband has gone. Sadly, we've found him.'

CHAPTER 10

I sat on a tall stool with my head in my hands, staring at my reflection in the metal of a kitchen counter. No longer paying attention to what was going on outside, I suddenly felt very tired. Gregg's hand rested on my shoulder and a mug appeared below my nose. He pulled up a stool next to me.

'Everyone's happy out there. We can forget about them for a while. You okay?'

'Yeah, fine.' But I didn't really feel it. 'I can't believe I didn't check who it was. I didn't want to get too close once I saw the knife and realised he was dead. Then Pat and Rog called the police and none of us wanted to contaminate a crime scene and… well, I'm useless without coffee.' Gregg nodded – my inability to cope without my first caffeine of the day is legend among the Charleton House staff. 'I just wasn't thinking straight. He looked like Dickens, he had the same hair, his book was on the desk, his hat, and who else would have been in the breakroom dressed like that? I should have checked.'

I took a long breath out and sat up.

'Well that changes things. I could have guessed at a few people who had a grudge against Charles, I mean Conrad, but I don't know anything about Thomas, let alone who might want him dead.'

'So you're already thinking about it, eh?' Gregg smiled at me. 'Lining up your suspects, working out their motives. I swear, it wasn't me.' He held his hands up in surrender. It wasn't all that long ago that Gregg had been wrongly accused of murder, so I was pleased he could joke about it.

'Yeah, you got me. I was thinking about it.'

'Gooooooood morning.' The kitchen door swung open and Mark waltzed in. 'Get the coffee on, we have a crime to crack.' Bill followed close behind. He rolled his eyes and mouthed 'Sorry' at us.

'How did you get in?' I asked. 'Isn't this place a crime scene?'

'I worked last night, so the police want to interview me. Plus security were distracted trying to keep the press at bay, and I'm married to the relative of one of the investigating officers. Add it all together and I'm almost as important as the Duke himself. Now, if you've finished with the questions, it's my turn. What *do* you look like? Did you sleep in that outfit?'

Gregg burst out laughing and stood up. 'I'm going to check there's still enough food out there, I'll make you both a coffee on my return. I'm assuming the urn isn't good enough?'

Mark screwed up his face in disgust and took a seat on the stool Gregg had just vacated. Bill gave me a hug and leaned against the counter. I was about to explain where I'd spent the night when the door burst open again and Joyce marched in. So much for the house being a crime scene, but then I couldn't imagine even a police officer having much control over Joyce.

'Right, someone tell me what's going on. Who's dead this time... Heavens, Sophie, did you sleep in that outfit?'

We'd moved to a table in the far corner of the café, away from prying eyes and flapping ears. Most of the guests were eating, and then heading home. There was no reason for any of them to stay, and it was only hunger and shock that were making some of them take their time. Every so often, another couple of guests would appear, loaded up with their overnight bags and costumes, grab some food, and then be escorted to their cars. Occasionally a police officer would come in and fill up a takeout coffee cup. Tina had arrived and taken charge, and I'd sent Gregg home. There was a strange atmosphere that made everyone talk in hushed tones – well, almost everyone. I'm not sure that Mark or Joyce are familiar with the concept.

'So, fill us in,' Mark demanded. 'I believe we now have the death of one of the world's finest authors on our hands. It seems rather appropriate that the man who wrote some of the most dramatic scenes to be found in a novel – think of when Bill Sykes kills Nancy – should die twice.' He shuddered dramatically. 'Shame he had to do it here, though.'

I tried and failed to get a word in to correct him. Joyce came to the rescue.

'Let the woman speak, for heaven's sake. You're not short of the overdramatic yourself, Mark Boxer, now quieten down. Sophie, you were trying to say something.'

'It wasn't Charles – I mean, Conrad. I thought it was, it looked just like him from behind, but I was wrong. It was another of the guests.' I looked at Mark. 'Thomas Hattersley. How well did you know him?'

'Blimey, I'd seen him at events, but I didn't know him to talk to.'

'I know him.'

We all turned to face Bill, who took another drink of his coffee. He was calm and collected, like knowing a murder victim was the most natural thing in the world. But then he was surrounded by some rather melodramatic people, so it was probably an unfair comparison.

We all continued to stare at him like he was a specimen in a test tube.

'What? We go to the same pub quiz, he was on an opposing team. He was good, too.'

'You're going to have to tell me more.' Joe had walked in and pulled up a chair, squeezing in between Joyce and me. 'So go on, then. I never thought your pub quizzes could help on a case, but fill me in.'

At first glance, the brothers didn't look at all similar, although they had the same soft brown eyes and their smiles were mirror images. Bill was an ex-professional rugby player with the broken nose to prove it. He was stocky and still looked to be made of pure muscle, with the exception of the little belly he was developing now he no longer played. I knew he went to the gym, but it wasn't enough to combat his increasing age and his love of good food. He was still very good looking, in a rugged way.

His brother Joe was taller. I used to describe him as being like a teddy bear, rather cute with a little extra weight on him, but since his move out of uniform as a police motorcyclist and into CID, he'd slimmed down. I credited it to the nerves and stress of a new job.

Mark had long been convinced that Joe had the hots for me. I had tried to dismiss it, but it was getting increasingly hard to disagree, and right now it was hard to focus on anything other than the heat of his leg against mine. But, I'm not looking for a relationship, as sweet and fun as Joe is.

'His team was always in the top two. To be honest, I think it was beginning to irritate some of the others who didn't stand a chance. I didn't mind, it's just a bit of fun. He was able to answer questions on almost any subject, but history, now that was where he was guaranteed to win.'

'What kind of history? Did he specialise?' Mark was clearly interested.

'Britain, Derbyshire, politics. I'd sometimes think he should have a job here. Only he could be dismissive if other people got things wrong or didn't have an answer. He wasn't very understanding.'

Joe was making notes, and without looking up asked his brother, 'Did he annoy anyone, have any fights?'

Bill thought for a moment, and then shook his head.

'No, he could be irritating, he was the kind of person to smirk when someone got a question wrong, laugh quietly to himself, but other than his team, he didn't really talk to anyone.'

'I'll need the names of his team mates before you go.' Bill nodded and went back to drinking his coffee. 'Do you remember him?' Joe asked me.

'Sort of. He dressed like a lot of the men, like Dickens. I didn't speak to him. He didn't look like he really wanted to be here; he went outside a couple of times and I saw him on his phone.' I felt myself start to go red; I still couldn't believe I'd been so wrong. Joe must have spotted the change as he gently nudged my leg with his.

'Hey, it's okay, it was an easy mistake to make.' He turned to the rest of the group and his voice returned to its normal volume. 'He was at the event with his wife, Annie. Yeshim told me that she's friends with a blogger, Philippa Clough, and they spent a lot of the evening with her.'

Mark glanced at me. 'After an evening with Philippa, he probably killed himself.'

'Well he'd have been pretty talented,' Joe replied. 'We need to wait for the report, but from first glance, the angle of the knife means there's no way he could have done that to himself. He was stabbed from behind.'

Joyce grimaced. 'Please, Joe, you're in the company of ladies. Do we really need the details?'

'Sorry, Joyce.'

'Clear fingerprints?' I asked. Joe shook his head.

'Clean.'

'What about his wife?' I asked. 'Surely she's somewhere near the top of your list.'

He shook his head again. 'You'd think so, but she takes sleeping tablets and slept like a log until everyone else started getting up. She has the packet of tablets, with one missing. Plus she's one of the few guests that the warders remember clearly for not getting up in the night. Unlike most of the others, she slept near the windows. Most people were on the far side trying to keep warm, but it seems she's the kind that likes to sleep with all the windows open, gets too hot otherwise. She was in the direct sight line of the staff member on duty by the door. She never moved. And she seems genuinely distressed – her mother came to pick her up.'

'But it was still someone at the event, that narrows it down for you,' I observed.

'Well yes, if you consider sixty guests and however many staff that were working "narrow". Plus you have a dark warren-like building where it's easy for people to sneak around undetected. You know as well as I do that a lot of the security here is smoke and mirrors. Your basic perimeter isn't too bad, and more cameras were installed after the murder at the food festival, but it's still easy to get around this place without anyone spotting you.'

'So,' I was thinking out loud, 'we need to determine what links Thomas had with people onsite. We can rule his wife out, but there's Philippa.'

I looked up to see three faces grinning at me, and Joe had 'Are you kidding me?' written across his features. He waited patiently to be sure I'd finished.

'Sophie Lockwood – and note I didn't say Detective Lockwood, because you're not – I'm beginning to wonder if there's a way of locking you in this café so you can't get involved.'

Mark laughed. 'Come on, she'd still solve it before you lot.'

That was below the belt and Joe looked hurt. I agreed with

Mark, but the last thing Joe needed was someone to take a stab at his ego. I felt bad for him.

'I could say that I'll stay out of it...'

Joe smiled. 'But you'd be wasting your breath. Just stay out from under our feet and keep a low profile when DS Harnby is about. She seems particularly tense about this one. Speaking of which, I should find her and let her know about Thomas. Thanks, Bill, I'll give you a call later and get a formal statement from you.'

Joe rose from his seat and my mind immediately started whirring, playing back the events of last night and trying to recall who I'd seen Thomas talking to during the evening.

'Now, girl,' Joyce tapped one of her long fingernails on the table in front of me, 'before you slip into Sherlock mode, you're coming with me. You look like the Wreck of the *Hesperus* and we need to make you look a little more like someone who works in Charleton House. You don't run a greasy spoon caff, you know.'

I looked down at the creases that had remained in my outfit and picked a couple of clumps of cat fur off my skirt.

'Come on.' Joyce rose from her chair and led the way, balancing perfectly on her pale green heels. They made me think of pistachio ice cream. I was rather nervous about what I was going to look like when she had finished with me.

Joyce's office was surprisingly tidy. It was normally packed to the rafters with containers and packaging, items that she'd been sent by people hoping she'd stock them in the gift shops, posters and cardboard displays. A huge box full of uniforms for her staff usually sat next to her desk, and there was always a mountain of paperwork that looked as if it was about to topple onto the floor. This time more of the carpet was visible than hidden and her desk was virtually clear.

She read the expression on my face perfectly. 'Spring clean.

Well, autumnal clean. Once the visitor numbers drop, I have more time to shut myself away in here and sort it out. Now, what have we got?' She pulled open a large cupboard door to reveal a wardrobe full of brightly coloured clothing. From a distance, it looked like a child's dream dressing-up box – Joyce has a rather striking taste in clothes. I was envious of the space. My office is so small, my only option is to hang my spare clothes on the back of my door. I was cursing myself for sending them all off for dry cleaning earlier in the week.

'I know you're a little more... subdued than I, shall we say, but I think this will do the trick.'

I held my breath; I knew I wouldn't dare turn down anything she offered me, but I was afraid of looking like an entertainer at a child's party. She held out a navy-blue pleated skirt. I was shocked by its simplicity, and just how much I liked it.

'Hardly wear the thing. I only pull it out when I have to give a formal presentation to the Trustees. Now, let's find something to brighten it up.'

It was hard to imagine the Duke and Duchess allowing Joyce loose in front of a group as important as the Trustees. I'd never known her not to speak her mind, but perhaps there were circumstances where that was useful. Plus she was never actually wrong, just less than delicate in the way she put things across.

'There we are.' Joyce whipped out a pink blouse with a large bow at the neckline. I couldn't quite make out the pattern and took a closer look. 'Tulips. A little spring-like for now, but everything else is too low cut for you.' She stared at my chest. 'You should show yourself off a bit more, you'd have a decent cleavage if you... well, shall we say, managed things a little better there.'

I groaned inwardly; I was never, ever, *ever* letting Joyce take me bra shopping. I wouldn't let her buy me a pair of shoes, let alone underwear.

'Go on, tuck yourself behind that filing cabinet in case anyone comes in.'

I quickly whipped off my crumpled clothes and pulled on Joyce's choice. I couldn't fasten the skirt at the back, but figured a safety pin would do the trick, and I'd just let the shirt hang out a bit to cover it. I twirled in front of Joyce so she could give her approval, or not. She laughed and handed me a pin from a pot on her desk.

'Ah yes, there is a bit of a height difference. That skirt is normally at my knee.'

I looked down at the skirt that was sitting mid-calf. At 5 foot nothing, I was hardly surprised that what on her probably looked like a sexy schoolgirl outfit made me look like a Sunday-school teacher.

'The blouse seems to fit.' I said the only positive thing that had come to my mind.

'Hmmm, yes,' she agreed. 'And that's probably the best we can hope for right now. At least you're free of cat hair and they don't look like you slept in them. Now, shoes…'

'No way!' I exclaimed. 'I mean, thank you, but I… I don't think we're the same size.' I stuttered out the best excuse I could think of. She ignored me.

'Try these.' She passed me some rather nice pale blue shoes with small heels. 'Wore them once and felt like a dwarf.' My feet vanished in them. 'Ah yes, I see what you mean.' She looked at my flat navy shoes. 'Well, at least the colour matches, even if you do look like a nun from the waist down.'

CHAPTER 11

I couldn't remember the last time I'd felt more conspicuous. If it were possible to blend in with the walls, I would have done, but that was even harder than usual now that I was dressed like a child who wanted to emulate 'Auntie Joyce'.

I left the shop and walked across the Tudor courtyard. The cobbles were shiny and slick after a short burst of rain and I watched my step.

'Sophie? It is Sophie, right?' Betsy was looking me up and down. I decided to assume that her expression was one of admiration for my uniquely combined clothes.

'Hi, yes, that's right. Excuse the outfit, I didn't get home last night. What are you doing here?'

'I got in early to collect a few things, and ended up being interviewed by the police. It's just awful what happened.'

I nodded. 'It had been such a great event, you were all fantastic.'

Now that she was in jeans and a waterproof hiking jacket, she looked jarringly modern compared to the last time I had seen her.

'Thanks. It was fun, it's a good team and we work well together.'

Running into Betsy like this gave me an opportunity to start piecing together what had happened. Regardless of what Joe had said, there wasn't a chance in hell I was going to leave this one alone.

'I was wondering, what time did you leave the house last night?'

'Well, I got changed after the reading, and then when everyone was ready, we all had a drink.'

'We?' I asked.

'Yeah, the live interpretation team. We were a fairly small group, so we decided to hang around for a while. Conrad had a bottle of sherry for us to share. It was Dickens's favourite and Conrad wanted to continue the theme of the evening. A couple of us had bottles of wine that we took over.'

'So you stayed onsite?'

'Yeah, we were in that little art gallery near the entrance. There are sofas in there. Conrad stayed in costume and kind of hosted it. I never tire of him playing the role.'

'How did you all get in there? Wasn't it locked up?'

'No, it doesn't have a separate door, it's basically a large alcove off a corridor. We saw Roger from security, but he didn't seem bothered and let us carry on.'

'Have you any idea what time you all went home?'

She thought for a moment. 'I reckon about 12.30. It started to get a bit tense.'

'In what way?' I'd only been hoping to get some idea of timings and where people were, but this was sounding interesting.

She sighed. 'Well, once Lycia had got changed and joined us, Harvey started making comments about Dickens and his mistress. We all knew this was aimed at Conrad. Eventually the others managed to change the conversation, but then it got tense between Harvey and Lycia. Then Harvey stormed out and Lycia went after him. After that, none of us were in the mood. I went home.'

'Did any of you go back up to the breakroom?'

'No, not that I'm aware of.'

'Okay, thanks, Betsy.'

She smiled and left the courtyard. So, they'd all been drinking and tempers were running high. If Lycia and Harvey were having an affair, they were obvious suspects – assuming, of course, that like me, they'd mistaken Thomas for Conrad as he sat at the desk. The question was, which one of them would resort to murder to get Conrad out of the way?

I watched Joe escort a couple of guests past the security gate, and waited for him. He smiled as he saw me and walked over. I watched his expression change to confusion, and then to amusement. He was fighting to conceal a smirk as he reached me.

'Don't say a word,' I commanded.

'I wasn't going to say anything, I was just wondering when story time starts. You do work in a library, right?'

'A library? What is it about me? Why do Joyce's clothes make me look like I should be serving tea at a Women's Institute meeting, and on Joyce they look like... like...'

'Like she has questionable morals,' Joe finished.

'That's a bit harsh, but yes.'

'Because you have anything but questionable morals and your goodness is transforming the way we see the clothing.'

I laughed. 'You're full of rubbish. How's it going?'

'Slow. We're trying to piece together where everyone was throughout the night, and we haven't had the pathologist's report back yet, so we're still working within a really wide window of opportunity. Although logic dictates it was between 12ish and 5.30 when you found him.'

'I was thinking, Joe. When I first saw the body, I thought it was Charles... I mean, Conrad. So is there a chance that the killer made the same mistake, and the intended victim wasn't Thomas at all?'

'Yep, we're pursuing two lines of enquiry. Double the work, double the fun.'

That meant Harvey and Lycia could go on my list of suspects.

'Might Conrad still be at risk?' That had only just struck me as a possibility.

'He might,' Joe agreed. 'He's with Harnby now. No one would be stupid enough to try again while he's here at the house, especially while we're still swarming all over the place. But we might put an officer outside his house when he goes home, until we know more.'

Joe sounded confident, self-assured. He hadn't been a detective for very long, but he seemed to be finding his feet. I was proud of him, like a big sister would be. Maybe that was the problem – I viewed him more as a brother than a potential boyfriend. Perhaps the romance would come later, who knew?

'Sophie?' Joe pulled me out of my thoughts and I was grateful he couldn't read my mind. 'Sophie, I have to go. I'll drop by later.' He let his hand brush against my arm as he walked past me. I had to admit, he did look really good in a suit.

Back in the Library Café, I sat down in front of Mark, who was flicking through a magazine.

'Where's Bill?' I asked.

'Shopping. Apparently we'd starve if it was left to me. Supermarkets are just such soulless places.'

'He's not your slave.'

'No, no, he loves it. He's one of those people who will spend fifteen minutes comparing two different kinds of cheese, and look them up online to see what wine they'll pair with.' He shook his head, a look of wonder on his face.

'I doubt you complain much when that cheese and wine appear in front of you.'

'Never. Now there's a thought, is it too early for a drink?'

'It's 9.30, so yes.' Wow, 9.30. It felt more like the middle of the afternoon, but then I had been up since 5.30 am.

'Really, you look like you've had a head start on the alcohol.' He waved his finger in my general direction. 'Is Joyce responsible for this?' I nodded. 'I'm saying nothing.'

'Very wise.' I had expected him to pile on the jokes at my expense and was grateful for whatever had distracted him. 'What are you looking at?'

'It's a history magazine. I'm reading Douglas's article. It's surprisingly good. No mistakes so far.'

'That doesn't sound like him.'

'I know, but I guess if he's writing with all his research to hand, he has no excuse. If he's not bothering to remember it properly, then he'll struggle on the tours, so perhaps this is his forte. Maybe his book won't be so bad after all.'

'What's the article about?'

'Capability Brown, the landscaper, and the work he did here on the estate, especially the area closest to the house. Douglas knows his stuff, so he probably spent some time with the gardeners as well. He's got a real handle on the management of the grounds.' Mark had an expression on his face I'd seen before when he was carrying out his own research, or was buried in a book he found genuinely interesting. 'I might view Douglas a bit differently now.'

Tina had told me that the Stables Café had been overrun with the press. There'd been no reason to close the café that was housed in the old stable block a short walk from the main building – there would still be plenty of dog walkers who wanted a hot drink, and now there would be people who would come to gawp in the hope of seeing something gory, or watching a killer get led off in handcuffs. Then there was the press, and to be honest, I'd forgotten about them.

As soon as I turned into the courtyard, I could see that the café was busy. A few people were standing outside talking on their phones, a takeout cup in the other hand. Inside it was heaving and my glasses steamed up as I walked in. I'd made the mistake of leaving my staff name badge on and I was immediately faced with a barrage of questions about what I knew or had seen. I replied with the standard 'No comment' and walked quickly round the back of the counter. Nick, the café supervisor, looked pleased to see me.

'Sophie, what's it like at the house? Are the police still there?'

'They'll be there all day, and maybe tomorrow. How are you faring up here, are this lot giving you trouble?'

He shook his head. 'They're fine. When they first arrived, they were digging for dirt, but once they realised we weren't going to give them any, they settled down. Now they're just using us as a base. I figure it helps keep them in one place.'

'Okay, but if they start causing trouble or hassling the other customers, let me know and I'll get security over here.'

Nick looked utterly unfazed by all the activity around him. 'So long as they have coffee, they're fine, but thanks.'

I stepped back out into the cold.

'Do you work at the Manor House of Murder?'

'The what? Oh, very droll.' I rolled my eyes at the reporter and stepped around him. He wasn't going to have any luck with me.

CHAPTER 12

Charles Dickens was sitting in the corner of the Library Café. His coat was hanging over the back of a chair and he'd removed his necktie completely. His unbuttoned waistcoat hung loosely open and he'd lost his geranium. Despite looking dishevelled and tired, he still managed to appear rather dapper. It was easy to picture him straightening himself out and within minutes having the other customers in the café enthralled with his stories.

I could see that his coffee mug was almost empty, so I fetched him another. He was miles away.

'Conrad? Conrad?'

'Oh, hello. Sorry.'

'I thought you might need another.'

'Thank you.' He took a swig, showing no signs of the hot liquid burning his mouth. Sitting back in his seat, he pulled out his overstuffed wallet and started to ease a five-pound note out. I waved it away.

'It's on me.'

'Thank you. I'm afraid I don't know your name.'

'Sophie.'

'Thank you, Sophie. I saw you last night. I hope you enjoyed it.'

'You were fantastic. I love Dickens.' He smiled weakly. I nodded at his waistcoat. 'Do you dress like that all the time?'

He followed my eye line. 'Oh no. Last night, I was... well, I guess I was distracted. I didn't go home.'

'I heard about your little party. I'd love to share a glass of sherry with Charles Dickens.'

He looked momentarily confused. 'You mean last night? Oh, it wasn't a party, not really. Certainly didn't finish up that way.' All the energy I had seen in him had gone and he just looked as if he needed to go to bed, but I guessed that he didn't feel much like going home if there was someone out there who wanted him dead.

I decided to push him. If he was tired, then maybe his defences would be down.

'Where did you spend the night if you didn't go home?'

'The Black Swan. I was lucky they had a room free.'

I was reminded of the couple who had done the same thing and gone to the Black Swan for the night. How lucky they were to avoid all the drama. I wondered if they had attempted to get back in the house for breakfast, or if they just hadn't bothered and had gone home.

'Are you worried?'

'What about, that someone is out to kill me?' He shrugged. 'Yes, no. It seems so ridiculous and the police aren't worried, but there is a man dressed like me who is now lying in a morgue, so I suppose I should take it seriously.'

'Do you have any idea who would want to kill you?'

'You sound like the police. No. I'm sure I've rubbed a few people up the wrong way, but not kill me, no. At least I hope not.' He stroked his beard, gently pulling it into a point.

'What about Lycia?'

A bark-like laugh burst out of him. 'My wife? Now I know

I've made her mad, but it wasn't that bad. Anyway, things are better now, or they were.' He stopped and looked at me intently. 'Hmm, my own fault. I guess my stupidity will haunt me forever and I have no one to blame but myself.'

'You said things "were" better?' Of course I knew what he was alluding to, but I wanted to get as much as I could from him. He sat in silence for a moment or two, staring into his coffee cup, then he started to talk.

'I thought we had it all sorted, I thought she'd forgiven me. I did everything she asked of me. I didn't take any jobs that involved travel unless she could come with me. If there was an event Philippa was likely to be at, then I would ensure that Lycia had a role so she could be there too and was visible. A sort of warning to Philippa, and me, I 'spose. I did it all, and willingly. I love Lycia and I kick myself every single day. I thought we were working it out, but I guess not. Harvey does a lot of work here at Charleton as well, so the more time we spend here, the more time they spend together. I know he's trying to win her over; I don't know if they've acted on it yet, but that's definitely what he's after.' He looked heartbroken. 'I guess last night wasn't short in irony.'

'What do you mean?' I asked.

'I was playing a man who has brought his mistress to an event, leaving his wife at home, and all the while my actual wife is thinking about running around with another man. He was probably trying to snatch stolen kisses in the shadows and alleyways of this place.'

I thought back to last night, and watching Lycia and Harvey emerging from the shadows. Sadly, Conrad was right.

'What about Harvey?

'What about him?'

'Do you think he would go to such extreme lengths to have Lycia to himself?'

'Heavens, no. He's classically handsome, I suppose, but that's all he has to offer. The ladies fall at his feet, but he's weak and insipid. He'd run a mile rather than confront the opposition.'

'Anyone else?'

'You make it sound like there might be a queue of people waiting to get rid of me. I'm really not that bad, you know.' He gave me a little smile.

'I'm sure you're not. But was there anyone else there last night who you've had a disagreement with? You're not aware of any strange behaviour? No one has threatened you, or tried to make contact with you? Sent you notes, phoned you and hung up when you answered? Anything odd that you dismissed at the time?'

'Only Philippa, but they were hardly threats. I was apparently the best thing since sliced bread.'

'How did she take it when you broke it off?'

'Broke what off? It was a one-night stand. A stupid, regrettable one-night stand. You think Philippa might have done this? A delayed response to it all?'

'Possibly. How has she been since you, well, you...'

'Slept with her? There were a couple of times she tried to make her way to our breakroom. I had to talk to Yeshim, and the staff were told to keep an eye out for her. We didn't want to make a fuss, just gently dissuade her from getting too close. Then of course Lycia was always with me, and boy can she give someone a good glare. That probably scared Philippa off on a couple of occasions. But after a while it all calmed down and Philippa just returned to being a devoted history fan and appeared to put her energy into her blog, which has gone from strength to strength. She's always here for events, and she has travelled to see some of the other stuff I do, but she's kept her distance. Some days it's actually quite nice to see her, a familiar face in a crowd, and I'm sure her glowing reviews have helped me get jobs.'

'So there's no hard feelings?'

He shook his head. 'Not that I'm aware of. It's Lycia that hasn't seemed able to let it go.'

Despite Conrad's confidence, I lodged the idea of Philippa being involved firmly in my brain. After all, she had motive and she clearly knew where the breakroom was. It wasn't impossible that in the dim light, after a few glasses of wine and whilst in the grip of passion and frustration, she had mistaken Thomas for Conrad.

'What connection do you have with Thomas?'

'Nothing solid. He comes to some of the events, but not often. I get the feeling he's dragged along by his wife. I've been pulled into a few conversations with him when I was talking to Philippa and I have lost my temper with him a couple of times when he's pushed me too far, been disrespectful.'

I mulled over what he'd said.

'What are you thinking?' Conrad looked curiously at me. I wondered if he could hear the cogs turning in my brain.

'I'm thinking I've not had enough sleep, or coffee.'

With a takeout coffee in one hand, and a bag containing a chocolate chip cookie in the other, I stretched my legs in the direction of Yeshim's office. She had one of the more attractive offices amongst my colleagues. A repurposed bedroom that had views of the garden, it was the perfect example of understated elegance, rather like Yeshim herself. A large fireplace stood half way down one wall, on top of it a display of the various awards that Yeshim and her events team had won. The soft grey carpet was spotless and the pale yellow walls added a warmth to the room. Neatly framed photos of beautiful brides and handsome grooms adorned the walls – happy couples who had tied the knot under the watchful eye of Yeshim's team members.

The room smelt of delicately scented candles. I took a deep breath in – pinecones and cinnamon. The smell of Christmas which, it disturbed me to remember, was only next month. Three of the desks were unoccupied, unsurprising for a Sunday with no events other than the sleepover planned. Yeshim was sitting at her desk in the far corner, her legs curled underneath her and a soft grey blanket round her shoulders.

'Are you cold?' I asked as I put the coffee and cookie on her desk.

'No, I just find it comforting. Thank you.' She did a double take at my outfit, but didn't say anything. I spotted a pair of pink slippers on the floor beside her chair and she followed my eyes down. 'We all wear them round the office, gives our feet a break after walking around on hard floors all day.'

'Good idea, although I doubt health and safety would let me get away with that in the kitchen.'

She took a bite of the cookie. 'Still warm, yum. Thank you.'

'I think Tina was bored. She hardly ever bakes, but there's not a lot to do now. It's mainly just the police coming in to grab a coffee and get back to work. Have all your guests gone?'

Yeshim shook her head as she dropped crumbs onto the desk. 'There's still a few to get through. Harnby said she'd let me know when she'd done with them all.'

'I've got a question for you.'

'Of course you have.' She grinned. 'I'm rather disappointed you haven't figured out who did it yet.'

'I'm trying, give me a chance. I was wondering, you had a warder on the door all night? So wouldn't they be aware of who was coming and going, and who had left the room long enough to kill Thomas?'

'You're assuming the killer was one of the guests?'

'Not necessarily, but there were sixty of them.'

Yeshim pointed at an empty desk chair. I wheeled it over and sat down.

'We had a warder on the door and one downstairs. They were a point of contact in case there were any problems, and they made sure that people could find their way to the toilet without getting lost. But, it's a boring job in the middle of the night, cold too if you're downstairs. They're allowed to read and they were swapping posts so they had time to warm up. They also need to take toilet breaks as well. So, two warders isn't really enough, but we're running these events on a tight budget. Can I guarantee that no one could sneak out when one of them took a break, or they were distracted helping another guest? No. But having said all that, you'd be surprised at what they do remember. We also make sure that we have reliable staff working events like these – they're usually pretty on the ball, and over the course of the evening they start to recognise the guests. So, I can't guarantee it, no, and there may well be someone that slipped by unnoticed, but the warders will be able to remember a lot of things about many of the guests.'

'We didn't check the guests were all there when they went to bed.'

'You mean a head count? No. Maybe we should have done, but there's nowhere they can go that would cause any harm. Security lock the rooms we've been using once we're done, so the only places they could have gone are the cloisters and out onto the back lane where they'd be face to face with security.'

I thought about the open door into the Duke's library, but decided not to say anything if it meant that someone would get into trouble. Pat and Roger had a lot more to think about than usual with so many people sleeping over, and forgetting to lock a door only showed they were human.

'Does that help?'

'Kind of. It means there is a small chance one of the guests had the opportunity to kill Thomas.'

'But only if they knew where the breakroom was,' she pointed out.

'True, unless they followed him. Which is entirely possible.'

'We've not narrowed it down any, have we?'

'Nope, I just wish I knew more about him.'

'What about Joe? Can't he give you some insider information in return for a lifetime's supply of coffee?'

That made me laugh. 'He already has that. I can't push him; I'll save that for when I'm really struggling.'

I got up to leave and Yeshim muttered another thanks through a mouthful of cookie. At least now I knew that Philippa would have had the opportunity to slip out from the Long Gallery. It was another mark against her.

CHAPTER 13

As I stepped out into the back lane, a blur of black and white shot round the back of my legs and off towards the garden. It was Romeo, and another larger black-and-white blur was hot on his tail.

'SCOUT, HEEL!'

The Border collie came to a stop with an 'Oh pleeeease, let me play' look on his face.

'Come on, boy.'

Scout slowly walked back towards the muddy Land Rover that was parked outside the security office. His owner, Seth Mellors, the estate gamekeeper, was chewing on a sandwich and chatting to a police officer. Seth and I had exchanged the occasional hello, but he was mainly out and about looking after the 40,000 acres of land – in between being endlessly teased about his surname. Mark for one never called him by his actual name, instead referring to him as Lady Chatterley's lover.

I watched as DS Harnby appeared, escorting a couple of guests out. The day seemed strange and grey, and I felt deflated. I needed to go home, take a long, hot shower and come back tomorrow, ready to start again.

'Hello, Sophie, you look a little more alert.' I had nearly walked into the Duke who was smiling at me, an amused look on his face.

'Afternoon, Duke. I am sorry about this morning.'

'Oh please, don't worry. You gave the Duchess a bit of a laugh when I told her. I take it you've been home.' He glanced at my outfit, but unlike everyone else, he maintained a polite, shock-free expression.

'Oh, no. Joyce had some spare clothing onsite.'

'Ah, that explains it. Do you think we'll be able to open the house to the public tomorrow? The police still seem to be all over it like flies on a corpse.' He paused as he realised what he'd said. 'Oh, I am sorry, that was very inappropriate.' He looked embarrassed, but I waved his comment off. I'd said worse in my time. 'You must have met the victim if he was at the sleepover.'

'I didn't talk to him. He didn't seem too interested in it, the kind of guest who has been dragged there by his wife. But then he was interested in history, so you'd think that he'd be engaged with some of it.'

'And he wasn't?'

'Not really. He didn't seem too happy. In fact, he avoided some of it.' I remembered seeing Thomas outside through the window during the Dickens reading.

The Duke gave a small wave and I turned to see who he was acknowledging. DS Harnby was chatting to someone, but it looked as if she was trying to get away and talk to the Duke.

'Hopefully she'll fill me in, maybe they'll have learnt more about Thomas. Thomas Hattersley, isn't it? You know, I recognise the name. I'm not sure why, but it's ringing bells.' He was staring off down the lane, distracted, presumably trying to work out the connection. 'Ah, she's free. Now go home, I'm sure you're tired.'

I watched as he walked off. Even in jeans and a sweater, he was able to look elegant as he stopped and spoke to DS Harnby. He seemed very calm about the whole affair, the perfect display of the British stiff upper lip. I was keen to follow his instructions, but before I left, I wanted to see Mark. If there was one person who could perk me back up, it was him, plus he'd kill me if I went home without saying goodbye.

Mark shared a big open-plan office with a couple of other tour guides, including Douglas. It was unglamorously located above some of the visitor toilets and overlooked a courtyard, which was eerily quiet for a Sunday afternoon. The door was open. Mark had his feet on his desk and was covering the pages of a book with little pink sticky notes. Douglas was on the far side of the room, reading something on a computer screen, occasionally turning away in order to feed paper into a shredder.

'Can you believe it?' he was complaining. 'She must have written it the minute she got home.'

I remained in the doorway. 'Gentlemen. Working hard?'

Mark didn't move. 'Always,' he responded. I stared at him.

'Don't you stand when a lady enters the room?'

'Refer to my previous answer.' I couldn't help but laugh. He could be so predictable. 'You're letting all the heat out.'

I closed the door behind me, feeling like a nagging mother. I wheeled a chair next to Mark and collapsed into it.

'I've just come to say ta-ra, I'm going home. Caffeine is keeping me standing, but I can feel it swilling round my brain and I'm no use to anyone. I'm done in.'

Douglas let out a loud sigh. 'I wish someone had done *her* in.' He sighed again.

'What are you moaning about?' Mark asked. 'Spit it out instead of huffing and puffing.'

'That sodding woman, she's already written up a review for last night. Trying to get in on the action, I bet, get some publicity for her blog.'

'You mean Philippa?' I asked.

'Who else would take such pleasure in tearing me to shreds in front of the whole world? She's not right in the head, I swear.'

Mark got up and walked over to Douglas, leaning over his shoulder, reading the review.

'Wow, she really doesn't like you.'

'Tell me about it. She's also commented on Lycia's age, not being young enough to play Ellen, and that not all the guests did their research before signing up for the event.'

'That'll be a reference to those who went to the Black Swan,' I commented.

'But then she goes on to talk about Conrad. She reckons he continues to give the, and I quote, "finest portrayal of Charles Dickens in living memory". The rest of the evening gets the thumbs up as well. Of course, she revels in the drama of the night, makes it sound like she was personally at risk and only narrowly escaped the clutches of death. If only.'

He sat back with an air of defeat.

'Wait, she wasn't on your tour, she was on mine. How could she review your tour?'

'She can't, but it doesn't stop her. If you look at it, she's worded it very carefully: "known for his inaccuracies... ever the showman, yet unable to convey the significance of the Fitzwilliam-Scott family's role in British history"...'

Mark glanced up and caught my eye. I saw a very slight smile in the corner of his lips.

'You had that mate of hers. Was he rolling his eyes at every other word?'

'Who?' Douglas had leant forward again and appeared to be re-reading some of the review.

'Thomas, the guy who died. It can be really distracting when he's tutting away, or standing there with a look of disbelief on his face. But you learn to ignore it.'

'Oh him. I didn't notice – I'd never seen him before last night.

She doesn't actually say she was on my tour, but she sure makes it sound like she was.'

'Ignore her.' Mark slapped him on the shoulder in a display of manly support. 'She's just a two-bit blogger with an overblown sense of her own worth.'

'And with 5,000 followers,' Douglas replied dejectedly, feeding more paper into the shredder.

'Why does she hate you so much?' I asked. 'Mark tells me this has been going on for a while. Was she like this when you were working as a tour guide elsewhere?'

'Always. As soon as she found out I'd started doing it, she came along, and the next thing I knew she'd created a blog, and one of the first things on there was a review of my tour. I have wondered if the whole reason she created the site was so she had the chance to get back at me.'

'Why? What did she want to get back at you for?' Philippa was starting to sound a bit obsessive.

'Years ago, we both entered a competition, the Dr Archibald Vogler Award – some old bloke wanted to encourage recent history graduates from Manchester University to pursue careers in the field. You needed to write a history essay. The prize was a couple of hundred quid and your piece went in a national history magazine. We both entered and I won, and she came a close second. That was it, I've had her on my back ever since.'

'I guess you could keep an eye on it and see if she ever gives you reason to pursue her for libel.'

'She's too clever for that.' Douglas turned his computer off with a hard shove of the button. 'I'm done for the day.' He marched out of the room, his frustration clear in every heavy footstep.

'I feel for him,' Mark offered, 'but she's not entirely wrong. He doesn't deserve that, though. I hope enough people have the measure of her. He's still young – well, compared to me – he's got time to improve. Talking of my age, how's my cake coming along? Am I going to have a display of edible artistic magnificence presented to me over dinner, or are you going to poison us all and add to the body count round here?'

'The cake was meant to be a surprise.'

'Look who you're talking to, everything makes it back to me. Every word of gossip or news, every secret can be followed, and at some point it will land on my lap. I'm like a magnet, a walking repository of everything that should be known, everything that shouldn't be known, and everything that is complete and utter rubbish. You baking me a surprise birthday cake was never going to be a surprise, to me or anyone else.'

'Then what flavour is it?' I asked, testing him.

'Carrot cake,' he declared confidently. He was right and laughed at the expression on my face. 'Go home and get some sleep. I'm sure that fat cat of yours is missing you and needs feeding. Although it will probably do her some good to skip a meal or two.'

I playfully flicked the top of his ear as I walked past. Leaving Mark to it, I walked across the courtyard, thinking about a comfy sofa, a soft blanket and a log fire.

Heaven.

The Library Café was empty and the lights off when I returned. Tina had left a note pinned to my office door saying that she'd see me in the morning and to get some sleep. I stuffed my clothes from the previous night into a bag and was about to turn off my computer when curiosity got the better of me.

I typed Douglas's name and 'Dr Archibald Vogler Award' into a search engine and waited. There it was, the 2012 list of winners and runners up, and amongst the names were both Douglas and Philippa. There were also links to their essays. I pulled up Douglas's and started reading. It was about Victorian trade unions; I didn't really know the subject, but it seemed well written.

'You still here?' Joyce had appeared at the door and was looming over me.

'Hmm, I'm just reading through something Douglas wrote years ago.'

'Full of mistakes, I assume? Mark told me he's not exactly a detail man. What is it?'

'Actually it reads pretty well, but I've no idea if it's accurate. It's a competition entry.'

'He cheated,' she said quickly, and with absolute certainty. I laughed.

'You cynic.'

'I mean it. I bet he cheated. His work is always full of mistakes, yet you say it's very well written. Why are you reading that stuff anyway?'

I told her about the review and Philippa's unfair assassination of Douglas's skills.

'Oh dear, sounds like she didn't have a good time. Did she not sleep well?'

'She had a great time. She thinks Conrad was amazing, and the rest of the evening got five stars too. Have a look.' I opened a new window and searched for Philippa's review of the sleepover.

'Oh yes, her darling Conrad. Of course she thought he was fabulous, she's probably still hoping she's in with a chance.'

'She might be now.' I filled Joyce in on Lycia's relationship with Harvey.

'There you go, then.' She was reading the review over my shoulder. 'That's more than a review of Conrad's performance, that's a love letter. He should look out, she doesn't appear to be the full shilling. Does Joe still think that Conrad could have been the actual target?'

'He said they have two lines of enquiry because of the circumstances, yes.'

'Then make sure he has a closer look at that girl. She sounds like she's got a screw loose – who knows what she might do if the man of her dreams has turned her down? And if she isn't aware of Lycia's expeditions into foreign territory, then she might still be mad at him. If she does know about it and thinks he just doesn't want her, then she'll be *really* mad. Either way, he can't win.'

She started buttoning up her jacket.

'I'll see you tomorrow. I presume you're not planning on waking up with the Duke again?' She smirked, and then turned on her heels. 'Goodnight,' she called back over her shoulder as she crossed the café.

I turned off the computer. It was time to finally head home to what was bound to be a very grumpy cat.

CHAPTER 14

I threw my dirty clothes on the floor in front of the washing machine and Pumpkin pounced on them. She burrowed her head in amongst the folds of cloth, a habit she has whether the clothes are clean or dirty, but this time she buried hard for a minute or two, and then quickly pulled her head out and turned to face me with a look of fury. She'd smelt Romeo on my clothes – I was in trouble.

Pumpkin is a large, affectionate, very sociable tabby. She has learnt to offer me the top of her head so I can kiss it when I pick her up after arriving home. But she can also perform award-winning sulks, and like most cats, if she isn't in the mood for attention, she lets me know with her claws. I decided that tonight I would steer clear; she could tell me if she wanted stroking. I didn't want to end the day with bloody scratches.

I made sure her food bowl was full and she had clean water, and then I poured myself a drink. I didn't have the energy to craft a decent cocktail; instead, I slugged a double shot of gin into the first glass I could lay my hands on and threw some tonic on top. Not too much; tonight my gin did not need watering down. I took it with me to the bedroom and put on my pyjamas; this glass wasn't leaving my hand, even for a minute.

Next it was back downstairs to the fire. I had become pretty adept at getting my log fire going and it wasn't long until it was roaring away and I was sprawled out on the sofa, a furry blanket over my legs. Pumpkin had taken up position within a whisker's length of the fire and was cleaning herself.

I closed my eyes. I wanted to be able to put some clear thought into the events of the last twenty-four hours, but all I ended up with was a dead man who had no apparent connection with the house and fifty-nine other guests about whom I knew nothing. I started to drift off. The heat of the fire was sinking into my bones and the sound of the wood crackling gave me something to focus on, other than the image of a dead Charles Dickens that kept popping into my mind.

Ooomph! There was a sudden weight on my chest and the air shot out of me. My eyes popped open and I was nose to nose with Pumpkin. She sniffed my face, gave my chin a quick lick, and then settled down, staring at me. I wasn't sure if I was forgiven or if this was her unsubtle way of saying, 'I'm watching you.' There was something comforting about the weight of her on my chest and I closed my eyes again, only to rapidly open them as my phone rang.

I stretched my arm out and fumbled around on the floor. I couldn't find it.

'I'm sorry, Pumpkin, I'm going to have to…' She leapt off as I rolled over further than she was comfortable with. Finally, my fingers met my phone.

'Hello?'

'Were you asleep?' It was Mark.

'Not yet, I was having quality time with Pumpkin.'

'She's forgiven your betrayal?'

'Well I wouldn't go that far, but she hasn't drawn blood yet. What do you want?'

'Oh, very nice, "What do you want?" On the eve of my birthday, I'd expect a little more warmth.'

'Stop milking it, you only get special treatment on the day itself. So, my dear, how may I help your good self? Is that better?'

I heard him give a little harrumph. 'I thought you might like to know that DS Harnby came to see me after you left.'

I dragged myself upright. 'Go on.'

'They found a manuscript amongst Thomas's things and the content seems to relate to Charleton House. They needed someone to have a read through it and see if anything stands out.'

'Does it?'

'I don't know, I've only had it an hour. I'm going to head home and make a start on it. I'll let you know what I think as soon as I'm done, just thought you'd want to know as I'm sure the race is on to solve the case before the police.'

'It's never been that.' I was a little hurt. He made it sound like I had something to prove, some sort of vendetta against them. Joe was my friend, I just kept getting caught up in these things.

Mark must have picked up on my feelings. 'I'm only kidding. You need to get some sleep, girl, you're getting sensitive.' He was right. I'm never at my best when I'm tired. 'I'll come by the café in the morning and tell you all about it while you stick a birthday candle in a chocolate croissant. Goodnight.'

He hung up and I swapped the phone for what remained of the gin and tonic. With my glass drained, I lay back down. Mark would be in his element, under police orders to read a book about Charleton House. It was the perfect birthday present.

I had no idea how long I'd been asleep when my phone rang again, but the fire was down to embers and needed another log. Pumpkin was asleep at my feet and I was groggy. I looked at the screen on my phone: 'Joe Greene'.

'Hey, Joe,' I slurred. 'Hang on.' I got up slowly, trying not to disturb Pumpkin, and threw another log on the fire. 'Okay, I'm back.'

'I hope it's not too late to be calling?'

'I have no idea what time it is, so I'll let you be the judge of that.' Trying to keep my tone light, I wandered through to the kitchen. 'So, have you cracked it?' I asked. 'Is the killer at the station now, sobbing out a confession?' I grabbed a block of cheese out of the fridge; I was hungry and fancied a toastie. Quick and easy, that was the kind of food I needed tonight.

'Ha, I wish. No, I wanted to run something by you. Did you know about the drinks party that Conrad and the others were at after the sleepover?'

'I wouldn't call it a party, but some of them stayed for a drink. I heard about it from Betsy, and then Conrad mentioned it to me, and that there was a disagreement. I had no idea it was happening. I'd probably fallen asleep in the library by then.'

He laughed. 'You give new meaning to "the body was found in the library".' I noticed that he didn't comment on my chat with Conrad. Normally he'd tell me off for sticking my nose in. Maybe he was getting used to it, maybe he realised it was a lost cause. It was hardly my fault if people found me easy to open up to, or at least that was my excuse.

'Okay, I'm just wondering where Lycia and Harvey went after the arguments started, but there are a few discrepancies about the timing of things. They could have gone straight home, or they might have been hanging around the house another hour or so before they left, depending on who you talk to. Everyone seems a bit cagey, and security don't have a full record of people coming and going. We'll get the thumbscrews out in the morning and try and pin the timeline down.'

'You think that Lycia or Harvey might have stayed onsite long enough to kill Thomas, thinking it was Conrad?'

'I'm just trying to be sure of people's movements, but we're not ruling out their developing relationship as a possible motive.'

'While we're talking about relationships, what about Philippa?' I asked.

'What about her? She's reached your list of suspects?'

'Well she's part of that whole love triangle thing, and Joyce made a comment this afternoon that got me thinking.'

Joe laughed. 'Joyce? Don't tell me she's taken on the role of detective as well?'

'Oh God, no, can you imagine? She has the subtlety of a sledgehammer. Mind you, she could terrify people into confessing with a single glance. No, she made a comment about Philippa still being in love with Conrad. He reckons it's all calmed down and everything is fine, but Joyce thinks she's still harbouring a passion for him.' I told him about the review, and about Philippa's reason for resenting Douglas. 'She seems able to fixate in a really unhealthy way. She's still taking her anger out on Douglas, in public, seven years after the competition. That's not exactly the action of someone who is of sane mind.'

Joe was quiet, then he said something I never thought I'd hear.

'You know, Joyce might be onto something. Obsessive, capable of holding on to a grudge, pent up anger. I'll call Harnby, discuss it with her.'

'It's a bit late, isn't it? What time is it?' I looked at my phone. It was nine o'clock, not as late as I'd thought.

'No, she'll still be at the office. I think DI Flynn is starting to put her under pressure, and anyway, I don't think she knows how to relax. Thanks, Soph.'

'Come on, anything else you can let me in on before you go?'

'You don't give up, do you. No, nothing new, although we did get the pathologist's report back. It seems that Thomas was punched before he was stabbed.'

'So there was a fight?'

'I wouldn't go as far as that, a bit of a scuffle maybe, and then what looks like a punch to the side of his face. It wouldn't have contributed to his death.' He paused. 'You know, I remember when we would talk about things other than murder. One of these days, we should have a drink, but rule that subject strictly off limits.'

He was right, it did seem to be one of our few topics of conversation.

'That would be lovely. We can make a start tomorrow night.'

'What's tomorrow?'

'Mark's birthday. You know he'll want to be the centre of attention all day, and probably for the rest of the week.'

'Oh hell, it had completely slipped my mind. I don't even have a card. He'll kill me, and I can't just go to an all-night petrol station and get a dreadful card and some battered flowers.'

'Luckily for you, I have a drawer full of cards. I'll bring one in for you. Just make sure you find me before you run into him. You can tell him his present is on the way but the delivery is late and it will help him stretch the fun throughout the week.'

'Sophie, you're a star. I owe you big time.'

'Yep, this is more urgent than solving the murder.'

After we'd hung up, I broke up the fire, and then set off up the stairs to bed, dragging the blanket behind me like a tired child, a cheese toastie in the other hand. I was done, the cogs were about to stop turning. I had to sleep in a proper bed, even if it did quickly become a crumb-filled one. I needed the energy to cope with the royal birthday in the morning – lots of energy.

CHAPTER 15

I was fully prepared for the moment that Mark burst dramatically through the Library Café doors. It wouldn't have been right for me to cover the café in banners and streamers, particularly as I'd been told we could reopen to the public today, but I had prepared a table for him. A 'Happy Birthday' napkin and paper plate awaited him, along with a tall pointy gold cardboard hat. His birthday card was on the plate, but he'd have to wait until the evening for his edible present.

'I see no expense has been spared,' was his sarcastic greeting. He grinned and kissed me on the cheek. 'I love it, thank you.'

'Take a seat, Your Majesty, I'll be back in a minute.'

I returned from the kitchen with a chocolate croissant, his favourite, a single candle stuck in the top. I carried it slowly, not wanting to blow out the flame. Behind me, Tina carried his mug of coffee, and together we sang a rather disturbing rendition of 'Happy Birthday'.

Mark glanced around the room. 'No, no windows were shattered. Thank you both,' he said when we'd finished.

'I hope the candle sets your 'tache on fire,' Tina called over her shoulder as she returned to the kitchen. Mark took an enormous bite of the croissant, leaving a collection of flaky pastry crumbs along his moustache, which had survived the blowing out of the candle fully intact. He grinned at me.

'Thank you,' he mumbled. I passed him his card. He ripped it open and laughed at the picture of a muscular naked young man who was holding a strategically placed birthday cake.

'I hope *he's* coming tonight.'

'So, has Bill been pampering you all morning?'

'Not a chance. He had a staff meeting first thing this morning and he's giving a presentation. Something to do with the latest round of testing the poor kids are going to be subjected to.'

Bill was a history teacher at a local secondary school. I knew he loved working with the children, even the distracted teenagers, but disliked the amount of paperwork that was being added to a teacher's workload and showed no sign of letting up.

'But he did bring me coffee in bed before he flew out of the door, and when I went downstairs there was the most enormous bouquet of flowers on the dining table.'

'That'll be a yes, then,' I said. 'You're a lucky man.'

A gentle smile appeared on his lips and he nodded.

'I'm a *very* lucky man.' He pulled out his phone. 'Look at these, aren't they beautiful?' He showed me a photo of the most enormous bouquet of roses and carnations. I could see in the background that Bill had also hung up a 'Happy Birthday' banner.

'So lucky that I'll get you a second coffee before your first runs out.'

I went back up to the counter just as Tina walked out of the kitchen.

She leant over and whispered, 'There's a strange man at the window, I think he wants you.'

I left her to make Mark's coffee and went into the kitchen, wondering what I was going to be dragged into next. I needn't have worried. I was greeted by Joe Greene's face peering through the glass.

'Sophie...' I couldn't make out the rest so I opened the window 'Do you have the card for Mark? I know he's in there with you.'

I laughed and fetched it from my office. 'I hope this'll do.' The card joked about Mark looking great for his age, if you squinted.

'Perfect, I don't want him getting complacent. Have you got a...' Before he could finish, I handed him a pen. 'Thanks, be there in a minute.'

I returned to the café to find Tina and Mark admiring the young man on his card. They were still discussing it when Joe walked in and stuck his head between theirs.

'Not bad. You'd only need a cupcake though, eh, Mark? Here you are, happy birthday.' Joe handed him the card and slapped him on the shoulder.

'Bill mentioned he came with baggage,' said Mark. 'It's only recently that I've realised he meant you.' He read the card and raised his eyebrows at his brother-in-law. 'Cheeky sod! Thanks, Joe.' His smile was genuine. 'You still coming tonight?'

'I hope so, assuming we make some kind of progress on the case.'

Mark glanced up at me. 'It looks like you might be first past the post, Mistress Poirot.'

I was pleased that Joe decided to ignore the comment.

'Now I've done my brotherly duty, I need to go and get some work done. I'm meeting Harnby.'

Tina placed a takeout cup of coffee in front of Joe. 'I'm sure you'll be needing this. Do you want me to make one you can take to your boss, start the day on the right side of her?'

Joe grinned. 'Yes please, Tina. How did you know I wouldn't be staying?'

'Because you're not stupid enough to be lounging around here while your boss is trying to solve a murder. A takeout cup shows you've not settled in for a chat, but you're ready to spring into action at a moment's notice. I'll be back in a minute.'

Joe watched her walk off. He looked a bit sheepish.

'To be honest, I never thought of that. Maybe I should always have my coffee in a takeout cup. It'll make me look more dynamic.'

'Absolutely,' confirmed Mark with a little too much assurance. 'It can be your new superhero symbol. Rip off that spectacularly pedestrian-looking shirt and underneath is a Lycra vest with a picture of a takeout coffee cup on it. The stronger the roast, the more crimes you solve. Captain Coffee to the rescue.'

He mimed a salute. Joe shook his head.

'If it wasn't your birthday...'

Tina arrived just in time to interrupt.

'Two coffees, and one detective sergeant walking down the lane. You should get your skates on, Captain Coffee.'

Joe raised his eyebrows at his new nickname, but smiled at Tina.

'Cheers. Well, I guess Captain Coffee better go save the day. See you motley lot later.'

I turned back to Mark as Joe left. He was staring intently at me.

'I'm getting old.'

'What?'

He looked down at the card of the muscular young man. 'It's finally happening, I'm getting old.'

'You're two years younger than me!' I exclaimed.

'And you're almost entirely grey. Is that what I've got to look forward to?'

'Yes, and you're going to shrink a foot too.'

'Do you think Bill will want a younger model?'

'He already has one, you're ten years younger than him.'

'Precisely. He met me when I was *much* younger, so maybe I'm getting too old for him. Maybe he prefers men under forty.'

'Then you've got three years to convince him to hang on to

you. Anyway, I wouldn't worry. Mentally and emotionally, you're barely out of your teens.'

He stuck his tongue out at me. He needed distracting.

'So, what did you discover?'

'Where?'

'The book. The manuscript that Harnby asked you to read. Have you finished it? Was there anything useful?'

He took a deep breath and appeared to refocus himself.

'Almost. I have no idea if it will help the case, but it makes for a decent read. There's some general history, and then it focuses largely on the Fitzwilliam-Scott family's role in British politics. A rehashing of some old arguments about their significance, but it comes firmly down on their side.'

'Do you think Thomas wrote it?'

Mark had pulled the manuscript out of his bag and was idly flicking through the pages as he spoke.

'Possibly. Bill said that he was very keen on history and wiped the floor with the other teams at the pub quiz. I would guess he's local, so he'd be familiar with the house and the family. It would make sense for it to be a subject he wanted to write about. I'd need to see something else he's written to check it's the same style to be certain, but I don't see why not.'

'Do you think this was why he was killed?'

'The book? No idea.'

I drank the cold dregs of my coffee and thought about Thomas. We knew next to nothing about him, except that he might not actually have been the intended victim. When I looked up, it was nine o'clock and staff were starting to trickle in, wanting to get a coffee and pastry to take back to their desks. Although today I knew they would linger and chat with their colleagues, hoping to get some gossip about the events of the weekend. Tina and Chelsea seemed to be coping fine and I was desperate to start digging around for more information. I was feeling like a caged animal; it was time to escape for a little while.

'Come on, birthday boy, you must have work to do.'

Mark pushed his chair back and started to gather his things.

'I need to finish the book before Harnby gets back if nothing else, then I've promised to write an article for a local newspaper, "Life as a Tour Guide" sort of thing. I figure that will be enough – I don't want to overexert myself on such a historic day.'

'Historic?' I queried, and then realised. 'Oh, your birthday. Yes, one for the history books.'

CHAPTER 16

After tidying up the evidence of our little birthday breakfast, I had a quiet word with Tina, grabbed a couple of bags of Charleton House chocolates and a jar of honey, and jumped in my car. Normally I'd enjoy the scenery as I drove, relishing the sweep of the narrow country roads and the rolling hills beyond the dry stone walls. I'd play my music loud and, if it wasn't too cold, wind the windows down and enjoy a blast of fresh air.

This time, however, I was on a mission. I wanted to know more about Douglas and his relationship with Philippa; I figured it might tell me about Philippa's state of mind. Finding out more about her relationship with Conrad was also on my to-do list. I ignored the claustrophobic fog that had crept over the fields and shot around the bends much faster than was safe, heading to one of my favourite Derbyshire villages. Tina lived in Hathersage, about twenty minutes' drive away, and so did Philippa. With a concerned but resigned look on her face, Tina had told me exactly where Philippa was to be found.

. . .

Hathersage is a picturesque village that would be overrun with visitors in the warmer weather. St Michael and All Angels' church is famous for being the reputed burial site of Little John, Robin Hood's sidekick. Philippa lived a few hundred yards away from the church in a small stone cottage. As I stood outside, I recognised Tina's house further down the lane from photos she'd shown me of her garden.

I grabbed the chocolates off the passenger seat, took a deep breath and walked up the path to the front door. Philippa opened the door before I'd finished knocking and peered at me with a quizzical expression on her face. She looked rather ordinary now she was out of her straw yellow dress, an oversized t-shirt hanging over tight-fitting jeans, her impressive, curvy figure not quite as eye-catching. I could only assume that Conrad had fallen for the persona she created at events.

'Oh hello, you're... weren't you at the sleepover?'

'Yes, I work at the house. I'm Sophie, Head of Catering.'

'Do you often make house calls?'

'No, no, I'm just... here.' I thrust the bags of chocolate at her. 'We wanted to check that our guests were okay – the local ones, anyway – and we hope you'll come back again soon.' I was rambling and talking rubbish, but I wanted to get in the front door. 'How are you?'

'Fine.' She still looked rather confused. 'I guess I should invite you in.'

'Thank you.' I brushed past her before she had a chance to change her mind. 'Should I go in here?' I walked through an open door and into a sitting room with a rather old and tired-looking moss-green sofa. The rug on the floor had seen a lot of use and was bare in patches. She took a seat in a matching green armchair and indicated that I should sit on the sofa.

'How are things at the house?' Philippa asked. 'Are the police still there?'

'They are. We're open to the public again, but they're still finishing off. I'm sorry about your friend. Were you close?'

She laughed, and then started coughing. 'Thomas? Oh God, no. I'm friends with his wife, but Thomas and I have never exactly seen eye to eye. Still, it is shocking.'

'You must be so relieved it wasn't Conrad.'

'Conrad? Why would I have thought it was Conrad?' She looked at me blankly.

'You didn't know? It was initially thought that the victim was Conrad, they were dressed very similarly.'

She let out a puff of air and slumped back in her chair. 'I had no idea. I'm glad I didn't realise at the time.'

'You and Conrad are close?'

She sat up and eyed me suspiciously. 'I'm guessing you know the answer to that question. I know how quickly gossip spreads around that place, so why don't you tell me why you're really here? And don't tell me it's to deliver chocolates.'

I stared at my hands for a moment, wondering how to approach the subject. We'd got to the point quicker than I'd intended.

'You're right, I know about what happened. Conrad says you've remained on good terms.'

'As much as we can under the circumstances. We don't talk anymore, it's better that way.'

'What about Lycia?'

'What about her? I'm sure she hates my guts. I'm not proud of what we did, of what I did. We just got caught up in the moment.' She was playing with the hem of her t-shirt, a thread gradually getting longer and longer as she wrapped it round the end of her finger.

'How did you feel when they got back together?'

'How did I feel? Do you mean was I wracked with jealousy? Had I been imaging a perfect life with Conrad? Two-point-four children, growing old together? I had a moment of envy, yes, but it *was* momentary, and I always knew nothing would come of our… our… well, I moved on. I had to. I knew Lycia had put rules in place for Conrad and I did what I could to make it easy for him to follow them. But I didn't stay away entirely. I wasn't going to stop attending events. I still have my blog to write, and anyway, I wasn't the only guilty party.'

She sounded so reasonable, almost too reasonable. There was a sadness woven between the words as she spoke, but I didn't detect any bitterness. It was time to change the subject.

'There's something else I wanted to ask you. Can you tell me anything about Douglas Popplewell? I know you knew him years ago, and I know you don't get on. What happened?'

She visibly relaxed as I steered the conversation in this new direction.

'Douglas? Do you think he might be involved?'

I shrugged. 'I don't know for sure, I'm just curious about a couple of things.'

'Douglas is a cheat, or at least he was, and my guess is he still is. You look surprised by my bluntness, but it's the truth.'

'Tell me.'

'He cheated in a competition we entered just after we graduated from university.'

'The Dr Archibald Vogler Award?'

'You've heard of it? It can kick-start people's careers. At the time it was considered really important for students who wanted to get research funding. Douglas entered an essay written by someone else and won.'

'You know this for sure?'

'I can't prove it, but yes, I'm sure. A group of students were found guilty of plagiarism around that time. There was a bit of a racket going on, students were writing essays for cash, and Douglas was friends with a couple of them. His name came up in gossip at the time, but he was never pulled into the investigation formally – as far as I know, anyway. His grades were okay, not great, but the essay he submitted for the competition was *really* good. Too good for it to be his work. But I couldn't prove it, so they dismissed my concerns and he won.' She sounded both angry and resigned to it.

'But why keep on attacking him in your blog? It was so long ago.'

'I only write what I see.'

'Maybe, but you're pretty harsh in the way you do it.'

'Perhaps. He deserves it, though. He's probably spent his whole career to date riding on other people's coat tails. I'm just trying to ground him.'

'Very publicly.'

'Is there anything else you wanted to ask me? Only I have work to do.'

I'd tested her patience to its limits. I shook my head.

'No. Actually, I'm sorry to ask, but could I use your bathroom? I don't think I'll make it back to the house.' I'd had four mugs of coffee since I'd got out of bed and I was regretting at least one of them.

'It's up the stairs on the left. You can see yourself out.'

The stairs were steep and narrow, and I was grateful for the light that was suddenly flicked on for me. Before I turned into the bathroom, I peered into the room opposite. A large antique wooden bed dominated the room – it must have been hell to get it up the stairs. At the foot of it, a heavy wooden chest of drawers held a number of photos.

I stepped closer; they were all photos of Charles Dickens. Well, I say all, but some were postcard reproductions of paintings, and all of them were of Conrad. Joyce hadn't been wrong. Despite everything Philippa had just told me, it looked as if she hadn't let go of Conrad yet.

Beside the photos were multiple copies of Dickens's books, a dried red geranium, and a little figurine of Dickens. On the wall above were posters of Dickens's book covers and a framed collection of tickets from staged versions of his work she must have attended over the years. An article about Conrad and a reading he had given in London last month had been printed from the internet and lay next to the books.

I heard footsteps downstairs and dashed out of the room. Going into the bathroom to flush the toilet, I then ran down the stairs.

'Thank you, bye,' I called as I left. I was going to have to drive back with my legs crossed.

CHAPTER 17

After running from my car, elbowing my way past a few visitors and making it to the car park toilets just in time, I walked back down the lane, thinking about the shrine to Conrad that Philippa had in her bedroom. I was wondering how much of what she'd said I could believe when I spotted the Duke, who waved at me.

'Hold up, Sophie, I've remembered why Thomas Hattersley's name rang bells. We used to have a team of locals who would come and work as beaters during the pheasant shoots. They'd flush the birds out from the undergrowth for the hunting party. Arnold Hattersley was one of the regulars and he'd sometimes get extra work with the gamekeeper throughout the rest of the year. But he got caught up with some sort of poaching.'

'When was this?' I asked.

'I had a quick look back over some of our annual reports. Early nineties. I think it all came to light in 1992, but the poaching had been going on for a while.'

'And how is Thomas linked to all this?'

'Arnold was his dad and a young Thomas used to come to work with him from time to time. I asked the Duchess about it and she remembered a rather chubby, spotty teenager. He must have been about eighteen. I don't remember a lot more about it, but the current gamekeeper might have some files in his office. I hope this is of some use?'

'Yes, absolutely. Thank you.' My heart was starting to race; this was the first bit of really useful information I had, although it opened up the field of people who might have known Thomas. Maybe he had been the intended target after all.

Seth Mellors had been the gamekeeper for less than a year; he'd started not all that long after me and I knew him by name and sight only. He was always in a green wax jacket and a flat cap, his Border collie by his side. He'd park his muddy Land Rover on the back lane and spend time with the security team; their jobs often crossed over and they helped each other out, but I'd had no reason to be in meetings with him. For all I knew, he wasn't a coffee drinker, unless he made his own. I'd never seen him in any of the cafés.

His office was just off the yard that was home to the gardens team. He had a small room in a single-storey stone building, his desk was in front of the window, and I could see him working on his computer as I approached. He looked up and I gave a little wave, pointing at his door questioningly. He stood up and opened it.

'Hi, do you have a few minutes?' He stepped back to let me in and Scout quickly got up to take a sniff of me.

'Scout, back to your bed. Course. I've seen you around, but I don't know your name.'

'Sophie, I run the cafés. Here, it's a chocolate brownie.'

'Thanks. Is this in case I don't believe you?' He smiled and ripped the bag open, making a start on its contents before he'd even sat back down. 'Pull up a seat. I'm just working on some reports, but I'm happy to take a break. How can I help?'

'I'm trying to find out about an incident a few decades back, around 1992. I was hoping you'd have some record of it in your files.'

I turned to look at the row of shelves on the back wall, packed with battered folders and boxes, surprised at how plain the room was. I'm not sure what I was expecting. Guns leaning in the corner, maybe; perhaps a couple of rabbits hanging off the back of the door. But this was just a regular office. A tall locked cabinet was in one corner, Scout making himself comfortable next to it, and a couple of pairs of muddy boots were in another. An enormous map of the entire estate took up one wall. A small fridge was next to Seth's desk with a kettle and jar of instant coffee on top.

'What sort of incident?' he asked.

'Poaching.'

'Well, there's been a bit of that over the years. You might have to help me narrow it down.'

'It was one of the staff, a beater by the name of Arnold Hattersley.'

Seth stood up and reached for a file. 'I know exactly what you mean. I've been going through all this lot, trying to tidy things up, plus plenty of people have been happy to tell the new boy all the gossip. Especially when it relates to previous people in this job.'

He sat back down with a tired-looking brown file.

'This should really be with Human Resources cos it relates to an ex-employee. It shouldn't just be sat on my shelves. I'll get round to it eventually.' He flicked through the papers until he found what he was looking for. 'Bernie Stubbs was in my job then. He was the gamekeeper from 1962. In 1990, after a couple of quiet years, poaching started up again. Just bits here and there, but regular. No one could figure it out. Eventually someone pointed the finger at Bernie. It was always on his days off and holidays, or when his own small team was involved in a big project and not doing their day-to-day work. On those days, security were also short-staffed or preoccupied. All that required inside knowledge, and for some reason the powers that be decided it was Bernie. He denied all knowledge, but was suspended anyway.

'Turned out it was actually the work of Arnold Hattersley, a beater. He knew most of the team, game keeping and security. He'd drink with them down the pub so he knew all the goings on, and used that information to work out when the best time was to come and set traps. I don't know how they caught him, but he was arrested and eventually pleaded guilty. Bernie came back to work, but in 1993 he retired. Died a couple of years later. Is that what you're looking for?'

'That's exactly it. Is there anything in there about a Thomas Hattersley?'

Seth took a few minutes to go through the file.

'No, nothing. Who was he?'

'He was Arnold's son.'

'The dead guy from the other night?' He sounded surprised. 'It really is a small world.'

'I was wondering who might know Thomas from back when this all kicked off with his dad.'

'Well, the gamekeeper that took over from Bernie in '93 left in 2002. His successor left last year, and that's when I came along. So there's been a few of us since then.'

'What about family? Wasn't there a lot of jobs for the family in those days?'

Seth nodded. 'Yeah, key way to get jobs then, but as far as I know, Bernie didn't have any kids of his own. The two gamekeepers that followed on were father and son, so in that case, yes. But they weren't related to Bernie, they were a new lot.'

'And you?' I decided to risk the question for no reason other than curiosity. 'Are you related to anyone here?'

He laughed. 'No, my dad's a plumber. The closest my family

ever got to the great outdoors was sticking a bird feeder in the back garden.'

'So how did you end up doing this?'

'School. I had an amazing geography teacher who was a volunteer park ranger in the holidays and also loved to clay pigeon shoot. Took me under his wing. And with a name like mine, what else was I going to do?' He grinned. 'Is there anything else I can help you with?'

'No, that's great. Thanks, Seth.' I looked at the jar of instant coffee. 'And pop round the café anytime you want a decent cup of coffee, it's on the house.'

'If you chuck in another brownie, you'll see me before the week is out.' He winked and I let myself out of the door.

So Thomas had had a connection to the house, but he hadn't been the one poaching, as far as the records showed. I did the maths – as the Duke had said, he would have been about eighteen when his dad was caught, so old enough to be involved. Still, it could just be a coincidence that he was here when he was killed. He was a local man born and bred and he loved history. There were plenty of people who lived in the surrounding villages with connections to Charleton House, he was in no way unique. He was, however, the only one of them who had been murdered here.

I left behind the warmth of Seth's office and nearly fell over Romeo. He was patrolling the yard – this was very much his home turf – and he paid no attention to me.

'Romeo, here.' I clicked my fingers and crouched down. I couldn't resist a cute cat or dog – make that anything with fur. Romeo stopped, looked back over his shoulder at me, made an assessment that didn't go in my favour and carried on his way.

I wasn't giving up that easily, so I followed him towards the tall stone wall that ran the length of the yard. Finally he turned and allowed me to pet him. I picked him up. He was feather light compared to Pumpkin, who was going to put my back out one of these days.

'Why did you say it if you didn't mean it?' The man's voice sounded desperate and angry. I looked around; I couldn't see anyone in the yard.

'I'm sorry.' Now it was a woman speaking. The voice was familiar – both were.

'I thought you wanted to leave him.'

'I did, maybe... I don't know, but he's tried so hard. And when I thought he was dead...'

'You realised you couldn't live without him, is that it? I can't believe this! You've made a fool of me.'

I could hear the man start to walk away, then stop and return.

'There isn't anything I wouldn't do for you.'

It sounded like a row between Harvey and Lycia, but I needed to be sure. I looked around. There was a heavy-duty golf cart parked further along the wall with a flat bed at the back so the gardeners could carry equipment round the house gardens. It would be easy to stand on.

I put Romeo down, took a handful of skirt and pulled myself up onto the flat bed. From there, I had a clear view of the walled garden, and sticking my head over a bit further, I confirmed the source of the voices.

Harvey was pacing up and down.

'I've been a bloody idiot.' He punched the wall and I winced – that had to hurt. 'I told you I'd do anything, and I still would. He doesn't deserve you. This all would have been so much easier if it was him who'd been killed.'

'Oh my God, Harvey, you can't mean that...' Lycia looked horror-stricken.

'Can I help?' The voice came from behind me. 'You can get into the garden through a gate, climbing the wall isn't necessary.'

Seth was standing next to the cart, looking bemused and offering me his hand. I wanted to stay, hear a confession from

Harvey – if that was where the conversation was going – but I guessed I'd have missed it by now.

I took Seth's hand. 'I was just checking to see where… where Romeo had gone.' That was the best I could do at short notice.

'Romeo is fine. In fact, if you ask him nicely, I reckon he'll drive you back to your office.'

He nodded towards the driver's seat of the golf cart. Romeo was sitting facing the steering wheel, looking for all the world like he was about to turn the key and start the engine.

'Thanks, but I think I'll walk.'

Seth nodded, looking like he was stifling a laugh. I couldn't blame him. As soon as I was out of earshot, I burst out laughing myself. I must have looked like such a fool.

But I soon stopped laughing when Harvey strode past me, his face full of fury. Conrad hadn't been convinced that Harvey was capable of murder, but maybe he'd been wrong.

CHAPTER 18

I was still smiling to myself about Seth finding me perched on top of a golf cart when Betsy ran past, dressed in full servants' garb. She waved at me.

'Betsy,' I called after her. 'Do you have a minute?'

'Hang on, I need to get this to an education group in the courtyard. Come with me.' She was carrying a hessian sack in one hand and her long skirt in the other. It looked a little like the outfits Tina and Chelsea had worn on the night of the sleepover when they were serving dinner. In fact, she was probably wearing some of the exact same items. I had no idea what live interpretation piece she was working on today, but she was clearly a 19th century servant.

I followed on behind, ducked through a low doorway, down a narrow whitewashed corridor and into a courtyard full of schoolchildren.

'Betsy, thank God.' A young woman grabbed the sack from her and dashed back to the group of children before bellowing, 'Follow me, everyone, we'll head to the classrooms.'

'You wanted me?' Betsy turned to face me. 'I've a few minutes before the next group turns up, let's sit over there.' She led me to a bench in a far corner and pulled a shawl around her as we sat down. She didn't look dressed for the weather; I just hoped she had plenty of thermals on under her costume.

'I wanted to ask you about Conrad and Philippa. Just how unpleasant did all that get?'

'Pretty bad. Lycia blew her top a couple of times. Most of the time, everyone was very professional – in public, at least.'

'Was Philippa... well, did she keep pursuing it?'

'Do you mean was she some kind of crazed stalker who would do anything for Conrad, and when she didn't get him, she killed him? Or someone she thought was him.'

I smiled sheepishly; I wasn't being very subtle.

'I actually started to feel sorry for her. She's brash and doesn't have complete control of her volume dial sometimes, but I don't think she's as bad as people say. I get the impression the whole thing just got out of control. She was devastated when things got so nasty between Conrad and Lycia, and I think she regrets it all as much as he does. She became the fall guy.'

It made a change to talk to someone who sounded like they actually had some sympathy for Philippa.

'What do you mean?'

'I know that Conrad had wanted to handle it all a bit more carefully, tell Lycia himself. He knew what he'd done was wrong, but he at least had the decency to want to take responsibility.'

'And he didn't?'

'Didn't have the chance. Someone beat him to it. Whoever it was found out, and then broke the news to Lycia.'

The peace of the courtyard was broken as another school group flooded in, screaming and running, a teacher struggling to get them to pay any attention to her.

'I need to go, introduce that lot to the world *below stairs*.'

'Wait, do you know who told Lycia?'

'No, but it happened after an event at Berwick Hall, that much I remember. We were all getting ready to go and I saw Lycia reading a note. The next minute, she was driving out of the car park so fast, I thought she was going to kill someone. It all came out the next day. I have to go, sorry.'

I watched as Betsy effortlessly took charge of the group, leaving the teacher to resemble a spare part. It wouldn't be long until the teachers abandoned their charges and found their way to a café. Completely against the rules, but it hadn't stopped them before.

I warmed myself up by assisting behind the counter and giving Tina a break. Staff that came in were continuing to gossip, and it hadn't taken long for people to find out that I was the one who had found Thomas, although the stories varied as to whether he had been stabbed with Charles Dickens's quill or beaten with a copy of *A Christmas Carol*.

Once Tina returned, I decided to distract myself with Mark's cake. I wasn't a professional baker, just a keen amateur, but my interest and reasonable skill level meant I occasionally helped out and made cookies and cakes for the cafés, taking the pressure off our part-time pastry chef.

I was standing in front of three rectangular carrot cakes that I was about to decorate to look like books – I must have been drunk when I'd offered to make Mark's birthday cake. I'd planned on making a pile of five books, but I quickly realised that was overambitious and cut it down to four. Then I'd dropped one cake while taking it out of the oven, so four became three. Right now, they looked less like books and more like squashed bricks lying side by side. It was time to place them in a pile.

I carefully slid a large knife under one and ever so slowly brought it over the largest of the three. I wanted the books to look a little untidy, like Mark's desk, so I turned it slightly and lowered it. Perfect. Now for the third. I repeated the process and held it over the other two, trying to decide which way to lay it. Did I want the books in a sort of spiral, or…

There was a knock at the window. I looked up. At the same time I could feel the knife tilt. I looked back in time to see the third and final cake drop off the knife, slide down the side of the other two, and then fall off the counter into a pile on my foot.

'NOOOOOOO! DAG NAMMIT, NOT AGAIN. WHAT?'

Joe stood in the window, looking very sheepish. 'Sorry,' he mouthed. I jabbed my thumb in the air, firmly indicating that he should come in.

'Bloody idiot,' I muttered to no one in particular, scooping up the cake off the floor. I was dumping the last handful in the bin as a white paper napkin was stuck round the door and waved in the air.

'Is it safe?' Joe's voice drifted through.

'You muppet!' I exclaimed, this time loud enough for him to hear. 'I'm coming.'

Joe turned down the offer of a coffee, but I felt the need to start mainlining the stuff again. Something had to get me through the next stage of decorating the cake, what was left of it.

'I'll buy you a new pair.' Joe was looking at my shoes, one of which was now smeared in cream and crumbs. I'd wiped off the worst of it, but it was still a mess.

'Okay, but they're very expensive designer trainers that you can only purchase in person in New York.' I grinned. 'Don't be soft; you'll do no such thing. Right, seeing as you're here…'

I proceeded to tell him about the conversation I'd overheard between Harvey and Lycia, missing out the embarrassing bit about Seth and Romeo's cameo. I decided to save the information about the note to Lycia until I knew more.

Joe took a deep breath. 'Our list of suspects isn't getting any shorter.'

'And I'm about to make it longer.' He tilted his head and waited. 'I have a confession to make. Please don't get mad – you know what I'm like and I'm only trying to help.'

'What have you done? Have you been wearing that damned deerstalker hat again?'

'What?'

'Have you been playing detective? I've told you before, leave this to the professionals. So what have you done?'

I told him about my visit to see Philippa and watched the storm clouds gather across his face as I spoke.

'Sophie, I can't believe you did that. Harnby will hit the roof.'

'Does she have to know?'

'She'll probably find out, especially as Philippa now seems to deserve a visit from us. You're bound to come up in conversation.'

'But if I hadn't gone, you wouldn't know to pay her a visit.'

'Don't you dare try to dig yourself out of this one, Sophie Lockwood.'

We sat in silence for a few minutes, until I decided to break it.

'Do you have any idea why Thomas had the manuscript on him? Presumably it was his own work.'

Joe sighed and shook his head.

'Not necessarily. He was a history teacher, but did a bit of editing work on the side. His wife said that he wasn't really qualified, but he'd help people out by reading through their work and giving feedback for a small fee. It helped subsidise his teacher's salary, and she'd been out of work for a while, so the money was helpful.'

'If he's a history teacher, doesn't Bill know him from school as well as the quiz?'

'I already checked, no. Thomas taught at a school on the far side of Sheffield, and he wasn't much of a talker at those quiz nights, so Bill never knew much about him.' He glanced at his watch. 'I should be off.'

'It's almost lunchtime, are you sure you won't stay for some food?'

Joe shook his head. 'I'd better get back. I'll take a sandwich with me, though.'

'Hang on.' I took hold of his arm to stop him walking away. 'Is there any evidence that Philippa got up during the night? Did any staff see her go to the bathroom?'

Joe pulled out his notebook and started flicking through the small pages.

'I think she did... yes. The warder in the room remembers her going because she was one of the loudest snorers. He said there was a brief respite from the noise when she went to the toilet. The warder downstairs didn't see her; he was walking someone to the gents' toilet around the same time, which was in the opposite direction.'

'Do you think she could have done it – killed Thomas, I mean – if she thought it was Conrad?'

Joe didn't look sure. 'I didn't think so, not until you told me about her little shrine. Now she's high on my list of suspects. But we don't have any evidence to tie her to the scene of the murder.'

'Maybe you'll find something when you pay her a visit. Perhaps she's kept a souvenir of the event.'

'You mean like a severed ear? I didn't know you were the gruesome type. Anyway, the body was intact.'

'No, I don't mean that. Maybe she took something from the breakroom – a handkerchief, something like that.'

Joe pulled his jacket on. 'Not impossible. We'll find it if she did. What sandwich do you recommend? I'm starting to get hungry.'

CHAPTER 19

I watched Mark as he spoke to a group of tourists. They were wrapped up against the cold as he pointed out some of the architectural features in the courtyard. You could see evidence of the original Tudor building here, and the cobbles underfoot helped you feel like you'd gone back in time, but I knew Mark would be trying to keep this part of the tour short. It was too cold to be out here for long. The sky was a steel grey and the air felt damp. It was the kind of cold that seeped into your bones and required a long steaming-hot bath if you were to stand any chance of feeling warm again.

Pat from security walked past the group, the large set of keys that hung from his belt jangling as he went. He made no effort to silence them. Then he spotted me and walked over.

'Imagine paying good money to stand in the cold on a day like this. Crazy.' He was wearing gloves, but was still rubbing his hands together to keep warm.

'What are you doing here? I thought you were on nights.'

'I am, but the police wanted another word with me and Rog, so we both decided to hang around, get some overtime in.'

I looked in the direction of the group. 'Mark'll take them inside as soon as he can.'

'Has your mate Joe told you how the police are gettin' on?' He continued to watch the group, his eyes following them as they walked to another corner of the courtyard. 'That Harnby doesn't give anything away.'

'Not really,' I lied. 'I just keep him topped up with coffee.'

'Hmm, well, I'll be glad when it's done. We've still got press sniffing around and getting in the way, and there's a couple of police cars blocking up the back lane. Dunno what we're going to do if we have to get a fire truck down there.'

He didn't seem to be in any kind of a hurry, so I thought I'd take the opportunity to see if he knew anything helpful.

'Thomas Hattersley's dad used to work here, did you know him?'

'He didn't exactly work here; he helped out when we used to have shoots, but we're talkin' thirty years back. Cash-in-hand work, nothing serious. They were a bad lot, though, the whole family. It's hard to feel sorry for Thomas, he was no better than the rest of them.'

Pat's eyes followed the group as they went under a stone archway and through a worn wooden door that looked as old as the cobbles.

'Did you know him, then? Thomas, I mean.'

'Nah, it all kicked off a couple of years before I got here, but I 'eard all about it. I like to keep my ear to the ground, always have. You don't know what's going to come in handy, and in this job, you need to be well informed. We have the security of this place to think about and I've always taken that very seriously.' As he spoke his final words, he seemed to grow a little taller and puff his chest out. He'd always had an air of self-importance about him, and I'd just witnessed it take a physical form.

'But Thomas seemed to have left that behind him and done quite well for himself. A respectable job, a love of history.'

'People like that don't change. Once a bad 'un, always a bad 'un. I'm sure that Douglas agrees with me.'

I spun my head round to face him. 'Douglas? Why Douglas? Did he know Thomas?'

'I don't know if he knew him as such, but they certainly had words that night. I saw them arguing after everyone had gone to bed. If you're doing your Miss Marple act again then you ought to talk to him.'

Douglas had claimed never to have met Thomas before the sleepover, and yet they were arguing. Either Douglas was lying, or they'd found a way to annoy each other very quickly. Pat was turning out to be useful. For all his arrogance, he had been here for years and probably had a mine of amazing information in that head of his. I wouldn't dismiss him quite so quickly next time.

Mark looked frozen as he walked into my office. I had a moment of panic, but then realised that his birthday cake, which I'd yet to finish, was under a box and out of sight. I scooted my chair against the far wall, which in practice meant I'd moved about a foot, and Mark shoved some papers aside before sitting on my desk. He didn't attempt to remove his coat.

'I should be spending my birthday on a tropical island somewhere, not freezing my digits off with a bunch of hungover architecture students.'

'Was that the group I saw you with?'

'Probably, yeah. They were alright, but one of them admitted to me that they'd been on a bit of a bender the night before, so I was lucky they stayed awake. I don't know why I bother sometimes.'

'Because you love it,' I told him firmly. 'Besides which, you've been in their shoes on plenty of occasions, so you can't be too annoyed.'

'Me? Hungover? How dare you! Not since, ooh, the weekend before last.' He grinned. 'So, how's my cake coming along?' He glanced over his shoulder in the direction of the box.

'I have no idea what you're talking about. Have you finished that manuscript yet?' I asked, hoping to distract him.

'I have.'

'Were there any revelations?'

'No, it continued in the same vein. It's well written, a lot of the information reasonably well known already, but it will make a good addition to the books about the history of the family. It looks like it's finished, apart from the bibliography and author bio. There are a number of notes that reference books that aren't listed, so I reckon whoever it belonged to was still working on it.'

'Joe told me that Thomas would look over manuscripts for people, a sort of unqualified editor. Do you think it belongs to a client rather than him?'

Mark nodded. 'That would make sense, but there's nothing to give away who the author is, if it's not Thomas. One thing did cross my mind, though.'

He paused for too long. I didn't have the patience for his amateur dramatics today, birthday or not.

'Get on with it.'

'Who do we know that is going on endlessly about a book he's writing – a book about Charleton – and whose work, if his tour performances are anything to go by, is going to need plenty of help?'

'Douglas. Of course.' I stood up. In the tiny space, we were nose to nose as I reached around Mark for my coat, which was hanging on the back of the door.

'Where are you going?'

'Where are *we* going. Come on, we're going to talk to Douglas, and I'll fill you in on the chat I had with Philippa this morning.'

'But I've still not defrosted,' he whined, 'and it's my birthday. Wait, what about Philippa?'

'Then you'll acclimatise back into the cold quicker,' I reasoned. I knew curiosity would get the better of Mark if I mentioned I'd spoken to Philippa. 'Out of my way, birthday boy.'

Mark's office was deserted. There was no sign of Douglas or the other two tour guides who had desks in the room. Making my way straight to Douglas's desk, I started to go through the piles of paper that littered it. I guessed that he must have his own system of filing, but there was no way I could tell what it was.

'What are you doing?' Mark exclaimed.

'There might be other printouts, copies of sections of the book, something you recognise from the manuscript that ties it to him.'

'Why don't we just ask him?'

I looked around the room. 'I don't see him, and I'm not waiting. Besides which, he claimed that he'd never seen Thomas before Saturday night, but he was seen arguing with him by Pat, so I doubt we'd get the truth from him.'

'Well noted, someone's on the ball. Surely there'll be a copy on his computer.' Mark leant over me and switched the computer on. As it starting humming into life, he pulled off his coat and sat down at the desk.

'It'll be password protected, especially if there's stuff he wants to hide.'

'True, but he complains every time the IT department emails to tell us to change our passwords. He asked me to log on for him once when he was working from home and send a document to him. I just need to remember what it was. You know, I still can't believe you went to see Philippa without me.' He looked at me and shook his head.

'Focus, man,' I said, pointing at the computer.

He stared at the screen until it blinked into life, and then tried a couple of different words.

'I remember it was the name of his dog, and...'

'If he comes in, there'll be hell to pay. Do you know where he is?'

Mark didn't look up. 'No idea.'

I dived into stacks of paper and flipped through files, but there was nothing.

'Hang on, he was shredding stuff yesterday. What if that was it?'

'Then it's shredded and we'll have no idea. Buster, Bobby, Billy...' Mark was pounding on the keys.

'What if it's not completely destroyed?' I'd heard of crimes that had been solved because someone painstakingly recreated documents from their shredded remnants. Grabbing the shredder, I lifted the lid, pulled out a handful of paper and put it on the desk. If we could tie Douglas to Thomas via the manuscript, then we had another solid lead.

'Are you completely out of your mind? How much coffee have you had today?'

'Enough to know we can do this. Come on.'

He didn't move from his seat, just kept trying different passwords.

'Firstly, it's my birthday, which means I should be spending the day being waited on hand and foot, and secondly, this is going to be like looking for dandruff in a snowstorm. Not possible and not much fun... Got it, Bertie, and then its age. Douglas just kept upping that number with each password change.'

'Alright, old man, get on with it.'

I stared at the screen as Mark took us through a series of folders, the only noise in the room the click of a computer mouse. Then the quiet was interrupted by the sound of Douglas's voice over the radio.

'Security, this is Art Tour 1, this is Art Tour 1. Just to let you know I've finished the last tour of the day and the Long Gallery is locked and secure.'

'Thank you, Art Tour 1,' came the reply.

Mark and I looked at each other, and then scrambled into action. He rapidly closed down files, while I madly stuffed paper back into the shredder bin. I couldn't help but giggle.

'What are you laughing at? I'm the one that has to share an office with him if he finds us.'

'Sorry, I can't help it, we must look ridiculous.'

'You look ridiculous, fighting with that stuff. There's bits all over the floor.'

On my hands and knees, I started trying to pick up all the tiny bits of paper I could.

'Come on, he won't notice that.'

We ran to the door, down the stairs and into the courtyard, where Mark came to a sudden stop.

'Why are we running? That's my office too. We could have just moved to my desk.'

I gasped for breath; I wasn't used to taking exercise.

'Good point. Would have been… a better point… if you'd said… it in there,' I replied in between gulps of air.

'Any errors of judgment can be forgiven on my birthday.'

'You and your bloody birthday.'

'Did someone not get enough sleep?'

'No. What next?'

'Come with me, I've got an idea.'

'I should get back to the café. You're welcome to join me and spend what is left of the working day skiving in a corner, making snarky comments at my staff.'

'Marvellous. Throw in a chocolate brownie and I'm in, only I'm going to use your computer.'

I looked his skinny frame up and down. He seemed to spend half his life eating cakes and pastries, but there wasn't an ounce of fat on him. I, on the other hand, only had to inhale a whiff of freshly baked cookies and I could feel my hips expanding.

We pulled up our collars and braced ourselves against the rain that was starting to fall in big bloated drops.

I set Mark up in my office with cake and coffee. He told me he needed an hour to pursue an idea he had. After half an hour of cleaning tables, loading the dishwasher and generally getting under Tina's feet, I couldn't wait any longer. I pushed my way into the office.

'Budge up.'

'Hang on.' Mark shuffled the chair as far as he could. 'I'm not done yet.'

'I want an update, so you better not be online shopping for a new set of curtains.'

He turned and stared at me. 'Curtains? Why would I want curtains?'

'I dunno, it was the first thing that came to mind.'

He turned back to the screen. 'You worry me. I'm using the online archives of the British Library. I often use them as a resource when I'm researching tours. Most people don't realise what you can get access to without leaving the comfort of your own home.'

He was tapping and scrolling like his life depended on it; he knew what he was doing. I'd still be trying to log on, even after half an hour.

'I've only found three so far, but I'm right. Look.'

He held up a page of the manuscript against a paragraph of text he'd highlighted on the screen. I read one, then the other. They were the same, almost word for word, just a couple of minor changes here and there.

'What am I looking at?'

Mark swivelled the office chair round so he was facing me.

'Thomas has highlighted certain passages, like this one. He's noted the name of the book it's taken from. Those books don't appear in the manuscript's bibliography and I imagine they were never going to be added. My guess is that whoever wrote this was plagiarising texts and hoping no one spotted it. None of them are popular books, they're all pretty old and difficult to get hold of. It's unlikely they appear on any university reading list, and I would imagine there aren't many people around who remember them or have copies. Of course, if you know exactly what you're looking for, it's really not that hard to find, but no one would have known to look. But Thomas knew his stuff. He's also a details man. If he got wind of a problem, he would have hunted it down.'

I playfully punched Mark on the shoulder. 'You're not as green as you're cabbage looking. So, now we need to prove who wrote the manuscript. Are you still convinced that it's the work of Douglas?'

'I'm more convinced than ever. We know he's lazy when it comes to the behind-the-scenes stuff, so he's bound to take a shortcut if he can. I also reckon he's daft enough – or maybe naïve or arrogant enough, depending on how you look at it – to think he could get away with it. Come on, get your coat on. You're at risk of being demoted to Watson status.'

CHAPTER 20

The rain hadn't let up as we walked quickly across the courtyard. In the distance, I could see a hunched figure, equally bundled up against the cold, make its way towards the staircase that led up to the live interpreters' breakroom. I was struggling to make out who it was as the rain ran down my glasses and turned everything into a grey misty blur.

'Wasn't that Douglas?'

'It was. Come on, we need a word with our soon-to-be-published history writer.'

I hadn't returned to the breakroom since yesterday morning when I'd found Thomas's body. The worn wooden staircase and roughly painted corridors now seemed eerie and the atmosphere still and cold. It hadn't always felt that way, and I knew logically that nothing had changed, but a little part of me wondered if I was going to stumble on another disturbing scene.

We climbed slowly, carefully placing our feet to avoid any creaking planks of wood – a largely pointless exercise. Winding our way up two floors, we stood outside the breakroom. The entrance was actually two large wooden doors, the kind you could burst through to make a dramatic entrance, and one was slightly ajar. We could hear a scrabbling inside – a chair moving, a drawer being opened. I stepped closer and peered through the gap. Douglas was looking for something and muttering to himself.

A wave of tiredness swept over me. This was not where I wanted to be right now; I was low on patience.

'Douglas.' I stepped into the room with a determination to get this over with.

'Soph...' It seemed I'd taken Mark by surprise, and he was still outside the door as I reached the middle of the room.

'Lost something, Douglas? Do you need a hand?'

'What? I... no.' He stood up, guilt and surprise plastered across his face as he looked back and forth between the two of us.

'You know the police have been over this place multiple times. If you've lost something, they're bound to have it.'

Just the thought of that seemed to horrify him. I was painfully aware of the desk and chair to my left, sitting in front of a window that looked out over the gardens to the side of the house. Less than forty-eight hours ago, I had found Thomas's body slumped over that very same desk, but right now, that didn't seem quite so important.

'Are you looking for this?' Mark stepped forward, holding a large brown envelope in the air. I hadn't realised he'd brought his bag with him, but I was glad he had. It made for a fabulously dramatic moment, and was just Mark's style.

'I... I don't know what it is, what you're talking about.' Douglas didn't take his eyes off the envelope; he knew very well what it contained. He straightened himself up as though trying to project an air of confidence. 'I'm just looking for some paperwork I might have left here. Nothing important.'

'What time were you here until on Saturday night?' I asked, wondering if I could get anything out of him. 'I know you didn't go straight home after you finished the tour.'

'No, of course not, you saw me at the Dickens reading. I

stayed to chat to the guests, and then left as they started going to bed.'

That didn't match with what Pat had said, and for all his bluster and arrogance, I was inclined to believe Pat.

'You were seen later than that, and I'm guessing that security can confirm what time you left the house. If that's what you told the police, then it won't be long before they work out that your story has some big holes in it.'

He looked briefly nervous, but seemed to gather himself and made for the door.

'I'm wondering what Thomas was doing with this?' Mark had stepped into Douglas's path and made to open the envelope. 'The more I read it, the more I recognise the style, or some of it at least.'

'I still don't know what you're talking about.' Douglas no longer sounded so sure of himself. 'It's not my manuscript.'

'How do you know there's a manuscript in here?' Mark feigned surprise. 'It could be a magazine article, a blog post. I never said it was a manuscript.'

Douglas was looking increasingly lost.

'For heaven's sake, Douglas!' I snapped, taking him by the arm and steering him to the sofa. 'Sit down.'

Mark looked wide-eyed at me.

'What? I'm tired, I've had too much coffee and he's starting to irritate me.'

Douglas made to get up, but I glared at him and he stayed where he was.

'Mark's read the manuscript. We know you're writing a book, you can't stop talking about it…'

'And,' Mark interrupted, 'now I think about it, this is definitely written by the same hand as those articles that appear under your name in this.' He reached for one of the history magazines that sat on a coffee table – I recognised it as the one Mark had been reading in the café. He opened it up and pointed at a page. 'This is your work, right?'

'Yes,' Douglas replied hesitantly. Mark turned to me.

'It's the same author, I'd put money on it.' He looked back at Douglas. 'So, if you wrote this article, you wrote this book. Well, most of it.'

'It's not finished, there's still a lot of work to be done. I'd like it back.' He stared at Mark and reached for the envelope, but Mark didn't move. Douglas went quiet and sat back in the sofa. 'I haven't finished it, Thomas didn't give me a chance.'

'But you told me that you'd never met him before the night of the sleepover, that you didn't know him. Why didn't you want us to know you were working with him? I assume he's editing your book, or at least giving it a once-over before it goes to your publisher.' I couldn't understand what the problem was with Douglas admitting he knew Thomas.

'Thomas spotted something, didn't he? Something you hoped you'd get past everyone? Correct me if I'm wrong, but I reckon those books that aren't in the bibliography were never going in, were they? Thomas spotted some familiar passages. I'm sure a lot of this is your own work, but there are places where you've just stolen someone else's. You've got a track record, after all.'

'What are you talking about?' Douglas glanced back and forth between us both, eyes wide. He was starting to sweat.

'The Vogler Award.' I was seeing the same links that Mark had spotted. 'That time you paid someone else to write the essay, took the easy route. You knew winning would give you the exposure you wanted. This time, you just took someone else's work and Thomas spotted it. After getting away with something similar once, you thought you'd try it again. But you hadn't realised just how in-depth his knowledge and reading was. Have you really got a publishing deal?'

Douglas looked up. 'Yes. I returned the signed contract to them on Friday, and then Thomas called. Threatened to tell them. I'm an okay writer; I could manage a couple of articles, but

I just kept getting stuck. I'd run out of ideas. There was never enough for a book, and I was going to lose the contract. No one else wanted to take me on, this was my only chance. I thought no one would spot it. I needed this, I knew it would help my career.'

'Is that why Thomas kept leaving the activities on Saturday night?' I asked. Each time I'd seen him outside or at the back of a room, I'd just thought he'd wanted some fresh air, or didn't want to join in. Now I remembered Douglas arriving breathless as Dickens was reading from *Oliver Twist*, moments after I'd seen Thomas through the window, in the courtyard.

'Yes. He kept pestering me all night.' I could see the colour rising in Douglas's cheeks; he was getting riled. I wondered if we were about to see a display of the kind of temper that could lead to murder.

'Was that what you were seen arguing about later?'

He nodded, his hands fidgeting in his lap and his gaze occasionally lingering on the envelope that Mark still had in his hands.

'He would have destroyed me, I'd have lost the book deal and no one would have touched me again. I told him I was sorry, I'd rewrite it, make sure it was all my own work, but he was furious.' Douglas was angry himself now and just let it all spill out. 'People kept seeing us talking, but he wouldn't back off. I knew the breakroom would be empty, so I brought him up here where we wouldn't be seen and tried to talk him round. He wouldn't take no for an answer. Even when I offered him money, he wouldn't accept it, said I'd got the book deal under false pretences. I didn't know what to do.'

He stopped suddenly. I finished for him.

'So you killed him.'

'No! God, no, I didn't, I couldn't.' He sounded angry, but now there was a hint of desperation in his voice. 'We argued, I grabbed him, there was a bit of pushing and shoving, but I couldn't even hit him. I left him in here and went home, drank a bottle of wine, and eventually fell asleep. I had no idea he was dead until I got a message off a colleague. I know you've been involved in this sort of thing before, Sophie, you have to help me. I didn't do it.'

I glanced over at Mark, who shrugged his shoulders. I didn't know whether or not to believe Douglas. He'd certainly shown a full range of emotions and it was easy to imagine him losing his temper. Plus he was desperate and I knew that could make people do crazy things.

Mark stood up. 'You know the police have seen this already,' he brandished the envelope containing the manuscript again, 'they know it exists, and I'll need to tell them everything.'

'No you don't, not yet. Can't you wait, give them more time to find the killer?'

'And give you the chance to do a runner? I don't think so.'

Douglas glared at Mark. 'I told you, I didn't do it.'

'We can't promise anything, Douglas, I'm sorry. But if there's nothing to tie you to the murder, you'll be fine.'

I'd tried to sound soothing, but I realised it just sounded hollow. Mark looked at me and nodded in the direction of the door. I followed his lead and we left a dejected-looking Douglas on his own.

'You're a feisty little ankle biter,' Mark said as we made our way down the stairs.

'I'm tired, plus I don't think he's the strongest of characters, so I figured if I pushed him, it would all come spilling out of him.'

'What next?' he asked.

'We find Harnby and tell her everything.'

We didn't get very far. A bloody-nosed Conrad came round the corner, trying to stem his nosebleed with a handkerchief. The knuckles of his hand looked red and sore.

'You've been in the wars,' Mark observed.

'It's nothing, I'm just going to clean up. Is the breakroom open again?'

'It is, but you should have someone take a look at that.' I moved towards him, but he backed off.

'It's fine, just leave it.'

'Did you walk into a wall?' Mark asked with exaggerated innocence.

'I walked into a Duke.'

'You did *what?*' I tried to imagine the Duke of Ravensbury taking a swing at a member of staff. Conrad spotted my confusion.

'No, Harvey Graves. He said it's my fault that Lycia has dumped him. Didn't give a damn that I'm her actual husband. I went for him. If he hadn't got involved, we'd still be working it out and our marriage might have had a chance.'

'Where's Harvey now?' I hoped he wasn't bleeding to death somewhere in a darkened corridor.

'Security had hold of him, told me to make a swift exit and they'd send him home. Said they wouldn't tell the police and would put it down to the stress of recent events. I just want to go and get cleaned up.'

He walked past us and up the stairs. Mark watched him intently.

'If he's anything to go by, Harvey has a mean right hook, and quite a temper. Do you think he...'

'Killed Thomas thinking it was Conrad? He's been on my list since we found the body, and I might have overheard him confessing to the killing.'

Mark raised his eyebrows at me. 'You *what?*'

'Oh yeah, I haven't told you that bit.' I went on to fill him in on the argument I'd overheard between Harvey and Lycia, this time including the fact I was disturbed by Seth before I'd had a chance to hear the crucial words from Harvey. Mark was so deep in thought, he didn't even give me a hard time about having been caught in a compromising position by the gamekeeper.

'Put him up at the top of that list, young lady. I know security said they wouldn't tell the police about the fight between Conrad and Harvey, but I reckon I should give that brother-in-law of mine a call.'

I didn't get much closer to my office before I heard my name being called. It was the Duke – the real one. Dressed in a dinner jacket, he looked like an aging James Bond. Suave and debonair were two words that came to mind.

'Sophie, I found something you might be interested in. I have an old *Year in the Life of Charleton House* book from decades ago. It doesn't mention the Hattersleys, but the gamekeeper is featured in it. There are some marvellous old photos. I've left it with Gloria so you can collect it anytime. I must dash – I'm a brand ambassador for a whisky and they're dragging me along to some dinner. I've told the Duchess not to wait up.'

He grinned like a cheeky schoolboy and set off at a quick pace that I couldn't have kept up with if I'd tried. I blame my short legs, not my lack of exercise over the years. It amused me to think of photographs from the nineties as old; it was a sure sign I was getting on myself.

I thought about what the Duke had just told me. Gloria, the Duke and Duchess's personal assistant, is a terrifying woman of mature years who could give Joyce a run for her money. I briefly thought about putting off seeing her until the morning, but common sense got the better of me and I decided to get it over with. If facing Gloria could throw some light on recent events, then it was worth a moment of feeling like a terrified schoolgirl in front of a formidable headmistress.

CHAPTER 21

Gloria Dewhurst's office is really an alcove in a corridor. Her desk is stationed outside the door to the office the Duke and Duchess share, and no one has access to them without first being vetted by Gloria. I presume that she takes coffee and lunchbreaks, holidays, leaves early for dentist appointments or to take her car to the garage, like most people, but I have never seen her away from her desk, nor has anyone else I have spoken to. I wouldn't have been surprised to discover that she sleeps there. No piece of mail reaches the Duke and Duchess without first being inspected by her. She receives every phone call and decides who gets to be put through. I have heard a rumour that the Duke tried to have a direct line put into his office, but Gloria objected and he was too afraid to argue. I doubt the Queen is quite so well guarded.

Gloria wears her glasses on a chain around her neck, slowly placing them on the bridge of her nose to scrutinise whoever is standing across from her. Her loosely curled grey hair remains exactly the same, day after day, as does the string of pearls she wears and the bottle-green polo-neck sweater, no matter what time of year it is. Having never seen her stand, I have no idea how tall she is, and the only way we would find out her age would be to cut off a limb and count the rings. The woman is a mystery.

I arrived to find her tapping away on her keyboard. Her fingers froze above the keys as I walked around the corner and she reached for her glasses.

'Sophie Lockwood, I believe this is for you.' One hand moved swiftly and reached for a brown envelope at her side. She remained in pause mode while I opened it. 'Do you have everything you need?'

'Yes, yes thank you, Gloria.' I was about to walk away when I thought she might be able to help. 'Actually, I was wondering, do you remember Bernie Stubbs? He used to be a gamekeeper here.'

'Of course I remember him.' It was clearly a very stupid question.

'I believe there was a bit of an incident with some poaching?' Silence. 'Do you remember anything about it?'

'I'm not one to dwell on the past, nor do I engage in tittle-tattle... However, there was a very difficult period for Bernie, which I'm sure is on record somewhere. The current Duke's father was well aware of my feelings at the time, and that it was not one of his most auspicious moments. But he did the best he could with the information he had. Bernie's reputation remained an extremely positive one.'

'But didn't he retire early?'

'He did.' For a moment, I thought I glimpsed a flash of sympathy. 'The poor man was exhausted and wanted to spend time with his family. Now, if there's anything else you wish to know about his departure, then I would imagine that Human Resources are the people to talk to. Although I doubt there's anything they can tell you. I'm sure anything else remains confidential.'

'Of course. Thank you, you've been very helpful.'

She waited until I was out of sight round the corner before I heard her start typing again. That had been a painless encounter, but then I hadn't been trying to get beyond her to the Duke or

Duchess without an appointment. I decided I'd send up some pastries for her in the morning. Keep your friends close and your enemies closer.

I'd planned on returning to my office, but before I turned in through the door to the café, loud, angry shouting led me down the dark stone corridor that staff could take as a shortcut into the back lane. Harvey was still trapped against the wall by Pat, who was continuing to try to calm him down.

'I'll let you go when I know you're not going to do anything stupid.'

Harvey wasn't trying too hard to escape, but then Pat presented quite a barrier. In fact, Harvey looked more frustrated than violent; I doubted he would have run if he'd been freed. Even from the other side of the lane, I could see a smear of blood below Harvey's nose and more on his white shirt.

Lycia was over by the security gate, talking to Roger before walking off in the direction of the car park. He didn't look any more cheerful than he had the last time I'd seen him, and it seemed that Lycia was done with men fighting over her. It was hard to feel sympathy for her. If she didn't want to continue trying to repair the relationship with Conrad, she should have told him. She should have also been more upfront with Harvey, not given him hope, making the whole situation even more murky in the process.

I looked intently at Harvey. Was he really capable of murder? I had no idea if the police viewed him as a possible suspect.

I watched as the security gates rose into the air and an unmarked police car was let through to park across from my office windows. DS Harnby got out of the car and spoke to Roger. She followed up with a quick word with the officer who had been driving the car, who then walked over to Harvey. Pat stepped away and ambled back into the office. Security's plan of keeping the fight from the police had just fallen through.

'I was on my way back to the station when I got a call to

return. They're like kids. Did you witness the fight?' Harnby was standing next to me.

'No. I ran into Conrad on his way to clean up; he was a bit of a mess.'

She nodded, but didn't look at me, her eyes still trained on her officer and Harvey.

'Does this push Harvey up the list of suspects?'

'You know I can't answer that, Sophie, but he's not doing himself any favours.' I wondered if Joe had updated her following my conversation with him. She appeared to take a moment to think before asking her next question. 'You found the body. Do you really think someone could have mistaken Thomas for Conrad, got close enough to kill him and still not realised?'

As much as I didn't want to, I ran back through the events of the morning when I had found Thomas. I had assumed it was Conrad, but then I hadn't got too close.

'Possibly. It would have been pretty dark. The only lamp was a small Anglepoise in the far corner. Everything about him screamed Charles Dickens. He was wearing the same kind of coat and shirt. From behind, you couldn't see that he had on a much plainer waistcoat. Their hair is similar, he was surrounded by Dickens's props. If you were in a rage, then I guess you might see what you wanted to see.'

I had seen the geranium on the floor, the book and the hat on the table, and that had been it. As far as I knew, I had been looking at a dead Charles Dickens. Once I'd reached that conclusion, I didn't hang around long enough to double-check.

'You have a reputation for being quite good at this sort of thing, Sophie, do you have any ideas?'

I looked up at DS Harnby; she looked tired. Since we had first been introduced, I'd done a good job of avoiding her, mainly because I knew she didn't approve of me sticking my nose in, and I didn't feel like getting a lecture that I would find harder to ignore than Joe's friendly warnings. But this time, something felt different. I saw a woman in a really tough job who was probably being watched closely by senior officers and could never relax, not for a moment.

'I have ideas, but I also have some information. Come on, I'll make you a drink.'

'Coffee, or is it too late in the day?'

'It's never too late in the day. Black, please. So what do you have to tell me?'

DS Harnby was standing by the counter as I made her coffee. The café was closed and the team had done a swift job of clearing up and heading home. I had flicked on a couple of lights as it was already dark outside and the café was gloomy and grey, but I couldn't be bothered taking any of the upturned chairs off the tables, so I grabbed some stools and we sat at the counter.

'Has Douglas Popplewell been on your radar?' I asked.

'He's appeared on it, but then so have you. You did find the body.' She smiled. I hadn't expected her to say that out loud, even though I knew it to be true. She was trying to keep me on my toes.

'Fair enough. It seems he had a lot of dealings with the deceased.'

I was telling her about Thomas and his link to Douglas, coming to the end as Mark walked in.

'Roger said he'd seen you both head this way. Detective Sergeant, hello.'

'Mark. Sophie's just been filling me in. Do you want to tell me about the manuscript?'

Mark's eyes lit up. He loved talking about research, books, the house – you name it. If DS Harnby wanted a brief summation, she was about to be disappointed.

I left them to it.

CHAPTER 22

I wanted to try to get my thoughts together, but the café was starting to feel too closed in. I felt like I'd spent far too much time in there over the last couple of days; I was used to being out and about, attending meetings, visiting the other cafés. It was still less than forty-eight hours since the sleepover began, but it seemed like an eternity, and as though I hadn't left the place in a week.

There was no point going home before Mark's birthday dinner at the pub. I could fill my time with paperwork, but first I wanted some fresh air. It was dark, but there was enough light coming from the house to allow me to take one of the short walking routes that had become a favourite when I needed thirty minutes away from either my team or a tray of burnt cookies.

Pat was standing at the security gate, a bouquet of autumnal flowers in his hands, the oranges, greens and reds a burst of colour in the diminishing light.

'Very pretty, Pat. You got a secret admirer?'

'They're for the Duchess, she gets 'em all the time. They're probably for opening a supermarket or somethin'.'

'What are we meant to do with those?' Roger had appeared by

Pat's side. "Spose it's our job to get them delivered, like we've not got enough to do. Give me that.' Roger roughly took the flowers from Pat and marched back into the office. Pat watched him leave, and then turned to me.

'Rog has a lot on his mind. He's a bit... distracted.'

'Is he okay? Has something happened?'

'It's not my place to say. It's his business, but I didn't want you to think his mood was aimed at anyone in particular.'

'Okay, thanks, Pat.'

'I'll keep an eye on him, don't you worry.'

I turned to set off on my walk. Maybe Pat did have a heart after all.

My route took me through the walled garden I had seen Lycia and Harvey in, across the top of the car park and round the back of the stable block. From there, it was a quick ten-minute pull up a steep, wide path to a folly that overlooked the house. Follies were never built to serve a purpose, extravagant garden ornaments that were just fun to look at and demonstrated the owners wealth; this one was a twenty-foot tower that afforded wonderful views over the estate, it was decorated with finials in the shape of pineapples along the edge of the roof. Pineapples had been a rare delicacy in the 18th century and a symbol of power and wealth, perfect for the Fitzwilliam-Scotts.

A weather vane, also in the shape of a pineapple, sat on the roof. The spiral staircase that took visitors to the top was closed to the public, but in warmer weather, Mark and I had come here with a bottle of champagne and a promise to Roger that I'd bake him a cake if he would slip us the key to the gate at the bottom of the stairs and keep our little adventure to himself. It was hard to imagine him doing us that kind of favour today.

I dragged my tired legs up the hill, panting and telling myself to do this more often, then my thoughts drifted back to Roger. His sullen mood was so out of character. We'd had a spate of dead bodies onsite over the last year, so it couldn't be the shock, unless it was all getting a bit much for him. He was such a good-hearted man, it was easy to imagine him finding evil acts difficult to stomach. Perhaps this recent case had upset him in particular.

Roger hadn't known the victim, as far as I was aware. His current state of mind meant that I didn't feel able to have a heart-to-heart with him – I instinctively felt it was best to leave him in peace. It had been good of Pat to tell me that I wasn't the cause of his bad mood, but still, it worried me.

I touched my hand to the cold stone, paused briefly to take in what little I could see of the view now the sun had gone down, shivered and immediately headed back down. The path was slippery and damp, so I stuck to the side and the longer grass as I half ran, half walked, not quite in control of my speed.

It felt wonderful to be out in the fresh air, to focus on something physical, instead of endlessly trying to solve the puzzle that surrounded Thomas. This was exactly what I needed. I ran the last few yards and tumbled into the rear wall of the stables, laughing to myself at the childish simplicity of it all. Now I just had to work my way through a couple of hours of rotas, holiday requests and emails, and then I would have nothing more challenging to face than which gin to choose off the menu at the Black Swan.

The car park was quiet; only a few staff cars remained. As I walked past one, I noticed that someone was sitting in the driver's seat; it was Lycia. She must have been there a little while. I knocked on the window.

'Are you okay?' She jumped, then wound her window down. 'Sorry, I didn't mean to startle you. Are you alright?'

She nodded. 'Yes, thanks, I'm just leaving.'

'Are you sure you're alright? You've been sat here a while, don't you want to go home?'

'No, I just needed time to think.'

'I couldn't help but overhear your conversation with Harvey earlier, in the garden.'

'How? I didn't see you.'

I remembered Seth finding me on the golf cart and decided not to answer that.

'Can we talk, just for a couple of minutes?' I was getting cold; the sweat I'd built up running down the hill was now making me shiver. Lycia nodded and I heard the click of the door lock. I walked round and got in the passenger seat. 'Thanks. This must have been a tough couple of days for you. Harvey can't be making it any easier.'

'No, but it's not his fault.'

'He really seems to like you. I guess he'd do anything for you.'

She looked at me intently. 'I think he probably would. He's a romantic and a gentleman, in the old-fashioned sense.'

'Do you think he'd kill for you?'

She laughed, and then quickly quietened down. 'You're serious?' She thought for a moment. 'You know, it crossed my mind – for a second, that's all. But Harvey could never do that. He's prone to grand displays of emotion, but he doesn't have what it takes to kill someone. I can't imagine him getting the two men mixed up, either. He knows Conrad too well, and as far as I know, he has no history with Thomas.' Warming to the subject now, she had turned to face me and stopped playing with her car keys.

'Did you know Thomas?' I asked.

'Only from the occasional event. He didn't go to many; I think he looked down on what we do, never really understood all the hard work and research that goes into it. I tended to avoid him, he just wasn't very pleasant. His wife Annie is lovely, though I have no idea what she saw in him. It was always a little more stressful when Thomas was around, and it was already bad enough when Philippa was there. Conrad had words with him a couple of times.'

She paused and looked out of the window before continuing.

'Conrad and I talked about moving when we decided to stay together. We could both find work elsewhere, especially in London, but we love it here. Derbyshire is our home.'

I could understand that. After all, I'd moved back here after ten years in London. It was my home, too.

Something she'd said reminded me of my conversation with Conrad.

'Conrad said he and Thomas had words on a few occasions, do you know why?'

'Thomas could be sarcastic. He'd try and test your knowledge, trip you up if he could, but he did it in a mean-spirited way, not like the visitors who do it in order to have some fun and maybe learn something at the same time. I think he just pushed Conrad too far on a couple of occasions.'

'This is rather a personal question, but I believe someone told you about Conrad and Philippa. Who was it?'

She nodded. 'I've always assumed someone wanted to make sure I knew, yes. A note had been dropped in the pocket of my costume. I found it later when I was getting changed. We were at a big event over at Berwick Hall. There was dancing and I spent a lot of time talking to the public. Thomas was definitely there, and at the next couple of events he seemed particularly smug, making comments about illicit liaisons and secrets. I wouldn't have been able to prove it, and anyway, it didn't seem important. Conrad and I just needed to try and work at fixing things.'

'Did you see Conrad after the gathering you all had on Saturday night? Do you know what time he left?'

'After he refused to come home with me, I left him in the security office with Roger, waiting for a taxi. I don't know what time the taxi picked him up, though.'

'And you just went home? How come the police were struggling to get hold of you the next day?'

'I was annoyed at Conrad for refusing to come home, so I

turned my phone off. I wanted some peace and quiet, time to think, and I guessed Harvey would start texting me.'

'What are you going to do now?'

'I don't know. I still love Conrad. Maybe we need to get away from here; maybe staying in Derbyshire wasn't the right thing. None of this is his fault, not this weekend. I've been stupid; I was leading Harvey on. He's uncomplicated. Conrad had been working so hard at being the perfect husband, but it just didn't feel relaxed, normal. I don't want us to give up, not yet.'

To me, it all sounded exhausting, and I briefly thanked my lucky stars that I was single. The most complicated relationship issue in my life was judging Pumpkin's mood swings; no wonder I was in no rush to get a boyfriend.

'I hope you figure it out. You should get home.'

Lycia nodded and started the engine. I got out of the car, resisting the urge to run back to the office. With any luck, Harnby would still be in the café. It was time to catch up with her.

CHAPTER 23

Harnby had gone, so had Mark. I called Joe, but there was no answer so I left him a message. I doubted Roger's ability to register Conrad's whereabouts if he'd sat on his lap, but I wanted to be sure, and Joe would have seen Roger's statement. There was nothing I could do but wait.

I lifted the box that was covering Mark's cake and gave it a once-over. Dammit. I'd put a layer of fondant over the books and they now looked like worn leather, but that was as far as I'd got. While I prepared the icing so I could add titles, I started to run through everything in my head. I knew I wasn't thinking clearly; I hadn't had enough sleep, was still largely running on caffeine and had far too much information buzzing around my head, so I needed to try to make sense of it all.

Despite there only being one body, there were two potential victims. Conrad – I wasn't convinced that Philippa was involved. She was a spurned lover, but the more I thought about her pictures of Conrad, the more it seemed like a shrine to Charles Dickens. Maybe her interest wasn't really in Conrad, but the idea of him as someone else. Conrad didn't seem threatened by her and had said it could be nice to have her around: a fellow Dickens aficionado. Maybe it was Lycia's response that had turned all that into such a drama, rather than Philippa, who had simply continued attending events as normal.

Harvey was frustrated and passionate, his emotions running high, but if he had killed Thomas thinking he was Conrad, then I found it hard to imagine him starting a fight with Conrad in full view of anyone who wandered down the back lane. It was too risky. No, that was the overemotional response of someone who was running out of hope. I was doubting Douglas's involvement, too; he was naïve, but that wasn't a crime, and his attempt at plagiarism hadn't actually seen the light of day. He'd also been genuine when he'd pleaded with me to help him.

I tried to focus on the cakes in front of me; I couldn't get the decorative swirls consistent, and one was slipping off the book entirely. The gold letters in one title were getting smaller and smaller; I should have put a guide in place, but it was too late now.

Checking my phone, making sure the ringer was on full volume – I didn't want to miss Joe calling – I watched out of the window as Roger walked back to his office. He must have delivered the flowers to the Duchess; they'd been as beautiful as the ones Bill had bought for Mark. I couldn't remember the last time I'd been sent flowers.

I remembered the poor, lonely geranium I'd stood on in the breakroom and thought about Charles Dickens. Something was niggling at me. Thomas wasn't a popular man, but other than Douglas, I wasn't sure anyone hated him enough to kill him. And Douglas couldn't even find the strength to hit him. Someone had, though; someone had not only hit him, but stabbed him too. But Conrad had gone straight to the Black Swan, and everyone else had been caught up in their own dramas.

My wrist was aching and my hand was starting to shake; the writing was getting worse, but it was still legible – just. I was done, and anyway, it wouldn't take long for it to be devoured and all evidence of my artistic failings to vanish.

I threw everything in the sink and covered the cake; I'd tidy up tomorrow. Picking up my phone, I went to sit at my desk. It was covered in notes that my staff had left me: scraps of paper with requests for holiday, or shift swaps, or items of uniform that needed replacing. We had forms for all that and they knew it, but I was too tired to be cross.

I picked up one of the notes and folded it into tiny squares. Lycia had been given a note, and the one person who had been described as unpleasant was Thomas. If Thomas had given Lycia the note and Conrad had found out, then he had a reason to want him dead, but Conrad had gone to the Black Swan. He'd had drinks with his colleagues in his costume, so presumably he hadn't returned to the breakroom straight after the event to get changed, but he would have needed to return to get his wallet later. Conrad had told me he'd gone to the pub to spend the night, but he couldn't do that without his wallet – a wallet he wouldn't be allowed to have on him when he was performing and which he would have left in a locker, in the breakroom. He must have gone back and found Thomas where Douglas had left him, the geranium falling out of his buttonhole while he was up there.

My phone beeped. I grabbed it and read the message.

'On my way, stay put. X'. It was Joe. Okay, there was no need to rush.

My eye was caught by the envelope Gloria had given me that I'd tossed on the desk when I'd returned with DS Harnby. What did Bernie Stubbs have to do with all this, if anything?

I dialled Joyce's mobile; she picked up after two rings.

'This had better be good. No one disturbs my bubble baths, but I'll make an exception for you.'

I squeezed my eyes tight shut, trying to keep that image out of my head.

'You've worked here a while, Joyce.'

'That's putting it mildly. Some would say I was present when the foundations went down, but that's pushing it. Why?'

'Did you know Bernie Stubbs, the gamekeeper?'

'No, he was before my time – just. I remember it was my first week of work and I got left in the shop on my own as most people went to his funeral. You should ask Roger, he was here then. Been in his job a couple of years when I arrived.'

As she talked, I pulled the book out of the envelope. It was a large, slim hardback, more like a photo album.

'Okay, I will, thanks. See you later.'

She hung up. I flicked through the pages that captured food festivals, weddings, building renovations, lambing seasons, car shows and a visit by the Queen, turning to a page that had been marked for me by the Duke. There were photos of Bernie Stubbs. In one, he was feeding the deer; in another he appeared in a group shot with a couple of park rangers. They were lined up in front of their Land Rovers and pickup trucks, a very sweet-looking brown-and-white spaniel sitting at their feet, staring into the camera lens, its tongue hanging out.

I felt a stab of sympathy for Bernie. To have worked for thirty years in a job he loved, and then been falsely accused of an act so serious, he could have lost that job. He was a big, hearty chap, his ruddy cheeks and tough-looking skin a sign of the life he spent outdoors. His enormous hands were on his hips and he stood looking proudly into the camera, appearing approachable and friendly. I would have loved to have met him.

He also looked very familiar. I felt like I *had* met him, but I knew that was impossible. There was just so much about him that was recognisable, I expected to be able to look out of the window and watch him walk down the lane.

Then I realised I had, sort of.

I called the security office.

'Yes?' It was Roger. I paused, wondering if I should try to talk to him, but I'd seen something in the photos that was more pressing.

'Is Pat there?'

'No.'

'I just wanted a word with him, any idea where he might be?'

'He went to lock up the shop.'

'I'll track him down.'

He hung up.

The gift shop was deserted. All the lights were off, but an orange glow filtered in from the courtyard outside, the shelves and display cases taking on a ghostly quality. The outlines of the gifts and toys were unnerving, especially the dolls, or if faces from the front of books suddenly peered out of the gloom. I couldn't be sure I wouldn't walk into something at every turn.

Once the shop staff had left for the day, security would come and do another check. They'd also do patrols around the building throughout the night. Pat would be making the first patrol of the evening, ensuring none of the day staff had missed anything. There was no need for him to put the lights on; he would know the place like the back of his hand.

The steps into the shop are made of worn stone; hundreds of years of footsteps have left a big dip in the middle of every one. Barely a week goes by that someone doesn't trip over the 'mind your step' sign. The old door at the bottom looks like something left over from the Tudor period: dark wood with enormous metal hinges that takes two hands to push open. Fortunately it had already been open enough for me to slip through, so I didn't have to exert myself this late in the day.

'Pat? Pat, it's Sophie. Are you in here?'

There was a rustle in a far corner.

'Pat, is that you?'

The sound of a fire exit being tested was followed by a jangle of keys.

'Who's there?' Torchlight shone across the room and I squinted as it hit my eyes. 'Sophie, what are you doing here?'

'Looking for you, do you have a minute?'

'Not really, but you ask your questions while I finish up in here.'

I saw the outline of his bulky figure head towards Joyce's office.

'You've worked here a long time.'

'Twenty-five years give or take, one of the longest serving. Not like those just chasing their careers these days, here one minute, gone the next.' He gave the handle on Joyce's office door a turn. It was locked. He moved on. 'Why?'

'You said you knew of Arnold Hattersley, Thomas's dad. Did you ever meet him, or Thomas?'

I could trace Pat's movements by the noise of his footsteps as he walked the length of the shop. They came to a halt.

'Why would I have done? Like I said, it was before my time.'

'Yes, but you knew all about them, you saw them around. I just thought you might have come and visited Charleton House, especially when you had a family member working here. Didn't you come and see him? Join him on the job?'

He still didn't move. 'Whatcha talking about?'

'Bernie Stubbs. He's family, right?'

When I had looked at the book the Duke had left for me, there was no mistaking the similarity. The photo of Bernie would have been a spitting image of Pat, if Pat had bothered to get some fresh air and exercise. Pat's face had stared out at me from the ruddy cheeks and sun-worn skin. But it had been taken a very long time ago, and as Pat had said, a lot of staff had left since then.

'I know Thomas didn't work here, but did you come across him? He must have spent time with his dad.'

I heard Pat move and listened as his footsteps got closer. He was one of the few people who might have personal knowledge of what had happened all those years ago, and if it had any bearing on Thomas's death.

'Arnold was a waste of space. Did as little as he could, and then spent every penny he earnt down the pub. Bernie only used him when he had no choice, and anyway, it was a small community. You were meant to help each other out. Bernie was a good man, loyal. I wouldn't have bothered. I'd have got rid of Arnold. Better in the long run.'

I still couldn't make Pat out clearly. There was a fuzzy dark mass not far from me, but it was impossible to judge its distance. I moved away from the bottom of the stairs, trying to get a better view.

'Was Thomas involved in the poaching? He must have been eighteen at the time, old enough to get mixed up in it all.'

'Nah, he wasn't made of the right stuff. Always had his head in books. He'd even have one with him when he came down the pub. Thought he was better than the rest of us.'

'So you did meet him, then?' I listened intently as his story shifted, as the truth slowly came out.

The dark shape moved towards some windows to check they were locked. Then I lost sight of him behind the shelves.

'He could be a vindictive little sod, though.' There was a change in Pat's tone. He really didn't like Thomas. 'Once Uncle Bernie was suspended, I saw Thomas in the pub a couple of times. He always looked like he had a joke running through his head. A smirk on his face. Of course, now we know it's cos his dad was getting away with poaching, right under our noses. Arnold would be down the pub too, playing it all concerned, saying what a good man Bernie was, 'ow he loved workin' with him. Rubbish, all of it; he was gloating.'

Pat's voice had become harsher, the words spilling out of him, and I realised what an idiot I'd been. Pat, more than anyone, had reason to hold a grudge against Arnold, and by association, Thomas.

'Bernie was suspended from his duties for a whole year. Have you any idea how hard that was for him? He became a hermit. He was heartbroken.' Pat's voice was closer now, but I couldn't be sure which direction it was coming from. 'He loved this place, worked every hour God sent. He wanted to die on the job. Then it would have come to me.'

'What do you mean, come to you?'

'Bernie didn't have kids. In those days, family mattered, and without him having a son to take over the job of gamekeeper, I should have been next in line.' He was starting to raise his voice and I could tell that he was getting closer. I stepped backwards and hit the wall just to the side of the door, close enough to make a run for it.

'Why didn't you get the job?'

'After all that? Don't be stupid. There was still a cloud over our family name, they didn't want to touch us with a barge pole. The powers that be had been sniffing out candidates while Bernie was suspended. He hadn't even been found guilty and they were already thinking about who to replace him with. I reckon they were embarrassed, didn't want one of Bernie's relatives reminding them of how wrong they'd been. But it was mine by rights.'

I could feel the cold stone wall behind me. I knew Pat was close.

'But you are here, you still got a job.'

'As a bloody security officer, sure. I had to apply three times. Third time they had no excuse. I reckon they hoped I'd screw up, give them a reason to get rid of me. But I kept my nose clean, did a good job. I thought that once I was in, I could apply to be the gamekeeper when the new one left. I wanted to do it for Bernie, to get it back in the family. But no, they only went and gave the job to the new bloke's son. I didn't have a chance.

'To make things worse, he was a mate of Thomas's. My God, did Thomas gloat. Every time I went in the pub, he'd ask his mate how the job was going, full volume like. Make sure I heard. I stopped going in the end. They did the pub up, hold quizzes and all sorts now. Lost its spirit, not the place Bernie would have remembered.'

There was a very slight edge of sadness in his voice, but I didn't feel sorry for him. The more he said, the more I was certain that I was on my own in a darkened room with Thomas's killer.

'What happened at the weekend, Pat? Did Thomas say something to you?'

'He didn't have to. It took me a while to recognise him in that stupid get-up. Once he clocked me, that was it. Arrogant sod even raised his glass to me when I stuck my head in the door during dinner.

'I came across him when I was doing my rounds. He should have been sleeping, but he was in the breakroom at the desk. I don't know why he was there, but he was in a foul mood. Started winding me up about how I carried a torch instead of a gun, and no one would trust me with anything more lethal. I was on my way out, he didn't deserve my time, but he just couldn't keep his mouth shut.

'"Bernie would be *so* proud," he said. He was so smug. I grabbed the knife, and before he knew what was going on... He didn't have a chance to fight. I'm not sorry.'

I glanced over at the door, turning slowly, hoping he wouldn't realise what I was planning. But as I was about to move, he appeared from the shadows and I was within inches of his bloated body.

'Don't think you're going anywhere. I've got this far, I'll be here till the day I drop, just like Bernie wanted to.'

I ducked and made for the gap between Pat and the wall, but I wasn't quick enough and he moved. I slammed into his thigh. He shoved me back against the wall.

'I told you, you're going nowhere.'

'Roger knows I was looking for you.'

'Roger's an idiot, too bloody soft. Anyway, I finished checking the shop long before you arrived, didn't I. I never saw you.'

His hand was pressing my shoulder hard against the wall and it hurt like hell. I didn't see any alternative, so I shouted out, but the sound was cut off as his other hand, cold in its leather glove, folded itself round my neck. I started to choke.

'Don't be stupid. You might think you're something special round here, but not this time.' He added pressure. I wasn't sure if I was blacking out or staring into the gloom of the shop.

Before I could work out what was happening, the lights were thrown on and I was blinded by one of the ceiling spotlights pointing right over Pat's shoulder.

'What the hell?' Pat shouted, turning towards the door. As he turned, I made out the figure of Joyce, standing on the bottom step. She spun towards Pat, and in a sudden blur of movement I saw her leg fly up. Pat screamed. He let go of my neck and both his hands grabbed for his crotch, where Joyce's foot had landed with force.

'You bitch…' he cried out, his voice suddenly high pitched.

Joyce looked at me. 'See, I told you I could high kick with the best of them.'

CHAPTER 24

'I'm so sorry, I'm so, so sorry.' Roger looked distraught. 'I couldn't forgive myself if something had happened to you.'

'It's okay.' I leant across Joe and took Roger's hand, giving it a squeeze. 'It's not your fault. Can you get me some water? I really need a drink.'

'I'll be right back.'

Roger hurried away. I looked at Joe.

'He's a sweet man, but I needed a break. It'll make him feel useful.'

'Something more serious could have happened, you know. If Joyce hadn't returned, you could be dead.'

Joe looked annoyed, but there was a softness in his voice. I rubbed my neck; it was still sore. We were sitting in the security office. Flashing blue lights cast a strange glow around the room, like an eerie disco. After Joyce had delivered a physical and emotional blow to Pat's manhood, we'd raised the alarm.

'What were you thinking?'

'I guess I wasn't. I just thought he might know something useful.'

Roger returned and handed me a glass. In his garbled apologies after the police had been called, he had admitted to being distracted the last couple of days, not picking up on signs that Pat might have been involved or realising that he didn't know where his colleague had been at key times on the night of the murder, missing discrepancies in Pat's statement. During the sleepover events, Roger had received a phone call telling him that his heavily pregnant daughter had been taken into hospital. I remembered him getting a phone call after he and Pat had been poking fun at the dancing.

'I wanted to go in and be with her, but my wife told me to stay here, that it would all be fine. The doctors just wanted to check and be sure that everything was okay. I knew I had a job to do here, I didn't want to let anyone down, but I couldn't think of anything else.'

That explained his bad mood over the last couple of days. I couldn't blame him; he doted on his daughter and was overjoyed at the thought of becoming a grandad.

'We got there in the end, Roger, that's all that matters.' I gave him the warmest smile I could manage.

'I'll give you some space, shout if you need anything, anything at all.'

If anyone needed anything, it was Roger. It was going to take a lot of cake and reassurance to help him lose the feeling of guilt he was carrying.

Another police car pulled up outside and the beam of the lights swung across the office walls. Joe looked out of the window.

'DI Flynn is here. Just in time to break the good news to the Duke, explain why you beat us to it, *again*.' The slight smile told me I wasn't in too much trouble. 'You better stay out of sight. I think Harnby is warming to you, but Flynn definitely isn't a fan.'

'Not a problem, I'll stay in here out of harm's way.'

'Great, now you decide to play it safe. Why didn't you do that with Pat?'

'Because I'd come to the conclusion it was Conrad who'd killed Thomas, so I didn't think Pat was a risk. Conrad said he'd gone directly to the Black Swan, that he'd decided to spend the night there. But he needed his wallet for that. He'd gone to the party straight from the reading, in costume. They're not allowed to have anything modern on them that's visible to the public and his wallet is a huge, bulky thing. That's why they have those little lockers in the breakroom, to keep their valuables safe. When Betsy arrived at the start of the evening to play the Duchess, she still had a watch on and I had to look after it for her.

'Conrad must have gone back to the breakroom after the party to get his wallet. I assumed that gave him the opportunity to run into Thomas after Douglas had left and kill him. He had motive enough. Conrad was hardly likely to tell us he'd been up there once he realised who the victim was, it would make him a suspect straight away. Add to that the punch that you said Thomas had received before he was killed. We know Douglas had been with Thomas, but when Mark and I confronted him, he said he'd been unable to hit him, so it wasn't him. I figured it was Conrad, mad at Thomas for vindictively letting Lycia know about his affair. He'd taken any control of the situation out of Conrad's hands.'

'But what about Philippa? It was thanks to your – well, Joyce's – concerns that we found her Conrad shrine.'

'Philippa was no longer a suspect in my mind when I realised that she was actually obsessed with Charles Dickens. Her interest in Conrad was secondary. She wasn't so fired up by passion that she was capable of killing him; the man she's crazy about is already dead. Apart from anything, if she had thought it was Conrad, killing him would deprive her of one of her favourite portrayers of Dickens. You haven't charged her with anything, have you?'

'No, unless a dubious taste in literature is a crime.'

I slapped his knee. 'Dickens was a genius. He wasn't such a great husband, I'll admit, but he had a rather natty taste in waistcoats, and he was a fan of gin.'

'That's all that matters, then. A gin drinker, he must be a good bloke. So let me get this straight. First Thomas has a barney with Douglas, who leaves him up in the breakroom. Next Conrad pitches up and smacks him because he made sure Lycia knew her husband had gone to a hotel with Philippa, and then Pat turns up and stabs him.'

'With his gloves still on,' I interjected, remembering the feel of the cold leather against my neck. Joe nodded.

'Thomas practically had a queue outside the door with a bone to pick – he wasn't a popular man.' He gave a wry smile. 'Come on, I'll ask someone to take you home so you can get changed and go to the pub. You can have your precious gin then.'

'I'm fine, I can drive. Are you coming?'

'Later, I have actually got a job to do.'

'I doubt Mark would consider tying up a murder case more important than his birthday, I'm just warning you.'

He laughed. 'I can't argue with that. Go on, drive safe.'

He kissed me on the cheek and was about to walk up the lane when I stopped him.

'Joe.' I took hold of his arm. 'You know they say police officers are getting younger every day?'

'Yes?'

'Well, it turns out they're getting hairier too.'

I pointed towards the open door of the nearest police car. Sitting in the driver's seat was a very confident-looking Romeo.

CHAPTER 25

The Black Swan pub wasn't all that busy on the face of it, which wasn't surprising for a Monday. The noise emanating from a large table in front of the open fireplace, however, would have competed with any Saturday night. Bill and Father Craig Mortimer, the Charleton House chaplain, were debating the merits of two locally brewed stouts. Joyce was refilling her glass from a bottle of champagne and howling with laughter at something Bill had said. Mark, looking happy and relaxed, was chatting to Steve the landlord and ordering another bottle of wine. A number of birthday cards were standing in the middle of the table, their torn envelopes scattered around. A bottle of whisky in a gift box stood next to some books and a mug that declared 'I'm a tour guide. To save time, let's just assume I'm always right'. Wrapping paper had been screwed up into balls that were now strewn around like table decorations.

It was chaos. Wonderful, warm, loving chaos.

'SOPHIE! She's here, everyone.'

Bill jumped out of his chair and gave me a hug. 'Are you okay?' he whispered into my ear.

'I'm fine.' My hand instinctively went up to my neck. I had no idea if I'd bruise, but I'd worn a loose silk scarf just in case. 'A little sore, but nothing a gin and tonic won't solve.'

'Consider it done.' Bill went to the bar as Mark scraped his chair back and came over to give me an equally bone-crushing hug.

'You're a bloody idiot, Sophie Lockwood. What were you thinking?'

'I was just after more information.'

'Well next time, remain in blissful ignorance until someone is free to go exploring darkened rooms with you.' He stared into my eyes, waiting for a response. 'Promise?'

'I promise.' I hid my crossed fingers behind my back.

'Good. Now then, where's my cake?'

'I lit all the candles to make sure they worked and burnt down the kitchen.' He frowned. 'Joe's bringing it when he drops by later.'

His smile returned. 'That's more like it. I wasn't expecting to see Joe. I thought he'd be spending the evening turning the thumbscrews on Pat.'

'It'll be brief, but he reckons he can make it.'

'Well he better bloody had if he has my cake.'

'What are you moaning about now, old man?' Bill pushed his way between us and handed me a glass. 'Let the poor girl sit down.'

'So she's poor and I'm old. Exactly whose day is this?'

Mark went back to his seat and sat down, Bill giving him a playful push on the way. I lowered myself into the seat next to Craig. He offered me his glass for a toast.

'Here's to catching the bad guys.'

I took a long, cool mouthful. It was bliss.

'I said a prayer for you.'

'Thank you,' I replied. Craig knew the only times he'd catch me at a church service were Christmas, weddings and funerals, but still it was a nice thought.

'God and I both wish you'd be a bit more careful, but we also both reckon you're badass.'

I loved the idea of God sitting up on high, declaring me badass. If Craig was anything to go by, He'd also have a pint of craft beer in one hand and, after a few too many, a cigar in the other.

A ball of screwed-up wrapping paper landed in front of me. I looked up to see the culprit staring at me across the table. Joyce, wearing earrings that would have easily doubled as chandeliers and matching jewels glued on each fingernail, was eyeing me over half-moon spectacles. She discreetly gave me a little thumbs up with a questioning look.

'I'm fine,' I mouthed. She nodded, winked, and then went back to perusing the menu.

A couple of hours later, Steve and one of his team were clearing the empty plates from our table. I had devoured a large portion of fish and chips, my favourite thing on the menu. Steve's chef always manages to get the batter to a perfect level of crispiness, and the chips are chunky without doubling up as doorstops.

'Here he is, and I reckon he has dessert,' called out Mark. Joe had arrived, carrying the box that held Mark's birthday cake. He placed it carefully on the table.

'I've not got long. Catching a murderer is great, but the paperwork is a killer.' There was a collective groan around the table. 'Alright, I'm a copper, not a comedian.'

'Too right,' confirmed Bill, giving his brother a firm handshake. 'What are you drinking?'

'Coffee, please, I still have work to do.'

Bill got Steve's attention as he walked by and ordered Joe's drink.

'Come on, my sweet tooth is feeling deprived. Let's see it.' Mark reached over the table and lifted the lid. I squirmed slightly, only able to see the defects – the wobbly writing, the squished corner on one of the books, the uneven colour – but if the look on everyone else's faces was anything to go by, I was the only one who could see the mistakes.

'I love it, Sophie, it's fantastic.' Mark beamed at me.

'Well done.' Craig gave a little clap and licked his lips.

'Let's get those candles lit.' Steve, who had hovered waiting to see the cake, leant across with a cigarette lighter. I'd limited myself to ten candles – any more and I might have damaged Mark's already fragile ego. We all sang a rather painful rendition of 'Happy Birthday' that left other customers in the pub in shocked silence and, I imagine, local dogs howling.

With the cake being cut into enormous hunks by Bill, the conversation quickly turned to earlier events.

'It's a small world,' Craig commented. 'I had no idea Pat was related to Bernie.'

'None of us did,' replied Mark. 'Different surname and Pat kept very quiet about it. A few staff have been here long enough to remember Bernie, but I guess he dropped out of general consciousness. Plus the current Duke hadn't taken over running the house then; his father was still alive, so he probably didn't know much about Bernie.'

'If the Duke hadn't given me that book, we'd still have no idea of the connection and we'd all be scratching our heads and following dead ends.'

Joe sat up straight. 'No, *we* – the police – would be scratching our heads and... hang on a minute...' There was laughter as Joe realised what he had been about to say. 'We would be working hard and would have caught Pat before the week was out.'

'Of course you would.' I grinned and patted his shoulder as patronisingly as I could. Joe laughed and swatted my hand away.

'How's Douglas doing?' I was asking Mark, but Joe hadn't realised this and answered.

'He's a bit of a mess, to be honest, fell apart when we were questioning him. From what I've heard, he's been banging on about his publishing deal for so long now, he's worried about the damage to his reputation if he doesn't get a book out there soon.'

Mark snorted. 'Reputation? That was mainly in his head. Anyone who thought he was a great tour guide just didn't know any better, and he was never going to become a curator, not if he was doing it for the celebrity alone. People would have seen straight through him. But, if he's prepared to get stuck in and take feedback, I'll work with him and get him up to a decent standard of guiding.'

Bill put his arm around his husband's shoulders and kissed him on the cheek.

'You're a good man, Mark Boxer.'

'Hmm, you've caught me in a moment of weakness.'

Joe coughed and raised his glass.

'Anyway, this time the credit does not all belong to Ms "Sherlock" Lockwood here.' Everyone looked at Joe, wondering where he was going with this. 'The star of the show is our marvellous, glamorous, flexible Joyce Brocklehurst.'

The table erupted into roars of agreement, applause and calls for her to give a demonstration of the high kick that had saved my life. She looked momentarily bashful – not a look I ever expected to see on Joyce's face – then she quickly composed herself and told us all to:

'Keep the bloody noise down. There will be no demonstrations. To be honest, I rather surprised myself, but it turns out I haven't lost the knack. Speaking of which.'

Joyce reached into her bag, pulled out a beautifully wrapped gift with an enormous gold bow and handed it to Mark. We all watched silently as he unwrapped it.

It was a photo frame. Although none of the rest of us could see the image it contained, Mark's smile reached from ear to ear.

'But I thought you said you never joined the Tiller Girls,' he said, a little confused.

'I didn't. That was for a charity reunion about twenty years ago. Mum had already died so I dug out her old costume and went in her place.'

Mark handed the frame across to me. A slightly younger Joyce was dressed in all the finery of a Tiller Girl: a fuchsia-pink sequin-covered leotard clung to her still incredible figure. She wore fishnet stockings, a feather headdress that added over a foot to her height and matching tail feathers, and she looked magnificent.

Joyce had signed the photo to Mark and written, 'Now you can tell everyone you're friends with a Tiller Girl'. It was perfect, and a wonderful irony that on Mark's birthday, it was a woman who had made his day.

READ THE FIRST CHARLETON HOUSE MYSTERY

Building a relationship with my readers is one of the best things about writing. I occasionally send newsletters with details on new releases, special offers, interviews and articles relating to The Charleton House Mysteries.

Sign up to my mailing list and you'll also receive the very first Charleton House Mystery, *A Stately Murder*.

Head to my website for your free copy and find out what happens when Sophie stumbles across the victim of the first murder Charleton House has ever known.

www.katepadams.com

ABOUT THE AUTHOR

After 25 years working in some of England's finest buildings, Kate P. Adams has turned to murder.

Kate grew up in Derbyshire, the setting for the Charleton House Mysteries, and went on to work in theatres around the country, the Natural History Museum - London, the University of Oxford and Hampton Court Palace. Every day she explored darkened corridors and rooms full of history behind doors the public never get to enter. Kate spent years in these beautiful buildings listening to fantastic tales, wondering where the bodies were hidden, and hoping that she'd run into a ghost or two.

Kate has an unhealthy obsession with finding the perfect cup of coffee, enjoys a gin and tonic, and is managed by Pumpkin, a domineering tabby cat who is a little on the large side. Now that she lives in the USA, writing the Charleton House Mysteries allows Kate to go home to be her beloved Derbyshire everyday, in her head at least.

ACKNOWLEDGEMENTS

DEATH BY DARK ROAST

Just as it takes a dedicated team to run a historic house, it takes a team to bring a book out into the world. I am lucky enough to have a fabulous, generous and extremely knowledgeable team of my own.

Thank you to my wonderful beta readers Chris Bailey-Jones, Elin Begley, Joanna Hancox, Lynne McCormack, Eileen Minchin, Rosanna Summers. Your honesty and insightful comments keep me on the straight and narrow.

I have always wanted to ensure that life in a historic house that is open to the public is portrayed as accurately as possible. I can bring my own twenty-year career in visitor experience to bear on this. However I have needed the expertise of those who work in specialist fields. My thanks to Kerren Harris - conservation, Rosanna Summers– live interpretation, Aileen Peirce - access to historical information, Mark Wallis – live interpretation and historical costume, Liz Young – event management. It was great working with you all again. Any errors are mine, not theirs.

Richard Mason, my police advisor who guides me on procedure and makes sure I am, largely, within the law. When I break the rules, that's all me!

My fabulous editor, Alison Jack, and Julia Gibbs my eagle-eyed proofreader. Both are a joy to work with.

Thank you to Susan Stark, whose constant encouragement means that I keep sitting at my computer, and finding out what Sophie, Mark and Joyce are getting up to.

There is, in Scotland, a historic house called Charleton that bears no similarities to my own. Many thanks to its owner, Baron St Clair Bonde, who was happy for me to use the name. I am extremely grateful to him.

ACKNOWLEDGEMENTS

A KILLER WEDDING

I've always enjoyed working as part of a team, and fortunately, writing a book isn't quite as lonely as you might think. I am extremely grateful to many generous and knowledgeable people.

Thank you to my wonderful beta readers Chris Bailey-Jones, Joanna Hancox, Lynne McCormack, Helen McNally, Eileen Minchin, and Rosanna Summers. Your honesty and insightful comments keep me on the straight and narrow.

I have always wanted to ensure that life in a historic house that is open to the public is portrayed as accurately as possible. I can bring my own twenty-year career in visitor experience to bear on this. However I have needed the expertise of those who work in specialist fields. My thanks to Chris Bailey, Father Anthony Howe, Daniel Jackson and Liz Young. It was great working with you all again. Any errors are mine, not theirs.

Nicki Fietzer, Sara Healey, Kathryn Oldfield, David Stout, Nate Thompson, and Mark Wallis all gave me their time and expertise in a range of subjects. I am extremely grateful.

Richard Mason, my police advisor who guides me on procedure and makes sure I am, largely, within the law. When I break the rules, that's all me!

Fellow author Alison Golden has given me great support and guidance.

My fabulous editor, Alison Jack, and Julia Gibbs my eagle-eyed proofreader. Both are a joy to work with.

Thank you to Susan Stark, who has made sure my coffee mug is always topped up and provides unwavering encouragement.

There is, in Scotland, a historic house called Charleton that bears no similarities to my own. Many thanks to its owner, Baron St Clair Bonde, who was happy for me to use the name. I am extremely grateful to him.

ACKNOWLEDGEMENTS

SLEEP LIKE THE DEAD

Thank you to my wonderful beta readers Chris Bailey-Jones, Joanna Hancox, Lynne McCormack, Helen McNally, Eileen Minchin, and Rosanna Summers. Your honesty and insightful comments help make my books so much better than they would otherwise be.

Many thanks to my advance readers, your support and feedback means a great deal to me. Thank you to all my readers. I love hearing from you.

Although I worked on a number of sleepover events at Hampton Court Palace, Liz Young, Frances Sampayo and David Packer, kindly gave me their own insights.

Mark Wallis and Rosanna Summers gave me invaluable information on historical clothing.

Richard Mason, my police advisor who guides me on procedure and makes sure I am, largely, within the law. When I break the rules, that's all me!

My fabulous editor, Alison Jack, and Julia Gibbs my eagle-eyed proofreader. Both are a joy to work with.

Thank you to Susan Stark, who makes sure we have enough gin and tonic to get me though the writing process.

There is, in Scotland, a historic house called Charleton that bears no similarities to my own. Many thanks to its owner, Baron St Clair Bonde, who was happy for me to use the name. I am extremely grateful to him.

THE CHARLETON HOUSE MYSTERIES

Death by Dark Roast
A Killer Wedding
Sleep Like the Dead
A Deadly Ride

Printed in Great Britain
by Amazon